The Next Best Thing

Sarah Long worked for several years in publishing before giving it all up to move to Paris with her husband and three children. Following several years of the Parisian experience, they now live back in London. Her first novel, *And What Do You Do?* was published to great acclaim in 2003. *The Next Best Thing* is her second novel.

ALSO BY SARAH LONG

And What Do You Do?

The Next Best Thing

—⁄⁄⁄—

Sarah Long

Century · London

First published in the United Kingdom in 2005 by Century

1 3 5 7 9 10 8 6 4 2

Copyright © Sarah Long 2005

The right of Sarah Long to be identified as the author of this work
has been asserted by her in accordance with the Copyright,
Designs and Patents Act, 1988

Century
The Random House Group Limited
20 Vauxhall Bridge Road, London, SW1V 2SA

Random House Australia (Pty) Limited
20 Alfred Street, Milsons Point, Sydney, New South Wales 2061, Australia

Random House New Zealand Limited
18 Poland Road, Glenfield
Auckland 10, New Zealand

Random House (Pty) Limited
Endulini, 5a Jubilee Road, Parktown, 2193, South Africa

The Random House Group Limited Reg. No. 954009
www.randomhouse.co.uk

A CIP catalogue record for this book is available from the British Library

Papers used by Random House are natural, recyclable products made from
wood grown in sustainable forests. The manufacturing processes conform to
the environmental regulations of the country of origin

Typeset by Palimpsest Book Production Limited,
Polmont, Stirlingshire
Printed and bound in the United Kingdom by
Mackays of Chatham plc, Chatham, Kent

ISBN 1 844 13180 7

For Julia

Acknowledgements

Thanks to my café friends for morning support, and to Mary Pachnos, Kate Elton and Nikola Scott.

'In love, there are no crimes or misdemeanours. There are errors of taste.'

Paul Geraldy, *L'Homme et L'Amour*

ONE

'Next Wednesday? I thought I had two more weeks!' Jane tried to keep the note of panic out of her voice. If she couldn't cope, they'd find someone who could. Freelance translators were two-a-penny, she couldn't afford to be difficult.

'Well yes,' she said, 'that should be OK, I'll just have to up the pace, that's all. Without compromising the quality, of course.' She laughed reassuringly. 'Nothing like a bit of adrenaline to kick the machine into action. Thanks Gus, I'll be in touch next week. Yup, you too, bye.'

Jane slumped back behind the kitchen table. It was a good thing Gus couldn't see her, still in her pyjamas, surrounded by last night's unwashed dishes. It wasn't exactly professional. The domestic squalor would have to wait, she thought, pushing aside a pile of papers to unearth her laptop. She was getting good money for this job, and no-one was going to pay her for cleaning the house.

She switched on the computer and listened to the opening chords of Windows ringing nobly round her kitchen-cum-office. Over to you, it said, now is the time to launch into your flawless translation of *Bridges of France*. It had seemed such a good idea at the time, working from home. It meant she could fit it round the rest of her life, leaving time for her daughter and her partner. Juggling on her own terms in a heroic bid to have it all, the way women were supposed to these days.

If she was going to meet this new deadline, she'd need to get at least three chapters done before she went to meet Liberty from school. She took a bite of her toast and watched the crumbs fall into the gaps between the letters on the keyboard. Disgusting really. There must be all kinds of detritus lurking down there, it could muck up the whole system. She picked up the laptop, turned it upside down and shook it gently. Bits of food and hair and dust showered onto the table. Even a couple of nail clippings – how vile. She brushed them onto the floor, then dabbed a tissue to her mouth and set about polishing the keys. You couldn't be expected to work when your fingers stuck to the plastic piano, made glutinous by a child's sticky hands.

She threw the tissue in the bin and ran her fingers over the smooth surface of the clean keyboard. That was better; she was now equipped for a full day's work. She pushed her hair back from her face and fastened it with a comb belonging to her daughter that had been discarded beside a plate of congealing gravy. It was no good, she'd have to load the dishwasher. Even for someone with her own low hygiene standards, there were limits. She didn't want social services coming round and seizing her daughter.

She swiftly loaded the plates and wiped down the table. It would be nice to have a cleaner, but Will thought domestic staff smacked of bourgeois exploitation, and it was cheaper for her to do it herself.

Now, where was she . . . *the Pont d'Avignon, rich source of a myriad of treasured folkloric history, not least the celebrated song beloved of generations of children* . . . Too folksy. She mustn't slip into whimsy just because Gus had cruelly brought forward her deadline. Start again. *The Pont d'Avignon, source of many legends as old as the noble stones themselves, and familiar to every French schoolchild.* Better. She typed on, silently, swiftly, and was soon nearing the end of the chapter, which she would celebrate by taking a swift bath and getting dressed. It was one thing to do the morning school-run in your pyjamas, safely hidden in the car, but you couldn't stand outside the gates of Leinster Prep at four o'clock dressed like a tramp.

With just two pages to go, Jane became aware of an unpleasant sensation in her feet. She was wearing a pair of Will's old socks – he found slippers depressing – and when she looked down she saw that, for some reason, they were now sodden through. Not only that, the entire floor was covered with water. The dishwasher, of course. Not again: fourteen years old, what could you expect? Will had retrieved it as part of his spoils from the divorce, determined to take advantage of its extended guarantee. It always broke down when he was safely out of the way.

She paddled her way across the kitchen, soaking her knees as she bent down and reached under the sink in a well-practised routine to turn off the water supply. Once again she'd have to call the engineer and face his incredulity as he patched it up. You should get a new one, love, he'd say, and she'd agree, only Will wouldn't hear of it.

Cursing, she pulled out the mop and bucket and started slopping around. It wouldn't be like this if she worked in an office. The whole house could burn down for all she'd know about it, whereas being at home meant she was always on hand to take care of domestic crises.

The phone rang again. If that's someone trying to sell me car insurance, Jane told herself, they are in for a bumpy ride.

'Hallo, you sexy beast.' It was Will calling from work. He'd already written his column and was sitting feet up on his desk, swigging from an Evian bottle.

'Will, great timing,' said Jane. 'Your nasty old dishwasher has just blown up again. It's got to go, otherwise I will.'

'That's a very Wildean threat,' he said. 'Just ring Zanussi, it's under guarantee.'

'I'm always ringing Zanussi, they hate me.'

'Don't dramatise, darling, it's only an appliance.'

'An appliance that's begging to be put out of its misery.'

'You know our views on needless waste,' he said, crumpling the plastic bottle with one hand and chucking it across the room towards the bin. 'Landfill sites are clogged up with perfectly serviceable white goods, we don't want to make any further contribution to the death of the planet.'

'Sod the planet, I've got work to do. Gus has brought forward my deadline and the kitchen's flooded.'

Will observed a brief silence.

'On a brighter note,' he went on, 'I've invited Chas

over tonight. I thought you might like to do your mushroom risotto. You could stop off at Fresh and Wild on your way to school.'

'Or you could stop off on your way home.'

'I'd love to,' he said regretfully, as if nothing would have given him more pleasure, 'only they'll be closed by then. We're not all part-timers.'

'Part-time cleaner, chief cook and bottle-washer.'

'And talented translator. You are an extraordinary woman, I realise that.'

She softened at the flattery. 'All right then. What time will you be here?'

'Dinner time. Have you got proper stock? You can't make risotto without it.'

'In the freezer.'

'Good girl. Love you.'

'Mmm.'

He was right, she thought as she put the phone down. It was only an appliance, there was no point getting hysterical about it. Will was good at putting things in perspective, he never lost his cool and often made her feel like a petulant child. Though, in truth, it was easy to be cool when you weren't the one who had to deal with things.

She threw some towels down on the floor and shuffled them round with her feet to dry it, then sat down at her computer. She'd call Zanussi later, better not to interrupt her concentration. So Chas was coming to dinner. Chas was Will's agent, and therefore worth courting. He also liked his food, and was always complimentary about Jane's cooking. She'd need to get in some more parmesan, too, for tonight. Will would be pleased with her for making the effort, and she did like it when he was pleased with her.

Sighing, she forced her mind back from the evening ahead and concentrated on her work. Double speed now, no time to waste. The phone rang *again*. Damn, she'd forgotten to plug in the answer phone. Maybe she should just let it ring? But what if it was Liberty's school to say she'd had an accident?

'Hallo darling.'

Lydia. Her old friend. Or to be more accurate, the daughter of her mother's friend.

'Lydia! What a surprise!'

Which it was, in one way, since Jane had no idea why Lydia still bothered to keep in touch with her. On the other hand, Lydia called her so often at this time in the morning that it was hardly surprising at all. They had been at school together, then on to Oxford, followed by parallel lowly jobs that involved a lot of photocopying. But whereas Lydia's career had gathered momentum and was steaming along a high-speed track, Jane's had ended up shunted into a cul-de-sac right here in her kitchen.

'How are things, Jane?' asked Lydia. 'What have you been up to?'

'Coping with an enormous flood. The dishwasher broke, my deadline's been cut short and Will's just rung to say he's invited his agent to dinner . . .'

But Lydia wasn't listening. It was always like this, she popped the question, ignored the answer, then roared in with a full account of her own glamorous life. 'God, I can't tell you how busy I've been, it's been wall-to-wall hectic here.'

So if she was that busy, thought Jane, why waste time – especially *my* time – making unnecessary phone calls?

'Really?'

'Yes, really. I had to go down to Highgrove last weekend, we're doing a thing on Charles's organic stuff. He's fantastic, by the way, couldn't have been more welcoming.'

'Did you curtsey?'

'Did I curtsey! This was a professional meeting, I wasn't there presenting him with a bunch of flowers!'

'Were his hands softened by luxury or calloused by honest toil?'

But Lydia was already off on a full account of what he said and what she wore and calf lactation cycles. It was disingenuous of Jane to kid herself that she didn't know why Lydia bothered with her. Beneath that high-gloss exterior, she was constantly seeking validation for her achievements and Jane's drab life at home was the perfect foil to her own giddy existence. Busy, busy me and dear old steady you.

'But that's enough about me,' said Lydia, 'let's talk about you. What do you think about me?'

'Ha ha,' Jane replied.

'No, really, how are you?' said Lydia. 'Still busy with the old translation?'

Jane ran her finger across her computer screen and examined the line of dust which it had accumulated. Dust was supposed to be made up largely of skin cells, so why did it look so grey and fluffy?

'Frantic, can I call you back? I've got to get on before school finishes . . .'

'Ah yes, that child. You're a saint, Jane, you know that?'

'Mmm.'

'But good for you, you've managed to keep some kind of career going.'

'Nice of you to say so. Must go . . .'

'No honestly, Jane, I take my hat off to you. It can't be easy working all by yourself, with no-one to bounce ideas off. It would drive me mad, I know that.' Lydia fell silent in a moment of true, shuddering pity. 'Anyway, the reason I called,' she went on, 'was to ask if you were going to Miss Lancaster's memorial service.'

'Who?'

'Miss Lancaster, you know, our old tutor.'

Jane cast her mind back to a woman with Margaret Drabble hair and large flat feet, pouring out three glasses of Stones ginger wine before their midday tutorial. 'Of course, I remember, she was nice enough but I think I'll give it a miss. No point in wallowing in the past.'

Lydia's motives were neither sentimental nor nostalgic. 'It's a great networking opportunity. All those people you haven't seen for ages, some of them really worth knowing. I've made some great contacts at memorial services.'

Jane was not convinced. The last thing she wanted was to run the gauntlet of polite enquiries from her peers. Holding up the unremarkable achievements of her life for general inspection, while Lydia glittered and whirled around her.

'No, I think I'm busy that day,' she said, 'I don't think Miss Lancaster will miss me.'

'Obviously *she* won't. I'm just thinking of you. It would do you good to get out more. Finger on the pulse and all that. Hang on, there's my other line, I'll call you back.'

And with a dismissive click Jane was dropped back into her fusty old life. Self-chosen, and therefore not pitiful. The life of the home worker. Independent, flexible, the mistress of her destiny. Or underpaid, lonely and unrewarded? Discuss.

Goodness me, it was nearly lunchtime and the place was still a pigsty. She'd better just take ten minutes out to tidy up, they couldn't have Chas sitting down to dinner surrounded by mountains of trash. She took a stray plastic bag and started to fill it with bits of Barbie outfits that were strewn across the counter: a tiny boucle jacket, a handbag the size of a thumbnail and minuscule stilettoes for deformedly small feet.

The best thing about working at home was being able to move around freely since you weren't stuck behind the same desk all day, though the benefits were debatable when you were constantly reminded of your household chores and other family commitments. She sighed, picked up the rest of the toys littering the floor and decided to relocate to the bedroom to escape the demands of her kitchen. Picking up the laptop, she stepped over the piles of clean sheets sitting on the stairs. Her sister-in-law had noticed her laundry-pile habit and last Christmas had given her a rectangular basket specially designed to fit on a bottom stair. The idea being that on your way up you would gaily seize it by the handle and swing it behind you, tra la la, all the way to the linen closet, that well-ordered place so loved by women with its crisply pressed Egyptian-cotton sheets interleaved with lavender nosegays.

Upstairs, she slipped under the bedcovers, placing the computer on her knees. It was cold up here – Will didn't believe in heating too many unnecessary rooms – and the computer generated a reassuring surge of warmth through the goose down. This is the life, she thought, tapping happily at the keys. Tucked up in bed in her pyjamas and the womb-like security of her very own sleep/workplace. You couldn't really ask for more. Lydia was welcome to her hectic schedule of royal encounters, jumping into cars in a flurry of pashminas and spiky heels. It made Jane feel exhausted just thinking about it. Though sometimes she wouldn't mind slamming the front door and clipping off to the office in a pair of noisy look-at-me shoes. But Will was right, it made more sense for her to be at home. As he pointed out, it was one thing going out to work if you were a top dog with a fat salary to pay for nannies and cleaners. But when you were a middle-ranking nobody, you were lucky to break even once you'd paid for a child-minder, and tube fares and lunch and decent clothes.

When she finally reached the end of the chapter, Jane leaped out of bed and ran a bath. While waiting for it to fill, she walked across to the window and looked out at the rainy street where two men in hooded sweatshirts were shouting at each other. It was funny how she'd ended up in this dodgy bit of London where, bizarrely, houses were twice as expensive as in the leafy suburbs of her upbringing. Her dream had always been to move to the country, but she knew it wouldn't ever happen. Will didn't do the country. Or at least he might do the country for a weekend provided he was staying in a stonking great house with no ribbon developments to spoil the view. *His* fantasy, as he liked to reiterate in his newspaper column, was to live in London for the rest of his life. Dear old dirty London: her clothes may be ragged but beneath them beats a heart of gold. Or words to that effect.

She quickly bathed and changed then went downstairs to call Zanussi. Two more chapters, then she'd have to rush off to Ikea to get those shelves for Liberty's bedroom. Will had been chasing her to get them for weeks now and she didn't want to tell him yet again that she hadn't had time, it sounded so feeble. She finished her work in silence, then picked up her coat and the Ikea catalogue, marked up in Will's neat handwriting. On the North Circular she stopped for petrol and bought a family-sized box of Maltesers, which she ate from her lap as the traffic stopped and started its way through the drizzling rain.

In the downstairs bar of the French House, Will caught sight of himself in the mirror. With the benefit of low lighting and three gin and tonics, he had to admit he liked what he saw. He turned his head to get the best angle of his cheekbones, and found it incredible to think that he was pushing fifty. That was no age, though, these days. Fifty was the new forty, or more like thirty-five in his case. He smoothed some rogue hairs back into his ponytail and turned to his companion.

'Another one before you go, Chas?'

He wasn't usually so profligate in buying rounds, but it was worth keeping his agent sweet. Chas had sounded pretty bullish about what he might get for Will's next book. Anyway, he could probably push the drinks through on expenses.

Chas looked at his watch. 'Better not, I'm late already. I'm sorry about tonight, do apologise to Jane for me.'

'Don't worry about it, she's cool. One thing about Jane, she doesn't get uptight about a change in plan. Not like Carol, she wouldn't have spoken to me for a week.'

'How is the ex?'

'I hardly know, all right I think. Best thing I ever did was walk out of that marriage. Tough at the time, but she's grateful to me now. Freed her up to start a new life with that dismal travel agent.'

'And left you free to set up home with the lovely Jane. You're a lucky man.'

'I know.'

'Clever, good-looking woman who knows how to cook. And she earns her own money.' Chas sighed as he thought of his own high-maintenance ex-wife. Lounging around at home between trips to the beauty salon. He had asked her once whether she ever thought about going back to work. Perfectly innocent question, you'd have thought, but her reaction had been savage. 'What am I supposed to do?' she'd snapped back at him. 'Get a job in a shoe shop?' That was the problem with well-educated women. A few child-rearing years out of the market and they became unemployable.

'That's the advantage of cohabitation over marriage,' said Will. 'Women understand it's not a meal ticket for life.'

'Rod Stewart said he wasn't going to marry again,' said Chas. 'He'd just find a woman he didn't like and give her a house instead.'

'Exactly.'

They sat in silence for a moment to consider this monumental statement.

'I'll be off then,' said Chas.

They left the pub and said their goodbyes on the pavement. Chas had been offered a ticket for the Donmar, and Will insisted he take it. If there was one thing life had taught him it was always to drop an engagement if something better came along. He wandered up Dean Street towards the tube, but then thought better of it. A man in his position shouldn't have to slum it on the underground, even if he was financially crippled by years of alimony. He hailed a cab.

'Shepherds Bush please.'

Shepherds Bush, that was bad enough. It had been Notting Hill before the divorce, and for the purposes of his newspaper column, it still was. The Portobello Road was his beat, and every week he wrote of its delights to lighten the journey of his poor readers as they headed off to their god-awful suburban homes.

The seductive smell of garlic cooking in olive oil greeted Will as he opened the front door.

'Hey baby,' he called out, taking off his coat.

Jane came up from the basement, looking delicious in a soft pink sweater. She didn't often wear make-up but he could see she'd made an effort tonight. Her hair was loosely pinned up, framing her heart-shaped face, and her delicate features were flattered by a pale lipstick.

'Where's Chas?' she asked, looking round as if expecting him to be hiding behind Will.

'Couldn't make it unfortunately. Sends his apologies, though he knows the loss is all his. You look gorgeous.'

Jane dropped her welcoming smile and frowned at him. 'Well, thanks a lot!' she said. 'You could have rung. I've been charging around like a blue-arsed fly getting everything ready; it would have taken you two minutes to let me know.'

She turned on her heel and Will followed her down the stairs. 'Be nice to me,' he said, 'you lovely creature. I was only telling Chas what a marvel you were, how un-uptight, how free-wheeling . . .'

The table had been set with three places, lit by candles and miraculously free of clutter. Will deftly removed one place setting.

'There we are, all the more for you and me. Just the two of us, much more romantic.'

It was unusual for him to be currying favour like this, mostly it was the other way round. Jane looked at him with a mixture of exasperation and amusement. She still couldn't resist him when he turned on the charm.

'Oh . . . all right then,' she relented. 'At least we can have a normal conversation and I won't have to listen to you and Chas talking shop.'

She liked it when he courted her like this. It reminded her of when they first met, and he used to bombard her office with flowers. He knew how to treat a girl, of course, being that much older; she wouldn't fall for it in quite the same way now she was in her thirties. She watched him pour himself a glass of vodka then hold the bottle out to her enquiringly. She nodded and he gave her his louche, lop-sided smile. She'd been mad for that smile back then, she'd thought he was James Dean and Dustin Hoffman rolled into one sexy bundle of charming sophistication.

He handed her the glass. 'Liberty in bed already?'

'Yes, she was exhausted. Long day for her – ice-skating and French after school.'

'You got the mushrooms I take it?'

'But of course.'

'Fresh and Wild?'

'No, I got some button mushrooms on special offer at Safeway.'

His eyes widened in disbelief.

'Only joking,' she said. 'You know I wouldn't risk offending Chas with anything from a supermarket. Just too bad he blew us out.'

'Never mind, Nigella, we'll just have to go it alone.'

She didn't mind the Nigella allusion. Posh and sexy, crashing greedily round a kitchen filled with giant cooking pots. She smiled her acknowledgement and took a long, objective look at him. He'd still got it, she thought, that confidence, the way he assumed the room. She'd still cross the party to talk to him, though if she was being brutally honest, she'd have to admit the last ten years had not been too kind to him. The beginnings of a soft belly hung over his belt, and his face had loosened. He should get rid of the ponytail, too, now he was thinning on top. She ought to have a word with him about it.

'They came to fix the dishwasher,' she said, 'just happened to have someone in the area, luckily. That was the high point of my day, how about you?'

'Oh, you know, another day, another dollar. Another crop of wise and witty insights for my grateful public.'

'Lydia rang this morning,' said Jane, emptying the bag of mushrooms into a colander and taking them over to the sink.

'*What are you doing?*' Will's voice had become shrill with alarm.

'Washing the mushrooms.'

'You mustn't do that!'

'They've got clods of earth sticking to them.'

'So wipe them off with a damp cloth, but you must never, never wash mushrooms. They're like sponges, they soak up the water then it all comes out when you cook them and they lose all their flavour. I'm surprised you didn't know that.' He turned away to top up his glass, and while he was rummaging in the freezer for ice, Jane surreptitiously ran the cold tap over the colander. She was damned if she was going to have her dinner ruined by lumps of soil.

Will turned back to face her. 'What did Lydia want?' he asked.

'This and that. She wanted me to go to some sad old don's memorial service. As if. You would have thought she had better things to do. She's always going on about how busy she is. Busy, busy, busy, I hate that, don't you? So self-important.'

'"*And yet, methinks, she semed bisier than she was*",' said Will, in the actorly voice that he liked to adopt for quoting Chaucer.

'It's like what business people go through when fixing a meeting,' said Jane. 'You know, all that fawning about how I'm sure your diary's fuller than mine – quite ridiculous.'

'I agree,' Will replied, reverting to his normal voice, a fashionable blend of public school and glottal stops. 'It's seriously uncool to bang on about being busy. Very second rank, and also suggests you're not coping. Although Lydia's always been a bit of a bustler though, hasn't she?'

He'd had a thing with Lydia a few years ago, a fact he'd never thought appropriate to share with Jane. It had fizzled out anyway and mercifully Lydia had never seen fit to spill the beans.

'Is she still with that dull banker?' he asked.

'So it seems. How do you know he's dull? We've never met him.'

'He's a banker, so he's dull. I don't need to meet him. I can just imagine.'

You could never accuse Will of not knowing his mind.

'You're probably right,' she said, 'but you shouldn't condemn people you've never met, just because you don't like the sound of their job.'

'Anyway, he's bound to be loaded,' said Will. 'Lydia wouldn't bother wasting time on him otherwise.'

'That's true,' Jane agreed. It made her feel better to think of Lydia as a gold-digger, just as it made Will feel better to think of her boyfriend as a yawnsville banker. 'You'll be able to judge for yourself soon,' she continued. 'We're invited for drinks at his place.'

'How unspeakable, do we have to? Where does he live?'

'Chelsea.'

'Of course, like all bankers. You know I try to avoid Chelsea, for ideological reasons.' On Will's map of moral correctness, there were certain no-go areas. Jane had long since given up trying to fathom his logic.

'I think it's charming,' she said. 'I'd love to live there.'

'You wouldn't! It's full of ghastly braying dimwits and people like Lydia's boyfriend!'

'Whom you have yet to meet.'

'Whom I have no intention of meeting.'

'Anyway, I know the real reason you don't like Chelsea, you told me once. It's because everyone there is so tall, and you feel like a short-arse in comparison.'

It was a cheap shot and Will responded with a chilly smile of disdain.

'It's only drinks,' she said in appeasement, 'we won't have to stay long.'

It was certainly true, thought Will, that drinks was better than dinner. He would stand aloof in his brocade jacket, a raffish bohemian in a sea of clean-cut city suits. And it was certainly better than Sunday lunch with other young families, which was what Jane liked to organise. Couples drinking wine to ease the boredom of family life while the children wreaked havoc around them. Followed by the obligatory walk to the park, where Will had once been mistaken for the grandfather of his young daughter. The memory stuck with him still. He had been remonstrating with a boy who was climbing the wrong way up the slide, leaving dirty footprints on the smooth silver surface, while Liberty waited patiently on the top step. 'That your granddad?' the boy had asked Liberty. She had glared at him, indignant and defensive: 'It's my dad, stupid.'

That was the problem with second families. Small humiliations waiting to trip you up at every turn. It was the price you paid for starting over. Although, as Will watched Jane ladling hot stock into the pan and smelt the rosemary and garlic, he had to admit it was worth it. To find himself with this woman looking slim in her jeans and with a wild mane of hair that did not yet need to be dyed. She could be a black and white photo from a fashionable guide to Italian cooking, whereas his ex-wife was a hangover from the *Hamlyn All Colour Cookbook*.

'Lydia said she'd been down at Highgrove,' Jane told him, 'inspecting the royal cows.'

'That would be right up her street,' said Will, 'hobnobbing with the old ruling classes.'

He preferred to hobnob with the new ruling classes. Writers, film people, opinion formers who had won their position through their own endeavours and not through an accident of birth. What the French would call *les intellectuels*, though the British were too damn philistine to use the word except as a term of abuse.

'Do you want your salad before or after the risotto?' asked Jane.

'I think after.' He picked up Liberty's drawing of a tall princess with big hair and tiny feet, decorated with this week's leitmotif: a big yellow cartoon sun wearing dark glasses. 'How's my monkey?' he asked.

'She's fine. Miss Evans doesn't think she's dyspraxic after all. She thinks she might just be clumsy.'

'Well, I could have told you that. People are so neurotic these days, always trying to find something wrong with their children.'

It wasn't like that with his first batch of offspring, they had surged into adolescence with very little fuss. Not that he'd been around much to notice, his wife had taken care of all that, as wives did back then. It was only recently that fathers had become such hands-on nincompoops.

'Do you mind?' he said after dinner. 'I really need to get on upstairs.'

'Go ahead,' Jane replied, 'I'm going to work as well, once I've finished off in here.'

Will squeezed her arm on his way out. 'Catch you later,' he said, 'thanks for dinner.'

He walked into the hall and up the dramatic concrete spiral staircase with its Perspex balustrade. The creation of a live/work space for Will had been central to the architect's brief, and the entire first floor had been made over to this purpose. Will called it his *galleria*, a magnificent open space that was his kingdom and his refuge. On the walls his art collection was an eclectic statement of his 'modern with a nod to the past' philosophy, while books lining the shelves bore testament to a crushing intellect.

To pay for the galleria Will had sold one of his more controversial works of art, a dead fox pickled in formaldehyde as an ironic statement about the proposed ban on hunting. The artist had given it to Will just before he became famous, and when Jane became pregnant, Will had found the perfect excuse to cash in on his unexpected windfall. The smell of the formaldehyde leaking from the glass case was making her nauseous, so Will sold it to a New York dealer. He regretted it now, it would be worth at least ten times as much.

The size of the galleria meant they'd had to compromise on the rest of the house, but Jane and Liberty seemed quite happy holed up in the semi-basement where they could perform the eating and telly-watching functions that were so disruptive to Will's creative process.

He lit a cigar and thought about starting work on his book. It was an exploration of Native American culture, a follow-up to one he had published a few years back. *Flames of Youth* had described the initiation rites endured by young Native Americans who leaped through fire to achieve maturity. It was a book about courage, a quality underestimated in modern Western society. He had focused on this angle in his publicity, comparing the courage of these boys with the courage that he, Will Thacker, had demonstrated when he decided to leave his marriage. That had put the cat among the pigeons in the ugly feminist camp, but it hadn't harmed his sales. It irritated him the way people sided with the wife and kids when a marriage broke up. What about the lone crusader, the man in all this, the one who was brave enough to say, *Enough! I will not compromise and spend my life crouched in the brackish shallows of a humdrum relationship*. It brought tears to his eyes just thinking about it. Will Thacker, a big, bold, beautiful traveller.

Before starting work, he would just visit his website and look up the reviews for *Flames*. '. . . brings a coruscating intelligence to a little-understood subject . . .' 'Never before had I understood the searing pain and glory that rhymes with coming of age . . .' 'Thacker wears his erudition lightly in this clear-eyed and deeply moving *tour de force*.'

He really was quite something.

*   *   *

Downstairs, Jane quickly cleared the plates and set off the dishwasher. It was all very well, this foodie business, but it did cut into her precious time. Of course she enjoyed sitting down with Will for a civilised dinner, but sometimes she wished she could just open a can of beans and be done with it. She'd need to fit in a couple of hours tonight, so as not to get behind.

First, though, there was the ironing to deal with. She took the ironing board from the kitchen cupboard and creaked it open, an unwieldy symbol of life below stairs, its shape unchanged since Victorian days. No mob cap and floor-length pinny for her, though, she was a modern woman, doing it all, aided by many gadgets that freed her up to maintain her career. Career was pushing it, she thought, pouring rose-scented water into the iron that claimed to bring the smell of the garden to your wardrobe. She had a job, not a career. It would only become a career if she gave it up. Women who stopped working always referred wistfully to their abandoned careers, lending glamour to something that was, in most cases, pretty mundane.

Even so, she was glad to have her work. It kept her in the land of the cruel: the bright, brittle world of positive achievements. If you didn't work, you were committed to life as a kindly sponge, absorbing the worries of your children while flooding them with your own anxieties. Anyway, Will wouldn't let her give up work, he'd made that perfectly clear.

She switched on the TV and took a small pink tee shirt from the basket. She always did Liberty's things first; it was like playing with dolls' clothes. There was a programme on about a couple leaving England to set up a guest house in the Dordogne. Just as they were being waved off by teary-eyed neighbours, the phone rang.

'Hallo,' said Jane, one eye still on the screen.

'Hi, it's Marion.'

'Marion!'

Lovely Marion, it was always a shot in the arm to hear from her. They'd met when they were temping at IPC, both hoping to move on to better things.

'Do you fancy meeting up one night?' asked Marion. 'It's been ages.'

'I'd love to,' said Jane, 'not this week, though, far too busy.'

'You don't sound that busy to me, sounds like you're watching telly.'

'Just while I do the ironing . . .'

'You are so quaint.'

Marion had someone to take care of the ironing. Just as she had someone to take care of her children while she raced round town spending her husband's money.

'Not quaint, just poor.'

'Come off it, Will can't be doing that badly. Tell him to spend less money on clothes. And get him to do the ironing.'

Marion was one of the new breed of stay-at-home wives. Not so much a drab run-down housewife as a bumptious force of nature, out to milk the situation for all it was worth. Jane wished she had her nerve.

'Another time,' she said.

'Well, make it soon. You're turning into Norma no-mates.'

'OK, next week maybe.'

'I'll hold you to it. I'm not having you becoming one of those boring working-mother martyr types, huffing and puffing about having so much to do.'

'All right, you spoilt old bag, I'll call you.'

Jane replaced the receiver and turned her attention back to the TV, which was perched on a table alongside the computer, at the far end of the kitchen/dining/family room. A multi-function room for a multi-functioning woman. She honestly didn't mind the ironing, and so what if she did iron Will's shirts? They both agreed the great cause of sexual equality should not be reduced to a petty spat about the housework.

The couple on the programme had now arrived at the dilapidated *gentilhommière* in the French countryside: holding back the tears they contemplated the disastrous plumbing. This was when the viewers' *Schadenfreude* really kicked in. Dear oh dear, went up the sigh from a million sofas, we could have told you it was a bad idea.

Jane moved on to the Egyptian-cotton duvet cover and wondered whether she really was turning into Norma no-mates. True, she saw less of her friends than she used to. But she had Will and Liberty and her work and that was enough, most of the time.

Will appeared at the door, an elegant urban figure, his hand running through his boyishly long grey hair. 'I'm making tea,' he announced, as though this was of earth-shattering importance, 'would you like camomile or hibiscus?'

'Camomile, please,' said Jane, squirting some instant starch onto a pillowcase. Although he was used to roughing it on his travels, Will insisted on certain luxuries at home, and crisply pressed bed linen helped him overcome his insomnia.

'I see you're indulging in your usual fix of escapist nonsense,' said Will. 'What is it this time, an olive farm in Italy for a couple of no-hopers?'

'A guest house in France. I really admire them, getting up and making a go of it.'

Will switched on the kettle and turned a dismissive eye on the screen. 'Christ, look at those matching bedspreads and pelmets, and that horrible fake stone floor! What's the point of going to France and staying with Brits? You might as well go to Surrey for your holidays.'

'You must admit it's brave of them, though,' Jane countered. 'They had an idea and they've followed it through. They have achieved their fantasy.'

But Will wasn't having it. 'I don't think fantasy is the appropriate term for the aspirations of a suburban couple who've had a nice holiday abroad and think they can extend it into some kind of bed and breakfast never-never land. I don't buy it. Now *my* fantasy . . .'

'Yes, yes, I know,' Jane interrupted him. 'Your fantasy is to live in London for the rest of your life.' She had heard it once too often for her patience. 'It's all right for you,' she added sharply, 'you're always hopping off abroad. Most people don't get the chance to whizz off and live among Native Americans for months at a time.'

He looked at her in surprise. It was unlike Jane to get all chippy, maybe she was going down with something. 'That's for work, Jane, and hardly luxurious. Damned uncomfortable for much of the time.'

He brought her a cup of tea and set it down on the

ironing board. 'I only wish *I* had time to watch television,' he said self-righteously, 'but I'm afraid I'll be at least another couple of hours.'

It was churlish of her to snap at him like that, Jane thought, she hated sounding bitter. 'Thanks, Will,' she said, 'I'm sorry if I was a bit ratty, I'm tired, that's all, and worried about the deadline on that bridges book, you know what it's like.'

Though of course he didn't know what it was like. He never got in a state about his work. She was the one who flapped and panicked while he remained serenely in command. It was further proof, as if she needed it, of his all-round superiority.

He nodded his forgiveness and went back up to his galleria. The man of her life, absorbed in higher thoughts. She still couldn't believe her luck that he had chosen her, a two-bit translator, when he could have had his pick of minds more equal to his own. They'd met ten years ago at a publishing party, where she got stuck talking to a miserable crime writer who had recently left London to live alone with some cats on a Welsh mountain. 'I gave up my full-time job four years ago,' the writer had told her, staring moodily ahead. 'It was a big mistake.' Jane was just wondering how best to sidle off and refill her flaccid paper cup when Will drifted into her orbit, the star of the party and way out of her league.

'Do please excuse me,' he had said to the cat-lover, 'I have some urgent business to discuss with this woman.' And he had quite simply whisked her off her feet.

He had been wearing a beret that night. This was a detail that Jane now preferred to leave out of the story;

she had her doubts about men who wore hats indoors. Or outdoors, for that matter. She knew his name and had read his newspaper column, but not his books. Travel writing bored her on the whole, as she admitted to him after a few more glasses of wine. She took the view that if you had nothing to say at home, you were unlikely to find anything to say a long way from home. It wasn't as if a few thousand kilometres would change anything.

Will took her home that night to try to change her mind with a dazzling display of learning. She'd never met anyone so brilliant, who could quote world literature in fifteen languages including Mandarin. Looking back, you could say he'd been showing off, but she was mightily impressed at the time. She'd been used to boys of her own age, well-educated on paper but with little curiosity beyond the sports pages. After that night, Will started taking her to parties, hip bars, restaurants where they all knew his name. She knew it was pathetic to admire the way he asked for his usual table, but she couldn't help it, being that much younger.

Naturally, he came with baggage. You didn't expect to find a brilliant, passionate man approaching forty without a past. But he was already separated from his wife, there was no question of Jane being a home-wrecker. When his sons came to stay, she was tactful and accommodating, and made no demands for children of her own. He'd actually taken it rather well when she'd told him she was pregnant. Though like the Chinese birth-control granny police, he had insisted that one was enough.

Not being married was a condition Jane enjoyed. It

made her feel more exciting than she feared she was, though she still hadn't worked out what to call Will. He was too old to be her 'boyfriend', and 'live-in lover' sounded overly vigorous. The 'father of my child' implied they were divorced before they were even married, and 'companion' brought to mind a frail old person in a bath chair. The only real option was 'partner', although it always made her think of sex manuals like *The Joy of Sex*, where a bearded man is depicted pleasing his partner like a caveman crawling over his prey.

Mind you, nobody talked about living in sin any more, it had become as conventional as tea and toast. Only Jane's grandmother thought it was a scam devised to bring financial benefit to men and heap misery upon women. 'Of course no man would get married if he didn't have to,' she had raged when Jane had told her she was moving in with Will. 'Why buy the cow if you can get the milk for free?' This reactionary view had left Jane lost for words and sent her home to run through the reasons why she and Will had decided marriage was out of the question. Who had presented the arguments and who had agreed? She couldn't remember now.

Jane packed up the ironing board and went upstairs to bed, past the galleria where Will was still sitting at his desk, head bent over his work, classical music tinkling in the background. She reached the top floor of bedrooms where her daughter's Roald Dahl tape was still quietly playing in the dark. Jane switched it off and kissed her child's silky head. A little later Will joined her in bed and they lay there, folded together like two of

Liberty's bendy stickle bricks. Yin and yang, mutually complementary, the senior and junior partner in the business of family life.

Next morning at breakfast, Liberty was playing her questions game. 'Mum, would you rather die or break a leg?' Her eyes were glued to the TV screen where a large bear was making slow, child-friendly movements.

'Break a leg. Do you want crisps or Hula Hoops for your snack?'

'Hula Hoops. Mum, what is worse, losing all your money or your daughter dying?'

'My daughter dying. Do you want more milk?'

There was no reply but Jane topped up her glass anyway. Slimy rings of chocolate cereal floated in Liberty's bowl, a strange choice of breakfast but supposedly packed with all the appropriate vitamins.

'Are you ready then?' Jane said.

Liberty stood up slowly, still watching the screen, then without warning flipped over to turn a perfect cartwheel in the cramped space between the table and the wall. Her grey school skirt fell away, revealing a supple, well-muscled pair of legs. Jane loved those legs, she could eat them for breakfast.

'You'll be sick,' she said. 'Now, where are my keys?'

Liberty turned a second cartwheel then stood to face her mother. 'What is worse,' she asked, 'losing your keys or having an accident?'

It could go on forever, this game of choices. For the past week Jane had been forced to play the patient stooge as Liberty bombarded her with questions. That was the thing about having an only child, you had to act the part of sibling and playmate, subjugating the adult mind to the demands of a seven-year-old.

Liberty was bored with it now. She was staring at Jane in a considered way. 'Mum, if you died, I could be adopted by a celebrity,' she said, cocking her head to one side as she ran through the possibilities.

'I suppose you could,' said Jane, 'but let's hope it doesn't come to that. Have you got your ballet things ready?'

Liberty pulled a Mickey Mouse bag off the chair and waved it under her mother's nose. After-school activities were the trademark of a posh private school and gave Jane some precious extra time. She adored Liberty, but also valued the quiet hours when she was away.

'Good girl, now go and say goodbye to Daddy, it's time to go.'

Liberty leaped up the stairs to the galleria two at a time, on an important mission, her shiny school shoes clomping loudly on the stone treads.

Will was already seated at his desk, leafing through *The Sexual Life of Savages*. It was the book that Paul Theroux had taken with him when he went travelling through the Isles of Oceania to recover from a broken heart. Will considered Theroux a kindred spirit; they both needed a big canvas to explore their private emotions, unlike less adventurous souls who would just tuck it away and get on with it.

He looked up and saw his daughter beaming at him from above that repressive school uniform with its grey-and-purple-striped tie. Uniforms were something Will felt very strongly about. They were almost as insulting to personal liberty as the suggestion that people should carry identity cards, both notions carrying strong fascist overtones.

'Hallo, big face,' he said, 'are you off now?'

She nodded and kissed him briefly before turning away to make her noisy way back down the stairs.

The tie was bad enough but what really did it for Will was the outerwear – that purple cape and silly triangular hat. As if his daughter were some kind of fat-cat prelate. Jane didn't seem to share his discomfort, she just shrugged and said at least there wasn't an argument every morning about what to wear. Just as there was no argument in the Gulag, was Will's retort. Unthinking obedience. Mindless dehumanised discipline. He scribbled on his notepad. He might do a short piece on school uniforms in next week's column.

Jane shut Liberty, caped and hatted in papal splendour, in the back of the car and edged out into the morning traffic. She hadn't put her lenses in yet, so she was driving with the aid of an old pair of spectacles that made her look like Nana Mouskouri. It hardly mattered now that Liberty was old enough to be dumped on the pavement outside school; Jane could remain unseen in the car, engine throbbing, dressed like a fright.

'Mum, M.U.M,' came her daughter's voice from the back seat, spelling out the letters from beneath the papal crown. 'What is worse, having an injection or being run over by a car?'

Jane slyly tried to deflect the question. 'What do you think?' she asked, hoping to break the pattern.

'I'm asking *you*,' shrieked Liberty, indignant at her mother for changing the rules.

'Don't shout, darling. Let me see,' she went on ingratiatingly, 'I think it's worse to be run over, definitely.'

The morning run took them through the traffic-choked nightmare of the Shepherds Bush roundabout and on to the favoured reaches of Notting Hill where Liberty attended her prep school for girls. This was only a matter of faint embarrassment for Jane, but for Will it was a huge loss of face. Private education was so against everything he stood for. Apart from it being grossly unfair, he understood the burden it imposed on a child. He knew from experience how vindictive people could be. Kids from comprehensives didn't know how lucky they were, stepping freely into the world, untrammelled by the trappings of privilege.

Jane was not sure she agreed with him on this. Having attended what Will enviously described as a 'bog-standard comprehensive,' she couldn't honestly see it as an advantage. But on the other hand, they could hardly afford to throw money away on school fees. 'Let's move further out,' she had said, 'all the decent state schools are in the suburbs.' Will had blanched at the 's' word, so Jane had suggested the Home Counties, which he had found even more insulting. Could she honestly imagine him joining a golf club and hosting barbeques?

They tried to get Liberty into the only decent local state school, but there were ten applicants for each place. Unsurprisingly, most people seemed to think the best school was right for their child, nobody wanted to exercise their 'right to choose' the crap ones. So Will caved in and Liberty ended up kitted out in a purple cape in a class of children with even sillier names than her own. Boudicca, Olympia, Cassandra, Ianthe, a full galaxy of Greek and Roman deities, a canon of sainted military heroines, as well as the usual sprinkling of monied bohemians called things like India, Sky and Panda.

Jane turned into Leinster Square and joined the queue of big shiny vehicles searching for somewhere to park. Crouched low in her unremarkable Vauxhall, she was the beggar at the rich man's feast, presuming to infiltrate a world beyond her reach. Plain Jane from Nowheresville getting above herself, scraping together the school fees because she thinks her daughter's too good for the local comp.

Liberty kissed her mother goodbye and walked purposefully towards a stuccoed pair of townhouses. Brightly painted butterflies decorated the window of the front classroom. Girls with neat hair were escorted by expensive blonde mothers. Jane watched Liberty go through the door, serious and dignified. She felt a rush of pity. It wasn't what she wanted for her, this precious little academy of girls from well-off homes.

On the way home, Jane played her own version of Liberty's game of choices. What was worse, having a child or not having a child? Not having a child. What was worse, a posh little prep in Notting Hill or a failing school on a sink estate? It had to be the sink estate. What was better, a terraced house in Shepherds Bush or a country rectory with a gravelled drive and an orchard? She wasn't sure she wanted to think about that one, she'd better come back to her reasons for living in London. Who would you rather live with, a well-connected travel writer who was a personal friend of Salman Rushdie, or a sad old commuter whose idea of fun was taking part in the village quiz-night? No contest, and anyway, she'd made her choice now. She had chosen Will and the whole urban package that came with him.

Two

Lydia Littlewood leaned back into the seat of the train and pulled her coat (Nicole Farhi, a classic wrap) more tightly around her. The window wouldn't shut, and the wind whistled into the tatty, half-empty carriage. This country was a disgrace with its third-world transport system. Expensive, too: it had cost her an arm and a leg to take a day return to Oxford and put in an appearance – and a much-needed dose of glamour – at Miss Lancaster's memorial service.

It had been worth every penny though. The sight of all those dowdy academics made her realise how right she had been to turn down the chance of post-graduate research. Not for her a lifetime dressed in library clothes, shuffling around in an old cardi and a depressing pair of tan lace-ups. Lesbian shoes, she called them. Not lesbian shoes in the modern sense, those clumpy black fashion-statements of political indignation. But lesbian in that faded blue-stocking way of marriage being out of bounds to a woman with a mind. It was hard to imagine now that she might have been a research fellow, with all its mannish overtones.

No, she had done well to turn her back on the groves of academe. She lacked the gnat-sized vision required for the work of a scholar. How could you spend years of your life – the only life you had – poring over the minute details of a medieval French manuscript and speculating on what might have been written on the bit of it that had broken off? How unspeakably dull was that? Far better her own giddy existence in the magazine world, fluttering like an exotic butterfly from one colourful story to the next.

There had been a few other high-flyers at the memorial service – it wasn't entirely wall-to-wall pedants. You could tell the ones who had made something of themselves by the way they glanced swiftly at their watches, and scanned the church with a professional eye, making a mental note of those worth talking to after the service. She had managed to touch base with one or two useful contacts, which was the whole purpose of these events. Funerals were for grieving, but memorial services were different. They were for reflecting on a life well lived (you didn't get one if you were a complete nobody) and lent themselves to networking. There was one girl there she remembered from school who had done terribly well and was now practically running *Condé Nast*. She'd mentioned a school reunion that was taking place next week, and Lydia fully intended to go along. Her Essex roots weren't something she liked to make a song and dance about, but she'd make an exception for *Condé Nast*. Jane should come along too, get out of her rut for a change.

It was a shame that Jane had missed the memorial service, but Lydia wasn't surprised. You only wanted to be seen at these public functions if you were feeling good about yourself. And since Jane had given up her proper job in favour of a joyless life of working at home, she seemed reluctant to go anywhere.

Working at home. A slow death. Lydia had joked to Jane once that she was like the miller's daughter in Rumpelstiltskin. Instead of having a roomful of straw to spin into gold, she had a heap of French manuscripts to turn into tuneful English prose. Locked up with her laptop by the cruel Svengali that was Will.

She would ring Jane now, tell her about the service, and see if she could be persuaded to show up next week. No doubt she would be hunched behind her computer, in that messy basement room, while Will was lording it upstairs in his stupidly named *galleria*. She was probably wearing library clothes, too, come to think of it. No point in dressing up when the only conversation you'd have all day would be with the postman.

Jane answered quickly, in the distracted tones of someone breaking off concentration. 'Yup, hallo.'

There was no need to be quite so graceless, thought Lydia, for all Jane knew this could be a very important phone call.

'Darling. It's me. Heading back to London, thank God. Talk about drowning in a sea of tweed, you've never seen a more dismal bunch.'

Jane pulled her mind away from her translation to imagine Lydia in all her glory, surrounded by dusty academics.

'They're above it all, aren't they?' she said. 'More into the life of the mind. You don't work in that world in order to wear fine clothes. The more you study, the more you come to despise human vanity, wouldn't you say?'

Lydia felt a surge of irritation. Jane could be so sanctimonious sometimes, sitting at home, ploughing through her work. 'Anyway,' she continued, 'I'm ringing for two things. First of all, to make sure you're both coming to my party.'

'Of course, wouldn't miss it for the world. A beacon of light beckoning through the dark tunnel of my daily life.'

'There's no need to be sarcastic. I'm sure you have a very busy social life.'

Though Lydia doubted it. Will seemed to have a reasonable time – drinks at Soho House, poker games, gallery openings – but Jane was more interested in staying in for her child, and rarely hired a babysitter. Lydia couldn't understand it herself. If she ever had a child, it would be on her terms, which were loosely based on a photo of Tina Brown taken when she was editor of *Vanity Fair*. Tina had been wearing a spangly evening dress and was perched on the edge of her child's bed alongside her black-tied husband, like a dignified visiting fairy godmother. Popping back from the office to kiss the daughter goodnight before sweeping out to a function. Pure class.

'I'm looking forward to meeting Rupert,' said Jane. 'Crazy name, crazy guy. I can't believe you've managed to keep him from us for so long.'

'You'll love him. I do. Not sure that he's quite Will's style, though.'

'Will's determined not to like him because he hasn't got an interesting job. You know what he's like.'

'Dear Will.' Lydia thought back with a flicker of affection to the time of their affair. It had been really rather exciting.

'But I'm sure he'll come round,' said Jane. 'What does Rupert look like? I imagine he's tall, dark and chisel-jawed.'

'Certainly tall, and possibly chisel-jawed, but not dark.'

'And he's got a very good address.'

'Fantastic address.' Lydia's pulse quickened as she thought about the lateral conversion. 'Hugh Grant and Liz Hurley nearly bought the one above, when they were together. It's rather horribly decorated of course, as you'd expect from a bachelor pad. You know, those nasty oil-painting imitations of old masters.'

'You mean he doesn't own the originals?'

'Not in London. He's got a few hanging in the country seat, apparently. I haven't seen that yet, it's been let out to some oil sheiks to pay off the new roof.'

'He's obviously a good catch, well done.'

'It seems to be going well for us at the moment, touch wood.' That's all you could say about a relationship nowadays, wasn't it? That it was working well at this moment in time. No promises, no unrealistic expectations, enjoy things as they are. It was the way Jane treated her relationship with Will, wearing kid gloves, as though he was a precious ornament that she was incredibly lucky to have out on loan.

Well, actually, no, not in Lydia's book. It didn't work that way. She had invested a great deal of time and energy in her courtship of Rupert. And now, thank God, it was payback time. He had finally done the decent thing and popped the question, without her even having to issue an ultimatum. That would have been very unstylish.

She realised the omens were good when he'd told her he'd booked a table at the Ivy. This was promising in view of his growing fondess for TV meals. It also reminded her that he was someone who could get a same-day booking at the Ivy. Lydia had ordered champagne, as she always did, and when Rupert told the waiter to make it a bottle, she realised the deal was in the bag. He usually preferred a Scotch before dinner.

'I think I'll have the lobster,' Lydia had said.

'Me too,' Rupert had concurred, which Lydia had taken to mean – quite correctly – that she would soon be over the final hurdle.

Jane really needed to get off the phone now, she was reading back over her last paragraph, making her corrections. 'What was the other thing?' she asked briskly. 'You said you were ringing about two things.'

'Oh, yes, that's right,' said Lydia. 'Toni Vincent was there, do you remember her? Anyway, she's now huge at *Condé Nast*, and she told me about a school reunion on Sunday week, so I thought you and I should go along.'

Jane sighed. It seemed Lydia was always trying to get her to do things she didn't want to. 'What for?' she said, fiddling on her computer and changing the font size to make her work look more substantial.

'For laughs. Come on, Jane, let's stand up and be counted as Essex girls. In an ironic spirit, though there's no shame in it these days, look at Jamie Oliver.'

'I'm going to have to let you go, Lydia,' said Jane, 'I really need to get on.'

'Course you do, I'll see you next Sunday then.'

'I'll think about it.'

'I'll pick you up at five.'

Lydia put her phone away and gazed out the window as the train sped past the suburban gardens backing onto the track, ugly patios with clothes hung out to dry on triangular washing lines. She was glad she'd never have to live anywhere like that. Lydia Littlewood had homes in Chelsea and Gloucestershire. And the South of France, she musn't forget that little bonus. *Lydia Littlewood Beauval-Tench divides her time between Chelsea, Gloucestershire and the South of France.* Yes, that would do nicely for her bio at the front of the magazine; with three homes you didn't need to invent any wacky hobbies to make yourself sound interesting.

It had been her idea to keep the engagement secret and to announce it at their Christmas drinks party. It kept the excitement going for a while longer. She would tap on the side of her glass with a silver spoon – very appropriate – and pray silence please, and Rupert would then say they had something else to celebrate this Christmas and would everyone please raise their glasses to his bride-to-be.

At this point Lydia would look at Jane to see her expression of surprise, mingled with a reassuring dose of envy.

Because poor old Jane had fallen into the dreadful trap of 'living together'. Lydia had seen so many of her friends taken in by that one. They didn't realise it was feminism's BOG – Big Own Goal – saying you didn't need to get married. Whereas from where Lydia was standing, marriage was always of financial benefit to a woman.

Unless you were very rich like Madonna, in which case you had a pre-nup. If you didn't marry and made the fatal error of moving in together, that was it: you had played your trump card and completely scuppered your chances of getting him up the aisle. Either he liked what he had, so saw no reason to change things, or he believed he could one day do slightly better, so might as well keep his options open. Either way it was a no-win situation for the live-in girlfriend.

Mindful of the need to avoid the BOG trap, Lydia's tactics had been exemplary. Like Anne Boleyn and Catherine Zeta Jones – who had both held out for a ring on the finger – she knew you needed to maintain a bit of distance to keep him interested. She always kept her own apartment, most recently a shoebox in unlovely Balham. Rupert respected her independence and they enjoyed mutual visiting rights. And now they were going to do things properly. She had a wedding to plan, and a home to decorate as well as her day job. Busy, busy, busy.

The train was pulling into Paddington and Lydia checked her make-up in her compact mirror. Green eyes, an unusual colour cleverly emphasised by her use of eyeshadow, luxuriant auburn hair, her best feature, which she often wore brushed forward over one shoulder. She traced a finger lightly over her slim white neck that was gratifyingly free of lines. Come to think of it, Anne Boleyn was not an ideal role model. She got her man all right, but then look what happened to her.

Lydia thought she'd work at Rupert's flat this afternoon, since everything about Prince Charles's farming methods was loaded onto her laptop. There was no need to be too technical; her readers were more interested in her insight into HRH at home than his views on dreary old agriculture. Who cared what the calves ate, what really mattered was whether the valet who served them tea looked as though he might be enjoying an unhealthy relationship with another member of the royal household. Though she wouldn't couch it in those terms. She worked for a society glossy, not the gutter press.

'Cadogan Gardens please,' she said to the taxi driver, who nodded his approval. What a relief it was, after two years of remonstrating with cabbies to take her to the black hole of Balham, to know you wouldn't have to put up a fight in order to get home. 'Sorry love, I don't go south of the river,' they usually said, 'can't get a ride back.' She quite sympathised; she wouldn't go there herself given the choice.

It had been such a come-down, after her return from New York. Two years of *Sex and the City* glamour, the feted British expat, then home to roost in Balham. It gave her a frisson of panic to think what might have been if Rupert hadn't come good on the proposal. A lifetime of Balham, although it was surprising how many posh people seemed to emerge from the tube, mostly temporary inhabitants on a staging post to somewhere more respectable. Young blonde mothers would drift westwards to Wandsworth to join horrid playgroups and children's music clubs twixt the commons in Nappy Valley. Nappy of the Valley of Living Death. Lydia would stick to Chelsea, thank you very much.

She paid the taxi and let herself into Rupert's building, picking up his post from the hall table. She would take care of all the admin once they were married, she was good at it and liked to feel in control. She walked up to the second floor and let herself into the apartment, throwing down her coat and breathing in the atmosphere of what would soon become her home. The maid hadn't been in and Lydia made a mental note to change that: you needed someone every day or what was the point? A bowl of half-eaten cereal sat discarded on the kitchen table, and a cup of cold tea stood on the drainer, next to the supper dishes piled up in the sink. Well, they'd just have to stay there; Lydia had no intention of starting as she didn't mean to go on.

She wandered down to the bathroom, where Rupert's spartan collection of toiletries stood on the shelf above the basin. Razor, shaving foam, deodorant, toothbrush, it didn't take much to get him ready for the outside world. Her own overnight bag was kept in the cabinet, containing a small sample of the range of beauty products that would soon be crowding Rupert out. She frowned as she looked round the room. Those black and white tiles would have to go, they were so desperately Eighties. She was planning to completely redo this bathroom anyway, to turn it into a wet room. This meant you lost the boundaries between shower tray and floor (*so* suburban, the idea of a shower tray!) and just stood in a mist of beautiful mosaic tiles while the water came at you from all sides in a sort of Moroccan nirvana of spiritual cleansing. If Rupert made a fuss, she could always have a jock-style power shower fitted in the guest bathroom.

Her mind buzzing with design ideas, Lydia went back to the sitting room and sank down on a large and ugly leather sofa. It was like Rupert himself, she thought disloyally, big, beige and comfortable, and directly facing an extremely large television screen. The room was given over to the needs of a man coming in from work with no thought in his head beyond kicking off his shoes to watch Sky Sports over a takeaway chicken tikka masala. Needless to say, it would have to change. You couldn't have smart dinners where the guests were expected to have their drinks sitting in a circle around the council-house-style monster telly.

It gave Lydia a rush of excitement to think about briefing a designer. No wonder brides always lost weight, there was so much to do that you forgot about food. She had a short-list of three interior architects and was waiting to see who would give her the best price in exchange for a four-page spread in the magazine. It was lucky the photos were always taken of interiors without any people sitting in them to ruin the view. Rupert, bless him, was a lovely guy, but hardly likely to enhance a mood shot of the kind of Soho Loft meets the Andes vibe that she was aiming for. He was more Johnnie Boden meets happy-clappy schoolmaster.

She remembered the first time she had met him, in New York, in the piano bar of the Pierre Hotel, a stately establishment where the corridors were lined with unctuous staff. Very old money, and just what Lydia thought she was looking for. During her brief affair with Will, he had brought her to New York to stay at the Paramount, a Johnny-come-lately kind of place, done out like a nightclub so you couldn't see anyone's face in reception. John Malkovich had held the door open for her, which was nice, but it was all a bit too cool for its own good.

In contrast to the darkness of the Paramount, the Pierre was all gold and magnolia, fatly upholstered chairs, ten sheets on your bed. Rupert had been looking very at ease; he was big enough for this place, whereas Will, had she brought him here all those years ago, would have looked small and displaced, like a street busker who had somehow made it through the wall of bouncers.

Rupert and Lydia had been set up on a double date, which they undertook in the ironic spirit of the British abroad, the idea of 'dating' being beyond hilarious in their home country. With their trademark haplessness, the British expected to just fall into the right relationship, whereas the Americans worked earnestly to establish the best possible base from which to proceed. Luckily, the date had paid off, and she had hit the jackpot.

Sod the work, thought Lydia, I've got a wedding to plan. She put her coat back on and decided to check out Kelly Hoppen on the Fulham Road where she was thinking of having her list. They had nothing in the window except three white vases at astronomical prices, which all looked very promising.

The rain was sheeting down as Lydia walked up the road to Sloane Square where the Peter Jones courtesy bus arrived just in time to rescue her from those damned nuisance charity workers patrolling the Kings Road with their clipboards. As if she didn't have enough to spend her money on right now. She sank gratefully into the luxuriously upholstered seat. At the age of thirty-seven, she was a short engagement away from being a rich Chelsea wife, with an interesting and successful career to boot. When she could so easily have slipped into the life of a sad freelance hack with a bedsit in Balham. It had been a gamble, moving to New York, but one that had paid off. You won't make the scene if you don't hit the green, to quote one of those mottos of self-improvement so beloved of Americans, the masters of reinvention. Don't ask, don't get. Go for broke. Marry a millionaire.

The bus drew up outside PJ2 in Draycott Avenue and the passengers got off, politely thanking the driver as though he were the family chauffeur. Lydia cut back to Sloane Avenue, past Bibendum and left into the Fulham Road, when she heard the sound of low-flying aircraft so loud she feared an attack by the axis of evil. But it was just a red Virgin helicopter coming down to land in the private gardens of Onslow Square. Richard Branson coming home for his tea, perhaps. How fabulous.

And wasn't that Nigella and Charles going into Theo Fennell's posh jewellery shop, the tall façade prettily illuminated by a mesh of white fairy lights? It was here that the Duchess of York's poor ex-dresser had been working before she clubbed her boyfriend to death with his own cricket bat for failing to marry her and referring to her as a pair of old slippers. Lydia would not have gone that far, but Rupert's proposal had certainly brought things to a very satisfactory conclusion. She pushed open the door to Kelly Hoppen and greeted the lofty assistant with a smile. 'I'd like to open a wedding list, please,' she said. Was it her imagination or did she see a flicker of envy cross the girl's face?

Jane wished she had gone to the memorial service now. She always did that – said she was too busy to do things, then wasted time dithering around. Lydia's call had knocked her off her stride, and she might as well have gone for all the work she'd achieved this morning.

Maybe she really should go to that school reunion next week. Last time she'd checked on Friends Reunited, she'd been cheered by the all-round lack of achievement. The cleverest girl in the class was now working part-time as a receptionist at the local opticians which fitted in nicely round school hours. Former prefect Janet Bowles volunteered the information (with three exclamation marks) that she could usually be found browsing the aisles of her second home, aka Waitrose. It must be lovely to feel so little pressure to succeed.

She switched off the computer and thought about lunch. She could make herself a macrobiotic salad using the salad leaves and seeds she so conscientiously hunted out at farmers' markets. Will swore by them, hoping their virtuous influence would stamp out the after-effects of his decadent youth. He was always telling Jane what she should and shouldn't be eating.

She decided that what she really needed was a Chicken McNugget Meal with large fries and large non-diet Coke. It offered the double satisfaction of being nutritionally void and creating an unseemly amount of non-recyclable waste. That polystyrene box alone, she thought, as she slipped her coat on and pulled the door behind her, could push Will over the edge.

Walking back home with her McDonald's, Jane disposed of the evil packaging in an anonymous bin, and wondered what thoughtful present she should buy to take tonight. They were invited to supper with an art-dealer friend of Will's. Jane knew better than to say they were going to a dinner party. Will had told her early on in their relationship that he didn't do dinner parties. All that fuss about the seating plan, boy, girl, boy, girl, it was so damned couply. Instead, he did supper with friends, which was far more bohemian. Ossian was quite nice, but the wife was a worry, a glamorous actress who knew everybody. You couldn't very well hand over a box of Celebrations. I know, Jane thought, I'll go to that pretentious shop on Westbourne Grove and get them a glass boot of cassis balsamic vinegar. Wildly original.

Hunched over her computer with her Chocolate Chip Flurry, she pulled out her Christmas list to see what else she should look for while she was out. Not many shopping days left now, and she had Will's family to think of as well as her own. His mother was the most difficult, since she only approved of useful gifts, and had a withering contempt for anything that suggested unnecessary expense. The problem being that by the time you got to eighty you didn't need anything except for medical accoutrements, which hardly made for a festive feeling.

Three hours later she arrived at school, the car piled high with booty. Liberty was standing alone in the playground, her face thunderous. She made a throat-slitting gesture as Jane rushed up to collect her.

'Sorry darling, terrible traffic, I was doing some Christmas shopping.'

She opened the car door and Liberty climbed in, turning round to peer into the boot. 'Did you get me a pet?' she asked, as though hoping to see a puppy or a kitten snuggled up among the carrier bags. It was all she wanted this year, an animal to call her own.

'You know we've discussed that,' said Jane, 'and you agreed a goldfish would be very nice.'

'Oh, aren't *I* a lucky ducky?' said Liberty sarcastically. She often came out of school with a new piece of posh slang. 'Can't I at least have something you can hold?'

Jane did sympathise. You might as well drop a slice of carrot in a bowl of water for all the reward a fish could give you. 'Maybe next year,' she said.

Liberty slumped back in her seat. Next year didn't count when you were seven. 'Are we going anywhere for Christmas?' she asked.

'No, we're staying here and everyone's coming to us.'

'Oh. Lutetia's going skiing, Apple's going to Thailand. And Panda's going on a safari.'

'Bully for Panda. Maybe she'll be captured and forced to live in a tree.'

Back at the house, Jane ferried in the Christmas presents and hid them in the cellar, away from Liberty's curious gaze. The boxes of shelves she had bought at Ikea were still sitting in the hall.

'I'd better take those up,' said Jane, 'you know how Daddy can't bear things cluttering up the house.'

'I'll help,' Liberty offered. She had changed out of her school uniform and wanted to be useful.

'Too heavy for you,' Jane said, heaving the first pack onto her back, 'but you can help me put them together.'

'Why don't you get Daddy to do it?'

'He's got a bad back, you know that.'

Jane was stronger than she looked, which was just as well, since Will was reluctant to lift things. Not that he was lazy. When he had been married to Carol, he'd done all the decorating himself, with disastrous consequences for his back. Second time round he felt he deserved an architect. It was a measure of his success. My architect, my agent, my lawyer, my sleep therapist; it suggested that all these people belonged to you, that you sat on the apex of an important pyramid as chairman and managing director of the large business that was your life. The architect had been ruinously expensive. Personally, Jane would have preferred to spend the money on a cleaner, or holidays, or else put it away for school fees – his monstrous bill sat oddly alongside the careful economies she made to stretch the household budget.

'That's the last one.' Liberty handed over the final screw to Jane as she finished constructing the shelves and they admired the results.

'Excellent work,' said Jane, 'you'll have somewhere to put your fish tank now. Why don't you come and talk to me while I get ready for this boring dinner.'

Liberty followed her into the master bedroom and helped her lay out suitable outfits on the bed. She then produced her box of Barbies and lined them up on the floor, their dresses piled up in a chaotic heap.

Jane frowned at the thought of the evening ahead. Dressing for supper with Will's friends was always tricky. To be avoided at all costs was looking as though you had tried too hard; on the other hand, she was no longer in quite good-enough shape to slouch up in an old pair of jeans. She pulled on a rather short skirt and a white shirt under the critical eye of her daughter.

'Your arse looks good in that,' said Liberty, nodding her approval.

'Don't say arse,' said Jane absent-mindedly, turning in front of the mirror and wondering if Will would agree. She rifled through her jewellery box for what she hoped was a bohemian pair of hoop earrings while Liberty turned back to talk to her dolls. Jane wished she'd been able to give her a little brother or sister but Will had been adamant, his nerves couldn't take it. The fact remained that he had three children and she had just the one. It seemed a bit unfair but she wouldn't dream of springing another surprise baby on him. You didn't do that sort of thing in a reasonable modern relationship.

'Come on, darling,' she said, 'let's get you to bed.'

Her mind roamed freely as she read chapter five of *The Enchanted Wood* at breakneck speed. Three hundred and sixty-five stories a year, no wonder it got a bit dull. I have measured out my life in bedtime stories, she thought. But that was child-rearing for you, an accumulation of mind-deadening routines. If you don't like repetition, don't have kids. It was a choice you made and you shouldn't expect any sympathy. What else was life for anyway? The one thing she could never regret was her beautiful, demanding daughter.

She slapped on some lipstick and rushed downstairs to tidy up for the babysitter. Ianthe's nanny from Estonia was arriving at eight. 'I'm making the most of her while she's fresh,' Ianthe's mother had said. 'Once they've been over here for a couple of years, they quite lose that Eastern Bloc work ethic.' Hardly surprising living in that house. Ianthe's mother wasn't exactly a model of industry, swanning around having lunch and discussing her winnings in the Hearts pyramid scheme.

Listening to the wailing police sirens, Jane worried, as usual, if she was doing enough for Liberty. Ice-skating, French lessons, violin, tennis, pottery classes. It sounded a lot, but what about tai chi and chess and drama classes? And Japanese was supposed to be very good for stimulating the left side of the brain. What if Liberty grew up stunted because an unexplored area of her consciousness had not been properly stimulated at a young age? She might be like a wilted plant potted in the wrong soil, her leaves yellow with neglect, and all because her mother had failed to identify an obvious childhood need.

Will told her she worried too much, but it was different for men. They didn't feel viscerally responsible for the well-being of their children the way that mothers did. While she was putting Liberty to bed, he had been out for drinks with some writer friends, being big and clever and exchanging ideas that transcended the small domestic arena. She fought back her resentment. The last thing she wanted to become was a dreary nag. Naomi Wolf said men believed the sanctuary of the Edwardian home had become a domestic hell, filled with vituperative harridans. There was no way that Jane would become like Will's ex, moaning and needy and unsympathetic to his creative requirements. Will Thacker, the acclaimed writer — she couldn't say she hadn't hit the jackpot.

She heard a key in the lock.

'Hallo, sexy,' Will said, slurring slightly as he looked her up and down, 'you look hot, in a waitressy sort of way. Shall we go?'

* * *

Ossian and Bella lived in Notting Hill and had an outside shower on one of their roof terraces. It was Bella who opened the door, wearing plastic flowers in her hair and what looked like a floor-length nylon housecoat with a brown and orange floral theme. Jane would have looked like an escapee from a mental hospital in such an outfit.

They followed her into a kitchen/dining room of gargantuan proportions. The doorways had been widened to bring them into proportion with the high ceilings, and extra-deep work surfaces had been installed to give an Olympian feel to the room. It was not a house for little people.

Although a bit on the small side, Will fitted in perfectly with his Jasper Conran jacket that had been deliberately frayed at the edges to look as though it was twenty years old. By comparison, Jane felt like the suburban school girl she was, dressed up in her trendy weekend wear for a day up in town. In her short black skirt, she felt she should be passing round the canapés.

'Hey, you look gorgeous,' said Bella's husband Ossian, sidling up for a better look. He'd always had a soft spot for Jane, and there had once been an embarrassing incident when he had pressed himself up against her at a gallery opening. She hadn't told Will about it: he might have thought her a prude, or else that she had been flirting. In any case, it was all water under the bridge, and she was grateful for his attention tonight.

'Let me introduce you.' He put a hand in the small of her back and propelled her over to where a gouty-looking man and his effete companion were sitting on a Moroccan couch.

'May I present the estimable linguist Jane Locksmith? This is Roland Edgeworth and Jeremy Markham.'

It was the kind of party where everyone was introduced by their full names, so it was clear they were people of substance. There was none of that 'James and Amanda, this is Phil and Jenny' stuff that you got at the sort of dinner parties Will hated.

Jane had heard of Roland Edgeworth, he was rich and wrote erudite books on London's history. Jeremy sat beside him, his thin legs in tight silver trousers crossed, lady-style, to one side. He started to talk to Jane about champagne, while Roland puffed away at a cigarette, ill at ease so early in the evening and only three glasses to the wind.

Jeremy leaned towards Jane, a confidential hand on her thigh. 'I know everyone goes on about the Louis Roederer vintage being the bee's knees,' he said, 'but do you know, I actually prefer his *non*-vintage.'

'Interesting,' said Jane. She smiled politely and tried to think of something clever to say, but her mind had gone blank.

'Cheap to run,' guffawed Roland, breaking his silence and topping up his glass.

'That's me,' said Jeremy. 'Low-maintenance Larry. Actually, the only champagne I can't stand is Moët.' He pronounced it correctly, sounding the hard T at the end. 'I find there is something about it that just hits the back of the throat. Quite undrinkable.' He shook his head at the impossibility of it all.

'You're a linguist, Jane, you'll be able to help me,' he went on. 'What does *blanc de blanc* actually mean? Blankety blank, blankety blank, what's all that about?'

There was a silence as they waited for her answer. White of white, of course, but what did it *mean*? She dithered around until Roland took pity on her.

'White wine from white grapes,' he pronounced, coughing then extinguishing his cigarette, 'whereas the best champagne is made from a mixture of red and white grapes. Pinot Chardonnay and Pinot Noir, to be precise.'

'Champagne made from red grapes,' said Jeremy, 'who'd have thought it? Shall we go through?'

They moved across to join the others at the table. Will was well into his stride now, talking to a fat man with a twirly moustache and pointy beard, and a freakishly tall model like a child distorted by the Hall of Mirrors. Jane tried to think of interesting topics. Would they be curious to hear about her recent trip to Ikea? She could talk about her work, if pushed, but it was unlikely that the translation of a guide to French bridges would hold them for long.

'You have to be Catholic if you've got children,' Bella was saying, 'only fools and Protestants pay school fees. I know that church is the ugliest building on Kensington High Street, but come on, one hour on a Sunday morning to save twenty grand a year, you'd be stupid not to. Schmoozing the priest has been my most lucrative role ever!'

Everybody laughed except Ossian, who had heard it all before.

At the table, Will was enthralling the model with his tales of life among the Amerindians. It was fascinating to watch him – he still had an irresistible effect on women, a magnetism that Jane remembered all too well from their own early days. 'It's a need with me, Ali,' he was saying, his eyes on a level with her flat chest, 'to get beyond the pedestrian, to test myself to the limits.'

The model nodded down at him. 'I know what you mean. I always say to myself, come on Ali, you really could look even better, just give it all you've got.'

Will looked insulted by the comparison. Scowling into a camera was hardly on a par with his own spiritual journey to the heart of another culture. He carried on regardless. 'As I was saying only the other evening to David Hare, most people in our society can't see beyond their couple. They get locked into their little lives, can't see that there's a fascinating world out there . . .'

'I'm single at the moment actually,' she interrupted him. 'I've got a few issues to deal with before I enter another relationship.'

Would the bloody woman not shut up and let him finish? 'Whereas I strive constantly to explore, to understand, to recognise that I am just a tiny cog in the greater scheme of things,' he continued. 'In essence I suppose you could say my work is an exercise in humility . . .'

Jeremy cut across him. 'What exactly are your issues, Ali?' he asked, unable to resist the scent of psychobabble.

Ali jumped at the chance to talk about herself and her problems. 'Oh, eating issues for one,' she said. 'You've always got them if you're a model; and then I've got confidence issues, of course, but I do feel I'm becoming stronger . . .'

Jane caught Will's eye and smiled sympathetically. She knew he couldn't stand the language of personal growth.

But Will frowned and turned instead to talk across to Roland, by now dangerously red in the face.

Jane was rescued by the man with the twirly moustache. 'I understand you're in the translation game?'

This was her chance to talk herself up a bit, make herself sound fascinating. Instead she took the easy option of turning things back to him.

'That's right,' she said. 'And I would guess you're an artist of some kind, judging from your appearance.'

Twirly gave a dismissive gesture to his velvet jacket and floppy bow tie. 'Might as well look the part. I'm a novelist, actually. Do you translate fiction?'

'No, I don't do literary. I'm more on the practical reference side. Less scope for misinterpretation.'

Dull, dull, dull, she thought. He gave her a pitying nod.

'I know it's a bit of a poor relation,' she apologised. 'Will can be rather cruel about it actually. You know, if you can't do, teach. If you can't write, translate.'

'Oh rubbish,' said Twirly, unconvincingly, 'we must each do what we can.'

'Well, yes. I used to have an office job, but I wanted to change to something I could do from home so I could be there for my daughter.'

She saw his interest waning and was annoyed with herself. Everyone knew it was social suicide to start on about your kids as if you had nothing else to talk about.

The model broke away from Jeremy to join their conversation. She clearly had the concentration span of a flea. 'Don't you find it boring working at home?' she said. 'It's a bit nerdy, isn't it, all by yourself. I'd be watching Kilroy all the time. Or Trisha. Mind you, I could never be a translator, I'm useless at languages.'

'I work at home too,' said Jeremy, 'keeping myself gorgeous for Roland, and let me tell you, that is a full-time job.'

'With splendid results,' said Twirly, his eyes feasting on Jeremy's biceps bulging out of his tight little tee shirt. 'Give us your secrets, Jeremy, I might make you a character in my next novel.'

Jeremy settled back in delight at this invitation to hold forth on his favourite subject. 'Jojoba oil,' he said, 'with a few drops of rosemary to help build brain cells. I rub it all over my body and scalp before I exercise. And the moment I wake, I programme myself to admire everything so that every new day provides something beautiful.'

With Roland's funds at his disposal, it would be easy to find beauty, thought Jane. The only ugly thing Jeremy had to encounter each morning was Roland's bloated body lying in bed beside him.

'Next I do aerobics and yoga before I shower. I floss three times a day and once a month I hang the enema bag on the bathroom door, run the hosepipe up my bottom and do a handstand. Wonderful clear-out.'

'Ugh!' said Jane before she could stop herself.

Jeremy looked at her in surprise. 'Just basic body-management, darling. You need to look at your body as a business and the organs as executives. They each have job descriptions you know, and hang on to emotional memory. Especially the thalamus.'

'The what?'

He ignored her. 'The heart and liver need a lot of nour-ishment and motivation. I pay them special attention in my morning meditation. You need to nurture yourself to heal yourself. That's why I'm never ill. Plus I only buy organic.'

Yes, it would be easy to stay healthy when you led such a spoilt and pampered life.

He seemed to read her thoughts. 'But my number-one tip is, get yourself a nice rich man and the rest will follow.' He blew a kiss to Roland who grunted in acknowl-edgement as he filled his glass to the rim. He was grateful to Jeremy for providing floozy glamour, it was just what he needed after a hard day in his study.

Jane did her best through dinner, helped along by Ossian who seemed amused by her account of her daily life, egging her on for details, asking her to talk him through the school run. She couldn't help wondering if he was taking the piss.

'Hey, Bella,' said the model, who had eaten nothing all night. 'I really like your curtains. That is just so cool, blankets held back with leather belts.'

Bella leaped up to finger them and demonstrate their authentic roughness. 'Belgian surplus army blankets. And the belts are from Gap Kids.' She shrugged. 'Simple ideas are always the best.'

'I absolutely agree,' said Twirly. 'It's a hard and fast rule in my novels. Particularly in my latest where I had the rather straightforward notion of twins separated at birth who then meet up . . .'

'Green tea, anyone?' Bella cut him off quickly. Writers

could be terribly dull; clearly it had been a mistake to invite three at one sitting. Actors were so much better value, dishing up hilarious theatrical anecdotes instead of droning on about their dreary books.

Jane declined the tea, to her hostess's surprise.

'Would you prefer a tisane? Or raspberry leaf? Ayurvedic?'

'No thanks. Have you got any coffee?'

Jane's request was met with the astonishment you might expect if you asked for Class A drugs at a prayer meeting.

'Let me see,' said Bella, getting over the shock, 'I think one of my au pairs bought some last week . . . yes, here we are.' She searched in a cupboard and brought out a packet of instant-cappuccino sachets as though she were holding a filled nappy sack.

'*One* of your au pairs, how many have you got?' asked Jane, then immediately wished she hadn't. How mumsy was that, to show an interest in the home help? 'Just two. Work it out, instead of paying a fortune for a nanny, you get two nice girls for a pittance each, they share a room and have each other for company and you have twenty-four-hour cover. I can't think why more people haven't cottoned on.'

Afterwards, they moved across the sitting area, where Roland spilt wine over the Moroccan throw and passed out in a large snoring heap. Will went off to the loo with the model in order to 'talk to Charlie'. Which left Jeremy centre-stage to talk about his latest therapy.

'It seems that Sudden Wealth Syndrome is quite common

now,' he confided. 'They identified it at the Money, Meaning and Choices institute in San Francisco. Roland wanted me to see someone after we were talking about *Who Wants to be a Millionaire* at a dinner and I happened to say that thirty-two thou was nothing to us. Which it isn't. It wasn't as if I was in a room of social workers, either, most people there would have spent at least that on their fortieth birthday parties. But then when I ran up a bill of twenty-five thou redecorating the bedroom, he insisted I take myself in hand. So to speak,' he added with a lewd wink.

Was he serious? Since when did striking it lucky mean you had to go into therapy? Jane had had enough now, she wanted to go home.

'Guilt is a terrible thing,' Jeremy was saying, 'it can ruin your life if you're not careful.'

'So give your money away to charity if that's how you feel,' said Ossian with a shrug, 'rid yourself of the cause.' Personally he'd never lost any sleep over his millions, but then again he'd been born to it. Unlike Jeremy, who had gone overnight from hotel receptionist to kept man and crazed spendthrift.

'It's not really mine to give,' said Jeremy, nodding towards his prostrate companion whose snoring had now reached a deafening level, 'and to be honest, I don't want to give it away. I like being rich, I just want to stop feeling bad about it.'

'Shrinks are the new priests,' said Ossian, 'it's the secular version of paying a cleric to say mass for you.'

Will was animated on his return from the lavatory, and it was well into the small hours before they finally did leave.

Roland was roused from the dead by Jeremy and assisted into a taxi, while Twirly and the model went home on foot. Jane had her eye on the clock as she drove away, calculating how much she needed to pay the babysitter, and whether she had sufficient cash in her purse. She knew better than to ask Will. He couldn't really be bothered with tedious stuff like this after a good night out.

Will was wide awake on the journey home. 'I couldn't believe you, Jane, sitting there with your instant coffee, like you were at girl-guide camp.'

'Ging gang goolie,' she said, slowing down as they approached a roundabout, 'I can't help being conventional, blame it on my upbringing. And at least coffee is cheaper than cocaine, you should be grateful I'm so cheap to run.'

'I hope that wasn't a sly dig at me. I'm allowed to enjoy myself now and then, aren't I?'

'Of course. And I'm allowed to indulge my quaint old-fashioned habits. At least my needs are simple and you don't have to fork out for a therapist for me. Or an enema bag. That Jeremy was quite something, wasn't he?'

'Colourful, at least.'

'And incredibly narcissistic.'

Will sighed. 'You're so . . .' he was searching for the right word '. . . sensible. That's the word for you, Jane. You are such a sensible woman.'

'I'll take that as a compliment, shall I?'

'If you like.'

'I do like. Unless you're trying to say that I'm a boring person without an original idea in my head.'

'Hmm.' He was laughing now, but Jane wasn't going to let it go.

'So, if I am so uninteresting, why did you . . . why do you live with me?'

'Interesting question. And one to which there are many answers.'

'One will do.'

'Just one, now let me see.' He drummed his fingers on the window and gazed out thoughtfully at the deserted London streets.

'Your wild-mushroom risotto, perhaps. Or the way your hair springs up at the front. Your smile. Maybe it's because you don't cramp my style, you know how to give me space . . .'

'Not very convincing so far . . .'

'Or because you've offered me the chance to be a father again without ramming it down my throat . . .'

'Useful breeding stock . . .'

He frowned and tried again. 'I suppose I live with you because I am happier with you than I would be without you. Yes, that's it, it's like Cyril Connolly said, if we want to be happy "we must select the illusion which appeals to our temperament and embrace it with passion." And you are my illusion.' He smiled across at her in triumph, and added in an American accent, 'You are my illusion of choice.'

They drove on in silence for a bit.

'And what about you, Jane,' he asked. 'Are you happy with your life?'

She drove in silence for a while, thinking about everything she had to be grateful for. Her precious daughter, her job, her house. The fragile construction of their family life. You had to be so careful the whole thing didn't come crashing down around your ears.

'Of course,' she said. 'I make it my business to be happy.' She took her hand off the wheel to squeeze his leg.

Jane drove the babysitter home to avoid paying for a cab. Will was already asleep when she got back, wearing his British Airways blindfold to keep out the morning light. His ears were blocked with special wax ear-plugs that he'd bought in France. The normal ones were hopeless, they fell out in the bed like rabbit pellets, whereas Boules Quies could be lovingly kneaded to size. He lay there, his chest rising and falling, all orifices defended from attack by the outside world.

Not wanting to wake him, Jane slipped into bed without turning on the light. She stared up at the blackness and thought about their conversation on the way home. It should be obvious, shouldn't it? Ask yourself whether you are happy, and you cease to be so: that's what John Stuart Mill thought.

She was happy enough for sure, with her lovely daughter and a man to share her life, and her work to keep her occupied and drive away the demons. Those were the most important things. Then there was the accumulation of small pleasures that made up the rest of happiness. Cooking and gardening and the occasional treat to look forward to, like her trip to the cinema tomorrow lunchtime.

It was a habit she had acquired when Liberty started school, and she finally found she had some time to herself. Often on a Friday afternoon, she switched off her computer, turned her back on her domestic duties and took the tube to South Kensington to see a film at the French Institute. She always went alone, that was part of the pleasure. With no-one to defer to, she was anonymous, silent, and free to please herself. In three years she had revisited the *oeuvre* of Bunuel, Godard, Truffaut, and kept up with the new releases. She sat near the back, surrounded by empty seats, sipping on a mini bottle of Evian and letting the Frenchness of it all wash over her. Dark gallic eyes, suffused with unspoken meaning, the banal stirring of a cup of coffee somehow conveying the looming shadows of tragedy.

Tomorrow she was going to see an old favourite, *A Bout de Souffle*. It had all the ingredients. A heroine with a Joan of Arc hairdo and authentic striped tee shirt; fantastic black and white shots of Paris in the days when you could just draw up and park your 2CV on the Champs Elysées; the suggestion that happiness was contained in a simple room with a bare mattress, two glasses and a bottle of wine. Young people with their lives ahead of them. She couldn't wait.

She snuggled into Will's back, her non-seeing, non-hearing partner, who was now snoring loudly. Thanks to his ear plugs he was sealed in a soundless world, but it didn't mean he couldn't be heard. Jane reached out a hand to pinch his nose and cover his mouth. There was a silence, then the familiar pig-like snort as he wrenched his face away to take a desperate breath. Then he settled back down to regular, quiet breathing. If there was one thing Jane had learned in ten years of non-marriage to Will, it was how to stop him keeping her awake at night.

That night she dreamed she was on a safari with Panda and half of Liberty's classmates. They were wearing their purple uniforms, packed into one giant Jeep under Jane's supervision, while Will followed in a separate vehicle, scowling at them from under his weathered Drizabone hat.

THREE

Rupert Beauval-Tench slipped on his jacket and glanced down at Lydia still asleep in bed. She wouldn't wake up for at least two hours, which was perhaps why she looked so serene. Though come to think of it, she always looked serene. She was blessed with the peace of mind that came from knowing what she wanted, and being in no doubt that it would all come her way in the end. It was what had attracted him to her, this presumption that life was a party to which she had been invited as chief guest of honour. He only wished he felt the same.

He quietly closed the door to the apartment and went downstairs, letting himself out of the front entrance where the taxi was waiting, engine purring, black and shiny against the redbrick terrace. Considering this was such a chic address, the architecture was pedestrian, like a series of Victorian school-buildings.

Climbing into the back of the cab, Rupert stretched out his long legs and reminded himself that London taxis were one of the few reasons he was glad to be back in

Britain. In New York the sullen drivers refused to get out, and left you to pull your own suitcase out of the trunk. In London, you felt they were on your side; they were engaged and chatty, with firm opinions, and often alarmingly well-read.

'Mayfair please,' he said. 'St James Street.'

The driver nodded, and Rupert disappeared behind his copy of the *Financial Times*. He might as well face the worst and check out this morning's figures, though doing so always left him with a creeping sense of gloom. At the age of forty, he knew he should feel much happier than he did. Not only did he have a lovely new fiancée, he had his very own new business to run.

'Looks like you're in finance.' The driver had raised his face to speak, obliging Rupert to meet his gaze in the rear-view mirror.

'Sorry?'

The driver pointed at his *FT*. 'You want to take a look at that book by Roland Edgeworth I've left out in the back,' he went on. 'He's got a good section on you lot. "In sawcy State the griping Broker sits." John Gay. Wrote *The Beggar's Opera*,' he added, seeing Rupert's blank response.

Rupert politely put down his paper to take a flick through the densely worded tome bulging out of the back pocket of the front seat.

'I'm not a broker, actually,' he said. 'Good God, have you read the whole thing? How on earth do you find the time?'

'Lunch break. I get a sandwich and sit in the rank. What d'you do then?'

'Me? Oh, I used to work for a bank, but I left to set up a hedge fund.'

'A what?'

'It's . . . a bit tricky to explain really. Not sure that I quite know myself.' He acquitted himself with a self-deprecating smile in the mirror. 'Speaking of which, I'd better get back to the markets, if you don't mind.' He replaced the book and retreated behind his newspaper. On reflection, there were times when a silent driver would be preferable to a chirpy London cabbie.

He glanced down the figures printed in small tight columns on the pale orange paper, then sighed and closed his eyes. It must be his age. There had been a time when he was genuinely interested in all this, but since his return from New York he just felt he was going through the motions, marking time until he found a way out. This was unfortunate, since he had just gone into partnership with a colleague whose enthusiasm made Rupert feel like a sodden old rag in comparison. After eighteen years in the corporate fold they had decided with *Boys' Own* bravado that it was time to go it alone, but Rupert was no longer so sure it was such a good idea.

Turning forty, that's what had done it for him, though he had played the occasion down with a low-key dinner for two with Lydia, rather than one of those bells-and-whistles parties that people gave to show how well they'd done. His business partner Richard had also hit forty this year, and had chartered a large ship to convey three hundred close friends in a Disco Inferno-themed evening to the Thames barrier and back. He always did things properly. He already had a wife and four kids flourishing on a country estate in Kent where he reared organic venison and hosted quiz nights in his spare time. Rupert had a country pile too, but his was unfairly inherited rather than earned through his own talent and energy. It was unavailable anyway, having been leased to a Saudi prince for eight years. And even if he and Lydia started a family right away, he knew he'd never catch up with Richard.

The cab dropped him outside his office in Mayfair. They had chosen St James Street because London's most successful hedge fund was based here, and it was hoped that this success might rub off on them like gold dust. To Rupert, it felt increasingly that they were rats on a sinking ship. He climbed the stairs, trying to work himself up into a positive frame of mind. It was easier in New York where the money-making ethic ran through the streets and was contagious, like a happy plague. Plus he had been there during the late Nineties boom, when everything you touched turned to gold. Not like now in this age of uncertainty, beneath grey British skies and a bear market and the rebellious British public rising up against fat-cat salaries. Rupert sympathised, he always considered himself grossly overpaid compared to real people who did real jobs. It's just that he couldn't really think what else to do.

Richard was already at his desk, which was festooned with photographs of himself surrounded by his large family. Having ten photos of yourself on display might be considered vain, but for some reason this was not the case if your kids were in the frame with you. Richard's wife was there, too, beaming out confidently, candy-striped pink trousers cropped beneath the knee, white shirt with upturned collar, headband and gold earrings. She was one of those girls from a comfortable background who seemed entirely fulfilled by her role as homemaker. Rupert couldn't quite see Lydia in that vein, nor would he necessarily want her to be hovering with a G and T the moment he stepped in the door.

Richard greeted him with a hand upstretched, like a policeman stopping traffic. 'Rupert, sound fellow!'

The hand was square and strong, confident of a lifetime's success and happiness, emerging from a thickly folded double cuff from one of those swanky Jermyn Street tailors that were so square they were hip. Richard's smile was unfairly dazzling for someone who got up each morning to catch the 6.59 train, and his skin was the colour of caramel.

Rupert's skin was fair and freckly and he hated it. When he caught the sun, or drank more than a few pints, it turned bright red, which he hated even more. Among the photos on Richard's desk was a picture of the two of them celebrating the launch of their business, in a pub in Shepherd Market. Richard looked like Mel Gibson, small and dark and sexy, while Rupert loomed behind him like an ungainly beacon, his ginger-blond hair clashing violently with his beetroot complexion. He wanted to ask Richard to take the picture down, but everyone knew that Rupert didn't care two hoots about his appearance and he didn't want to rock the boat.

He waved a hearty greeting to Richard, who then returned to his phone call. Rupert took off his heavy coat and settled at the opposite desk, fixing his face in an expression of purposeful zeal as he focused in on the screen.

It was awful being in partnership with a friend. When he'd worked for the bank, he used to complain about it: the hierarchy, the red tape, always being accountable to someone else. Now he was only accountable to himself, and to Richard. And to the investors who had entrusted them with millions of pounds. It made his blood run cold just thinking about it. His younger self might have relished the challenge, but his new couldn't-care-less self wished the whole thing would just vanish in a puff of smoke.

Richard finished his phone call.

'Brian Timmons. Looks like he's going to come through with a few hundred thou.'

'Great.' Rupert's voice sounded phoney even to himself. 'I've got lunch with a prospect myself today. Ex-banker, husband works at the French embassy, she sounded pretty interested.'

'Good.'

'Yup.'

'Big Hairy Audacious Goals, let's go for it.'

It was such a strain, all this encouraging mutual back-slapping and talking positive. When all he wanted to do was go up to Richard and say 'fooled you!' and they'd have a laugh about the whole thing then go off to the pub.

Rupert knew he was not the first to feel disaffected by his work. Other people called it burnout, and fell into dramatic crises of depression, harming themselves with penknives and receiving therapy on BUPA. But Rupert was too humble for all that. He wasn't theatrical enough to cast himself as the flawed hero of his own private tragedy. And besides, he wouldn't say he was depressed exactly. It was just that he didn't really want anything any more. He suspected it might simply be the onset of middle age. Which was a bit of a joke, as he was about to become a blushing bridegroom.

Richard came over and dropped a brochure on his desk. 'Take a look at this, Rupert, old boy. Let me know what you think.'

Richard called him old boy in jokey deference to his breeding. Whereas Richard was an Essex boy made good, Rupert had an entry in *Burke's Landed Gentry* and family money of such noble distinction it had gone yellow with age, like those treasure-island maps that kids dip in cold tea to give them an authentic look. Richard liked to imagine Rupert still had a soft spot for old Nanny, pensioned off in some cottage on the family estate while the big house with forty-seven rooms and its own chapel crumbled into elegant decay. All rubbish, of course. But the name of Beauval-Tench brought a touch of class to their outfit. And Rupert was a good bloke, solid and dependable, which was more than you could say for some of the toffs who ended up in the city.

Rupert glanced through the brochure, admiring the chiselled jaws of the men it featured. He was particularly taken by one of the main board who called himself the Director of Ideas. As though he sat in the brain of the company, pulling strings to initiate movement among the lesser organs. Heavy lower limbs dragging on the spark of his own creative genius. Was this company one they should invest in? How the hell was Rupert supposed to know? Could he really spend the rest of his life doing this job?

He looked across at Richard, so at ease behind his desk. Richard loved this work, he was made for it, his eyes lit up at the thought of a deal, and he fed off adrenaline. His very body oozed confidence and dynamism. He was absolutely certain that life would give him what he wanted. In fact, he was rather like Lydia, which made Rupert wonder if there was something in him that was sub-consciously attracted to go-getters, to make up for his own wishy-washiness.

He had hoped that formalising things with Lydia would help him feel better. It was a positive step, the right time, and quite frankly the decent thing to do. He had been amazed that she had fallen for him when a girl like that should have had the whole of New York at her feet. He was, let's face it, no matinee idol. They had hit it off immediately, united by their Britishness in the artificial hothouse of Manhattan. They enjoyed defending crooked yellow teeth and cynicism against orthodontics and preppy wholesomeness, it had been fun. He didn't consider the bond strong enough to survive the move back to London, but Lydia had proved him wrong, re-organising her work so she could follow him home and showing a flattering willingness to fall in with his plans. It became clear that she saw their future together, and to be honest he felt he owed it to her. She was so funny, clever and beautiful, you really couldn't ask for more.

Lydia's euphoria at being engaged more than made up for his own indifference. She had moved into the flat and begun writing lists in a red notebook that she kept in the kitchen drawer. The book was segmented into different sections, each headed up in her rounded handwriting. Surprise engagement party, wedding guest list, reception venues, Cadogan Gardens – redecoration, joint finances with a question mark. Whenever they spent an evening in, she would pull the book out and run through the details with him over their drinks. Rupert would crash on his beige leather sofa and wish he could turn the TV on, while Lydia perched on the matching pouffe, crossing her ankles like the queen as she quizzed him about his views on a remote Scottish castle versus the In and Out Club. Should they go for romantic medieval heritage or faded London chic? There's so much to think of, she would say, as she flipped the book shut. It's rather wonderful, isn't it, having all this to plan, just as we were running out of things to talk about. Rupert couldn't help wondering what Lydia would do for a hobby once the whole wedding business was over.

Richard was pacing up and down now, speaking into a cell phone the size of a matchbox. His voice filled the room, and Rupert wished not for the first time that they had opted for two separate offices. Open plan was all very well when a whole floor of people were involved, but when it was just the two of you, it felt like an unconsummated marriage, sharing a twin-bedded room with someone you didn't have sex with. Hideously intimate. When you worked in an office of two hundred people, nobody could hear you on the phone, but now he had to wait for Richard to go out if he wanted to make a private call.

He checked his emails and tried not to listen into

Richard's conversation. It was easy to look busy in front of a computer. All you had to do was scrunch your face up into a frown and peer intently at the monitor, one hand on the mouse, and everyone thought you were super-industrious.

Staring at the screen, Rupert wished he was at his house in France. He wished he could walk out through his garden, fragrant with lavender and rock roses, push open the high metal gates and make his way down the stony track until he reached the village and the *Bar des Sports*. There he would sit up at the bar, on a stool upholstered with cracked maroon fake leather and drink a *pression* and smoke a Gitane, even though he gave up cigarettes a decade ago. He would order a fat *steack frites* – *saignant*, naturally, and a *demi* of house red. After crème caramel and a small, dark coffee in a proper little cup – certainly not a Starbucks abomination with an inch-thick rim – he would walk back to the house and stretch out on the swing seat in the garden. Although, as it was December, he might prefer to make a fire in the wide stone chimney and lie down on the day bed, reading Rabelais or Baudelaire or Jeffrey Archer or the sports section of yesterday's *Times* that he had picked up in Marseille. That was all he wanted, wasn't it?

The phone rang, and it was his lunch date, Marie-Helene, ringing to cancel because of a breakdown in childcare, they would have to fix another time. Rupert put the phone down and thought what a shame it was. She sounded attractive in that breathy, neurotic way of Parisian women, always in a hurry and permanently tense in the face of imminent catastrophe. He could imagine the vein throbbing behind the fine skin of her forehead as she gave the failing servant a good old bollocking down the phone. Lovely French girls, lovely Paris, *Paris mon Amour*.

So that left him with a free lunchtime. Except there was no such thing when you were creating your own business, time famine being the executive's number one enemy. Even so, Rupert felt disinclined to tell Richard of his change in plan. Instead, he pulled an envelope out of his briefcase that he had been carrying around for a while. It was a mail shot from the French Institute – they must have got his address through something to do with his French bank account. It listed details of the winter season of films, and, if he remembered rightly, they often had lunchtime screenings. Yes, there it was, today at 12.50, *A Bout de Souffle*, the Godard original of course, and not the jumped-up remake. It was perfect, he wouldn't even need to cancel the taxi; instead of dropping him at chez Max, it could go on to South Kensington, and he would be just in time to get a ticket. It was hardly likely to be sold out. Most people had other things to attend to during the working day.

Jane often went in for a guilty bout of housework on Friday mornings. Knowing she would soon be sloping off to the pictures, the least she could do was wipe round the kitchen beforehand. The problem being that she really had no idea how to go about it. Cleaning was not something she had ever been taught. Her mother had been more interested in encouraging her schoolwork. She didn't want her daughter's fine mind going to waste on mopping floors.

She sloshed the mop around the rubber floor then lifted its heavy, drooping head onto the strainer thing that sat on the bucket. Was this correct, or were you supposed to go down on your hands and knees with a scrubbing brush, like the kitchen maid in a costume drama? She had once bought something called a Swiffer, a nervy little stick with a flat end to which you were supposed to attach disposable cloths. One swiff round the floor and it was all clean, and it could even swivel round to turn corners and climb walls. Jane soon worked out it was for very clean people who used it twice daily to supplement the proper operation that was carried out with heavier equipment. In her home, it was like taking a feather duster to a coal face.

She left the mop leaning against the wall and tiptoed over the sopping wet floor to make herself a coffee. That was another reason she couldn't stand cleaning: you always ended up having to change your socks. But she couldn't leave the room right now because she had to stay and listen to *Desert Island Discs*. She'd just realised the castaway was a girl she used to work with who had won acclaim for a slim novel about alienation and then achieved a dazzling marriage to a business tycoon.

Self-deprecation was the style adopted by most guests on *Desert Island Discs*, and Fanny Lipman was no exception, undermining her success with a skin-deep veneer of modesty. Jane bent down to take a bottle of bleach from the cupboard. She liked the way it worked its mysterious alchemy, removing the brown stains as she poured it round the white sink. The phone rang, and Jane turned down the radio to answer it, soaking her socks further as she made the return trip across the film of dirty water that covered the kitchen floor.

It was Lydia, though as usual she didn't bother to clarify.

'You took a while to answer, so I can tell you're not at your desk. I'll tell you what, I just woke up, in Rupert's fabulous extra-king-size bed, and realised I had a free lunch today. Do you fancy meeting up? I rather thought Fifth Floor at Harvey Nicks.'

'And I rather think that sounds beyond my budget,' said Jane, 'we can't all be ladies who lunch.'

'I'll pay.'

'Too busy, I'm afraid, I'm actually cleaning the kitchen.'

Damn, how did she let that slip out?

'Then I need to get on with my proper work,' she added quickly.

She didn't mention the film at the French Institute. Lydia might want to join her and end up in the next seat, whispering loudly and ruining the atmosphere.

'Cleaning, how very avant-garde of you! You know housework is supposed to be the new gardening, though both are menial beyond belief if you ask me. Are you wearing a Cath Kidston pinny?'

'Certainly not, Will won't hear of anything floral in the house. And I don't know how you can compare planting a rose with wiping grease off a cooker. At least I know which I'd rather be doing.'

That reminded her, she must put her seed order in. It kept her going through the winter to imagine how the garden would look later on, bursts of blue speedwell against the pale yellow verbascum, sweet peas running riot through the trellis. She wanted to try nasturtiums this year, pale orange flowers and heart-shaped leaves they could eat in salads. Gardening was so much more rewarding than housework.

'Well, if you really can't spare the time, I'll have to look further through my little black book,' said Lydia, thinking that maybe she'd treat herself to a pedicure instead, 'but I'll see you on Sunday anyway, don't forget I'm giving you a lift.'

'I won't. Let's hope it won't be too ghastly, suppose it's just you and me and Toni? That would look really feeble, like we'd just trailed along to get in with her.'

'Oh buck up, it'll be fine. What else would you be doing on a Sunday night, apart from humouring that child of yours? Let her father deal with her for a change while you get out and enjoy yourself for once.'

Jane could hear the music had ended and Fanny was speaking again. 'Quick, turn the radio on, Fanny Lipman is on *Desert Island Discs*.'

'Fanny Lipman! That secretary from your old office?'

'Turned lady authoress and multi-millionairess.'

'Oh puh-lease. They must be getting desperate to ask her on.' Though Lydia had nothing but admiration for the way she'd got her claws into Number Ninety-seven on the *Sunday Times* rich list. 'I'll let you go then.'

'Bye.'

Jane returned to her bucket, then decided to call it a day. The useless thing about cleaning was that everything only got dirty again, so what was the point? When you planted a shrub, it stayed there for years, growing, changing with the seasons. You had something to show for your efforts. All she would have to show for a gleaming kitchen floor two days later would be more sticky traces of fruit juice, bits of blackened carrot peel, rogue seeds escaped from Will's breakfast selection.

She poured herself a coffee and sat down at the table to listen to Fanny eulogising motherhood. It had transformed her, she said, redeemed her from her selfish existence, and given her a rich subject for her writing. Oh yes, thought Jane, turn the whole thing round to glorify yourself, why don't you. And the tycoon had been so supportive, he'd made a point of being there this time round, having missed out so much on his first family due to pressures of work. Fanny's next choice of record was for him: '*I'm looking for someone to change my life.*'

And what about the tycoon's ex-wife in all this? Her life had been changed all right, when her husband left her. She'd probably done the diets and the maintenance work, but there was no way a fifty-year-old woman could compete with someone twenty years younger. And did it make the children from his first marriage feel better to know that Dad was making up for the neglect he had shown them by drooling like an old fool over the new babies?

Jane thought about the first time she had met Will's two sons. It was in a pub in Notting Hill, and she had been struck by how close in age they were to her. For a moment it seemed that they were three school-leavers out for a drink together, with Will the English teacher on hand to buy them a patronising round of drinks to welcome them to the adult world. Their youthfulness had made him seem middle-aged. They were nice to her, though, and she was glad that she had not been the cause of their parents' break-up. That honour belonged to her predecessor, long-legged Louise, who had been the catalyst to bring the failing marriage to its inevitable conclusion. Or at least that's what Will said, and she had never enquired further.

Jane opened the doors into the garden and breathed in the sharp air. She liked this time of year, when you could think about your plans for spring planting. Even in a London garden you got the exciting, rotting smell of vegetation that had finished sinking down for the winter.

She went to the bottom of the garden, to a hidden patch on the other side of the shed that she had earmarked for a makeover. It was to become her hot and vulgar garden. Will favoured elegant grey and green plants; she had always indulged him with hostas and santolini, white lilies, stern Edwardian specimens that complemented the décor of the house as you looked out of the galleria window. All very tasteful. But behind the shed in this little suntrap she was only going to plant bright orange and yellow plants. French marigolds, zinnias, wallflowers, red-hot pokers, black-eyed Susan, sunflowers and – Will's particular bugbear – dahlias. She had ordered the naffest ones of all, the sort that looked like artificial pompoms. Next summer, she would lie here on a plastic sun-lounger and eat synthetic ice-cream and let her eyes be dazzled.

The steps of the French Institute were wide and grandiose, backed by a vast Art Deco window with square panes of pale green light. After the film, Jane made her way down the staircase, looking at the young man sitting behind the curved reception desk. With his earnest spectacles and cropped hair, he was so authentically New Wave, he could have stepped straight out of Godard's 1950s Paris.

Jane looked away and realised that the vision in her left eye had become out of focus. Damn it, she had lost a lens. It happened quite often, and was not a big deal. It just meant you had to freeze and very slowly inspect every inch of your clothes and the floor around you. She stood still on the step, and waited for everyone to walk past her so she could take her time and search for it properly. It wouldn't take long, there hadn't been many takers for the lunchtime screening.

After running her fingertips over her face and body, she carefully crouched down and began combing the surface of the step she was standing on, then the one below.

'Can I help you?'

She became aware of a pair of stout black brogues coming to rest a few inches away from her face. She was no expert on men's shoes, but these looked the sort that came with a thirty-year guarantee. Above them rose a pair of socks decorated with red and green diamonds. She looked up further and saw they belonged to a large man with kind eyes wearing a blue pinstripe suit. A pair of red braces nudged out over one of those stripey shirts with a plain white collar that had just become fashionable again, though he clearly didn't know that. He looked like the last person you'd expect to run into at an art-house movie. And he had stopped for the sole purpose of helping her. It had been so long since anyone had unexpectedly offered to do something nice for her, that Jane felt at a loss.

'Thank you, yes,' she said, 'I've lost a contact lens.'

'Bloody nuisance, aren't they? I'm always losing mine.' He lowered himself beside her and ran a hand across the step with surprising finesse. She noticed he wore big cufflinks, another hangover from the yuppie Eighties, and that his tie was decorated with miniature stags' heads.

'I can't see it,' he said, 'but in my experience they don't usually get as far as the floor. Let me check your face.'

Still crouching beside her, he put his hands on either side of her head and stared intently, clinically into her eyes. His fingers felt warm and comforting as they pressed against her temples.

'Look up . . . now look down. Now try looking to one side.' Jane followed his directions, rolling her eyes like a mad woman being exorcised.

'You don't look like someone who wears lenses,' she said, treating him to a view of the whites of her eyes as she swivelled the pupils up into her skull.

'How do you mean?'

'You don't look vain enough.'

He laughed. 'I'll take that as a compliment, though I probably shouldn't. I actually got them when I was twelve and we were reading *Lord of the Flies* at school. I got fed up with being called Piggy, after the one who broke his glasses. You know how cruel kids can be.'

'Yes. I got mine because everyone said I looked like Olive from *On The Buses*.'

'Hang on, I can see it. Right down in the corner. Just

hold it there and I'll see if I can nudge it out.' He applied the lightest flick with his little finger, and the lense dropped out into his palm.

Jane looked down at it, a fragile semicircle of grey plastic lying in his steady open hand. She licked her finger and picked it up, slotting it back into her eye.

They got up and faced each other. He stood head and shoulders above her, but Jane thought the Piggy label was unfair. He was big-boned, that was all, which people sometimes used as a euphemism for fat, but in his case it meant just that. Big-boned, with sandy hair and those kind brown eyes.

'Well, that was all a bit *Brief Encounter*, wasn't it?' she said breezily. 'Or should I say *Brève Rencontre*, as we're in the French Institute?'

'You speak French?'

'Yes, it's my job. I'm a translator.'

'I see.'

He looked genuinely interested. Surely he should be moving on now, he must have a job to go to, dressed like that. You wouldn't bother to put on red braces just to sit in a darkened cinema.

He made no attempt to leave, so Jane felt obliged to carry on talking.

'Do you often go to the cinema? During the day, I mean. On your own?'

Why was she trying to make out he was some kind of pervert? He was only doing the same as her.

'Never.' He shook his head. 'But I had a lunch cancelled and I suddenly just fancied it. *A Bout de Souffle* is one of my favourite Godards.'

Jane couldn't help smiling at the idea of this ungainly Englishman being a disciple of the French New Wave. He was about as Continental as roast beef and Yorkshire pudding.

'Me too,' she said.

There was a moment's pause, then they both began speaking at the same time.

'Well, thanks for your help . . .'

'I don't suppose you'd like to . . .'

They both stopped and laughed. This was ludicrous, they were like tongue-tied teenagers.

'I was going to suggest that we might . . . have a coffee,' said Rupert. 'To celebrate the lens and its non-disappearance.'

If she said no, that would be that. He would never see her again and life would go on as usual, he'd go back to his computer and Richard's booming voice across the room. You couldn't go organising your life around chance encounters, pretending it was like the movies. He had Lydia, after all, and this woman was nothing special anyway, you might even say she was rather plain. He almost hoped she'd say no.

'All right,' she said.

It was only because he had been kind to her. Considerate, nice manners, something Will couldn't always be relied on for. It wasn't that she fancied him or anything, good God, hardly! Definitely not her type, in fact about as far as you could get from her type. Those awful socks, and the soul-destroying pinstripe suit with the maroon tie, like a caricature city gent, it was a miracle he wasn't wearing a bowler hat. What on earth had made her agree? She had to pick up Liberty from school, too. Still, a quick coffee wouldn't do any harm, would it?

They left the French Institute and crossed Harrington Gardens to walk down Bute Street, a narrow road that pretended it was in Paris, with its French bookshop and patisserie and a café where Jane said they served the best cappuccinos. Le Raison d'Etre, it was called, and Rupert wondered aloud as they went in whether they would have to take part in the kind of 'café philo' discussion that the French were so keen on.

'I hope not,' laughed Jane, though she thought it might be less embarrassing to have an impersonal debate on a finer point of philosophy than to make small talk with this man whose name she didn't even know. What if she bumped into a friend, how on earth would she introduce him? As 'Piggy'? Fancy him telling her that, it hardly cast him in a flattering light, but ex-public schoolboys were all like that in her experience. So hung up on their formative years in prep school that they clung to their nicknames. They didn't seem to move on, like normal people.

He pulled out a chair for her and they ordered two regular cappuccinos. Jane realised she hadn't told him her name. 'I'm Jane by the way,' she said.

Plain Jane, he thought. Which she was, sort of, or maybe hers was simply a cleaner, less-made-up look. She didn't look as well groomed as Lydia, with her freckly face, regular, well-spaced features and medium colouring. But when he looked at her he felt uneasy and his throat was dry.

He coughed. 'Your jacket reminds me of the tablecloth on the kitchen table of my house in France.'

Jane pulled at her sleeve dismissively. 'Why, this old thing?' she said, in a Southern Belle voice, 'I've had this since gingham was in fashion last time round. Where's your house?'

'Near Marseille.'

'How lovely. Do you love it?'

'I do.'

They remained silent, contemplating how much he loved his house in France.

'I'm sorry,' he said eventually, 'that was a very pretentious thing to say, about my tablecloth. It's just that it really did remind me.'

'It's OK.'

She smiled at him. Her smile was nice; open, a bit shy. He smiled back at her.

'I wish I was there now, actually,' he said. 'I was just thinking about it before I went to see that film.'

'I'd love to live in France,' said Jane. 'Or Spain. Or deep in the English countryside. I'm afraid I'm one of those tragic Londoners who dreams constantly of escape. My partn— some people think it's pitiful, like going after some kind of never-never land. What do you think?'

I think you're beautiful.

'I think . . . It's nice to have both. If you can. But it's not essential. Home is where the heart is. And other clichés.'

He lightened up. 'So, tell me about being a translator. It sounds very glamorous. Are you one of those people who sit around talking into headphones at international summits? In those conference rooms that look like space labs?'

'No, you're thinking of interpreters. I'm just a nerdy anorak who works at home on my computer. At the moment I'm translating a book about French bridges for an American publisher. I'm just on the chapter about the Pont de Normandie.'

There, that should put him off. Though strangely enough, he seemed to be gagging for more information. Claimed to have a degree in civil engineering and had a special interest in bridges. She could just imagine Will rolling his eyes in mock boredom when she told him. If she told him. He might even lie down on the floor and pretend to go to sleep, which was his favourite jokey response to something he found truly, deeply boring.

But the odd thing was that when she talked to Rupert about bridges, she actually found it interesting. She had got so used to her work being considered unworthy of discussion that she had forgotten how absorbing a new subject became when you were working on it. You became an overnight expert, until you moved on to the next book.

When they had finished their coffee, Jane saw that she had cut it much too fine for the school run and stood up brusquely, quickly pulling on her coat.

'I'm sorry, I really must dash,' she said. 'Thanks for the coffee and the lens and everything.'

He followed her out onto the pavement. If he didn't act now, he would never see her again. But what could he do? He couldn't ask her out or anything. He was engaged to Lydia.

She was running up Bute Street now, on her way to the car park. 'I quite often go to the Institute on Fridays,' she called back to him over her shoulder. 'I'll definitely be there next week. Louis Malle. *Au Revoir les Enfants.*'

He smiled in relief. Next Friday then. He waved to her, then found himself confronted by an angry waitress. In his confusion he appeared to have done a runner. He tipped her five pounds, and went off to find a taxi.

Jane switched on the engine of the Vauxhall, willing it to stutter into life. She should be just in time for Liberty. Her new friend from the Institute had no idea she had a daughter. He knew nothing about her except what she did for a living. And that she liked going alone to the cinema, and would love to leave London if she could. And he would know how it felt to cradle her head between his hands on the stairs of the French Institute. She was sure he would be there next week, she was ninety-nine per cent sure of that. She didn't think she would bother to mention it to Will. They weren't joined at the hip, after all. They weren't even married.

FOUR

Sunday Brunch at the Bluebird Café on the Kings Road was Lydia's idea, not Rupert's. He couldn't understand why brunch had become so fashionable in England, because to his mind it was an American invention best practised in its country of origin. Brunch was perfect in New York. The city was so ugly that you had to spend all your leisure time in restaurants. You took refuge from the brown streets by diving into some joint to order sickly combinations of skinny blueberry muffins with bacon and maple syrup and banana smoothies. But in London, it didn't really work. It was almost sad to see Brits trying to be like Americans. What happened to a few pints of warm bitter followed by steak and kidney pie? Because brunch was only lunch by another name and was always served at lunchtime, in spite of its pretensions to be seen as a late breakfast.

Lydia shared none of his reservations. She polished off her eggs Benedict with rocket side-salad and ordered another glass of buck's fizz, glancing round with satisfaction at the tables filled with successful people pretending to read the Sunday papers. Obviously, they were only pretending, because everyone knows it is impossible to read a broadsheet newspaper over a small table laden with glasses and plates, even if the plates did only contain 'brunch'.

'Well, this is the life!' she said brightly, raising her glass to her secret fiancé who was sitting across the table, looking stout in a pair of jeans that had a horrid ironed crease running down the front of the legs. It was the Filipino maid who did them that way, and Rupert couldn't be bothered to instruct her otherwise.

She lowered her voice and leaned confidentially across to him, to add *sotto voce*, 'Bye-bye Balham, hallo Royal Borough of Kensington and Chelsea,' then winked to show Rupert she was only joking, that of course she would be marrying him even if he lived in Streatham. Though it was a shame he didn't look more like the Italian at the next table who was right now giving her a very dirty look indeed beneath his Enrique Iglesias hair. His jeans were half the width of Rupert's, and seemed to be moulded to his energetic lower body, suggesting that if you were to remove them, you would be confronted by a fabulous Renaissance statue in rippling hot bronze. For two seconds she met his eyes to acknowledge that they could have great wild sex together, then she turned her attention back to her boyfriend. The good thing about being thirty-seven was that you were grown up. Ten years ago she might have hopped tables, but now she had clearer objectives and she was in it for the long term. Rupert stirred two sachets of sugar into his large cappuccino and pulled his navy Guernsey sweater off over his head. He'd had it twenty years and it didn't owe him a penny.

'Bloody hot in here,' he said, his sandy hair dishevelled and flattened over his pink face that had got pinker with the heat and the Bloody Marys he'd ordered to soften the effect of last night's dinner party. 'You seem bright as a button,' he added, 'considering what time you got to bed.'

One of last night's guests had been a food critic, so Lydia had taken care to spend as much money as possible on the ingredients, notching up £13 for a loaf of bread from the bread shop on Walton Street, £48 for a fruit tart and an impressive £76 on a piece of organic beef. There had only been one sticky moment, when the food critic had wandered out to the kitchen to help her and found her taking the meat out of the oven while wearing a shower cap to keep the smell out of her hair. He had shared his mirth with the other guests, and Lydia had felt foolish, swearing never again to stage a party without the help of the sexy Brazilian butler who was listed in this month's magazine as the 'must-have dinner party accessory'.

Rupert had not enjoyed the evening. He had felt like the stooge, the spectre at the feast. Lydia had once told him that the ideal proportions at a dinner were two shouters to five listeners, but last night had thrown up six shouters and just one listener, in the form of solid Rupert, the banker, who had singularly failed to sing for his supper, though at least he was paying for it. Bored by the conversation, he had sloped off to bed as early as possible to watch the end of *Parkinson*. From down the corridor he could hear the squealing laughter of what sounded like Lydia multiplied by six. Or rather, six times the worst part of Lydia, which didn't take into account her many redeeming qualities.

And now, the morning after, Rupert looked across the table of the Bluebird Café for evidence of those redeeming qualities. He was partially reassured. Lydia looked terrific, and he was not a high-minded hypocrite who pretended that looks didn't matter. Her rich auburn hair was a more intense version of his own reddish blond, and he hoped that any children they had would inherit it. She had the kind of sex appeal that turned heads. Even now he was aware of that good-looking chap at the next table giving her the eye. He liked that, it made him feel he was getting better than he deserved, better than the tubby, good-natured wife with a Sloaney moon-face that you might expect him to have by his side.

'What do you want to do today, Lyd?' he asked. 'Shall we go and look at the mummies in the British Museum?'

There was something about Sundays in London that made him restless. You needed to go somewhere, feel you had done something, otherwise they could be strangely unsatisfying. He would rather be pottering around his country estate, but that was let out. Or else he'd like to be planting some English roses in front of his house in France, but it was too far to go for a weekend.

Lydia rolled her eyes. '"There's many a poor bespecta-cled sod,"' she quoted at him, '"Prefers the British Museum to God." Varied couplets. W. H. Auden.'

And she was well read, too. Mustn't forget that on the plus side.

'Shall we do God instead, then,' he asked with a smile, 'score a few churches?'

Lydia made a yawning gesture, patting her hand prettily in front of her mouth. 'Darling, you surely know by now that I infinitely prefer Mammon, and luckily for me, Sunday is now just another shopping day.'

She whipped the scarlet notebook out of her handbag and his heart sank. He hadn't noticed her pick it up on their way out of the flat.

'I want to take you round a few interiors shops. Get a feel for how you see the refurb.'

Rupert sat back sulkily, and Lydia noticed how he got a heavy jowly look when he didn't get his way.

'I've told you, Lydia,' he said, 'I really don't mind. I leave it entirely to you, as long as I get to keep the sofa. But please don't make me join in. Especially not on a Sunday. Can't we enjoy ourselves instead?'

'But we are enjoying ourselves. Making plans. Nest-building, showing the world how we see our lives showcased. I don't need to tell you that interior design is the new sex.'

'What's wrong with the old sex?' asked Rupert. 'Stood us in good stead for thousands of years, hasn't it?'

The Italian at the next table looked up again, his nostrils flaring at the mention of sex: he could clearly smell it at five hundred metres.

'Fine, if you'd like us all to still be sitting around in caves. If we don't care about how our homes look, we might as well sweep away centuries of civilisation.'

Rupert sighed and called for the bill. 'All right then, but just for an hour. Then I want to go home and watch the match.'

'Fair enough. Anyway, I'm off to that school reunion later, so you'll be able to slob out in front of the telly as much as you want. Now, my theme for this afternoon's tour is that Colour is Back. I'm thinking of a move away from post-minimalism. I'm thinking eclectic, creative rejection of global blandness.'

She struck an earnest pose and Rupert laughed in spite of himself.

'And I am thinking that it all sounds deeply boring,' he said, pulling out his wallet.

'Just for one hour,' she pleaded. 'How bad can it be?'

As they stood to leave, the Italian watched Lydia's legs unfold with undisguised lust. Rupert pulled his sweater back on, a sweater better suited to a hearty stroll on the moors than an afternoon mincing round Designers Guild and William Yeoward. A fine weekend this had been. Saturday night listening to fashionable people talking about how your bag shouldn't match your shoes any more as that was too obvious, and Sunday afternoon being patronised by designer shop staff. Then back to the office on Monday to a job he had come to hate, though he couldn't admit that to anyone, least of all to Lydia.

It seemed to him that the week ahead held just one ray of hope, and that was the near certainty that he would see Jane again at the Friday afternoon screening of *Au Revoir Les Enfants*. He held that knowledge secretly inside him, like a tiny unseen torch, too fragile to be exposed to risk of extinction.

* * *

Later that afternoon Jane was hurriedly clearing away the lunch things while trying to explain to Will about Liberty's homework.

'Where is she supposed to write it?' he said irritably. 'Where? I can't see.'

'It's not exactly rocket science,' she said, 'just there, on the facing page. She knows, anyway, don't you, Liberty?'

Liberty shrugged. She was offended that Jane was deserting her on a Sunday evening, but not as offended as Will was.

'I do think you could have done this earlier,' he said. 'You've had all weekend to do it, but oh no, you have to wait until the eleventh hour so muggins here has to step into the breach.'

You would have thought she was asking him to write a fifty-page thesis instead of oversee six elementary sums. Pressed for time, Jane decided to resort to flattery.

'Come on, Will, you know you're so much better at it than me. Liberty takes notice of you when you put your foot down. Don't you, Liberty?'

The child shrugged again. It seemed they were both determined to stay in a huff.

'There goes the doorbell,' said Jane, relieved to know she'd soon be out of it.

Lydia swept into the kitchen in killer heels and a cloud of perfume. 'I'm parked at the end of the road,' she announced, 'let's hope no-one nicks my car. You are *so* brave to live round here, it would scare me shitless. Hallo, Will.' She kissed him on both cheeks, then stepped back so he could give her the once-over.

He dropped the exercise book on the table; he had to admit she looked pretty damn hot. 'I hear it's Chelsea for you these days,' he said. 'Fat chance of witnessing a crime there, unless you count living off a trust fund as a crime against humanity.'

'I'm not living there yet,' she said, 'but let's just say the wheels are in motion. How are you anyway, good weekend?'

'Not really,' he replied. 'Look at me, left here holding the baby.'

'I'm not a baby!' Liberty scowled up at him.

He patted her shoulder. 'I know, sweetheart, it's a figure of speech. No, Lydia, it's been a crap weekend to be honest. We had dinner last night with these vegetarian friends of Jane's who served wine with plastic corks and let their four-year-old crawl round our feet all evening, wearing a cloth nappy.'

'I don't know, all you young families saving the planet,' said Lydia. 'You make me feel so decadent. All I've got to worry about is my own pleasure.'

Will scowled at her, remembering when her pleasure used to be his pleasure.

'We'd better go,' said Jane.

'He's still quite prickly, isn't he?' said Lydia as they drove off. 'I mean that as a good thing. He hasn't gone all boring and domestic like most men do once they've got a kid. Mind you, he's been there before.'

'Yes,' Jane looked out the window, 'though I do sometimes wonder, seeing the way he treats Liberty. You feel he's never spoken to a child before, let alone brought up two sons.'

Lydia was surprised to hear Jane admit that Will might be a less than perfect father. She would usually never hear a word against him, always insisting he was an all-round wonderful person. That was partly why Lydia had decided to seduce him all those years ago, just for the satisfaction of proving her wrong.

'So what do you think?' she said. 'Via the Mile End Road or Islington, what's the best way to get there? It's been so long, I really can't remember.'

'Whatever,' said Jane, holding up her fingers and thumbs in the shape of a W, the way Liberty did, 'you're the driver.'

She settled back to enjoy the ride and moved her thoughts away from her family to focus on the night ahead. 'I'm looking forward to this, in a grotesque way,' she said.

It was good to break the routine, do something different. She and Lydia ran through all their friends from school, wondering who might be there tonight. They agreed it was bound to be the more dreary ones who turned up.

'It is a bit tragic, after all,' said Jane. 'I'm only going because you made me. I'd hate anyone to think I really wanted to go.'

'That's typical of you,' said Lydia. 'You always worry what people will think. I don't, I just do what I want.'

The lights were glittering on the London Eye as they drove along the Embankment, and a ghostly blue light showed off the new footbridge. London was spectacular these days, like a drab woman who had put on a party dress. Jane looked across the river at the Festival Hall and the National Film Theatre beside it. Only five more days, she thought, and she'd be off to the cinema again. He was bound to be there. She folded her arms and thought about him, how little she knew about him. What was he doing now? Was he sitting alone in a darkened room, thinking about her? Out at a pub with his friends? Or watching television with his children – he could be married, for all she knew. But then again it was none of her business, really.

The school hall looked smaller than Jane recalled, and the walls were still hung with portraits of the great composers. Jane remembered staring at them during morning assembly, whiling away the tedious minutes. Time dragged endlessly when you were young, you spent hours feeling bored, waiting for something to happen. Then suddenly you were grown up and there weren't enough hours in the day.

At the far end of the hall a small group of middle-aged people were standing in front of a trestle table, holding paper cups of wine. Jane's first instinct was to turn around and walk straight out.

'Let's go now,' Jane whispered to Lydia, 'pretend we've left something in the car, quick.'

'Don't be absurd.'

And Lydia made her entrance, heading for an apologetic-looking man who was passing round a bowl of Twiglets.

Jane ducked in behind her.

'Peter Griggs!' said Lydia. 'I'd know you anywhere, you've still got the same glasses!'

They exchanged life stories, though Peter's didn't take too long. Solicitor, stayed local, two kids. By comparison, Lydia presented hers as a richly embroidered tapestry, albeit with one or two embellishments that Jane knew were not entirely true.

'Gosh, you make me sound really boring!' he said.

'No!' said Lydia unconvincingly, looking round for an escape route. 'You remember Jane, don't you? Oh my God, there's Steven May!'

She slipped away to talk to a thick-set man who was still handsome, though grown jowly. Steven May, Jane thought with a jolt, my very first boyfriend. The love of her life, or so she had thought, until that Christmas party when Lydia had slow-danced with him to *Careless Whisper*. She looked away over Peter's other shoulder and saw two women who looked familiar, class swots who had now fulfilled their early promise of dowdiness. In spite of her reservations, it was comforting to be with people you hadn't seen for twenty years. It was like an old film, comically rewound to show the figures running backwards to their starting positions.

Peter Griggs seemed delighted by the whole affair. 'I'm surprised I haven't seen you at one of these before,' he said. 'This is my tenth, it's always a marvellous evening.'

Thank goodness I got away, thought Jane. The thought of living round the corner, never missing a reunion, was enough to provoke a panic attack of claustrophobia. Life was a journey, after all, you had to move on or you'd end up stagnating in the corner of the school hall with the likes of Peter Griggs.

'You're not married then?' he was saying, nodding at her empty ring finger.

'No, well, I live with someone. Same difference really. What about you?'

'Fifteen years. We had a weekend to Rome to cele-brate, it was wonderful, we got our flights for forty-eight pounds, and stayed in a marvellous hotel . . .'

Jane listened to him detailing the itinerary and thanked her lucky stars for Will. At least she didn't need to come out to functions like this to brag about her life. Peter was going on about his children now, how well they were doing. As if I care, thought Jane. Next thing he'd be bringing out their school reports to show her.

'Will you excuse me?' she said. 'I must just go and say hallo to Toni Vincent.'

She made a break for it and cornered Toni, feeling the need to talk to someone who didn't think that life began and ended off the North Circular.

'Hi, Toni, do you remember me?'

Toni frowned slightly.

'I was goal defence to your goalkeeper in the netball team.' She'd never thought she'd be using that line, but at least it put her on the map for Toni.

'Of course, how are you? What are you up to now?'

'I'm a translator.'

'That's right, I remember you being good at languages. Hang on, though, didn't you use to write for one of our magazines?'

'For a bit, but I went over to translating. Only room for one writer in a relationship. I think you know my partner, actually. Will Thacker, he does stuff for you occasionally.'

Toni's eyes widened in respect. 'Oh, gosh, so *you're* Mrs Thacker.'

'We're not actually married.'

'Well, rather you than me. I must say he's a brilliant writer but he must be hell to live with, I'd have thought.'

Jane felt herself colouring. 'Not really, no, he's terribly easy . . .' she groped for words '. . . I mean, obviously he can be quite demanding . . .'

'Demanding is putting it mildly, I'd have thought. Still, you look good on it.' Toni cast her hand round the room. 'Isn't this hilarious? We're doing a piece on school reunions so I thought I'd put in a little research.' She smiled at Jane. 'Let's have lunch,' she said. 'Maybe I could lure you back to do something for us. Don't bring Will, though, otherwise we won't get a word in edgeways.'

'All right, great,' said Jane, still a bit put out by her remarks about Will, but flattered by the suggestion.

'You and Will have got kids, haven't you?' Toni asked.

'One daughter.'

'I've got two, just gone off to boarding school. Fantastic arrangement, they love it, come home at weekends, means I can work late all week without feeling bad, you should think about it.'

For a brief moment, Jane thought it did sound like a very good idea. The tantalising carrot of all those free evenings, release from the bedtime routine. Then she remembered she didn't approve of boarding school. 'I couldn't do that,' she said, 'I'd feel terrible. I've always thought that having a child away from home would be like adopting an animal in London Zoo.'

Toni snorted. 'Like a chimpanzee, you mean? It's not that bad, you still see them at the weekends. And you shouldn't exaggerate the mother thing. She'll grow up before you know it, and you've got to think where that'll leave you.'

'That's exactly why you have to make the most of it,' said Jane. 'I'd hate to think I hadn't made her childhood as happy as it could be.'

Toni shrugged. 'I do think it's a bit of a trap, this business of putting the children first all the time. You aren't necessarily doing them a favour by making them feel they're the centre of the universe. They think that anyway.'

It's all right for you to say that, thought Jane. She remembered going to Toni's birthday party, in her large and messy house, surrounded by brothers and sisters, her parents happily sitting back and letting them run riot. How she had envied her that casual freedom, a normal family with two parents.

Jane was ten when her parents divorced. Nobody spoke of single-parent families then, they were still a rarity. When her father walked out, her mother had taken to her bed for several weeks. Jane remembered making breakfast for her one morning, setting out the tea and toast then carrying the tray carefully up the stairs until she tripped and sent the lot flying. Normally her mother would have been straight there, cleaning it up and telling her it didn't matter, but this time she just stayed in bed. So Jane had fetched a bowl of water herself, scrubbing at the stair carpet, hot tears running down her cheeks. The next time her father came to visit, she lay down in the road in front of his car so he couldn't drive away. He didn't come again after that.

This was why she was so adamant that she and Will should always stay together. She would do anything to shield Liberty from that kind of pain.

Lydia appeared between them. 'Oh my God, isn't this just a riot? Steven May, can you believe I ever went out with him, although of course he used to be considered quite a catch, his dad owned that garage.' She frowned at Jane, trying to remember. 'Didn't you have a thing with him at some point?'

Jane stared at her in disbelief. Could her memory really be that selective? 'I went out with him for three years until you stole him off me,' she said indignantly, 'I'm still not over it, you know!'

Lydia had the grace to look slightly guilty. 'Oh dear, so I did, I'd quite forgotten. How brutal we were then.'

'No, you were brutal, the rest of us just picked up the pieces,' said Jane. She could laugh about it now, but it wasn't so funny then. She had spent many happy evenings at his house where his mother cheerfully administered to the needs of her three sons. His father would come in after work and sit benignly in the bosom of his family. He had a bald head with a crown of hair, like the picture on the Daddy's Sauce bottle. When Steven went off with Lydia, his mother told Jane he'd made a big mistake, didn't know what he was throwing away.

He was coming up to talk to her now that Toni and Lydia had drifted off into conversation about magazines. She remembered his walk; it had a cocky lift to it that was still appealing. She'd tried so hard to get him back

– it was humiliating to think of it, the tears, the begging, the eventual acceptance of his rejection. She had refused to speak to Lydia for two years, which was childish of her, and difficult, too, with their mothers being so close.

'Hallo stranger,' he said, 'fancy seeing you here.'

She laughed, relieved that he no longer had the same effect on her. 'Glad to see your pick-up lines haven't moved on. It's good to see you, Steven.'

'Likewise.' He smiled at her. His eyes hadn't lost their twinkle, at least. 'Brings it all back, doesn't it?'

'Yes, though I'm not sure how much of a good thing that is . . . Anyway, how's business? Did you take over the garage?'

'Certainly did. As you can see, I'm as predictable as ever. You would have got bored with me, you were too clever for me by half.'

He wanted her forgiveness.

'I'm not sure about that,' she said, 'but you're right, it wouldn't have worked out.'

He smiled in relief. 'You look fantastic,' he said, then lowered his voice to a whisper. 'You've aged better than Lydia, to be honest.'

'That's nice of you, but you know it's not true.'

'I mean it! So tell me, who's the lucky fellow?'

'He's a writer, actually . . .' And she was off down the familiar track, giving a mouth-watering account of her fascinating partner, her gorgeous daughter, the perfect life/work balance she had worked so hard to achieve. But her version of the ideal life was slightly lost on Steven.

'Shepherds Bush, that's a bit rough, isn't it?' he said

in suburban concern. 'Still, I hope he treats you right. You deserve it.'

'He treats me just fine,' she said quickly. 'Shall we get another drink?'

On the way home Jane thought about Steven May and his life at the garage. He had a wife and four children – he said his wife had always wanted four because everything came in packets of six so five was a stupid number to make a picnic for. Jane imagined them on happy family days out, a giant coolbox in the back of the people carrier, packets of jam tarts being shared out on a blanket on the sand. He was so certain about everything, whereas she seemed to live in a fog of doubt these days, constantly wondering if she might be barking up the wrong tree.

They were on the Mile End Road now, and Lydia had put on Donna Summer at full volume. 'I remember driving down this road with Steven May in his Trevor Seven,' she said, tapping the wheel in time to the music and putting on a sexy pout for the benefit of the car that had drawn up alongside them at the lights. 'We were on our way to Stringfellow's. God we thought we were sophisticated, we thought we were just it. Isn't it funny how you move on. Though thank the lord we do.'

'I wish you'd shut up about Steven May,' Jane said. 'He was my boyfriend first, you know. Though he never took me up the West End; his idea of a night out with me was a quiet drink in a pub in Epping Forest.'

'Here we are,' said Lydia as they drew up outside Jane's house. 'Good fun, wasn't it. Are you glad you came?'

'Yes,' said Jane, 'I really am. Thanks for the lift.'

'Bit of a boost, isn't it, seeing all those boys who clearly still fancy us. Good to know that Peter Griggs is always there for me if all else fails.'

Good old Lydia, she always liked to keep her options open.

'I thought you were spoken for these days?' Jane commented.

'Indeed, you'll get to meet him at the party. Did I tell you we're going to South America for Christmas?' She smiled her dazzling smile. 'See you then.'

And she was off.

The house seemed cold and pretentious when Jane let herself in. That concrete staircase was a big mistake, she should never have allowed Will to talk her into it. She climbed up its minimalist treads, past the galleria and into the bathroom where the green glass washbasin mocked her, perched like a mixing bowl on its limestone base. Who did she think she was, living in this monument to cutting-edge urban design?

She slipped into bed and thought about Steven May, so confident about his life. Whereas it seemed that the older she got, the less certain she became about things, a kind of reversal of wisdom. If she was honest, there were only two things she felt sure about right now. First of all, she loved her daughter to death. And secondly, she was looking forward to her Friday cinema trip with a sense of anticipation that was way beyond the reasonable. And which had entirely to do with the prospect of bumping into her new friend in the foyer of the French Institute.

FIVE

On a filthy December night, the best place to be was holed up at home with a ready meal and a bottle of wine. This was Rupert's thought as he made his way through the rain down the Kings Road, towards his favourite source of comfort food. He'd had a horrible day at work and stepping into Marks and Spencer was like coming home to mother. Not his own chilly, spiky mother, but the mother he would have liked to have had. Quiet racks of ordinary clothes, blouses and trousers of the type worn by normal women, giving way to pretty underwear, cosmetics and flowers before you arrived at the shelves of easy-to-eat food. No effort required, microwave packs, heaven forbid that you should have to cut the ends off your own green beans. The only burden lay in deciding between Italian and Thai, gravad lax or sushi.

Rupert opted for beef casserole with dumplings, a smoked-salmon starter and treacle sponge, plus a lump of blue Stilton and a bottle of claret. It was the kind of meal he used to dream of when he lived in New York.

There, you could get any food you fancied delivered to your door, but then you still had to be on your toes with the cash and the tip and the obligatory pally exchanges with the delivery boy. It was nothing like the anonymous experience of shuffling round M&S with a wire basket, hovering over the Chinese Meal for Two as you projected the TV evening ahead. Britain was without doubt the cosiest country in the world.

Rupert's quiet night in was going to be spent alone, and he was looking forward to it. Lydia usually slept at her own place on Thursdays, which meant Rupert could do exactly as he pleased. He needed to take advantage of this luxury while he could. Very soon he would be entering the compromise and shared decisions of marriage, and in some respects he wasn't at all sure he was ready for it.

He wandered out of the food section and into men's underwear where he selected a three-pack of black socks which he placed in his basket on top of his dinner. Some men stopped buying their own clothes once they were married. Their wives picked out their pants and advised them on which suits to buy. He knew Lydia was already chomping at the bit to give his wardrobe a thorough overhaul.

The girl at the till filled a carrier bag with his meal and socks and took his bank card. 'Would you like any cash back?' she trilled.

'Yes, fifty pounds please.'

It amused him, this little ritual that took playing at shop to ridiculous lengths. Mr Brown went to town and he bought: beef and dumplings, sticky treacle pudding, three pairs of socks and fifty pounds. The first time someone had asked him if he wanted cash back, he thought he had won some kind of lottery, as though Britain had become a benevolent spoon-feeder during his years abroad, dishing out bonuses to random supermarket customers.

Back at the flat, Rupert went to the bedroom to take off his shoes and put on his favourite pair of slippers. Lydia couldn't stand them, she especially hated the nylon fur all flattened and brown around the edges, and the green and red plaid. She said they reminded her of Rupert the Bear, whereas she much preferred Rupert the hereditary peer. He saw she was right. It was what he had wanted when he proposed, for Lydia to bring up his standards and make him a more acceptable person. But he still enjoyed the chance to slob out when given a chance.

He hung up his jacket in the wardrobe and pulled on his old sweater, dressing the part for a night in with himself. In the kitchen, he poured himself a glass of wine and went through the post. It was a relief to open the envelopes in his own time, without Lydia chivvying him along, and he was particularly pleased to find the Beales list had arrived. He added it to the pile of favourite nursery catalogues he kept beside the phone then took them all through to the sitting room to make his final choice. He was planning to order some roses for his garden in France and even the names soothed him: damask roses, Bourbons, the thornless Zephirine Drouhin, Felicite and Perpetue, Roseraie de l'Hay, Perla de Montserrat, Mme. Isaac Pereire. It was like inviting a bevy of ghostly ladies to beautify your life, to come and lay their gracious white arms around your troubled soul. He couldn't show any interest in Lydia's refurbishment of the flat, but the plans for his garden were on a different level altogether. They spoke of passion and release, conjuring up a paradise of perfume and soft velvet petals and sunshine.

If he was a rose breeder, he could make one up called Jane. It would have apricot buds opening up into creamy buff petals. How many times had he run through their conversation in his head. Jane had said she dreamed of escape, and he imagined them leaving together, driving down to Dover in a Citroën 2CV, with nothing but a boot full of Austin roses and just the clothes they stood up in. They would catch the ferry and drive slowly through France, avoiding the autoroutes, taking the minor roads, stopping for lunch to eat tripe *à la mode de Caen* or horse casserole at roadside cafés with plastic tablecloths and lace curtains. When they arrived at his house in Provence, they would plant the roses and then . . . And then his imagination ran out. He didn't know this woman, he had no idea who she was, and no idea why he was placing her at the centre of his fantasy. But he did know he would be seeing her tomorrow, and that fact was exciting enough to make him almost lose his appetite.

Almost, but not quite. He filled out the order form for Beales nurseries and returned to the kitchen to prepare his supper. Setting out the smoked salmon on a plate with a garnish of rocket, programming the microwave to heat the beef casserole. He took pleasure in his solitude:

like a condemned man, he had the exquisite sense that each meal taken alone could be his last. The chair opposite him was blissfully, silently empty. Tomorrow it would be occupied by Lydia, noisily updating him on the plans for their party, pulling out a few more brochures of wedding venues. He should be glad at that thought, but he wasn't.

Rupert knew he didn't want to turn into a sad old bloke living alone, but the fact was he enjoyed his own company. There was a quiet satisfaction in finding your own space after a gruelling day at the office. Padding from room to room in your old slippers without being upbraided for being an old slouch. Freed of the obligation to make small talk. But then again, it was time he got married, otherwise people would start to think he was a bit of a pervert. If you got past forty without being married, everyone assumed there was something wrong with you. If you were a woman, it was because you were a hard-nosed bitch concentrating on your career, but if you were a man it was because you were unnaturally close to your mother, or commitment-phobic, or gay, or all three.

Maybe it was the power of thought, for as he was contemplating the need for marriage, the phone rang and it was Lydia.

'Darling, I just had a thought, we must get our jabs done for the holiday. Can you meet at the hospital tomorrow lunchtime? You're supposed to have it done three weeks before you go, otherwise you'll be done for by a tsetse fly the moment you arrive.'

Tomorrow lunchtime? Had she no idea how entirely

impossible that was? It was on the tip of Rupert's tongue
to explain why, to tell her that tomorrow lunchtime was
to be the high point of his week, when he realised how
out of order it would be. He was building his entire week
around the chance of meeting a woman he barely knew,
and he was about to share that with his fiancée.

'Not tomorrow, Lyd,' he said, 'I've got a work lunch.'

It was the first time he'd ever lied to her, and it made
him feel bad.

Lydia hung up on Rupert and sank back into the foaming
water of her scroll-topped cast-iron bath. The bathroom
was the best thing about her Balham flat. It was so
Eighties retro, she had laughed aloud when the estate
agent had opened the door to show it to her. All fake
Victoriana, gnarly gold taps, ruched blinds and dangling
lavatory chain, with the bath tub floating like a stately
galleon in the middle of the room. It took up nearly half
the flat and was the only part of it she would be sorry
to leave behind.

She slipped her hips forward and let her head fall backwards, running her hands through her wet hair to rinse
out the seaweed conditioner. The movement caused the
water to slop over the edge of the bath, drenching the
carpet, but Lydia didn't care. If her landlord had been
stupid enough to cover the bathroom floor with a wool
carpet, he only had himself to blame if it disintegrated.

A pile of holiday brochures was lined up beside the phone
on a bow-legged velvet stool that stood next to the bath
tub. They were all for spa holidays, though Lydia didn't use
that word any more. Last year it was OK to talk about

going to a spa; this year you had to say you were going on a retreat. Not that the brochures had caught up with this yet, they weren't nearly as ahead of the game as Lydia was. She wiped the water from her eyes and picked up her current favourite, which claimed that regular spa visits were essential if you were to achieve balance of mind and body. It implied that if you didn't spend two grand on a trip to a luxury health farm in the Indian Ocean, you would fail to achieve this balance, and therefore presumably end up in a mental hospital.

Personally, Lydia didn't buy into all that nonsense about our lives being so stressful. Stress was when you didn't know where your next meal was coming from. Stress was worrying about not having the money to pay the rent. It sure as hell didn't equate with overpaid people tossing up between a yogic Thai massage and a honey-and-sesame wrap. Where did it come from, this idea that we were all so hard-done-by that we deserved narcissistic self-pampering? But still, in her business, she owed it to herself to look her best. She was planning to spend a week on a retreat before the wedding, to make sure she looked truly fabulous. It wasn't so much a de-stressing exercise as an act of self-congratulation. A little 'well done me' present, to celebrate her success in pinning down lovely Rupert and his even lovelier – for she was nothing if not honest! – big fat fortune.

The choice had been narrowed down to two. She was torn between the Banyan Tree in the Maldives where you were pummelled in your own private tropical garden surrounded by high walls, and Ananda in India where they went in for those Ayurvedic treatments inspired by the

Hindu monkey god. Lydia loved all the eastern religions, especially Buddhism and Kabbalah Judaism. So much sexier than drab old Christianity, though perhaps that would become the next big thing: hair shirts and scrimping and saving and not coveting your neighbour's wife and those appalling fish stickers all over the family saloon.

She flicked from the Jacuzzi Ocean Villas of the Banyan Tree to the majestic turrets of Ananda. When she read that the Moorish palace was still home to a living maharajah, her mind was made up. Even if the treatments were a load of quackery, everyone knew you couldn't visit India without getting dysentery and losing half a stone, so any which way she would be the winner. She pulled the plug and stood up in the bath, like Botticelli's Venus in a giant shell, her auburn hair slapping wetly over her shoulder. The water pooled sluggishly round her calves. She should really clear the drains, but then again it was hardly worth it, she'd be moving out soon.

She stepped out of the bath and wrapped a towel round her body, picking up her hairbrush and standing before the full-length oval mirror. Free-standing and tilting awkwardly on its axis, it took up too much space, and made Lydia impatient for the sleek wet room she would be installing in Rupert's apartment, which would be far more suitable for her home spa treatments. She frowned as she brushed her hair and thought about one detail she had overlooked. Where were she and Rupert to live while the work was being carried out? It would have to be nearby, so she could supervise things. She rather favoured the Sloane Court Hotel, just up the road. It would be nice to be waited on and she'd have enough on her plate what with work and the renovation. The last thing she'd want to do was go home to a rented flat and fix Rupert's dinner. No, the hotel was the answer, and she just hoped Rupert wasn't going to be a tight-wad about it.

He was OK about money, though, she had to give him that. But she knew too many cases of girls marrying generous men who turned overnight into parsimonious old miseries. It was as if they were programmed to spend to attract a mate, and then the moment the cat was in the bag it was zip tight and batten down the hatches. She threw the hairbrush down on the vanity unit, which boasted soppy 'his 'n' hers' floral-motif washbasins. The 'his' basin remained unused: Rupert had never spent the night in Balham, she didn't want him growing to like the area and suggesting they move there instead of Chelsea.

She slowly unwound the towel from her body and reached for the body lotion that cost £75 a bottle, but in her case had been a freebie from the magazine. Soon she wouldn't have to rely on handouts, she would be able to go to Harvey Nicks and just buy whatever she fancied. She didn't love money for its own sake, she wouldn't say she was greedy, but it did make life so much more enjoyable. Knowing that she was marrying into the Beauval-Tench fortune meant she could relax, sit back and just enjoy the ride. You could hardly blame her for feeling pleased with herself.

For this was what we had come to, wasn't it? Religion was over, except insofar as it related to spa treatments. Guilt was finished: you no longer owed anyone anything, that was what therapy taught us. All that remained was a long luxurious journey into self-discovery, and the more sumptuous the journey, the more richness and colour and five-star hotels you could cram in on the way, the better you could say your life had been. And Lydia had every intention of making sure that hers would be a first-class Ananda-type experience.

In the foyer of the National Theatre, Jane sipped her gin and tonic and waited for Will. He was bringing a friend along for tonight's performance, an arrogant hippy from Wales who never washed. He came to stay once a year and Jane kept a special set of sheets for him that she laundered separately at a very high temperature.

She sat back to enjoy the sight of the middle classes at play, eating salad while listening to the pre-theatre jazz band. Three young men were playing that vague kind of music that doesn't bother with a tune, the sort that people listened to in the early Sixties, tapping their Hush Puppies in a fug of Woodbine smoke. You could see people looking pleased to have signed up for Tom Stoppard's new play to then find they got a bit of free jazz thrown in. There is nothing the British public likes better than a bargain.

Five minutes to go and still no sign of them, though there was no shortage of middle-aged men. Glasses and grey hair everywhere, as you'd expect at a play dealing with Shelling, Kant and Hegel. It wasn't exactly rock and roll. But that was the beauty of the theatre, it made you feel like a bright young thing, unlike at the cinema where too many people were under thirty. Except for the French Institute, where cinephiles came in all ages. She'd be there tomorrow. With or without her *Brief Encounter* hero. Only one more day to go.

She was just wondering whether to get herself another drink when she saw them coming towards her. Two old blokes with ponytails, she thought in a disloyal shock of recognition, before reassuring herself. Will had an elegant air of success, while his college friend looked like the loser he was. He had several degrees and lived on the dole in North Wales, having turned his back on working in favour of what he and Stendhal termed the tender sensations.

Will kissed her on both cheeks and Jane was glad that Phil made no attempt to greet her beyond a brief nod.

'I'm looking forward to this, aren't you, Phil?' asked Jane, deciding she had better make an effort. 'The reviews have been pretty good on the whole.'

Phil gave her a pitying smile. 'I never read reviews, I prefer to make my own mind up. You can't trust critics, no point expecting an honest opinion from people who are in the pockets of newspaper proprietors.'

'No, of course not,' Jane said. 'Horrible capitalists. Shall we go up?'

As the curtain went up, Jane was glad it was Stoppard and not Shakespeare. There was nothing worse than sitting through one of those so-called comedies and hearing the audience show off by laughing at jokes that weren't funny. *'T'was not a . . . t'was a pricket!'* Cue howls of phoney laughter. Any allusion to the horns of a cuckold and the house would be rocking in their seats to prove they understood the significance of sixteenth-century humour. Stoppard was much safer, particularly a new play where few could claim to know the lines.

After the performance, they made their way slowly down the wide stairs as Phil and Will dissected the play in loud detail.

'I'm surprised that Stoppard shows so little under-standing of deconstruction,' complained Phil, 'considering he was arguably the first postmodernist.'

Jane dropped back in the crowd and pretended she wasn't with them.

'I'm more staggered by his failure to treat Bakunin as a thinker,' said Will. 'It's well-known that he could have been just as tyrannical as Marx.'

'But surely you see that Stoppard is afraid of Bakunin?'

They stepped outside to face the rain driving in from the west, streaking the concrete façade of the theatre. After three decades of ridicule, concrete was back, but it still looked rubbish in wet weather. Will and Phil went ahead, walking in step, ponytails nodding. They cut up the stairs to Waterloo Bridge and waited for Jane while they completed their critique.

'Of course there are interesting parallels between Tsarist Russia and Blair's Britain,' Phil was saying, 'but if you're looking for brilliant absurdist fun with bio-dramas, I'd stick with Lenin and Joyce in *Travesties*.'

They stopped talking as Jane caught them up and Will hailed a taxi. They were going to The Ivy, which wasn't wildly convenient for the South Bank but that wasn't the point. Ordinary people couldn't get a table at The Ivy which was enough to ensure it was always fully booked by those who could.

The taxi cut through Covent Garden up to Soho and Jane stared out of the window at the young people laughing on the streets, in groups and couples, all enjoying a night out. They looked so carefree she felt like jumping out of the taxi right now and joining them.

At the restaurant, Will led the way in, nodding at one or two people he knew. Jane clocked Graham Norton on one table and wasn't that Joan Collins over there? There was also a table of dull-looking young men in suits, which brought into question the whole exclusive booking policy.

Will's easy manner with the maître d' evaporated when they were shown to a small table at the back of the bar.

'I'm surprised at you, Will,' said Phil, once they had been moved into the main room, 'making such a fuss about a table. I can't remember ever seeing you so worked up about anything.'

Jane was surprised to hear him say something sensible at last. It did seem an awful lot of bother to go to for a dish of pasta. Then again, worrying about the little things was a useful distraction from big, scary questions. Don't sweat the small stuff, wasn't that the message from one of those dreadful self-help books? Bad advice. Do sweat the small stuff, it will stop you worrying yourself sick about the big stuff. Jane glanced across the table at Will and quickly turned her attention to the menu. She didn't like the way her thoughts were going.

'I'll take the gnocchi with gorgonzola,' said Will. His eyes were all over the room, making sure he hadn't missed any opportunities.

'Will, how ya doin'?' A man with droopy jeans stopped by their table and punched fists with Will as a sign of 'respeck', in that way white people did in imitation of their cooler black counterparts. Jane believed they were known as wiggers.

'I'm good,' said Will, which was the required response to that American style of greeting, even when it was between two English ex-public schoolboys.

'Hot new TV producer,' Will bragged, as the man slouched off to the loo, but nobody was listening. Phil was busy ordering the faux working-class fish cakes, and Jane was choosing a salad. She was never hungry this late, she would rather be at home, reading in bed or watching repeats of *Sex and the City*.

While they waited for their food, Will turned the conversation back to Stoppard. 'I do think it's a mistake to get too hung up on the Bakunin question,' he began, but Jane cut across him quickly.

'Can we talk about something else now? I rather feel we've done the play to death.'

Will looked surprised. 'Excuse-moi!' he said. 'Didn't realise we were boring you, did we, Phil? Over to you then, Jane, maybe you can tell us what's new in *Heat* magazine?'

'What's *Heat* magazine?' asked Phil, who had no interest in celebrities.

'It's a trashy rag that Will thinks I enjoy reading,' said Jane. 'You may have noticed he doesn't think I'm up to the heavy stuff.'

'Unfair!' said Will. 'And anyway, as a cultural phenomenon those magazines are worthy of serious study.'

And he was off on a discourse about media reflecting society, which led them into reminiscing about the Oz trial and the Velvet Underground and Jimi Hendrix.

Jane remembered a friend once telling her how she could never go out with someone who didn't know what was in the charts when you were at school. Jane suddenly knew exactly what she meant: she was isolated by the age gap.

In the taxi home, she felt excluded again by their conversation. But as she stared out at the rainy streets, she rationalised that everyone gets bored sometimes, and that boredom at least replaced worry. She'd rather be bored than worried.

'I wish you wouldn't belittle me like that in front of people,' said Jane as they got ready for bed, 'making out I'm a bimbo just because I tried to break up a monotonous conversation.'

Will looked aggrieved as he turned back the duvet. 'I think if anyone should feel belittled, it's me,' he said, 'having you cut me off mid-sentence and making out I'm a bore.'

'But it was quite boring, hearing you going on like that, going over the same old ground.'

'Phil didn't think so.'

'I rest my case. You've got to admit he's heavy-going.'

'The finest mind at Cambridge at one time.'

'What's that supposed to mean? Why do you keep going on about it? I never go swaggering around telling everyone I went to Oxford, but you and Phil act like you're streets ahead of the pack. It gets on my nerves.'

'Don't be bitter, Jane, it doesn't suit you,' said Will, putting on his blindfold to let her know the conversation was over.

'But I am bitter. I can't help it, you always make me feel like I'm not quite there with you. I'm fed up with being treated like a dim relation. I'm beginning to think Toni Vincent was quite right about you.'

The blindfold came straight off and he was bolt upright at the prospect of hearing about himself.

'Toni Vincent the publisher? When did you meet her, what did she say about me?'

'She was at the school reunion. I told you, but you weren't listening as usual.'

'You went to school with Toni Vincent? How amazing, I would have thought she'd been somewhere a little more . . . you know, a bit classier.'

'It's amazing what crawls out of the suburbs,' said Jane. 'Anyway, she was reasonably complimentary about you as a writer, but she thought you'd be very difficult to live with.'

'And you agreed, I suppose.'

'No, I defended you, as usual. But it's true, you can be difficult.'

Will sighed. 'I'm an artist, Jane, you knew what you were taking on.' He shook his head. 'I'm disappointed in you. I thought you were different, interested in a better life, not just in plodding along like any old couple.'

'But plodding along is what life is about, isn't it? At least it is when you've got children . . .'

'Oh, don't start your martyr act again.'

'And you're never interested in what I'm up to. Like

when I went to that reunion, you never asked me how it went or anything. Sometimes I think you're not a proper person at all, you're just a . . . collection of opinions, about bloody Bakunin or Hegel or fuck knows who . . .'

She'd gone too far now.

'Of course I have opinions, Jane, that's what I'm paid for. Do you think I'd be given a column if I didn't? If you want a little lapdog to follow you around, you've come to the wrong man. And if you've got something to tell me, fine, but don't expect me to ask about every detail of your life. You know we agreed how important it was for us to keep our own space.'

'Except that my space has been built entirely round yours. I bend over backwards to make our life the way you want it to be, and I am beginning to wonder what it's all for!'

'You tell me! You're the one who pushed for us to move in together. Believe me, I would have been more than happy to stay as we were, but oh no, you wanted us to share our every waking moment.'

'Oh, I see! You'd prefer me and Liberty to be shut away on our own somewhere, so you could just drift in and see us whenever it suited you. We're a family, Will, doesn't that mean anything to you?'

'Of course it does, I've done it before, remember!'

'How could I forget! I'm always trying so hard to do the right thing, trying not to piss you off so you don't walk out on us the way you walked out on Carol and the boys!'

Will was having no more. 'That was low,' he said, and coldly turned his back on her, switching out the light.

Jane shut herself into the bathroom and sat down on the loo, trying to calm herself down. This wasn't like her, she and Will never rowed, he had taught her that it served no purpose. By the time she came out he was asleep and she was able to slip into bed and lie there wondering what was happening to her.

SIX

The next morning, Jane was making Liberty's breakfast and worrying about the row she'd had with Will. They'd never had an ugly slanging match like that before, it was quite out of character and Jane felt drained by the whole episode.

She shook a helping of porridge oats into a bowl and topped it up with milk. Jane was pleased when Liberty asked for porridge, it seemed like a proper breakfast to her, the sort of thing that sensible mothers prepared for their children. The breakfast equivalent of Clarks' flat lace-up school shoes, whereas those synthetic chocolate cereal rings were more like slut-bitch high-heeled platforms. The kind of cereal that would go off to meet strange men at afternoon screenings.

'Mum, can birds have heart attacks?'

Liberty's bright eyes followed her mother round the kitchen as she put the bowl in the microwave and tried to apply her mind to the question. She had barely slept last night, and had more or less decided to skip the cinema. The last thing she needed now was a extra dimension to her life, it was all far too complicated as it was.

Did birds have hearts? She supposed they must do, they weren't cold like fish, though barely more interesting.

'I guess they can,' she said, stirring the porridge and adding a generous helping of brown sugar. 'Why do you ask?'

'We found a dead one in the garden yesterday just after you'd gone out. Anna helped me to bury him. Can I have more sugar please?'

Jane passed her the bowl. 'Make sure you do your teeth after,' she said. The goody-goody breakfast was fast degenerating into the usual processed sugarfest.

'And I wasn't a bit upset.' She looked up, challenging.

Jane knew what was coming next.

'You always say it's not a good idea to have a pet, because I'd be upset if it died. But you see, I wouldn't be.'

'Do you want milk or apple juice?'

But Liberty wasn't falling for that diversionary tactic. She pushed on to play her trump card.

'And Cosima is getting a pony for Christmas!'

'Goodness me, is that the time?' said Jane. 'Run up quickly and do your teeth, hurry, hurry . . .'

On the way back from school, Jane wondered how Will would be when she got home. He had still been asleep when she'd got up this morning, so she had no idea how he was feeling about last night. People said that everybody had arguments, that it was good to clear the air, but that had never been Jane's experience. She was brought up in a house where you avoided confrontation, where you didn't want to risk your father's displeasure. Then after he left, she avoided taking on her mother's unhappiness, preferring to tiptoe round the edge, hoping everything would be all right.

Until last night she had always adopted the same approach with Will, making sure they didn't squabble, going along with his view of things. She didn't want it to go wrong between them, her life with him was the version of happiness that she had chosen. That was what you did in a relationship. After the first heady phase, you took a cool look at what you had and decided whether or not it was worth going on. She'd had a few affairs that had gone no further, but with Will she knew it was for life. She knew this after just three weeks, when they went to see a play and he took her backstage to have drinks with the cast. They were hanging on his words, laughing at his jokes, and she felt so proud to be with him. He was what she'd been waiting for.

When she got in, Will and Phil were sitting round the kitchen table drinking tea in their pyjamas. Or rather, Will was in Calvin Klein pyjamas and Phil was wearing a baggy pair of Y-fronts and a tie-dye tee shirt. They both wore their grey hair loose, like ladies in a costume drama waiting for their maid to come in and pin up their chignons.

'Ah, here she comes,' said Will. 'Jane, how the hell do you stop that bloody whirring noise over the cooker? It's been driving us mad.'

He didn't seem to be harbouring a grudge, but with Phil there it was difficult to tell.

'The extractor fan?' she said. 'You just need to turn it off.'

She had deliberately left it on all night. You needed all the ventilation you could get with a house guest like Phil.

'That's better,' said Will. 'Thank you. You know how challenged I am by domestic machinery.'

She need not have worried: clearly he was reminding her how much he depended on her, that they were mutually complementary. He had the big ideas, and she was queen of the household appliances. Each to his own.

'Do you have any toast?' Phil asked, looking vaguely round the kitchen as though hoping to catch sight of a couple of slices. 'Will wasn't sure where you might have put the bread.'

'Try the bread bin,' she said, opening it and putting two slices in the toaster.

'I wouldn't mind a bit of egg and bacon if it's not too much trouble. I know Will doesn't do breakfast, but I'm afraid I can't get going without it.'

Get going to what exactly? As Phil did nothing, Jane failed to see why he needed to start the day on a full stomach, but she'd happily cook him breakfast if it meant getting rid of him. Will would be off to the library soon, and she would go to the cinema as usual. Except it was not as usual. She felt a rush of butterflies in her stomach as she took a bag of organic bacon out of the fridge. Shame to waste it on Phil, but she didn't have the stuff that leaks white liquid into the frying pan.

'Do you want some, Will?'

He turned to her with an expression of mock surprise. 'Have you ever seen me eat a cholesterol-charged full English nightmare?'

'It's made a comeback now, with the Atkins diet, but I'll take that as a no.'

'I have to warn you, Jane,' said Phil, a ripple of concern crossing his middle-aged face, 'I'm a little bit picky when it comes to eggs. I can't bear it when they have that overcooked lacy edge.'

'I'll do my best,' said Jane. 'But then I'm afraid I'll have to turf you out. I need to get on with my work.'

'You see how clever I am, Phil?' said Will. 'I've got myself a woman to cook breakfast for my friends before sitting down to earn money all day at her computer. As well as bringing up my daughter. Modern women, I love them. Jane and I have a post-feminist relationship, we've put the sex war behind us. Haven't we, Jane?'

If he was calling a truce, that was fine with her. She squeezed his outstretched hand. Maybe it had been a good thing, to have a go at him last night.

'Well, it's good news for you, I can see that,' said Phil. 'But I think if I was a woman I'd prefer to do what I liked all day and let some man go off and earn the money.'

Will laughed and ran his hand through his long hair. 'That's because you're a lazy bastard, Phil. Whereas Jane has a strong work ethic, luckily for us all.'

He put his arm out and patted her on the flank as she walked past.

Three hours later Jane sat on the 49 bus as it crawled its way through the roadworks. New pipes were being laid, or cables, or sewers, in the never-ending upkeep of the crumbling city. Jane wouldn't be surprised if the whole lot came tumbling down one day. All those Victorian

houses and drainage systems and underground passage-
ways might suddenly reach their expiry date and collapse
simultaneously in a heap of dust.

She hoped she wouldn't be late. He might not bother
with the film if he thought she wasn't coming. He might
ask himself what he was playing at and just walk away.
Like she should if she had any sense. She looked at her
watch and frowned. It was a nuisance that the car had
refused to start, but at least she'd left home so absurdly
early that she had plenty of margin for error.

The bus picked up speed and Jane relaxed. She was
going to make it. Going anywhere in London was an
adventure: you never knew how long it would take, or if
indeed you would arrive. Buses inexplicably stopped
mid-route so the driver could get off, taking his cash box
with him. Tube trains stock-piled in tunnels or were
cancelled due to staff shortage or leaves on the line. In
any other country, it would not be tolerated, but the British
treated it all as a huge joke and a rich source of stories.

With three minutes to spare, Jane stepped off the bus
into a crowd of students from the French lycée who were
loafing around on the pavement, smoking cigarettes and
fiddling with their hair. They wore very flared jeans that
hung low on their hips then ballooned too wide and too
long over their shoes to form flaps that were wet and
muddy from the winter puddles. Almost adults, but clumsy
and unfinished, they seemed both exotic and intimidating
to Jane, who skirted past them, up Queensberry Place
and into the Institute.

Even without looking round too obviously, she could
tell he wasn't there. He must have had second thoughts.

She bought herself a ticket and went up the stairs, past the place where she had dropped her lens a week ago. She was careful not to look back over her shoulder; she didn't want to appear too desperate.

He was there, watching her coming up from his vantage point at the top of the stairs. She blushed when she saw him, then pleasure gave way to a very faint sense of disappointment that she remembered from her single days. When you spent all week looking forward to a date, your eager imagination couldn't help transforming a normal-looking person into a sex god. Inevitably, the reality fell a little short.

If her disappointment registered with him, he didn't show it. He smiled at her but made no attempt to come too close. She was glad, it annoyed her the way English people had got so continental, air-kissing at every opportunity as though they'd been at it for centuries instead of barely a few years.

'Perfect timing,' he said. 'Shall we go straight through?'

'Kingsley Amis said those were his least favourite words. Along with the question "Red or white?"'

He looked at her in admiration. Will would have sighed wearily, he would have heard it all before.

'How on earth do you remember what people say?' he said. 'I have an appalling memory for words.'

'I suppose it's because I work with them. You probably don't.'

'No.'

He held the door for her, then followed her down the aisle. They sat near the back, near the centre – there was plenty of choice. For the next two hours, Jane knew she would be sitting here, regardless of anything else going on in the outside world. That was the joy of the cinema, and it was all the more delicious to be here with this man that she didn't know, who felt so comfortable by her side.

He leaned across to whisper in her ear about the last Louis Malle film he had seen. She caught his unfamiliar smell, an aftershave, soap and something indefinable. You either liked a person's smell or you didn't.

He sat back and she was aware of how he filled his seat. Will's legs were slightly shorter than hers, he never had a problem in aeroplanes. In contrast, this man's knees grazed the seat in front, and the breadth of him meant her own shoulder was lightly in contact with his upper arm. In the darkness she found this contact warm and reassuring.

It was odd to experience the intimacy of the cinema with someone new. Jane was conscious of his breathing pattern, the way he shifted in his seat. At one point she stole a glance at his profile, noticed the point at which the stubble of his beard gave way to the soft skin of his neck. When it got to the part when the child is taken off by the Nazis, she discreetly wiped her tears away. You couldn't show emotion in front of a stranger like that, it was worse than stripping off naked.

When the film finished, they sat until the credits stopped rolling.

'Are you OK?' Rupert asked, passing her a man-sized Kleenex. 'It's always grim, isn't it, the jolt back to reality. Especially after a tear-jerker.'

Jane dabbed at her eyes impatiently. 'I'm terrible, I cry

at anything. Even the most kitsch and manipulative American piece of saccharine. So it's even worse when it's a good one . . .' She blew her nose. 'Let's go, shall we? Are my eyes all red?'

She held her face up for inspection and he looked down at her. Slowly, he took in her grey eyes, flecked with hazel, the long lashes stuck together by her tears, the fine high line of her cheekbones, the freckles undisguised by make-up. How could he ever have thought of her as Plain Jane? He sat entirely still, and wished they could stay like this forever. It was as if he'd been trapped in a stuffy room and had just discovered a way out.

'No,' he said eventually, 'they're not red, just a bit wet. And I can see both your lenses are in OK.'

'Good. I won't be needing you then. To crawl around on the floor, I mean.'

'I suppose not.'

They continued sitting there like that, then Jane suddenly stood up. 'Come on, everyone's gone except us. Shall we go to the café? If you've got time, that is.'

'Oh, I've got time all right. And even if I didn't, I would make time. Just for you.'

'Would you?'

'You know I would.'

How do I know? she thought, as they made their way out. I don't know anything about you.

They crossed the road and walked down to the café. The same waitress was there; she seemed to recognise them from last time.

'Two cappuccinos?' she asked.

'Yes, thank you,' said Jane. Then, to Rupert, 'Scary! Do you think she memorises the orders of every passing customer?'

'It's her job, that's how you get on in the restaurant business. The personal touch, remembering faces.'

'Yes.'

They both fell silent, they couldn't think what to say.

'It's funny,' Jane began.

'Yes?'

'How you can look forward to something, how our entire lives are geared up to making plans . . .'

'And you were looking forward to this afternoon?'

'Yes.'

'Me too. And now it's almost over, and we have to think about the next time.'

'Yes. And it's ridiculous. It's not as if . . .'

'Not as if we're on a date or anything.'

'Exactly. There's nothing between us.'

'No, nothing.'

She started again. 'It's just, you have your life sorted, you get what you wanted, or what you think you wanted. And then you suddenly panic, and turn round and start asking yourself, is this it? Is this to be my life?'

Rupert couldn't believe how she'd just put in words exactly the way he felt.

Jane pulled herself up. 'I'm sorry,' she said, 'I shouldn't be talking like this. I am happy, really. Or as happy as you can hope to be. I have a good and lucky life.'

'Tell me about it,' said Rupert, already envious because it didn't include him, 'tell me about your lucky life.'

'Well, I've got a lovely daughter. She makes me feel very lucky.'

His heart sank. She must be married. She didn't wear a ring, though, maybe she was a single mum, or divorced, or a saintly widow.

'That is lucky,' he said. 'I'd like to have kids one day.'

He didn't have children then. For some reason this made Jane glad.

'And . . . I have my work, which we talked about last time. I work from home which means I choose my own hours and don't need to get dolled up for the office. I can slouch around looking ugly.'

His eyes told her this was unlikely.

'And . . . I have a good social life with my partner.'

Ah, he thought, here comes the sting in the tail. Well, what did he expect?

'He's a travel writer,' she added.

'That's interesting,' said Rupert politely, though personally he didn't think so. Travel writers generally reminded him of those boys at school who felt they deserved to be gentleman explorers from a previous age. The sort who used to go off to the jungle for three years and come back with a loin-clothed manservant and a new species of insect.

'He thinks so,' she said. 'You may have heard of him, his name's Will Thacker.'

Rupert shook his head, which pleased her.

'Sorry,' he said.

'And he knows everyone,' she added.

'Everyone?'

'Anyone who's anyone. He's a journalist as well. Has a column in the *Messenger*.'

'I don't read the papers any more. I find them boring. And time-wasting. I found I was spending all weekend reading them and then, come Sunday night, I couldn't remember a single thing I'd read.'

'I know what you mean. It's good for getting invited to things, though, living with a journalist. Especially as I'm pretty tied to the home during the day. Though he goes out more than me. He's . . . quite a bit older,' she added.

'Is he now?' Rupert felt encouraged and leaned forward with a surge of youthful energy. Perhaps forty wasn't the end of the line after all. What did she mean by quite a bit older? Ten, twenty years? Was he over sixty? Maybe he was a white-haired old darling that she pushed out in his wheelchair to take the air, it could be that sort of relationship.

'But that's enough about me,' said Jane, 'you still haven't told me what *you* do for a living. I'm getting another coffee, do you want one?'

'Yes, I will.'

She signalled to the waitress while he shifted uncomfortably on his chair. It was time to come clean about his so-called career. She was bound to consider him dull beyond belief once she found out what he did. You could hardly compare number-crunching on incubator funds with the creative scribbling of a famous writer. Not so famous that Rupert had heard of him, but then Rupert wasn't a big reader. He pushed his chair back and looked sideways, couldn't quite meet her eye while he owned up.

'I run a hedge fund. Or rather, I'm setting one up, with a friend.'

She looked bemused rather than bored. 'What's that then, a charity for old gardeners?'

'Nothing so noble, I'm afraid. The only beneficiaries – if there are any – will be me and my business partner and our investors, who are already pretty rich otherwise they wouldn't be putting money our way in the first place.'

'So it's a sort of City job.'

'Yes. Except it's in Mayfair, just next door to a gym actually. I go there quite a lot, there's this rest room with a big sofa that you can lie on and watch fish swimming in a tank.'

'Sounds relaxing.'

'The thing is,' he said, 'my job, it's not really me. I'd much rather be a gardener.'

Her face lit up. 'You like gardening too? I love it! Will's always making fun of me for reading *Hortus*. He thinks I'm on a slippery slope to wearing big tweed skirts and fancying Alan Titchmarsh. My best-ever job was trans-lating a book on the great French gardens, most of them created by English gardeners of course. I thought, if I ever get the time, I'd like to drive across France and visit them all. You could come with me!'

She was teasing of course, but as he watched her laughing excitedly, he knew that he would like nothing better. They could leave tonight, throw a bag in the back of the car, take the night ferry and just drive. It was easy. Happiness was always easy, it was there for the taking, so why did people waste their lives getting tied up in knots of misery?

'You're on,' he said.

*   *   *

By the time they came out of the café they had sketched out their entire route, starting at Le Havre and working their way down through Normandy and the Loire valley, before heading down to the Dordogne and the Pyrenees.

'We don't even need to do it now,' she said. 'I feel that I've already been there.'

He shrugged. 'I still think it would be better in the flesh.'

She looked at her watch. 'I have to go, I'm afraid.'

'Don't be afraid.'

'No.'

She wished he would wrap his arms round her and kiss her right there in the street. 'Better go and get my daughter.'

'Better had.' He stood there, hands in his pockets.

'Next week?'

'Yes . . . no, I don't know, I've got a thing in the evening, so I really should work all day . . .'

She should take his number, that was the logical thing to do, but she couldn't do that. As long as it wasn't properly arranged, as long as it could count as just bumping into each other, there was nothing to hide. But if you started getting into phone calls and secret rendezvous, then it became something else.

He knew this, too.

'Maybe we should say Friday week then,' he said, pulling out the programme, 'they're showing *Belle de Jour*.'

'It seems a long way off.'

She blushed then, worried she appeared too eager.

'Not really,' he said. 'Not in the greater scheme of things. Two weeks is no time at all.'

* * *

Reliance on fantasy was what kept people going on the whole. You had to have a dream, or else why bother getting up in the morning? It was far more logical to lie there and wait for death to come.

These were Jane's thoughts that evening as she wiped down the kitchen table and shook the crumbs from Liberty's homework book before returning it to her school satchel. She had already put in an apple and a Penguin biscuit for Monday's snack. Getting in front, beating the clock, organising the week ahead to avoid an unsightly last-minute panic. The routines of domesticity were soothing and at the same time insufferably dull. No wonder you needed to project another parallel life, imagining yourself elsewhere. Driving through France, for instance, with a man whose name you didn't even know.

She set the table for two and turned her attention to a recipe for salmon with roasted beetroot that she had thought would appeal to Will's taste for unusual combinations. Phil had gone home a day early, which was cause for celebration, so she had made a panecotta for pudding. She always said 'pudding' these days. For Will, dessert belonged to a whole category of outlawed suburban vocabulary: serviette, settee, lounge, pardon – all so terribly lower-middle. Just like the set of avocado dishes and cut-glass decanter that she had been obliged to cast off, along with her fondness for doileys.

She put the salmon in the oven and washed up the pans from Liberty's tea. Will was working in the galleria and had requested a late dinner as he wanted to get on with his column. Jane had hoped to fit in a bit of work, too, but decided to go upstairs to clean the bathroom instead, fishing out long strands of grey hair from the plughole with a pair of tweezers.

Back in the kitchen, she peeled off the Marigolds and hung them to dry on the pair of upstretched chrome hands that a friend had given her. Rubber gloves scored high on Will's naff register, but Jane drew the limit here. It was one thing playing Cinderella and taking care of all the household chores, but she refused to let her hands turn into ragged old bits of meat.

Maybe it was the Cinderella thing that was the problem. She couldn't help thinking that going out to work might shake her out of this self-indulgent fantasy. If you got to chat round the water cooler, you wouldn't need to strike up conversations with strange men at the cinema. Whereas she spent her days in solitude, tapping away at her computer then tidying up the house, like the inmate of a closed order of nuns. She often went all day without speaking a word, until she went to fetch Liberty. It must have the effect of making her more eager for male company, mustn't it? Why else would she be thinking endlessly now about her new friend, and running this afternoon through her mind, and wondering when they might see each other again.

'Cinderella, you *shall* go to the ball.'

She jumped as Will came into the kitchen, waving an invitation in a flourish of mock excitement. Had she actually spoken aloud?

'It's from Lydia. That drinks party you were warning me about. It must have arrived a while ago and got caught up with my papers.'

He passed it to her and opened the fridge to fix himself a drink. The invitation was properly engraved, bobbly black italic letters on thick cream card. '*Lydia Littlewood and Rupert Beauval-Tench*' at the top, then the words '*At Home*' in the centre, and in the bottom corner '*Drinks: 6.30–8.30*'. Like Jane, Lydia had enjoyed an upwardly mobile education. She came from a home where you might be at home with a cold, but were never At Home in a posh, hostessy way. It meant that as an adult, she had adopted such habits with Dickensian energy.

'Better make sure I leave before midnight then,' said Jane. 'Don't want to lose a glass slipper or find myself in rags.'

'If we're not out of there three hours before midnight, I shall turn into a pumpkin myself with boredom.' Will was dipping the rim of his glass tumbler in a plate of salt, preparing a margarita. 'Have we got any limes?'

'Bottom of the fridge,' she said. 'I don't know why you're being so horrid about it. I thought you liked Lydia.'

'I like her well-enough. It's that stuffed shirt she's living with I'm worried about.' Will poured a generous shot of tequila into his glass and thought back to the time when he had liked Lydia well-enough to engage in regular sex sessions with her in her Bayswater apartment. It was when Jane was pregnant, and he had been suffering a terrible sense of *déjà vu*. Once again he had been trapped into the role of father provider, feeling the same itch as when his ex-wife had swapped her miniskirt and patent-leather kinky boots for a brown maternity smock and Dr Scholl sandals.

Lydia had been a release from the crushing burden of

domestic responsibility. While Jane was smugly preparing her nest, he had been going at it hammer and tongs with her best friend. It went some way to redressing the balance of power. And Lydia was a smart kid, she took it for what it was, a bit of fun, nothing more. It was just a pity that her taste in men had since hit rock-bottom. Going from one of the most talked-about writers of his generation to a stiff in a suit couldn't have been easy for her.

He sat down at the table with his drink and rocked backwards on his chair, his arms folded behind his head, watching Jane as she wiped up the saucepans and crouched down to replace them in the cupboard. She was a good girl, really: easy-going, and she had quickly got over that little outburst last night, thanks to some soft-soaping on his part. It had been easy to reassure her that of course he hadn't meant it about her forcing them into living together. Not strictly true, but it had all worked out in the end. He had no reason to complain. He wouldn't have wanted a live-in relationship with Lydia. She might have been hot, but she was endlessly demanding. Very keen on expensive restaurants – he couldn't imagine her knocking out home-made dinners the way Jane did – and she was ruthlessly out for what she could get. This was a quality he actually rather admired, but you only had room for one person like that in a relationship.

'Surprise me,' he said to Jane, putting his feet up on the table and brushing a fleck of dust off his moleskin trousers with the back of his hand. He raised his nose to breathe in the smell from the oven. 'I'm getting fish of some kind. Coriander, a hint of caraway. Lemon, obviously.'

'Sicilian unwaxed, you can rest easy,' said Jane. 'As gnarled and misshapen as you could hope for, and I got them from Alistair Little's deli.'

'That's my girl.' He took a sip of his drink and sniffed the air again. 'There's something else . . . no, it's no good, you'll have to put me out of my misery.'

'Beetroot. It's salmon with beetroot.'

'Well I never . . . how very original.'

Thank you, thought Jane, thank you for showing appreciation of the ingenuity I put into my menu-planning. It was good that they shared a passion for food. You needed something like that as the years went by, people said; common interests to tide you over once the sex had quietened down.

'You'll be pleased to know I've cracked it,' said Will, 'my idea for next week's column. Sorry, there I go again, talking about myself. How did your work go today? You see, I *do* care.'

He pressed his hand on his heart and Jane laughed.

'It's OK,' she said, 'I'll spare you the details. What is it then, your idea?'

'I'm going to speak out against this shocking new fashion for educated women to give up work to stay home with their kids,' he told her. 'An appalling and reactionary trend. As one of the first male feminists, I can only condemn it. Next thing, they'll be taking away a woman's right to vote.'

'I think people are getting fed up with the superwoman thing,' said Jane. 'You know, doing two jobs and only being paid for one.' She picked up the halves of lime that Will had left on the chopping board and returned them to the fridge, then took out some green beans. 'I think they're starting to ask themselves, what's the point?' she went on, slicing the ends off the beans, 'working their arses off at the office, then coming home and taking on the domestic shift.'

'But surely you realise, Jane, that it's just not fair on men!' Will had jumped up and opened the fridge to take out the bottle of tequila. 'Why should men have to go out to work all day while their lazy-cow wives play tennis and go on coffee mornings? I tell you one thing, I wouldn't tolerate it, not any more! The last thing men need when they get in is to hear about how their wives have had a gorgeous day spending all their money.'

Jane thought about how it might be if she had bottomless funds and no paid work to tie her to her computer. She could spend all day shopping, and having lunch, and could go to the French Institute cinema every day if she felt like it. 'Sounds all right to me,' she said, 'a glamorous take on the 1950s housewife, what's wrong with that?'

'At least the 1950s housewife did housework. These new jumped-up stay-at-homers all have cleaners and *au pair* girls. They bring nothing to the household. They are an economic drain, and should be forced to reimburse the state for the money wasted on their education.'

Jane said nothing and let Will rant on, rehearsing his argument for the compulsory employment for all mothers that he would later flesh out on the Apple in the galleria. She poured boiling water over a bowl of tomatoes the better to release the skins. She would chop them and mix them into the beans along with some garlic. Will always said plain boiled vegetables seemed just too school dinners for words.

After dinner, Jane cleared up and Will went upstairs to work for a bit, then they went to bed and had sex. It was like mowing the lawn, she thought; same motions, same frequency of once a week in the growing season. They weren't yet at the fallow winter stage, where the machine could be locked up for months at a time. Afterwards, Will picked up Wittgenstein and Jane went back to reading about the architectural uses of roses in *Hortus* magazine. After a few years of bed-sharing you didn't need to bother with post-coital intimacy. A comfortable fug of indifference replaced the probing conversations of the early days.

'I might go Christmas shopping again tomorrow,' said Jane. She addressed the remark to her bedside lamp, her back still turned on Will, 'if you wouldn't mind looking after Liberty.'

She twisted round to look at him.

'Of course not,' he said, after a pause. He put in his earplugs, pulled the British Airways blindfold into place and turned off the light.

'Preparing for lift-off?' she asked.

'You know I need my sleep,' he said, 'particularly now you've sprung a morning's childcare on me. Never mind that I've got a deadline. Good night.'

'Good night.'

Jane switched off her light and lay on her back, making mental lists for tomorrow's shopping. Already December, and she had barely started. What a bore. She thought enviously of Lydia going off to South America with stylish disregard for family obligations. Lydia was disdainful of what she termed the red poinsettia Christmas experience. Fat relatives watching telly in ripped paper hats while outside the rain drizzled down. Waitrose magazine said that Christmas dinner was 'probably the most important meal of the year', which struck a note of darkness in Jane's soul.

She turned her mind to happier thoughts. Her new friend at the French Institute. The word 'friend' sounded both coy and sinister when applied to an adult you barely knew. It carried dark overtones of an Internet chat room, a hairy man-sized version of a childhood playmate. She'd have to wait two weeks before seeing him again. But he was right, two weeks was no time. Not with everything else she had to get done. There was the Christmas dinner, still a while off but never too early to plan for. Mustn't forget the mincemeat, and brandy butter, or should they go wild this year and ring the changes with rum butter? Bronze-feathered Kelly free-range turkey, or a tasty but fatty goose? And the fill-your-own empty Christmas crackers that she thought would make an amusing change; she and Liberty could make things out of card and glitter to put inside them: it would be a good arts and crafts project for a Sunday afternoon. Faintly boring, but heart-warming, a bit like Christmas itself.

SEVEN

On the morning of her party, Lydia woke up early. Rupert was already dressed for work, and was performing the male equivalent of loading a handbag, sweeping the coins and keys from the top of the chest of drawers into his hand and then into his trouser pocket. It would be easier to have one of those Latin-style men's clutch bags, but he would look ridiculous, a large man like him, mincing out of the door with one of those under his arm.

Lydia stretched luxuriously into Rupert's side of the bed. 'Big night tonight,' she said, 'the day we tell the world that we are to be an item. Oh my God, that's just broken my dream!'

'What was it?' asked Rupert, rather hoping she'd say she'd learned in a blinding flash that getting married was a bad idea.

'I dreamed you took me to live in a horrid little house near Milton Keynes with Dralon furniture.'

'Is that all?'

She curled up on her side and pulled the covers over

her head. 'And now I'm awake too early and won't be able to get back to sleep,' she said, her voice muffled through the goose down. 'I'll have bags under my eyes and look hideous tonight.'

Rupert's heart sank. After tonight there would be no going back. The door would be firmly closed, and he would go from being an anonymous single person who happens to have a sort of live-in girlfriend, to being Lydia's fiancé, with everything that entailed. He would never know romance again, he would never sleep with anyone else ever again. It was a terrifying thought.

'I'll see you later, then.' He jangled his pocket, now filled with a ludicrous amount of loose change, and made for the door.

'Remember, darling, not too late,' said Lydia, blowing him a kiss from beneath the duvet, 'don't forget the caterers are coming at six.'

Climbing into his cab, Rupert thought about Lydia's dream and what it said about her. He was only averagely romantic, but even he knew that when you were in love with someone, you didn't care where you lived. When you loved someone and got engaged, the material details were immaterial, weren't they? They weren't living in the dark ages, after all, when marriage was a crude form of financial barter.

For instance, if things were different and he and Jane were to go off together, he knew for a fact that she wouldn't care where they ended up. She would show no interest in bathroom taps or kitchen flooring, or living within spitting distance of Sloane Square. And this he knew without ever having discussed it with her. He knew she didn't care about things that didn't matter.

But there was no point in thinking like this. He was forty years old and this was the real world, and Lydia was a fine match for him. For three years he had been proud to call her his girlfriend, and getting engaged was the natural next step. His fantasy about Jane was just another symptom of his mid-life malaise. Perhaps he should swallow his stiff upper lip and see someone about it. His aversion to therapy was making him feel unfashionable. Sadness and disappointment used to be accepted as part of life, but now you were supposed to label it depression and get cured by taking drugs or talking to a qualified person. There was a shrink who lived in the apartment below him who seemed to have a lot of men Rupert's age coming and going. He was gay and outrageously handsome, but most of his clients looked straight enough. Stiffs in suits, most of them, just like Rupert. It couldn't do any harm to have a trial session.

Lydia heard the taxi purring in the street below, then the door slammed and off it went, carrying her lover away. Recently she had been finding him sexier than usual, a little aloof, less easy to please. There was no denying that although one didn't want to marry a bastard, a little bit of bastard-like behaviour did wonders for a man's sex-appeal. No-one wanted an over-eager dog, wagging his tail and drooling over you with idiotic, unconditional love. She dozed on and off for another half hour, then thought she might as well get up. She had lots to get on with, though obviously she wouldn't be working today.

Lucky for her that she was editor-at-large, roaming free and expansive through the wide ocean of life, unlike those poor full-timers chained to their desks at the magazine like rats in a cage.

After a leisurely bath and breakfast, Lydia slipped on a pair of jeans and a low-cut sweater and lay on the ugly beige sofa watching *Trisha* on telly while she painted her nails. A hard-faced teenage mother was going to find out whether or not her pimply ex-boyfriend was the father of her baby. When it was revealed that he was not, the girl leaped up from her chair and punched the air in triumph while the youth sank back deflated, a useless cuckold already at the tender age of sixteen.

By the time Lydia got out onto the Kings Road, the boutiques were just starting to open. Shop girls were crouching down or reaching up at the glass doors, frowning as they negotiated large bunches of keys. Friday morning was a fine time to cruise the shops since you got none of the trippers who came up at the weekend. Sundays were the worst, it was the only time you could park for free, which meant the streets were all blocked solid.

Lydia was glad to count herself among the rich and leisured locals who could shop at hours to suit themselves. She was following one now, a classic Chelsea blonde wearing a full-length sheepskin coat over a baby-blue cashmere sweater, talking on her mobile phone.

'Yuh,' she was saying, in a loud, confident voice, 'there are some jeans that I'd raahly like you to look at. Yuh, eighty-four pounds but the length is perfect.'

Mobile phones could have been invented for girls like that. Girls like that were born without embarrassment, born to loudly bore everyone to death with the details of some purchase they were thinking of making. They never whispered into their phones like lesser-born types, never muttered an ingratiating apology, 'Hallo, it's only me, sorry I'm a bit late, I'm on the 6.16, shall I get the bread or will you?'

The blonde stepped into Karen Millen and Lydia continued on her course. Past Kenneth Cole, which she liked for its New York chic, past LK Bennett, which she disliked for its prissy assumption that modern girls wanted to look like little old ladies in two-piece suits and neat matching shoes. She crossed the road and glanced in the Jigsaw window, not bad but frankly a bit too high-street for her these days. She then slipped down a side road, where the pretty row of different coloured cottages made you think you were in a quaint fishing port, until you remembered that a two-up two-down worker's hovel round here would cost you well over a million.

Lydia's hairdresser was situated at the end of one of these falsely modest terraces. Not so much a salon as an artist's studio, it had an easel set up in the middle of the room, displaying a large, cheerful canvas. Klaus laid down his paintbrush as Lydia came in – he liked to add the finishing touches to his work-in-progress in between customers. Big and Austrian, he wore long leather shorts even in winter, and had his grey hair tied up in a ponytail. He greeted Lydia warmly and sat her down in front of a mirror while he rubbed the paint off his hands with a rag soaked in turps.

It was no coincidence that Lydia came to Klaus for her hair. He was expensive and off-beat, which was a plus, but the real attraction for her was the long list of famous ex-clients he could reel off for her benefit. Like a London taxi driver boasting about who he's had in the back of his cab, Klaus peppered his conversation with allusions to the stars who had passed through his hands. Most of these clients used to come in the Seventies, before he had downsized to make time for his painting, but Lydia loved it nonetheless.

Klaus brushed out Lydia's hair in his usual, blissfully unhurried way, pausing between strokes to shout at her in the mirror. She assumed he must be slightly deaf, or maybe Austrians always spoke in very loud voices.

'But did you know,' he boomed, 'that the Chelsea Pensioners are considered a very good catch as husbands?'

'What, those dear old veterans in red jackets, get out of here!' said Lydia. She loved seeing them cruising the Kings Road, often in electric wheelchairs, but didn't buy the idea of them as marriage material.

'I swear it's true.' He shook the brush at her in the mirror to make his point. 'The mothers from the council estate encourage their daughters to marry them. Then they die very soon and the girl gets the Chelsea pension. It's a well-known scam.'

'No!'

'Honestly. How much, one inch? Did I ever tell you that I had Sacha Distel when I was still in Knightsbridge? And Catherine Deneuve. Dear Jenny Agutter still comes, and Judi of course, Charlotte Rampling and Meryl, she likes a good haircut . . .'

And he was back on the star trail, occasionally breaking off to bend down and take a snip off the end of Lydia's long auburn tresses.

'Would you like some apple-cider vinegar on your hair?'
he asked as she lay back with her head in the basin, feet
resting on a high stool.

'Not really. Why would I?'

'Makes it nice and shiny,' Klaus bellowed, as though
she were at the far end of the street instead of right there
between his hands.

'I'm having a party tonight, I don't want to smell of
chips.'

'As you like.'

He wrapped a towel round her head and propelled her
back to her seat, then spun her chair round to face the
painting on the easel.

'What do you think?'

He always asked her, so she wasn't unprepared.

'A lot of verve.'

'Thank you. Do you think you could use it in the
magazine?'

'We only use figurative I'm afraid.'

He dried her hair and stopped talking for a while,
staring out of the window instead at a homely, large-boned
mother wearing an anorak and pushing a buggy up the
street. He turned back to face Lydia in the mirror and
jerked his thumb in the direction of the retreating
woman.

'She came in once to ask how much it was for a haircut.
It was too much for her, of course. If you have to ask,
it will always be too much. She is from Switzerland, lives
down the road, her husband works for a bank that pays
the rent on the house. But she is just a simple sort of
person. She is not for this area.' He shook his head in a

mixture of contempt and pity, then smiled broadly and shook his hand through Lydia's glossy hair.

'Not like you. You are perfect for this area.'

'I'll take that as a compliment,' said Lydia, who thought she wouldn't bother telling him that she actually came from Essex. She lived in the present, not the past, and anyway Klaus wouldn't know where Essex was.

After drying her hair, Klaus produced a hand-held circular vibrator that he applied to her back and shoulders. Lydia winced, it set her teeth right on edge. He then brought out a mirror and made her hold it herself so she could enjoy the rear view of his handiwork.

He nodded with satisfaction. 'Now that is a very good haircut.'

'Though you say so yourself.'

'Though I say so myself.'

By the time Lydia came out, the pub across the road was filling up with the usual crew of hoorays, big and braying in beige slacks or jeans and rugby shirts. As a fashion person, Lydia was fascinated to see the rugby shirt still living on here in the heart of Chelsea. As far as she was concerned, they belonged to the Seventies, when girls used to borrow them off their boyfriends and wear them with upturned collars and a string of pearls to look petite and vulnerable like Felicity Kendal in *The Good Life*. For the purposes of research, she went in and ordered a large glass of wine while she ran a thorough check.

She sat down in a battered armchair and noticed one of the customers looked like a younger version of Rupert. He was giving her the eye now, leaning against the bar, pint glass in hand. He was talking to the man next to him, but his body language was for her benefit: broad hips tilted towards her, one foot crossed in front of the other. He had a wide forehead and fair hair that sprung up with patrician virility. She shook her newly groomed hair and made eye contact for a few seconds before looking away. It was nice to know she could still pull if she needed to, although that was all taken care of now. By the end of this evening she would officially be recognised as the fiancée of the Hon. Rupert Beauval-Tench. She drained her glass and left the pub, brushing past her admirer on her way out.

'The Pont de Normandie resembles an elegant, powerful bird, soaring up in a gracious curve over the Seine estuary. Comparable to Concorde, it bears witness to man's capacity to scale the heights of technical brilliance, and stands, proud and erect, a lasting testament to the presidency of Jacques Chirac.'

Jane read back over the last sentence and pressed the back-space key. She couldn't say proud and erect in the same breath as President Chirac, it made the book sound like a soft-porn mag instead of a hymn of praise to French engineers. On the other hand, what did it matter? She doubted anyone would go so far as to read the book. Americans might line it up on the coffee table to prove they were well-travelled Francophiles, but they would be unlikely to do more than flick through the photos as they sipped that weak cinnamon-flavoured coffee they all raved about.

She replaced the words with '*magisterial*', one of her favourite adjectives for this kind of job. The art of Cellini, the oeuvre of Stendhal, the slopes of the Auvergne, all could be described as magisterial, which also served to flatter the reader with its assumption of a knowledge of Latin roots. Or 'routs', as Americans pronounced it. That always made her laugh, like the way they said 'erbs' for herbs. Not to mention those quirky differences in vocabulary she had to be aware of in her work: horse-back riding, eggplant, heavy cream, sidewalk: strange words that reminded us that a shared language in no way meant we spoke the same way. Except in the field of personal development where the Brits stood shoulder to shoulder with their American cousins, as they moved forward, resolved issues, drew a line under things and reassessed goals.

Surely it must be time for a coffee. Jane saved her work and stood up, bulky, in her favourite working cardigan, which used to be a smart knitted jacket until she'd washed it and doubled its size. On her feet she wore a pair of Will's woollen expedition socks, and her hair was messily piled up on her head, held in place with a clip like a claw. She looked a fright, but who cared. She'd get brushed up tonight for Lydia's party, she'd have plenty of time since Liberty was staying at her friend Portia's house. The Barbie overnight bag – on mini-wheels with an extendable handle, the sort that air hostesses pulled behind them as they clip-clopped onto the plane in their ladylike shoes – had been packed and handed over this morning to Portia's mother, who hadn't failed to notice Jane's dishevelled appearance.

'What time do you want to collect her?' she had asked, a pucker of anxiety forming on her smooth brow as she noticed a dirty mark running down the leg of Jane's jeans.

'Don't worry, I'll use the tradesmen's entrance,' said Jane. 'Joke,' she'd added. 'It was the car, problem getting it started this morning, and I ended up spilling oil all over myself.'

Portia's mum had been wearing jeans too, but hers were put together with stiletto shoes and a Jean-Paul Gaultier jacket. It had been a long time since denim was a byword for tough rebel or beat poet. Now it just said rich bitch, same as everything else.

The breakfast bowls were still hardening on the table, so Jane took advantage of her coffee break to soak them in the sink. After their argument, Will had made a point of being helpful round the house. He had done all the washing up for three days until he cut his hand on a glass. Nice while it lasted, but they had now slipped back into their usual roles. It was business as usual, though Jane didn't mind. She had other concerns.

She stared at the goldfish swimming around in the tank that she had placed on the counter beside the microwave. They would have to be hidden away in the cellar before Liberty came back, and then hibernate until Christmas, pretend they were in a snow-covered pond. It was perfectly safe, she'd heard of one woman who kept hers in the fridge when she went away for the summer, with no ill effects.

She made her coffee and padded back to the table, slopping some onto the floor as she went. It didn't really matter any more, since Will had noticed a discolouration on the rubber flooring. He'd had the architect over yesterday so he could give him a bollocking about it. Just beneath the window the colour had faded and was now much paler than the rest of the room. The architect had said it was due to UV rays of sunlight. Will had said it was a miracle any UV rays could get in, the room was so dark, but it was an even bigger miracle that an architect who was supposed to know his materials should have recommended rubber in the first place. Jane had left the room at this point, and taken refuge in the galleria, which luckily appeared to be UV resistant. Will would go completely bonkers if anything bad happened up there.

The washing machine whirred up to the hysterical pitch of the spin cycle, and Jane blocked her ears. She really shouldn't put washing on when she was working, it was too distracting. Fingers still in her ears, she read on into the next chapter. She should be able to get a chunk of it done today, since she didn't have to do the school run. The day stretched ahead of her, a solid block of time that for once would not be fractured by the demands of childcare. Without Liberty, the *raison d'être* for her present life had been suspended. The benefits of working at home, choosing your own hours to fit in with your child's routine, suddenly became redundant. She could dress up and go to an office today if she wanted. Except she didn't have one. This was her office. Surrounded by zero companions and silent walls. And discoloured rubber flooring and the sound of domestic machinery. Chilly, in the daytime, and pretty damned lonely. Only those fish to look at.

She should have gone to the cinema, it was stupid to have said she'd be too busy. What was she afraid of? But then, she had next week to look forward to. And looking forward had become a delicious secret.

* * *

That evening, Rupert's flat was full to bursting and he had been cornered by a director of creaticity, whatever that was. She organised ideation sessions for a living but was now talking about her clothes.

'Oh yeah, I do it every season,' she nodded, 'I merchandise my wardrobe. Thank you.' She took a canapé from a passing tray and turned her attention back to Rupert. 'You know, people always say to me, how do you manage to look so fashionable, without looking too fashion victim, and I say to them, I'll tell you how.'

'Really?' said Rupert, hoping she wasn't going to tell him. 'Yeah. I cut pictures from *Harpers* magazine of this season's looks that I know will suit me, and paste them to my closet door. Then I go through all my clothes, identifying everything that will contribute to that look. Then I buy one or two key items to bring the whole thing together . . .'

'I see,' said Rupert, casting his eyes desperately round his crowded living room in search of redemption. No-one caught his eye, but at least here was a waiter with a bottle of champagne. He held out his glass for a top-up.

'Yeah. And you know what, I'll let you into a secret.' She leaned into him confidentially, obliging him to lower his head towards her. 'I'm going to be fifty next month.' She stood back and waited for his astonished reaction.

'Is that so?' Rupert said vaguely, taking a step back and hoping to somehow drift off into the crowd. She sensed he was making a break for it and closed in again.

'And just this week I was given another promotion. Kind of an early birthday present. And that's on top of the loyalty bonus I received six months ago.'

What was it with Americans? Were they programmed from birth to talk endlessly about themselves, or was boastfulness part of the school curriculum?

'Lovely, well done,' said Rupert, looking over her shoulder. Thank God, there was Richard just arrived, he'd have to go and greet him.

'You know, I love this country,' she went on, 'but I cannot get over how much you drink. I've never been a drinker myself. I used to be the national swimming champion in backstroke.'

'Course you were . . . will you excuse me?'

And he made a break for it. A bit abruptly, but sometimes rudeness was the only way to deal with rudeness.

The noise was deafening, eighty people shouting at each other. As he weaved his way across the room, Rupert tried to remember how long ago it was that people had stopped playing music at parties. It must have been around the age of thirty, when people start to think that what they have to say is far more interesting than anything that comes out of the sound system. The noise was still at nuisance level, but without any tunes.

'Richard, there you are, and Caroline . . .'

Rupert had been working with Richard all day as usual, but it had been a while since he had seen Richard's wife. She had thickened out and was overdressed in the manner of someone who doesn't come up to town that often.

'Hallo, Rupert, where's Lydia?' she said, pulling her silk stole down over her shoulders and peering around the room. Rupert wasn't observant about clothes but he did notice that the purple spangles in her headband matched both her evening bag and the brooch pinned to the bosom of her full-length dress. She looked ready to dine on the captain's table on a cruise liner.

'Over there.' He pointed to Lydia, who was talking to a man with a shaved head and a girl with emaciated thighs in knee-high boots. Caroline barged her way over, a beacon of Home Counties confidence.

'Caroline looks well,' said Rupert, then stopped in his tracks.

Standing some way behind Richard, just in front of the door, was Jane. Her hair was piled loosely on her head and she was wearing an orange lipstick that seemed to bring out her freckles. Her skin was luminous against her black dress. She caught sight of him at the same moment, and mirrored his reactions: surprise, then delight, followed by confusion. He went forward, ready to greet her, but then she frowned at him, just slightly, warning him off. Only then did he notice the man standing next to her, who must be her boyfriend, though he looked more like a footman in a powdered wig. He was older, but not impossibly old, not as old as Rupert would have wished. A bit of a short-arse, too, which was gratifying. But he was looking round the room with a world-weary nonchalance that made Rupert want to smash him into the ground.

Richard didn't seem to notice that Rupert's attention was wandering. 'Yes, doesn't she?' he said, looking round proudly after his wife. 'I tell you what, mate, best thing I ever did – apart from setting up shop with you, obviously – was marrying her and moving to the country. You and Lydia should do the same, you don't want to bring up kids in London.'

'Well, the lease is up on Lamington in five years' time, so it would be an option,' said Rupert, still watching Will and Jane as they made their way across the room, 'though I'm not really sure that Lydia is a country person, and she's got her job and everything . . .'

'She'd love it! You want to come down and stay with us one weekend, and Caroline will show her what she's missing.'

Jane had her back to him now and Rupert could observe the elegant curve of her neck rising out of the dress. He wanted to go over and plant a kiss right there on the back of her neck. What was she doing here? Why hadn't Lydia told him she was coming? She probably had, but the names had gone in one ear and out the other whenever she'd started talking about the party. It was all coming back to him now, though: Jane from school, or was it from college? They were old friends, that was all he needed to know. What on earth had he got himself into?

Richard was still going on about the pleasures of country living, and Rupert tried to concentrate on what he was saying. Then he felt a hand on his arm and turned to find that the director of creaticity had tracked him down again.

'So, Rupert, are you going to introduce me, or maybe I should just go ahead and introduce myself?' She turned to Richard and put out her hand. 'Hi, I'm Page Riley. I work in consultancy, but I'm also over here on a celebrity-author visa. I wrote a bestselling book some years ago about the effects of . . .'

Rupert backed off and left them to it. He should get across to see Jane now, he had to talk to her, maybe they could go somewhere more private. The room was so crowded though, it was hard to move, and as he began to negotiate a path he became aware of a good-looking man he vaguely recognised who was looking at him in amusement.

'You seem rather distracted,' said the stranger. 'I'm Andrew Firth, I live downstairs. So good of you to invite me.'

It was the gay shrink; Lydia had clearly lost no time in getting in with the most glamorous of the neighbours.

'Yes, of course,' said Rupert, 'you're the . . . psycho whatsit.'

He couldn't remember now whether he was supposed to be a psychiatrist or psychologist, so he just pointed to his own head and made a spinning gesture with his finger to suggest general looniness.

Dr Firth came to his rescue. 'Yes, just so, I'm a psychologist. Cognitive behavioural therapy.'

'I'm sorry,' Rupert said, 'I always get it mixed up, you must get sick of people doing that.'

'Don't worry about it,' said Dr Firth, taking a sip of champagne, 'I do it all the time. Memory like a sieve, which can be a disaster when you get your patients muddled up. You know, it's a bit embarrassing when you have to ask someone, remind me, are you the cot death or the premature ejaculator?'

Rupert snorted. He'd never thought of shrinks as having a sense of humour.

'Sounds very fruity,' he said. 'I wish I could have conversations like that in the course of my working day.'

'Best of all was when I was working in a prison,' said

Dr Firth, lighting a cigarette. 'You'd hear some great stuff from the lifers: telling you how it felt when they turned the knife in the stomach of their victim. I tell you, if I ever get tired of this game, I could turn my hand to writing horror stories.'

'Always nice to have a fall-back position,' Rupert agreed.

He looked over to where Jane was now in conversation with Lydia. There was no hope of talking to her now, he would need to wait and find a moment later on: she'd understand, of course she would. He saw that Will had floated off and was listening to the girl with the emaciated thighs. Rupert watched him nodding at her, then turning his face upwards while he took a deep drag of his cigar, narrowing his eyes in a macho Clint Eastwood sort of way. Tosser. What was Jane doing wasting her life with someone like that? He switched his gaze back to the girls, to find that Lydia was now looking right at him, pointing him out to Jane, giving him a little wave. That was that then. Jane would now be aware that he was none other than Lydia's boyfriend. Soon to be her fiancé. He gave a small wave back, the wave of a condemned man. Jane looked taken aback, clearly trying to hide the shock. The subject had never come up: he'd only ever met her twice, for God's sake.

Rupert's instinct was to rush over and sweep her up in his arms and walk out of there forever. But by the age of forty you've learned to overcome your instincts. You don't act on the spur of the moment, you take things in a measured and reasonable way. If you want to see somebody, you arrange something in your diary a month in advance, you don't just go crashing up to them like an uncivilised simpleton. This was his engagement party, after all. And he would see her next Friday at the cinema, that was already arranged. Unless she didn't turn up. Maybe after tonight she would think it was better not to see him again. The thought of it sent him into a panic.

'Rupert, darling, lovely party.'

Caroline was beside him now, her mouth full of canapés, and with three more lined up in her upturned hand. 'You could have done with plates, though, for the food. Mind you, there's a lot of faddy eaters here tonight. No wheat, no dairy, no this, no that. Don't know why they don't just call it a day and lie down and die right now.'

Rupert smiled at her refreshing good sense. He could see what Richard saw in her. 'Caroline, this is Andrew Firth. He's a psychologist, lives downstairs.'

'How very useful,' she said, 'though I do hope you don't keep any sharp knives about the place. You do hear some terrible stories, and you look just the handsome type that could turn a lunatic's head.'

Rupert left them to it and turned his attention to the grey suits who were his guests, as opposed to the silly haircuts and bum-revealing trousers that belonged to Lydia's list.

'We were just saying, Rupert, they've definitely softened round our way,' said one man with glasses and a rather daring bow tie. 'I think we could be looking at a thirty per cent adjustment.'

'Especially once interest rates go up again,' added another, popping a mini Thai crispy roll into his mouth.

'I wouldn't count on it,' said another, 'the economic situation is very different now to the late Eighties.'

Rupert sighed. Could one ever look forward to a time when people didn't talk about how much their houses were worth?

'We live on what we always describe as the coat-tails of The Chase, in Clapham,' said a plain woman, 'and we've seen prices double over the last few years.' She lifted a prawn canapé off a passing tray, and Rupert was glad to notice a blob of mayonnaise fall onto the scarf that was tied around her scrawny neck.

'Same in Windsor,' said a former colleague of Rupert's, 'luckily we bought at just the right time.'

'Bit of a hike, isn't it?' said Rupert, 'coming in from Windsor every day.'

'No! I drive, takes me fifteen minutes.'

Fifteen minutes my arse, thought Rupert. It sometimes took him fifteen minutes to drive from Sloane Square to Knightsbridge. Maybe if he travelled by Ferrari at four o'clock in the morning and ignored all traffic lights, it might just be possible.

A waitress reappeared with a tray of venison mini sausages which the man from Windsor took as a come-on for a bout of flirting.

'You little temptress!' he said to her, raising a Clark Gable eyebrow. 'You're trying to lead me astray again, aren't you?'

The waitress smiled noncommittally. She was earning thirty quid for this evening, not enough to put up with dirty old men.

'Oh go on then, you naughty little minx, have it your

own way! I'll even take two,' he added, popping them into his mouth in a lewd manner and washing them down with a generous slug of champagne.

Jane stood in the middle of the room, silent amid all the cocktail shouting. How come she had never asked him his name? She might have guessed if he'd told her, you didn't come across too many Ruperts. She'd dished out enough details about her own life. As well as her name and occupation, he knew the name of her partner and what he did for a living, and the fact that she had a daughter. And in exchange, she knew that he liked gardening and had a house in the South of France. He hadn't bothered to mention that he was going out with someone who just happened to be Jane's oldest friend.

'Hallo, you look a bit lost.'

Jane turned to see a woman in a grey suit with too-wide shoulders and a turquoise scarf standing beside her.

'I'm Jenny. My husband used to work with Rupert.'

'I'm Jane. I'm an old school friend of Lydia's.'

'And where do you live, Jane?'

'Shepherds Bush.'

'Oh yes, on the coat-tails of Notting Hill.'

'I'm sorry?'

'Well, you could say you lived on the coat-tails of Notting Hill.'

'I suppose I could, if I really wanted to.'

'And do you know Rupert at all?'

That was a very good question, but one to which she should give the official answer.

'No.'

'I used to work in the City myself, until I had my second child.'

That would explain the dated office uniform.

'But then it got too much,' she went on. 'I thought, what's the point? It's not as if my husband doesn't earn enough to keep us all. Very comfortably, I am happy to say.'

'Good for you,' said Jane, wondering if full details of his salary package would follow.

'Mind you, it's not as if I have an easy life. Overseeing the builders, ferrying the kids around, it's a full-time job all right. I'm on my knees by the time Jonathan comes home. Luckily he's very understanding, and knows that I don't cook. He always makes dinner. Or else we get a takeaway.'

She was irritatingly at pains to point out that she was no put-upon housewife. For some reason it had become a badge of honour for women to boast about not cooking. The modern equivalent of burning your bra, as though you were flying the flag for feminism by being inept in the kitchen. Making a virtue of incompetence. Jane didn't see it that way.

'Do you have children?' Jenny asked, hoping they might be able to gang up as homemakers.

'A daughter of seven. But I work too, while she's at school. I'm a freelance translator.'

What a relief it was to say that and therefore not be counted in the same category as this woman.

'Well, it's easy when you've just got the one,' said Jenny ungenerously. 'Didn't you want any more? It's such a shame, I think, for only children. They miss out on so much.'

Jane glanced around the room for someone to escape to. Rupert had his back to her. She had never seen him from that angle before, his shoulders broad and imposing. It made her feel like going up behind him and putting her arms round his waist and pressing her face into the space between his shoulder blades.

'Have you got any Irish in you?'

A very drunk man, not unattractive with his curly black hair and blue eyes, had appeared between Jane and the noble housewife.

'Not me, I'm a hundred per cent English, for my sins,' said Jenny, as though to imply anything else was a slur on her pedigree.

'I wasn't asking you,' said the man, rudely, 'I was asking this lovely looking woman here. Have you now? Got any Irish in you?' He was lurching, head on one side, waiting for Jane's answer.

'No, I don't think so.'

'Would you like some?'

He raised his glass in a suggestive toast, slopping champagne over the rim. Jenny turned her back in disgust and left them to it.

Jane laughed. 'Well, at least you saw her off with your vulgar proposition. I'm Jane, by the way.' She held out her hand which he grasped in a clammy squeeze.

'I'm Patrick. I'm in advertising. Do you want to know my motto?'

'Is it filthy?'

'Not at all, I only use filth in my opening lines, but we're beyond that now.'

'All right then.'

'It is, never leave a job voluntarily.'

'Is that it?'

'Yup. And that's how I got so rich. I've been fired so often I'm awash with redundancy payments. I am the walking embodiment of rewarded failure. That's how I got to buy my yacht. Guess what I named it? *Severance.* Get it?' He smiled winningly and stepped back onto someone's shoe.

'Ladies and gentlemen, your attention please!'

Lydia was standing on a chair in the bay window and banging a spoon on the side of her glass, just as she had planned it.

'Thank you so much for coming tonight, I hope you're all enjoying yourselves. This is as close as we get to celebrating Christmas, so do spare a thought for us when you're tucking into the turkey and all the trimmings. We'll be sweating it out in the desert sun – or else slithering around on a glacier, I can't remember which comes first in our tour of Chilean extremes.'

She waited for the waves of envious laughter to subside.

'I'd like to hand over to Rupert now, who has a rather special announcement to make. Rupert!'

The sea of faces turned expectantly towards Rupert, who looked down at his feet. When he glanced up again, he caught Jane's eye and she gave him a small smile. Sick at heart, he turned to face Lydia and prepared to deliver. Normally Rupert was a good speaker. He had been best man on six occasions, because people knew they could rely on him to be witty without giving offence. He had an innate sense of what was appropriate.

But tonight, Rupert's heart was not in it. He felt the way he did as a child when his mother used to force him to recite grace before Sunday lunch with his grandparents.

'Thank you, yes,' he began. He would keep it brief, get it over with as soon as possible. 'I, or I should say, we, do have something to tell you, and that is that we are going to . . . that I have asked Lydia to be my wife, and that she has agreed. So we are engaged.'

His diffidence was swamped by a deluge of enthusiasm. It was partly the drink talking. Ply a roomful of people with champagne and they'll celebrate anything. You could tell them you were getting your teeth fixed and they'd whoop with delight. And an engagement was best of all. The married people in the room took it as an endorsement of their own state, while those still single could cheer and thank their lucky stars it wasn't them. As he received the back thumping and handshaking, Rupert steeled himself to look at Jane once again. She gave him a small, ironic smile that cut him to the quick, then turned to join Lydia's coterie of well-wishers.

Rupert watched Jane as she kissed Lydia, then headed across the crowded room towards the door. He made his excuses to the director of creaticity who was going on about how she had learned to grow through the failure of her own marriage, then followed Jane out into the corridor. She was waiting alone outside the bathroom.

'You're not going, are you?' he said.

'No, I'm waiting for the loo. Why, did you expect me to walk out?'

'Of course not. Look, there's another bathroom down here, I'll show you.'

He took her by the elbow and propelled her into his bedroom, shutting the door behind them. The intimacy of the surroundings embarrassed them both. He pointed towards the en suite bathroom.

'It's in there.'

She laughed.

'Thanks. And are you going to wait here? Pass me a towel on the way out and hope for a tip?'

'Sit down. Please.'

The bed was piled high with coats, so he sat on the floor on the far side of the bed, leaning against its side.

She sat down beside him and he took her hand as though it were only natural.

'It's quiet in here,' he said. 'Such a relief to get away from that awful chit-chat.'

'Yes.'

'I saw your other half. I hate him of course.'

'Of course.' She smiled.

He squeezed her hand and she looked across at him. How could she have told herself he wasn't her type? From where she was sitting now, he looked like the most attractive man in the world, Russell Crowe meets Harrison Ford.

'I just want you to know,' he said, 'that all this was agreed a long time before we met. It was all sorted out, you see . . . I don't think . . . I know that I couldn't have suggested any such thing once I'd met you.'

'No. Well, there's absolutely no need to feel bad about it,' she said. She must remain reasonable and keep things in perspective. There was no point in going along with a wild romantic fantasy: he had his life and she had hers.

'I'm not exactly single myself, as you know,' she added.

'No.'

'Although I suppose you could have told me you had a girlfriend, a fiancée even. Who happens to be a friend of mine.'

'So it seems.' He hung his head.

'And anyway,' she went on, 'as we're always reminding ourselves, we've got nothing to hide. It's not as though there's anything going on between us.'

He turned to her, his face half in shadow from the bed. 'Now, we both know that's not true,' he said. And then, all of a sudden, they were kissing, passionately, wildly, sprawled on the floor like a couple of teenagers, and any pretence of them being just friends was quietly discarded along with the champagne glasses that they let slip onto the shag-pile carpet that would soon be falling victim to Lydia's renovation programme.

It was only when they heard someone clip-clop down the corridor towards the bedroom door that they sprang guiltily apart.

'Oh, excuse me, am I interrupting something?' Two bird-like eyes were peering at them from behind the door. It was the director of creaticity, from whom no hiding place was safe.

'Oh, my! Rupert, is that you? My goodness, it seems I really *am* interrupting.'

'No, no, honestly,' said Jane hastily, brushing herself free of the bits of shag-pile. 'It's my lens, you see, it fell out and luckily Rupert came in to help me find it . . . and just put it back in my eye for me. He's very good at that sort of thing, you see.'

'Apparently so,' said Page, holding her hand to her throat like she was the wounded party in a stagy old Hollywood film. 'I'll leave you to it,' she said. 'Let's just say I never came in here.'

And with that she closed the door.

Jane and Rupert giggled in nervous relief.

'We'd better get back to the party,' said Jane, 'before our reputations are ruined.'

They were standing now, and Rupert pulled her to him.

'Just once more,' he said, kissing her, 'just to remind me.'

Afterwards he stood back, and rested his hands on her shoulders. 'We're quits now,' he said, 'we've both got baggage.'

'Don't say that,' she said, 'it makes it all sound too serious.'

'All right, if that's how you want to play it.'

'How else could we play it?'

He didn't reply.

'So, we'll see each other on Friday, then,' he said eventually. 'At the Institute.'

Things were different now. It was a date instead of a chance encounter, with all the lies and deceit that went with that.

'I don't know . . .' she said, 'I don't know if I can do that.'

'But you must.'

'Must I?'

'Yes. Please don't refuse. We don't have to let things go any further. But if you refuse I won't have anything to look forward to.'

Only planning your future with Lydia, she thought.

'And neither will you,' he added.

She couldn't disagree.

'All right then,' she said, then slipped out of the bedroom to rejoin the party.

'Well, I daresay that could have been worse,' said Will, as he lowered himself regally into the car. 'I hope you're not over the limit, the last thing we want is for you to lose your licence, that would really screw us up.' He frowned as he imagined the inconvenience. 'Home James, and don't spare the horses,' he added, tilting the seat back as far as it would go, and closing his eyes.

'Don't worry, I only had two glasses,' said Jane, taking off her stilettos and slipping on a pair of sensible driving shoes. She used to laugh at her mum for keeping driving shoes in the car, and now look at her. Next thing, she'd be wearing tan-coloured driving gloves with that hole cut out of the back.

'Bloody funny when I went to say goodbye to that banker,' said Will. 'There was a group of them standing there in their appalling suits and ties, and I couldn't remember which one was him. They all look the bloody same! So I just said, "Bye, Rupert, thanks for the party," and waited to see which one answered!'

He gave a burst of smug laughter at the thought. Identikit bankers. You could never accuse him, Will Thacker, of not standing out in a crowd. No wonder Lydia had seemed so pleased to see him. She was looking pretty good tonight, too, he thought.

Jane reversed out of her parking place, and moved

slowly out onto Sloane Street. 'What did you think of him?' she asked casually.

'The banker?'

'Yes, the banker. Rupert,' she added, taking pleasure in saying his name.

'Just what you'd expect. Boring as buggery.'

'Did you talk to him?'

'Of course not. That would have been excessive. My duties as a guest did not extend to listening to someone bang on about the Dow Jones Index.'

Nor did mine extend to snogging the host on the floor of his bedroom, thought Jane, with a tremor of guilty delight.

'Anyway, the man's obviously a fool,' Will went on, 'getting himself hitched to that gold-digger. I know she's your friend, Jane, but she knows when she's on to a good thing. When will men realise that they've got to stop being taken for a ride by freeloading women? All in the name of 'marriage', that appalling, calculating, money-orientated trap of an institution.'

He reached across and patted Jane's knee.

'At least we've got the right idea, eh? Financial independence and mutual respect.'

In bed that night, Jane went through the motions of sex with Will and wondered about her own financial independence. The house belonged to him, but she paid all the bills. That had always sounded fair enough to her: it wasn't as though he was asking her to pay rent or anything. She had no idea how much he earned, but she knew he had heavy outgoings: alimony and club memberships and dining out that couldn't always be charged to expenses. She was usually pretty skint, but that was because of her lifestyle choice, working part-time from home. And anyway, thinking about money bored her. It was the life you led that counted, it was what you did every day that made you what you were.

They'd finished now; and with a theatrical moan and a self-satisfied smile Will slumped back to his side of the bed and took a sip of water.

'That's one thing Lydia won't be getting as part of the marriage package,' he said. 'An interesting and imaginative lover. Beyond all price, wouldn't you say, Jane?' He smiled a rakish, crooked smile at her, the kind of smile that she'd fallen in love with, but now she felt a chill in her heart. Was she destined to only ever sleep with this man for the rest of her life? Would she grow old and grey by his side, and never know the thrill of someone new? Married or not, that was what loyalty demanded. She turned her back on him and went to sleep, thinking of Rupert and reliving their stolen kisses at his engagement party.

EIGHT

He was there first, as she knew he would be. He was waiting downstairs, by the door, and touched her on the shoulder as she came in.

She turned to him and he wrapped his arms around her, bulky in his heavy overcoat. 'You came, thank goodness,' he murmured into her hair.

'Of course,' she said, detaching herself gently from his embrace, 'I promised, didn't I?'

'You did.'

He smiled in relief. The fear that had been plaguing him for the past week, that she wouldn't show up, that she would say there was no point, had evaporated, leaving him light-headed and full of plans.

'I thought we might skip the film,' he said. 'As we haven't got very long, I thought we should go somewhere we can talk. There's something I want to show you at the V&A, a tiny pair of Chinese shoes, from when they used to bind their feet. It's only a five minute walk from here.'

'Fine,' said Jane, catching his enthusiasm, 'whatever you want.'

He opened the door for her, and they stepped out into the cold, like two children excited at the prospect of an outing. The pavement was still sparkling with the morning frost, and the shop windows were filled with tinsel and Santa Claus, angels and the occasional Christ child.

Walking into the Victoria and Albert Museum was like stepping into an Aladdin's cave of possibility. An enormous green and blue glass chandelier hung like a giant bauble in the middle of the cavernous entrance hall, a modern head of Medusa bristling with snaky twists of glass. Off one side, there was a room of marble statues, cool and light and empty. Far busier, on the other side, the shop was packed with people thinking of Christmas, stuffing glittery tree decorations, miniature gothic treasure chests, Victorian jigsaw puzzles into wire baskets. Museums were so much more satisfying now you could take a bit of them home with you.

Rupert put his arm around Jane's shoulders, directing her straight ahead, on to the Chinese rooms. He then took her hand and led her to the glass cabinet where a pair of blue satin shoes were on display, the size of a baby's foot, but once worn by a woman. They stared at them, compared them to another purple pair above, talked about the pain the children must have felt, having their toes broken and folded back beneath their feet, then bound with tight bandages. They moved on to the next cabinet to see richly embroidered robes from the Qing dynasty, alive with flowers and birds, then back to the eighteenth century, a folding ivory fan and a cabinet laquered with a different landscape on each drawer. Everywhere were scenes of idyllic life.

Jane felt the warmth of his hand, and rubbed her thumb against his, feeling the dry skin. She had forgotten what it felt like to hold hands with someone other than her daughter. She couldn't remember the last time she had held Will's hand, and wondered if perhaps she never had.

'You know that Chinese proverb, don't you?' he said, as they stood in front of a screen panel from the Ming dynasty depicting phoenixes playing amid rocks and flowers. 'If you want to be happy for an hour, make love to a woman; if you want to be happy for a day, read a book; but if you want to be happy for a lifetime, plant a garden.'

'Why not all three?' she said, pulling at his hand to make him stand still, 'then you'd be really, really happy.'

'I suppose,' he said, standing closely over her. 'I feel quite happy now, actually, without doing any of those things.'

They finished with China and headed down a corridor in search of the café. On either side, rooms led off, revealing further treasures: 1950s ball gowns, Indian art treasures, fascinating artefacts from history, carefully assembled from all around the world and displayed for their pleasure. Jane felt lucky to be there, walking along beside this man.

They bought their coffees and sat down at a table behind a pillar. Around them were ladies who lunch, some dishevelled students, and a lot of older people making the most of their freedom passes to cruise around the city's treasures. Embarked upon the thirty-year jamboree that made up modern retirement, as opposed to digging the allotment for a year before dropping dead, which was how it used to be.

'I'm glad you liked the Chinese slippers, I thought you would,' said Rupert.

'We should always come here,' Jane said. 'There's so much to see, you could come every Friday for the rest of your life and still not have done it all.'

'What shall we do next time?'

'I quite fancy the Gothic stuff.'

'I quite fancy you.'

Her legs were crossed beneath the table and he slipped his hand between her knees.

She laughed at him across the table, she felt feckless and free. 'When are you off to Chile?'

By tacit agreement, they hadn't discussed the party, or Lydia, or Will; it was understood that their time together was not about the other stuff that made up their daily lives. But Jane felt confident enough now to ask the question: holidays were safe ground, it wasn't like she was asking him if they had set a date for the wedding. Even so, he looked uncomfortable.

'Tomorrow night. I wish I was going with you.'

'Only because you don't know me well enough yet to find me disappointing.'

He laughed. 'Do yourself down, why don't you?' Then, seriously, 'You could never disappoint me, I know that.'

'How do you know?'

'Because you're perfect. Scruffy perfect, that is, not shiny perfect.'

He rummaged in his coat pocket and pulled out a crumpled brown paper bag.

'I won't see you again before Christmas, obviously, so I've brought you your present. Sorry I didn't get round to wrapping it.'

She opened the bag and found it was full of tiny bulbs, like dolly-sized onions.

'They're fritillaries,' he said, 'rare and exquisite, they made me think of you.'

She ran her fingers over them and in her mind's eye saw how the flowers would look, dainty and bell-like on slender stems.

'I didn't get you anything,' she said.

He shrugged. 'It's not a barter, it's a present. They do quite well in pots, but you need to protect the shoots from frost.'

'It's a lovely present. I'll think of you when I plant them, then when they flower they'll remind me of you again.'

That would be in spring, the most exciting time in the garden, culminating in the Chelsea Flower Show. Maybe they could go together next year and look out for other fritillaries, make notes together on the back of nursery brochures. Have a glass of champagne in the Veuve Clicquot tent and argue about which garden they liked best. Her favourite this year had been a Mediterranean garden with a rusty old shed and mauve and grey herbs self-seeded in the cracks between the stones. She thought he would like that too.

'Did you go to Chelsea this year?' she asked.

'I went with some clients, which slightly took the edge

off it. Nothing like a dose of corporate hospitality to rob an event of its atmosphere, and for some reason they all want to go to Chelsea.'

'Just think,' she said, 'I might have seen you there, jostling along behind the rope to look at that dreadful garden with the double staircase.'

'I know the one you mean, with the grotto at the bottom.'

'In that fake stone that looks sort of luminous . . .'

'We'll go together next year,' he said, 'so we can spot the shockers together.'

He would still be single in May. The wedding was planned for June; it would be his last Chelsea Flower Show as a single man.

Jane carefully put the fritillaries into her handbag, zipping them up in the centre compartment. 'You should bring me back some seeds from South America,' she said, 'like a Victorian botanist returning from an expedition. I could be your faithful assistant, labelling them up and nurturing their growth at home while you go off round the world for another five years.'

'No, you could come with me. I'd like to see you in a pair of plus fours and knee-high explorer boots. I'd especially like to see you take them off in the flickering torchlight of our two-man tent.'

He touched her knee again, and his hand burned against her skin. She felt exhilarated. She was also aware that it was nearly time to leave.

'I must go.' Those three dreary, disappointing words.

'Have you got the car today?'

'Yes, it's in the car park by the Institute.'

'Good, you can give me a lift.'

'I'm going the wrong way . . .'

'Doesn't matter. You can drop me off by the school and I'll get a cab from there.'

'It'll take you twice as long . . .'

'But I get to see you for longer.'

There was a moment of panic when they arrived at the car and Jane thought she'd lost her keys, but they were eventually unearthed, hidden beneath the bag of fritillaries.

'Shall I drive?' Rupert asked as she unlocked the car. 'Only if you want me to, obviously.'

Jane threw him the keys over the car and walked round to change sides. 'I would *love* you to drive,' she said. 'Do you realise I have never once sat in the passenger seat of this car in the six years I've had it.'

'Does Will not . . . ?'

'Nope. He doesn't do machines.'

Rupert curled his lip in amused contempt. How affected was that, in the twenty-first century, to say you didn't do machines?

'Still uses a quill and ink does he, for his work?'

'Apart from his computer, I was about to say.'

She settled back and relaxed, enjoying the novelty of being driven. He drove calmly, confidently, as she knew he would.

'It's in Leinster Square,' she said, 'off Bayswater.'

He parked just round the corner, in Leinster Terrace, and switched off the engine. Jane went to open her door, but he reached across and caught her arm, pulling her towards him.

'You've got five minutes to go,' he said, 'let's not waste them.'

When he kissed her, she was squeezed over the gearbox, bringing back memories of teenage dating.

'We have to swap telephone numbers now,' he said, 'it's no use pretending any more.'

He passed her his phone and she gave him hers and they keyed in their numbers. They'd got each other logged now and there would be no more chance meetings, no more tragic thoughts of happiness lost if one of them failed to show. It was up to them and fate had nothing to do with it. She got out of the car and stood awkwardly on the pavement, waiting for him to join her.

'Have a lovely holiday,' she said, insincere and conventional all of a sudden. She wouldn't see him for three whole weeks.

'I'll think of you,' he said, standing beside her, unwilling to leave.

The moment was lost as Portia's mother appeared from nowhere.

'Hallo, Jane,' she said, looking approvingly at Rupert. Her eye was evidently trained to identify moneyed bankers from two hundred paces. 'Is this your husband?'

'No, no . . . as a matter of fact, I don't have a husband,' said Jane, as though that made things better. 'This is just a friend.'

Rupert nodded at Portia's mother. 'I'll be off then,' he said to Jane, 'have a nice Christmas.'

And then he was gone. As she walked towards the school, Jane saw him climb into a taxi and drive away. Beside her, Portia's mother was giving a detailed account of her holiday plans: Christmas in Cambodia followed by a river cruise in Burma; they wouldn't normally risk a cruise but this one should be all right as there were only forty cabins, totally luxurious and the obscure location meant it wouldn't attract the wrong sort.

Liberty came out bristling with rolled-up paintings and tinselly bits of stuff, and a plate piled high with gaudy marzipan angels. Her end-of-term excitement washed over Jane and lifted her spirits. That was the glory of children: they were the ultimate consolation prize, putting everything into perspective.

'We played a game today, mama,' she said. 'Miss Evans divided the room into five continents and everyone had to go and stand in the continent where they were going for Christmas.'

'Oh, so did you stand in Europe then?'

'No, I sat at the back, because we're not going anywhere. You weren't allowed to play if you weren't going anywhere,' she added, without resentment. 'It was only me and Phoenix sitting at the back: she can't go anywhere because her mum's having a baby. Guess which continent had the most?'

'Asia,' said Jane, thinking of Portia.

'Yes! Well done, Mum, you are the cleverest mummy in the world. And the prettiest.'

They got to the car and Jane began fishing around in her bag for the keys. She pulled out the fritillaries, her address book, her Christmas lists, a smashed-up Dime bar, but they weren't there. How stupid of her, she must have forgotten to take them back from Rupert. It was Portia's mum's fault, putting them off like that, but luckily she had his number, she'd have to call him right away. She walked away from her daughter, calling up his number. Come on, she wanted to say to him, please come here right now and take me away with you.

Clutching her Christmas booty to her chest, Liberty looked on resentfully. 'Why haven't you got the keys, mummy, who are you ringing?'

But before she had made the call, a taxi drew up alongside them, and Rupert was calling to her through the opened window, dangling the keys.

She ran up to take them, relieved.

'Sorry,' he said.

'No, my fault.'

'Is that your daughter?' He smiled at Liberty who glowered back at him.

'Sorry, she's not normally that cross, just a bit overwrought, you know, all the excitement.'

'Bye then,' he said, and as the taxi pulled away he blew her a kiss.

When she got into the driving seat, Jane had to adjust the seat, sliding it forward to the normal position, noting the disparity between the length of his legs and hers. It would be three whole weeks before they met again.

'Who was that man?' asked Liberty. 'Why did he have your keys?'

'He just helped do something with the car,' she said, surprised by the glibness of her lie, 'and then I forgot to take the keys back. Can I have one of your marzipan angels?'

While Jane and Rupert were getting romantic with each other in the Victoria and Albert Museum, Will was getting romantic with himself in the London Library, dreaming of the glory to come. His new book would be even better received than his last, offering as it did another penetrating insight into a vanishing culture. Like all great travel writers, he had a talent for drawing lessons from backward tribes and pointing out moral parallels with the modern world.

In front of him on the desk was a pile of relevant books: *Black Elk Speaks, The Wind is my Mother, The Way of the Shaman.* Today was his last opportunity for research before his creative life was put on hold for the enforced tedium of the Christmas break. It infuriated Will that he had to play along with the conventions of organised society. He was an artist, so why should he be bothered with Christmas shopping, school holidays and the inconvenient closing hours of his resource libraries?

He dropped *Neither Wolf Nor Dog* back on the heap and turned instead to an unrelated work by his mentor Wilfred Thesiger that he always carried with him.

'*Mountains have always attracted me,*' he read, '*early in 1952 I invited the mountaineer Eric Shipton to lunch with me at the Travellers Club when he suggested I travel in Hunza in northern Pakistan.*'

That was more like it, that was how Will's life should be. He didn't suppose Wilfred Thesiger had to worry about playing happy families round a turkey, he would have gone off for years at a time to fulfil his thirst for travel. There was a huge world out there, it seemed a crime to stagnate at home instead. A life less ordinary, that was what Will deserved.

He picked up another favourite, *The Great Railway*

Bazaar, and read with envy of Paul Theroux's escape by train to Istanbul.

'*I was doing a bunk, myself: I hadn't nailed my colours to the mast; I had no job – no-one would notice me falling silent, kissing my wife, and boarding the 15.30 alone . . . the train was rumbling through Clapham, I decided that travel was flight and pursuit in equal parts . . .*'

Yes indeed, Paul, thought Will, you and I both, we understand the importance of flight and pursuit, of going out in search of enlightenment rather than sinking slowly into homely nothingness. There was no doubt about it, Will would soon need to be making a journey of his own.

He decided to call it a day; the lights on his bike were on the blink and he wanted to get home before it got dark. He gathered up his papers into the battered old leather briefcase that had served him well for three decades. He nodded at the girl at the desk who had fancied him for ages – he knew what that blush meant, every time he caught her eye – and went outside to unlock his bike. It was an old-fashioned black sit-up-and-beg type, with a wicker basket attached to the front. It was not out of character, he thought with a smile, for him to have a bike that was unlike every other one in the rack.

The journey home was a good opportunity for reflection, and today Will's thoughts were centred around the theme of an extraordinary mind trapped in a life of domestic routine. He wondered whether he wasn't putting Jane into an unfair position. Would she really want to be held responsible for holding him back, for being the brakes on his creative talent? She was far from being a nag, he had her too well-schooled for that, but it was the reality of her and Liberty that kept him grounded in smallness.

He let himself into the house and picked up a handful of envelopes from the mat. On his one-to-ten scale of dull bourgeois habits, the sending of Christmas cards stood at around eight, and rose to ten when the cards contained round-robin letters. One of the envelopes felt suspiciously thick, and Will was not disappointed when he ripped it open.

'*What a year!*' it began. '*A promotion for Jim, a great first eleven season for Alex, a gold life-saving badge for Chloe, and as if all that wasn't enough, we rounded off with a super autumn half-term break in Tuscany! Lucky for us all I'd been taking Italian evening classes!*'

Christ almighty, thought Will, I should do Jane a favour and file it straight in the bin. She always felt obliged to reply to pitiful letters like this, didn't seem to have learned about moving on, about drawing a line, about not bothering to stay in touch with bores. He threw the cards down on the kitchen table and filled the kettle to make himself a herbal tea. Liberty's glittery angel stood on the windowsill, a testimony to what can be achieved with toilet rolls and kitchen foil. Will smiled at the thought of his daughter; he loved her, of course, but that didn't mean he needed to see her every day. His experience with his sons taught him that kids didn't disappear just because you were off the scene for a bit. Liberty would still be there when he got back from his travels, however long they took.

He heard a key in the lock, then Liberty came running downstairs to see him.

'Hallo, big face,' he said. 'Have you broken up?'

Liberty nodded and offered him her last marzipan angel.

'You can go and get changed then,' he said, helping himself, 'hang up that vile uniform and wear something normal for a change.'

Jane frowned at him as she came into the kitchen. She didn't want Will giving Liberty a complex about her school clothes. It was bad enough as it was getting her dressed in the morning, without him adding his unhelpful comments.

'You're back early,' she said, taking off her coat and throwing it onto the sofa.

'It's my concession to Christmas,' he said, 'my own little take on the seasonal go-slow, although naturally I despise the idea of normal life grinding to a halt for spurious religious reasons. A simple pagan festival appropriated by a corrupt and powerful church, and now degenerated into a materialistic riot of greed and gluttony.'

'Killjoy,' said Jane.

'What's materialistic?' asked Liberty.

'It's wanting things,' said Jane, 'you know all about that. And gluttony means eating too much.'

'Here's a thing,' said Will, holding up his finger as a prelude to the important information about to follow. 'Did you know that the average preparation time for a meal twenty years ago was sixty minutes, and today it is just thirteen minutes. So you should count yourself lucky!'

'Another one of Dad's useless facts,' said Liberty, unimpressed.

He was like a magpie, thought Jane, picking up shiny nuggets of information that he brought home to the family nest and expected them all to admire.

Will looked Jane up and down as she wiped the table clean and set out a glass of milk and a mini chocolate log for Liberty. She was looking pretty today in a slightly prissy way, wearing a neat green cardigan, and even a touch of make-up, which she didn't normally bother with during the day.

'You look a bit dolled-up,' he said. 'A bit Home Counties come to town, if you don't mind my saying so. Have you been on a date or something?'

Jane was annoyed to feel herself blushing. 'You know I often go out on Friday afternoons,' she said, plunging the dishes into the sink. 'It's my cinema day.'

'So it is,' he said, like a well-meaning uncle. 'What did you see, any good?'

'I didn't go actually, not today. I went to the V&A instead.'

So far, so truthful, there was no point in lying.

'What's the viannay?'

'A museum, darling.'

'Ugh, boring. I hate museums.'

'How perfect,' said Will, 'pretending you're up from the shires in your little twinset to take in our national art treasures. Leaving home at ten o'clock on a cheap day return, and hurrying back in time to make your husband's dinner. It's such a charming image, it's almost enough to make me marry you and whisk you off to the shires.'

Was this really how he saw her? Maybe she should

tell him she had been necking with her boyfriend in the family car, that might give him something to think about.

'It's not a twinset,' she said, 'they don't match.'

'It still looks like something your mother would have worn.'

He never seemed to tire of his familiar themes, but after spending an afternoon with Rupert, Jane suddenly didn't see why she should put up with it any more.

'Just cut it out, Will,' she said.

The sharpness in her tone surprised him; she never used to take offence at his teasing, but this was fast becoming something of a habit.

'Uh oh!' he said. 'Do I detect a sense-of-humour failure?'

'No, Will, it wasn't funny in the first place. You do whatever you like all the time, so don't have a go at me for seeking the occasional diversion from the endless treadmill of work and home and . . . boring, boring Christmas.'

She flung the cloth at the sink and sank down in a chair.

'Mummy, Christmas isn't boring, I love Christmas!'

Liberty flung her arms round Jane's neck, then remembered something. She ran over to her school bag and took out a Christmas card she had made for her parents. It featured a tall glamour-puss in full evening dress exposing an impressive cleavage and tiny stiletto shoes. Jane recognised that this was meant to be her; she was used to Liberty's flattering interpretations. The goddess was flanked on either side by two figures half her size: one was a flat-chested version of herself and clearly supposed to be Liberty, and the other was dressed like a toy soldier and barely came up to the woman's navel.

Will came over to take a look. 'How come I'm only the same height as you, Liberty?' he complained. 'You know I'm as tall as Mummy.'

'Only when you're wearing your stacks,' she said, borrowing the word Jane used when she wanted to be rude about a pair of Will's shoes that had a slight heel.

'Thank you, Liberty, it's lovely,' said Jane, setting it out in pride of place on the table. She sat down and pulled her daughter onto her lap, kissing the back of her head. Her hair smelt delicious.

'Boudicca didn't put her dad in her picture, only her mum,' said Liberty. 'They're getting divorced. I think divorce is dumb, don't you?'

Jane thought how terrifying it would be if children ruled the world. They saw everything in such black and white terms.

'It's not what anyone would choose,' she said carefully, 'but sometimes things don't work out and people don't have any choice. And it can be better in the long term, although it's difficult at the time.'

'Couldn't happen to me and Mum, though, could it?' said Will. 'We're not married so we can't get divorced.'

'Why aren't you married?'

'It's not necessary these days,' said Jane quickly, 'it's not like women are dependent on men the way they used to be.'

'What's "dependent" mean?'

'It means you have to wait to be given everything, instead of getting it for yourself,' Jane said.

'And your mother is an independent woman,' said Will, 'she's more than capable of paddling her own canoe.'

Am I, though? Jane wondered. Her version of independence had been entirely crafted around her life with Will.

'I forgot to say,' he said, as if on cue to remind her, 'I managed to get three tickets for that show you wanted to see on Saturday. Like gold dust they are, unless you know the right people. You'll love it, Liberty, and it's that rare thing, a play for children that might even entertain adults.'

'Daddy!' Liberty threw herself into his arms. 'You're the best daddy in the world!'

'How lovely, I thought you'd forgotten,' said Jane.

He was glad to see she'd lost that spikiness, he didn't like the way that was going.

'Forget my family? I don't think so,' he said. 'What's more, I think I'll make us all dinner tonight. I feel a surge of creative cooking coming on.'

He might as well push the boat out, it was easy enough to earn a little gratitude.

Jane smiled up at him gratefully. This was what it was all about: a happy nuclear family, enveloping their child with love as they prepared to bunker down for the two-week Christmas lock-in. This was her real life, the life she had chosen. And it certainly should not include flirting with her friend's fiancé on her afternoons off. What had she been thinking of?

Rupert didn't stay long at the office, just long enough to tie up a few loose ends. He straightened up his desk and thought how depressing it was that in a couple of weeks

he would be back to face it. He would rather have swept
it all into the bin and never crossed the threshold again.
Usually when he went on holiday there would be a surge
of adrenaline to get everything out of the way before he
left, and then the euphoria of getting on the plane and
feeling he was enjoying a well-earned rest. But this time
he felt no more enthusiasm for the holiday than he did
for his job. The thought of going to Chile with Lydia
filled him with nothing but cold indifference. He'd rather
be spending Christmas in his house in France, or else
watching telly in the flat. With Jane.

When he got home, Lydia had already filled a large
suitcase that was lying open on top of the bed. She herself
was in the bath, flicking through a copy of *London
Property News*.

'Do you know, darling, I'm beginning to wonder if we
wouldn't be better off moving rather than doing this place
up.'

Rupert opened a cupboard door and began pulling out
some underwear. It was a damned nuisance that they
were going to a hot desert *and* a bloody glacier. Why
couldn't they do one or the other? It was typical of Lydia's
greed that they had to pack for both. Woollen socks would
be needed, but he'd also need to find some cotton ones.
They should be on the top shelf, along with his summer
clothes. He reached up and pulled out three pairs of
shorts, throwing them onto the open suitcase.

'Really?' he said, without interest, 'I thought you'd got
it all buttoned up now with the designers.'

'Yes, but then this magazine came through the door
today, and it got me thinking Hot Tub.'

'Isn't that what you're in right now?' he said, taking five Lacoste polo shirts from a pile and adding them to his pile.

'You're not taking those, are you?' said Lydia, raising herself from the bubbles to cast a frown of disapproval over his choice. 'No-one wears polo shirts any more, you'll look like an escapee from 1980s yuppiedom.'

'Which is what I am,' he said, 'although unfortunately I have yet to escape.'

She ignored him and returned to her theme. 'Anyway, it's never bothered me not having a garden, but then I saw this place advertised,' she struck a wet finger on the page, 'just round the corner, with a roof terrace with a hot tub, and I thought, of course! Everyone's getting them now, and you can even use them in winter. It's on at two-point-two, but I bet we could negotiate and get it for less than two.'

'Have you seen my sunglasses?' Rupert asked.

'Hallo? Did you hear me?' She held her hand to her mouth, imitating a megaphone.

'Yes, I heard you,' said Rupert, irritated. 'And if you think I can rustle up two million pounds so you can enjoy an outdoor bath, you've got another think coming.'

Lydia didn't like what she was hearing, so plunged her head beneath the water, then emerged and started shampooing her hair. 'There's no need to be a prig,' she said, 'after all, nearly everyone's a millionaire these days. You know, the editor of the *Sunday Telegraph* banned the use of the word for that very reason. "We're all millionaires now," he said, and he's only a journalist, so if a successful banker like you can't afford to start his married life in a reasonable flat with . . .'

'Just shut up, will you!' said Rupert. 'I'm sick of hearing about what you want. What about me, don't I get a say in all this?'

Lydia looked at him in surprise. She hoped he wasn't going to get nasty once they were married.

'If you must know,' he went on, 'I hate my job, and I'm thinking of quitting.'

Oh dear, thought Lydia, this was beginning to sound like a touch of mid-life male angst. She'd have to handle it tactfully.

'That's fine,' she said evenly, 'it's not for everyone, working in a small office like that. You could easily get another job back in the mainstream, once you put the word out.'

'I don't want to go back into the mainstream. I'm sick of banking, I want to do something else.'

What did he have in mind, needlepoint?

'A different business, you mean?' she said. 'Venture capital, oil, property, commodity broker . . . ?' She couldn't think of any other lucrative-sounding jobs, apart from lawyer, but that was no good, he wasn't qualified and she certainly didn't intend to start her married life supporting a mature student.

'Gardening, actually,' he said.

'Gardening,' she repeated in disbelief, as if he had just announced his plan to retrain as a contract killer.

'Yes.'

'I don't see how . . . I mean gardening's a splendid hobby, though personally I've never quite seen the point . . . but of course we can get a house with a garden, if you'd prefer . . . or else you could get rid of those tenants and we could start going to Lamington at weekends . . .'

'I don't want a hobby, I want to do something meaningful with my life.'

'Like digging around in mud, you mean? Or driving one of those golf caddy things that cuts the grass? Or raking up dead leaves? Come off it, Rupert, I think you've gone a bit soft in the head. You've probably been overworking, it's a good thing we're going on holiday tomorrow, you need a break.'

She stepped out of the bath and wrapped a towel around her. Rupert the gardener was way down the eligibility scale from Rupert the banker. She needed to play this holiday to her advantage. Make it as special as possible, and just show him how grey life would become if he could no longer afford such luxuries. She'd make sure they kicked off with a spa treatment at the hotel, accessorised by a little private massage of her own. This situation would need careful management.

NINE

By the first week in January, everyone was usually relieved
that Christmas was over, and itching to get back to normal
life. The two-month-tyranny of tinsel was brought to an
end and a regime of plainness restored. People's rooms
looked bigger and starker without their Christmas trees.
The cards could be swept off the mantelpiece and into
the recycling. Which was exactly what Jane had decided
to do with Rupert.

It had been three weeks since she had seen him, and she
was beginning to wonder if she had made it all up. She'd
only met him four times, a flimsy basis for wrecking her
home life. A bit of pre-Christmas flirtation, and there she
was dreaming of skipping off into the sunset. It was pathetic.

So she had made a New Year's resolution. It was clear
she needed a change, and the thing with Rupert was
nothing more than an expression of her desire to escape.
It was London that was the problem; it was time for them
to move to the country. It was a realistic goal, and one
she should already have pushed harder for. How could
you be happy in a city where people were constantly

wishing they lived elsewhere, in a better street, where the desire for an excavated basement could become your overriding concern?

It wouldn't be like that in the country. Instead of looking enviously over your shoulder, you'd be dancing round the maypole in an equal sort of way. They'd have a big garden, Liberty could get a pony and apple cheeks, it would be just the exciting new start they all needed.

Fired up by the idea, she had planned a research trip. Her friend Alison had moved out to Sussex and was always inviting her to stay. Now was the time to take her up on it, and see what the local estate agents had to offer. Will was bound to go along with it once she showed him what they could afford out there. It wasn't far from Brighton, he could become a regular on that last train from London she had read about, where actors and bohemians held a non-stop party. He'd love it.

He was at work in his galleria now, so Jane decided to go and break the news. She wouldn't give him the full picture yet, just let him know she was going away for a couple of days, start testing the water. She brewed him a cup of green tea with ginseng and honey and made her way up the stairs to begin her campaign. He was sitting at his big desk, surrounded by paper. He could get an even bigger desk in the country, he could have an entire outbuilding to himself if he wanted.

'I've been thinking . . .' she began.

'Well, there's a first,' he said, then added quickly, 'only joking.' He had been trying to be nicer to her recently.

'I know,' she said pleasantly. 'The thing is, Liberty's got a few more days' holiday and I thought I might go away somewhere before she goes back.' She sat down in a low-slung chair and looked up at him.

Will frowned. 'I assume you're planning to take the monkey with you.'

'Of course.'

'Only I'm bogged down here, as you know. I really need to get going on my book.'

'I know.'

She had a deadline, too, but there was no point in telling him. Will was so autistically sealed into his own world that he was immune to other people's concerns. But when they moved to the country she wouldn't have any concerns, things would be so much better.

'And I need to get my column done,' he went on. 'I'm doing it on men: the new pariahs, you know, the feminisation of society, how everything's stacked against us . . .'

'I'll go tomorrow, come back Thursday.'

Will processed this information in terms of how it would affect him. On the plus side, he would have a couple of days of peace and quiet. On the minus side, he had only noticed this morning that he was a bit short on clean shirts.

'Fair enough,' he said, 'though if you wouldn't mind throwing in a load of washing before you go. I'd do it myself, only you know the difficult relationship I have with domestic machinery.'

That was it then. Like he was her commanding officer granting her leave. Or a headmaster authorising an exeat weekend.

'Don't you want to know where we're going?' Jane asked. He could at least show some curiosity.

He threw his arms up, feigning interest. 'But of course. Enlighten me! Where does one go for two days in the bleakest month of the year? Morocco, perhaps?'

'The countryside. Rodmell in Sussex, to be precise.'

'Aah, the country. *Rus nobilis*, your fantasy land of milk and honey. Well, I suppose you'll be able to report back to me on the parlous state of the local pond life.'

'Pond life' was the term Will used to describe country dwellers. Unless they had very large houses as well as a flat in London, in which case they were still worth knowing.

'I thought it would do us good to get some fresh air,' said Jane.

'Not my idea of a stimulating break. The country is where people who haven't made it go to lick their wounds.'

This wasn't encouraging, but he would see the light once she returned with details of the sumptuous barn conversions they could get for a song.

'Actually, Rodmell's not too uncivilised,' he conceded. 'The Bloomsbury connection does lift it, you could always visit Virginia Woolf's house, if you can bear to fight your way past those National Trust women in their boho headscarves As long as you don't fill your pockets with stones and walk out into the river.'

'I doubt if two days of rural living will push me over the edge. We're going to stay with Alison, now she's finished all the work on the house.'

'Ugh. Rather you than me.'

She and Alison had gone through their pregnancies together, locked into one of those close women's friendships that make men feel excluded. She'd forgotten that Will couldn't stand her.

'She's really very nice, you just never got to know her properly. Anyway, you can have a nice time here pottering around on your own.'

'I don't potter. That's what *you're* doing, pottering off to the country. I shall be working. Once I've done the column, I need to get going on the book. I still haven't quite got my head round the opening chapter. Fear. Courage. The two opposing forces, fighting for supremacy in the mind of the Native American.'

Jane shrugged. 'Don't worry, it'll be fine.'

He banged his cup down on the desk and pointed his finger at her. 'No, Jane, it won't be fine. I don't do fine. I do fabulous, brilliant, heart-stopping, intellectually breathtaking. But not fine.'

'Always the perfectionist,' Jane said, kissing his forehead, 'it's your artistic temperament talking, I quite understand.'

He grunted his acknowledgement, and grabbed her hand as she left. 'Sorry to be a grouch,' he said, 'I really don't know how you put up with me.'

'It's OK, it's just the stress of the city getting you down. It's a shame you can't come with us, I think you need the country as much as we do. You'd see it could be just the answer for us.'

Will didn't answer. He hoped she wasn't going to start that nonsense again about moving out. He had an altogether wider perspective in view.

Jane made her way down the concrete staircase. In the summer it was cool underfoot, but in the winter it was cold and harsh and reminded her of a fire escape. They should have stuck with the original Victorian stairs, it would have saved them a bomb. Still, that would soon be in the past, and they would have worn oak treads or cosy carpets leading up to a beamed attic room with a view across the South Downs. It was so right for them to make the move now. Will wasn't an office slave, he could work anywhere, and he would relax and become mellow in the country. He would become like he was when they'd first met, loving and attentive.

She cleared the kitchen then went down to the cellar to fetch a bag for her trip. The room was lined with bottles of mineral water, cans of food and a chemical suit that Will had bought to protect himself from the fallout of a terrorist chemical attack. If the worst happened, they would tape up the windows and eat baked beans until they got the all clear. Will would sit tight in his chemical suit, but Jane and Liberty would have to take their chances. When Jane asked him why he hadn't ordered similar outfits for her and Liberty, he said she wouldn't be interested in living on in a post-nuclear wilderness, and it would be no place for a child. Also, the suits cost nearly a grand a piece, and there was no point in throwing money away on something you'd probably never need.

Jane selected a small suitcase and took it up to the bedroom to begin her packing. In went the woollen socks and wellington boots, the outdated tee shirts and holey old jumpers. The good thing about the country was that she could indulge her puritannical fondness for wearing old clothes until they fell apart. She then went into

Liberty's room, and pulled out the jeans that were going
at the knee, the sweatshirt that had been once too often
through the machine. She was happy to be escaping
London, looking forward to breathing fresh air and
getting back to basics.

They left the next day after breakfast. Alison said it was
less than two hours' drive, so they should easily be there
in time for lunch. Jane hummed to herself as they crossed
the unlovely Hammersmith roundabout, and thought
about sitting round a big farmhouse kitchen table. Alison
was an enthusiastic homemaker, so it wasn't too much
to expect some home-made chutney and maybe even a
vase of early snowdrops to welcome in the new year.

'Are we there yet?' asked Liberty as they drove over
Vauxhall Bridge.

'Not quite. Shall we have a tape?'

'Video Rose.'

It was her current favourite, a grim modern tale of a
girl who does nothing but watch videos all day. At the
age of seven Liberty was through with witches and fairies.
It lasted them until they hit the motorway, then Jane
turned it off in relief.

'Have you got any more homework to do before you
go back to school?' she asked, looking at her daughter
in the mirror, small and perfect, strapped sensibly behind
her seat belt.

Liberty's face frowned in concentration. 'I've got to
write my New Year revolutions.'

'Resolutions,' Jane corrected her. 'That's a good idea.
What are yours?'

'I want a new pet.'

'You've only just got your goldfish. Anyway, New Year resolutions are supposed to be about becoming a better person, not just a list of things you want.'

'I would be a better person if I had a better pet.'

'We might all be better people if we got what we wanted, but that's not the point.'

They drove on in silence for a while, then Liberty was back on the case.

'Has Ella got a pet?'

Ella was Alison's daughter who used to be Liberty's best friend before they moved.

'I don't know,' said Jane. She saw an opportunity here. 'You could get a bigger pet if we moved to the country. Would you like that?'

'I'd like a better pet,' Liberty repeated, diplomatically refusing to answer on the wider point.

As they left the motorway, Jane felt a growing sense of excitement. Even in winter, the hedgerows looked appealing. She imagined meeting Liberty from school and walking her home through the lanes, stopping to pick up leaf skeletons and leaving frosty footprints on the stile as they took a shortcut through the fields. Instead of watching television she would be outside, feeding hens and rabbits and learning to ride.

The road to Rodmell was pretty, provided you turned a blind eye to the occasional flush of executive-home developments. Alison's house was in a perfect country lane, the kind you see on Victorian paintings, with boys in knickerbockers and flat caps using sticks to bowl along hoops. This is what I want, thought Jane as she pulled the old-fashioned doorbell. If she could live somewhere like this, she wouldn't be led astray by chance encounters at the cinema. She'd spend her afternoons alone in the greenhouse, and make nourishing dishes with home-grown leeks. Will might let her have another baby which would lie in a Moses basket in front of the Aga.

'It's gorgeous,' she gushed as Alison opened the door, 'you are so, so lucky.'

Alison looked gratified. She always took it as a personal compliment when friends were envious of her home.

'Thank you,' she said, 'but would you mind taking your shoes off, we've only just had the new carpet put down.'

'Oh, yes, of course,' said Jane, 'come on, Liberty, let's get yours off too.'

They placed their shoes alongside the others in a tight line by the front door. So much for easy country living; she didn't recall Alison being this way before.

'You look a little bit peaky, if you don't mind me saying so,' said Alison. She meant that Jane looked thin, but then people always looked thin when you had put on weight yourself.

'We're thrilled to be here,' said Jane. 'I'm terribly curious to see what it's like to live in the country, because I've been thinking . . .' She looked round to make sure Liberty wasn't listening, but she had already gone off upstairs with Ella. '. . . that we should do the same thing.'

Alison nodded her approval. 'Oh, you must,' she said warmly, glad to welcome a convert to the cause. 'I don't know how people can bear to bring up children in the city, it's an act of cruelty really.'

Steady on, thought Jane, you were there yourself a couple of years ago.

'Now,' Alison went on, 'you're obviously dying to see what we've been up to.' She picked up a large photo album from the hall table and gestured to Jane to follow her into the sitting room.

'This is lovely!' said Jane, though personally she found it a little too fussy. The best thing about it was the view out onto the garden that stretched enviably into the distance.

'We decided to go for the Modern Country look,' said Alison, settling into the sofa and opening the album. 'Come and take a look at these pictures, they'll give you a feel for how it was before.'

Jane turned away reluctantly from the window and sat down beside Alison to make the right noises at the pictures of dark and empty rooms.

'So then we had to strip out the joists,' Alison was saying, 'but only after we'd treated all the timbers . . . and of course, there was the DPC and the underpinning . . .'

We'd have to get somewhere that didn't need any work, thought Jane. It had been bad enough living through that galleria with Will, she didn't think they could survive another project.

Alison was talking about the roof damage now, flicking through the photos, showing where the holes were and how they had been carefully patched with matching tiles. Jane nodded, casting her mind back to when she had first met Alison, at the NCT meeting. She must have found her interesting then, mustn't she? She had worked in publishing, so that had got them talking. And they both loved cooking. But mostly it was just that bond of having babies together, it made you friends with people you wouldn't normally bother with.

'. . . a special lime-based distemper that actually allows the walls to breathe . . . based on the colours of eighteenth-century . . . we eventually found a plasterer who specialised in the distressed uneven look, no point in making an old cottage look like a Barratt Home.' Suddenly Alison stood up in a businesslike manner. 'Right,' she said, 'let's start at the top, shall we?'

'Why not?' said Jane.

She followed Alison's sashaying bottom up the stairs and into the attic rooms. Thank goodness she hadn't brought Will – he liked talking people through his own renovation, but he couldn't stand them reciprocating.

When they had finished, Alison called the children down for lunch and showed them into the kitchen, where a scrubbed oak table was groaning with quiche and home-made bread, just as Jane had hoped.

'It's such a relief, moving out of London,' said Alison, serving up monumental slices of quiche, 'it makes you realise what life is really for. I used to be so twitchy, always rushing around doing a hundred different things. Now I know this is as good as it gets. Proper meals on the table, making a real family home, it's enough, isn't it?'

'I suppose it is,' said Jane. 'Have you made friends? That is the one thing that worries me, finding like-minded people to talk to . . .'

'Oh yes, there are five or six couples that we're terribly close to, all with young families. We have tennis parties, Scottish dancing evenings, it's very social.'

Jane tried, and failed, to imagine Will taking part in a tennis party or doing the Highland fling.

'And when the men are off at work, we wives are always round at each other's houses. I've just started a book club actually, you need to make your own entertainment.' She jumped up from the table and stroked the handle of a kitchen cupboard. 'Do you like these? I'd been looking everywhere for matt nickel handles, couldn't find them for love nor money. I eventually spotted these on a freezer lorry and tracked them down to a warehouse in Hounslow.'

Living in the country was not so very different then. You could obsess about kitchen fittings just as well as in town.

After lunch the girls went upstairs to play while Alison made the coffee. 'I'm definitely a home bird,' she said, 'I don't miss working at all. You can only do the home thing properly when you don't have anything else to worry about. I actually feel sorry for neurotic career-women with children.'

Jane wondered if she was included in that category.

'Here, take a look at this,' said Alison, passing her a dog-eared catalogue. 'Lakeland Plastics, they do some marvellous things. I've got these special Sandwich Triangles that you put straight into the toaster.'

Flicking through the pages, Jane was struck by the number of handwritten comments that were marked alongside each entry. 'Oh yes, here it is,' she said, '"Spend over forty-five pounds and get a free Sandwich Triangle. Put a stop to battered butties." Who writes this stuff?' She turned the page to find a roly-poly-dog kitchen-towel holder and a decorative margarine-tub holder, '*as plastic margarine tubs aren't the nicest things to have on the table.*' There was also a hold-a-napkin clip, which was a tiny chrome hand designed to attach your napkin to your tie when you sat down to dinner.

'Don't you find it a bit depressing, Ali, all this glorification of homeliness?' Jane asked. 'The idea of nuclear families all over the country sitting down surrounded by their domestic gadgets. Cowering at home, safe from the outside world. I mean, how many people honestly need a document shredder? But to read this you'd think you were living on the edge if you didn't have one.'

'I know, it's a bit of a joke,' said Alison, 'but when your life is your home, as it is in my case, it's worth investing in.'

They took their coffee through to the sitting room so Alison could show her the 'after' photographs. As Alison took the first album down, Jane noticed with alarm that the bookcase was filled from floor to ceiling with similar volumes, all carefully labelled. Alison turned the pages reverentially, showing the rooms as they now looked, stripped and restored and draped with all the bustling energy of the urban professional come to the country.

Jane surreptitiously glanced at her watch: it was only three o'clock.

'Goodness me, you've been so busy,' Jane said as the last page of Volume 16 was turned, showing Alison in her decorating dungarees up a ladder, hanging an antique chandelier. It was in the seventh bedroom, which stood empty like most of them, dressed up in Cath Kidston bedcovers, ready and waiting for houseguests. 'Have you thought . . . that is, now that you've done the house . . . what you might do next?' Jane asked.

'Enjoy it, of course!' said Alison. 'I need a rest after all that work. Do you like this room? I was very torn between Gustavian and French Provincial, but looking at that Swedish armchair now I'm sure I made the right choice.'

They decided to go for a walk before the light went. Jane was determined to go home with a caseful of mud-spattered old clothes as evidence of happy splashing in puddles. She breathed in the wood-smoke from the chimneys of the pretty houses that lined the street and felt like she was really, properly in the country.

'This is so lovely,' she said. 'Just the smell of those log fires makes me realise I can't wait any longer, I must leave London right now.'

Alison had stopped to greet a woman in a stout coat and they talked about the produce show, and what a close thing it was for the best cabbage award. I could be like that, thought Jane, I could be a countrywoman with a pantry full of bottled pears and pickled walnuts. I want to get competitive about blackberry jam.

'You see how easy it is in a village,' Alison said, 'you get to know everyone. I never spoke to my neighbours once in Shepherds Bush.'

When the children were in bed, they moved into the TV Snug, a womb-like room off the kitchen, remarkable for its multiple layers of eiderdowns, blankets, coverlets, throws and any other words you could think of to define a length of fabric spread on top of a sofa. They lifted their slippered feet to rest on a suede pouffe. It was so cosy here you felt that nothing bad could possibly happen, the violent images on the TV news seemed so remote.

Around ten o'clock they heard a key in the door.

'The wanderer returns,' said Alison.

Robert appeared in the kitchen, wan-faced and besuited, padding across the floor in his socks to pour himself a glass of wine. Poor sod, he'd be up again at six o'clock.

'Nice day, darling?' Alison called out. 'Did you bring the *Standard*?'

'Just for you, sweetheart,' he said, pulling a newspaper out of his briefcase. He walked towards them in the Snug, then paused to feign surprise, peering ahead with his hand above his eyes like a pirate on lookout duty.

'Good Lord, what have we here?' he said. 'Is that a visitor I detect?'

'Hallo, Robert,' said Jane, getting up to greet him. 'I've been admiring your beautiful house.'

'Gorgeous, isn't it? It's changed our weekends. I never thought I could get so much pleasure from mowing the lawn.'

He chatted to her about the garden and painted a pretty picture of their new life, so much more fulfilling now than when they were a stressed-out double-income city couple. Nothing wrong with this, Jane thought. It came pretty close to that Ladybird book she had had as a child, where a ruddy-faced son swept the leaves with Daddy while the girl helped her smiling mother to do the dusting. It was easy to knock it, too easy to take a snooty view of normal family life.

Alison had got up to set out Robert's dinner on a tray. She wouldn't have done it in the old days, but it was part of the service these days. He was the one who made this dream possible, he deserved some reward for that daily commute.

'Mind if I join you for *Newsnight*?' he asked, setting the tray down on a small folding table then settling down between the women so they were sitting snugly, three in a row. Jane remembered reading that Princess Margaret had just such a table: not even royalty was immune to the horrid democracy of TV suppers.

'This is the life,' he said, pulling the TV table towards him so the plate was located in optimum feeding position. He took a paper napkin from the tray and fastened it to his tie with one of the tiny chrome hands that Jane had been observing earlier in the Lakeland catalogue.

'My TV-supper heaven,' he added, forking up an enthusiastic mouthful of food.

Jane felt uncomfortable in this intimate setting, an intruder in their daily routine. 'We went for a lovely walk,' she said, 'down your street and into the woods.'

He took another mouthful of food, and Jane looked away. While it was perfectly all right to sit across from someone at the dinner table, there was something repugnant about being down-sofa from someone eating off a tray.

'How's Will, by the way?' he asked, swigging his wine.

It was a jolt back into her own life after a day of drifting along on the edge of other people's.

'He's fine, thanks,' she said. 'Busy, but that's the way he likes it. I still have a go at him every now and then about moving to the country, but I'm not sure it's going to happen. I'm going to visit some estate agents tomorrow, though, see if I can find anything to change his mind.'

'Oh, he will, believe me. You get so much more for your money here, even now. Mind you, it's gone up again, there was a house down the road that went for . . .' His eyes lit up as he told her, and Jane noted that you didn't get any less greedy when you left town.

They could move out, of course they could, but suddenly she was losing her enthusiasm for the idea. Will would snub everybody and spend all his time in London, and she would be stuck here discussing house prices with Robert and trying to raise record-breaking marrows. Jane and Will would see each other less and less; far from being a new start for them, it could be the beginning of the end. She needed to get back to London, fast.

'And your work's going all right, is it?' said Robert. 'You don't find it too much of a strain, with the children.'

'Not at all,' said Jane, meaning it, 'and I've only got the one child.'

'Alison says she doesn't know how she ever found time to go to work.'

'That's what people always say when they retire. I just happen to think thirty-seven is a bit young for retirement.'

'Steady on,' said Alison indignantly, 'I never stop, Robert knows that.'

'I know, I know,' he said.

'I didn't mean you,' Jane added hastily, 'not with everything you've done down here. I think you're marvellous.'

Alison smiled her forgiveness. 'We'll look forward to

being neighbours again, once you've made the break. Won't we, Robert?'

'We certainly will,' he said. 'Do you both play tennis?'

Alison had put Jane in the Green Room, though the name was redundant. You only had to open the door to be assaulted by every permutation of the colour, from the white with a hint of mint woodwork to the apple-patterned pillowcases and the emerald bedspread and heavy olive curtains that puddled onto the eau de nil carpet. The theme was tirelessly carried over to the en suite bathroom with a leaf border on the tiles and a set of verdant bath towels.

Jane's thoughts on going to bed were that she was grateful for Will. She wouldn't want a namby-pamby husband who'd follow wherever she led. Will was right, he'd hate the country, and she would be asking for trouble to insist they left London. It was back to the smoke for her, and she was even looking forward to it. You can't run away from yourself, after all, it was foolish to think that where you lived could change anything. And maybe it wouldn't hurt to see Rupert again, now she'd calmed down a bit.

She slept late, dreaming of Rupert. He had taken her to China and was leading her through a garden where mythical birds perched on rocky outcrops. They were both wearing embroidered silk robes and she was tottering along on bound feet encased in tiny pointed shoes.

'OK, you win,' said Jane. 'I admit I had a hidden agenda but you can relax, we're not moving to the country.'

Will pretended to wipe the sweat off his brow. 'Thank the Lord for that,' he said, 'you only need to look around to see you made the right decision.'

They were out for lunch in Westbourne Village, Will's favourite part of Notting Hill, and so far up itself that even the public toilet was disguised as an upmarket flower stall, manned by a handsome young man in artfully ripped jeans.

The whole point of Westbourne Village was that you mustn't be seen to be trying too hard, and this extended to naming the restaurants. Why bother to come up with something when you could lazily use the address? 202 was where they were going for lunch. Obviously, this stood for 202 Westbourne Grove, and if you needed to ask, you were in the wrong place. The restaurant was owned by that dream-team couple, Nicole Farhi and David Hare. The understated designer favoured by Cherie Blair, and her husband the left-wing playwright. What could be more perfect?

The café was at the back of the shop, so Jane was able to admire the unstructured haute bohemian outfits on her way through. She was also rather taken by some attractive green and purple Italian rustic glassware, until she consulted the label. £55 per tumbler was a non-rustic price, but then nobody ever said it came cheap to be hip.

They were seated at a small table, and Will looked around him with satisfaction. People certainly knew how to dress round here: combat trousers tucked into stilettos, floor-length coats and trainers, the studied eclectic mixing that marked out the cognoscenti from the plebs. His gaze suddenly froze on one table, where a middle-management type was sitting by himself in a navy blue suit and a tie! How the hell did he manage to sneak in past the style police? Surely they had been briefed on the first new rule of door policy, that ties were strictly for losers.

'I'll have the chicken, black bean and feta quesadilla with mango coriander and chilli salsa,' he said to the waiter.

Jane was still frowning at the card. 'What is it about these places that they have to put "fish 'n' chips 'n' mushy peas" on the menu like we're living in a Guy Ritchie faux-working-class ghetto?' she said. 'I don't know why they don't make us sing along to "Roll Out the Barrel" while they're about it.'

'It's the fantastic melting pot of modern London,' said Will. 'All nations and classes, served up to Joe Public in a democratic cocktail.'

'I don't think many people here are on a Joe Public income,' she said, 'except for the waiters.'

'Don't be a bore,' said Will. 'What are you going to have?'

'Grilled lamb kofte with tabbouleh and tzatziki please,' she said, smiling at the waiter, 'and Liberty can have the fish 'n' chips, but without the mushy peas.'

She looked round the room, and admitted it was a relief to be back in town.

'We didn't see much evidence of cosmopolitan life in Rodmell,' she said. 'Alison made it sound really boring. Once you've done the house up, there's nothing to do except Scottish dancing.'

Now she'd changed her mind, she needed to bolster up her arguments.

'Correction,' said Will, 'it's Alison who's really boring.'

'That's not entirely fair . . .'

'That woman could bore for England.'

'She was a good friend to me when we were having our babies.'

Will rolled his eyes up into his sockets and mimed a yawn.

'But I don't think it would suit us down there,' she went on. 'It reminded me of when my grandparents retired to the country, but then they had to move back because grandma said that grandpa was becoming a vegetable.'

'He became one anyway.'

'Not until much later. And that was caused by a degenerative illness, not by lack of urban stimulation.' She twirled her glass and thought briefly about her grandpa on his deathbed, then pushed the thought away, not wanting to be troubled by intimations of mortality. 'Anyway, I didn't envy her, that's all I'm saying.'

'Of course you didn't, Jane. It's what I call the *Rasselas* effect. Setting off in hope of finding a better life, then realising you're better off at home.'

'Mmm,' said Jane.

She thought about her home life with Will, then opened a door of her imagination to think about a home life with Rupert. She remembered the touch of his hand on her knee under the table in the V&A, and imagined that table floating off somewhere, with the two of them, ending up who knows where: on a terrace of an Italian hillside cafe, overlooking slopes planted with vines; in an isolated pub on the North York Moors before a roaring fire; in the Chinese pavilion of a French garden with rambling roses climbing up the pillars and a thousand-bed dovecot next door. The rural fantasy might have been knocked on the head as far as living in the country with Will was concerned, but allow herself to imagine a change of partner and the dream was very much alive and kicking.

'I'm feeling generous,' said Will after lunch. 'Let's take you over to Emma Hope and see what she's got in the sale.'

They crossed the road where a couple of thin women in Ugg boots behind triangular pushchairs with fat wheels were looking in the Joseph window. For a quiet residential area it was very well served for clothes. You could easily nip out to buy a fluid range of separates from Agnes B or the concrete-façaded Laundry Industry that Jane at first had mistaken for a launderette. But it wouldn't be so easy to buy a pint of milk.

The young women who served in Emma Hope's shoe shop were far too classy to be labelled shop girls. They greeted Jane inclusively, while still managing to convey through their patronising smiles that they knew she was someone who could only afford to shop there during the sales.

Jane picked up a slim, purple shoe and turned it over in her hand, feeling the smooth leather against the tips of her fingers and admiring its gold buckle.

'It's like *The Elves and the Shoemaker*, Mum,' whispered Liberty, in awe of the pretty princesses in charge of the shop, 'when he leaves out the material every night, and they come in to sew up a beautiful pair of shoes.'

'That's right, Liberty,' said Jane, 'that's exactly what it's like.'

She slipped the shoe on and felt how soft it was, how it fitted like a glove instead of having hard edges that cut into your feet like you got with normal shoes.

'I'll try the other one please,' she said. So this was what all the fuss was about, why rich women paid hundreds of pounds for a pair of shoes that spoke of the rarified days of the bespoke shoemaker. They'd had a stab at democracy, at mass-produced footwear, but it just didn't cut the mustard.

'You're just like Cinderella,' said Liberty, proudly holding her mother's hand as they left the shop, 'and Daddy is your Prince Charming.'

'No need to romanticise,' said Will, 'I just get to pick up the tab. You deserve it,' he said to Jane, 'you work hard and, let's face it, you're not a self-indulgent creature, and you could pay a little more attention to the way you dress.'

They wandered down to Tavola to pick up some barrel-aged feta and elderflower presse for supper. On the way, Will waved at the owner of the Café Mandola. It proved you were a local to be on familiar terms with the restaurateurs.

'Sudanese cuisine in the heart of London,' he said.

'Do we need it?' Jane asked.

'Bang next door to yer regular old greasy-spoon caff,' he went on, waving at some dressed-down toff he knew who was enjoying what he doubtless called a 'cup of char' in The Windmill, so simple and much treasured by the locals.

'Can we go home now?' asked Liberty.

'Just one more stop, Liberty,' said Will. 'I want to get some flowers for the galleria, I've got someone coming over for a meeting tomorrow and she strikes me as the type who knows about these things, so I'm going to get them from *the* address.'

He led them up a road until they came to a small shop-front called Wild Things. Jane was interested to see it at last, because Will was always going on about it. The shop floor was grubby, and curiously empty of flowers.

'There's not many flowers here, Daddy,' said Liberty, staring at a stark handful of dull-coloured blooms on spindly stems.

'Of course not, darling,' said Will, 'we're not talking municipal park, we're talking less is more; when you get older you'll realise it's better to have a few perfect blooms than a vulgar great mass of colour.' His eye alighted on a plain white circular base which was supporting just four red roses. 'There we are,' he said, 'that's just what I need. Not so much a bunch of flowers as an installation. Jane, you'd better bring the car round, it's going to be difficult to carry.'

TEN

Heathrow in the early morning is a strange and silent place. The staging post on the way back to normal life, but still the unreal world of airport corridors and climate-less zones. It is also where you feel grateful to be back on firm land and reassess your life as you return to it.

After an eighteen-hour journey, Rupert knew he would be happy never to step foot on an aeroplane again. He switched on his phone as they went through passport control and listened to his messages. Nothing from Jane. Not that he had expected one, she knew he was going away. In front of him in the queue Lydia was also checking her messages, though in her case the process took much longer. Even at this ungodly hour she could turn in a good performance, frowning and smiling by turns as she flicked her hair and held the tiny phone to her ear.

At the luggage carousel, Lydia went off to the ladies, leaving Rupert in charge of reclaiming their bags. As the conveyor belt started moving, passengers dazed by the long flight gathered round to stare at the hatch, as though waiting for an oracle.

Rupert stroked his thumb over his phone, his Aladdin's lamp. Just a light touch and he could be speaking to her, it was that easy. The bags were coming through now, and Lydia would be back soon, but he just had time, it was quick enough simply to summon her number and press the button. The phone rang and switched straight over to the voicemail. Of course, it was early, she would still be in bed, but it was enough to hear her voice, apologising softly for not being able to take your call. It had none of the strident harshness of Lydia's voice which always reminded him of that jolly-hockey-sticks young woman on the *Today* programme. He hung up, then called the number again, to hear her once more. This time he left a message.

'It's me. I'm back.'

He then replaced the phone in his pocket and set about hauling their bags onto the trolley.

In the taxi queue, Lydia pulled on the llama-skin coat that she had acquired during the cold half of their holiday.

'Thank God we've got the sales to come back to,' she said. 'January would be quite unbearable otherwise. I might take a walk up Sloane Street this afternoon, it's better not to give in to jet lag otherwise you never adjust.'

'You're not seriously thinking of going shopping after that journey?'

'A change is as good as a rest. And much as I adored the desert, I can't wait to get back to some decent shops. Anyway, we can't afford to miss out on the sales, we can save thousands.'

'Only by spending thousands. The best way to save money is to stay home and watch telly, which is exactly how I intend to spend the day.'

They climbed into the taxi, Lydia taking care not to crush her souvenir collection of copper music pipes, and began the crawl into central London. She took out a small book and began making notes of what she needed to complete her winter wardrobe.

Rupert gazed out of the window and let the waves of tiredness roll over him. He felt dizzy with the travelling. It seemed they had spent days in planes and cars, transported from one extreme climate to another in the endless journey to satisfaction, punctuated by meals taken in luxury hotels. He had been like a heavy sledge, dragged along by Lydia through the blue-and-white granite colours of the southern glaciers, then hauled up to the burned umber northern desert where they boasted they'd had no rain in four hundred years. The pressure to see remarkable sights was endless and, in the end, self-defeating. You got wonder fatigue from everything being so extraordinary.

He thought of the message he'd left on Jane's phone. 'It's me.' That was a bit presumptuous of him, assuming she'd know who 'me' was. He should have left his name, but that felt too incriminating, especially a damn stupid name like Rupert, and you never knew if Will might go around checking her messages. He might draw the wrong conclusion, which would be unfortunate, because there was nothing wrong about their friendship, they had nothing to hide. A friendship was all it was.

Lydia's voice broke into his thoughts. 'You know, I think I'll see if I can book Clive for that dinner on the fourteenth.'

Clive? Dinner? What was she on about?

'Whatever,' he said. It wasn't a modern idiom that used to come naturally to him, but it was a useful way of replying to Lydia.

'Only it does lend a greater sense of occasion,' she went on, 'and it's not as if I want to spend my evening running in and out of the kitchen like a headless chicken.'

'Quite.'

He fell back into his reverie, trying to remember what it was he'd said afterwards, after 'It's me.' Something corny like, 'I'm back', like he was Arnold Schwarzenegger or something, as if she would give a damn. She'd probably not given him a thought, probably been caught up in her family Christmas: after all, what was he to her? It had been a mistake to leave that message, he should have just hung up and let her call him if she wanted to.

'Clive does come highly recommended,' said Lydia, 'and butlers are definitely in again. That's going to be the next thing, you know, a return to formal dining; people are sick of pigging it in the kitchen, surrounded by basalt work-tops and dangling pans. A separate dining room, that's what we'll be seeing, and let the servants get on with it in the kitchen. It's certainly a trend that gets my blessing.'

Rupert nodded and closed his eyes. She watched him rest his head on the back of the seat. He seemed quite exhausted by the holiday, whereas she had found it invigorating. Contrasts were definitely what she would be looking for in the honeymoon, maybe tropical paradise meets urban minimalism like on Cocoa Island. Rupert had seemed curiously reluctant to discuss it, kept saying they should enjoy the one they were on now, and not keep worrying about what they should be doing next. It was the nearest they had come to a row. Lydia had said it was all very well for him to say that, but things got booked up and you needed to get organised. And what task could be more enjoyable than planning the ultimate holiday that was your honeymoon?

He was sleeping now, which was probably a bad approach to the jet lag, but he needed to catch up before going back to work. Fortunately, there had been no more talk of him giving up his job, it was probably just a bit of pre-Christmas fatigue. It wasn't that she loved him for his money, but financial success was part of what he was. You couldn't separate him from his wealth any more than you could separate a peacock from his tail; it was one of his defining characteristics.

As for that ludicrous fantasy about becoming a gardener, that had really rattled her. A banker with his kind of earning potential must have mental problems to believe he'd be happier pushing a wheelbarrow. Would the owner of a factory suddenly announce that what he really wanted to do was sit on the production line and stick bits of plastic together? She didn't think so. The Chile holiday had been mercifully short on gardens. Burning hot deserts up one end and icy wastes down the other, with no time to hang around in the garden-friendly moderate middle ground. That had been more by luck than judgement, but thank God there weren't any dangerous moments of him going misty-eyed in front of a bougainvillea or whatever it was they grew over there.

*　　*　　*

At Cadogan Gardens, the usual mountain of post had piled up during Rupert's absence. He sat with his mug of tea, looking on as Lydia dealt with it, ripping open the envelopes and sorting the contents into piles. Junk post, catalogues, Christmas cards, many of them addressed to them both. Anything marked confidential she put to one side, then when she had finished she casually waved the pile at him. 'Shall I deal with this?'

He shrugged, so she opened them on his behalf. Bank statements, Christmas messages, invitations to sales openings, it was all the same to him. All of equal, zero interest.

He went into the living room and lay down on the sofa, closing his eyes and listening to Lydia bustling around, taking over his life. He'd have a couple of days to recover and then it would be back to the office, back to feigning interest and fiddling around with notional figures on the computer. He couldn't help thinking his job would be more fun if money was a physical thing as it was in the old days. He could sit like a king in his counting house, making shiny towers of coins, bagging them up in velvet drawstring pouches. Or even if you had chips like at the casino, where you piled them high on your chosen number, and your winnings were pushed towards to you by a sharp-eyed croupier in a low-cut silk dress. Where you could trade in your chips for wads of cash, where at least the money smelt of something, had physical form. Whereas the money he dealt with was formless: grey flickering images on a flat screen.

If he were in his garden in France right now, he could take a heavy-duty fork and plunge it into the ground, feel

where the stones lay and where the sandy soil allowed
the prongs to pass. Digging over the beds, he could reach
down to remove the roots of weeds, anaemic as bean-
sprouts. Afterwards, he would have a mug of steaming
coffee and be glad to think that he had rescued his
garden from those intruders, that later on, in summer,
the flowers would be all the more exquisite as a result
of his labours.

'Lovely card from Baz, thanking us for the party.'

Lydia's voice reached him like an unwelcome, distant
wake-up call.

'You might take him out for lunch, see if he wants to
invest in your fund. Now it seems we're well and truly
in the toy cupboard.'

Baz was the capricious chairman of Lydia's magazine
group, renowned for bullying his staff, who referred to
themselves as being in or out of the toy cupboard
according to whether they were currently in favour. Lydia,
being fearlessly self-confident, always assumed she was
well in, and Baz's note would seem to bear her out. Rupert
considered him a nasty piece of work he would rather
have no dealings with.

'You have lunch with him,' he said. 'I wouldn't touch
that piece of shit's money with a bargepole.'

'Ooh, you're so upright,' she said, clattering round the
kitchen. 'I do love it when you make a stand, such a
contrast to my own more fluid approach to people. Shall
I see if I can book Caraffini for tonight?'

'Surely we can eat in, we've eaten out every night for
the past three weeks.'

The thought of another evening in a restaurant listening

to Lydia's brittle talk was not appealing. This was hardly a good omen for their married life, but maybe he was just suffering from the over-exposure of three weeks' holiday.

'You're cooking, then, are you?' she said.

'Fine.'

'Because you needn't think I'm going to spend my first night back in London messing up the kitchen . . .'

'I said I'll cook.'

'But you're tired.'

'Let's get a takeaway then.'

'Might just as well pop down the road to Caraffini in that case.'

'OK, whatever.'

He closed his eyes again and returned to dreaming of his house in France. Jane would sit beside him and plan how to spend the rest of the day. Lunch might be a cassoulet that he would prepare in the big rough-cast iron pot that always sat on top of the cooker. The cannellini beans would have been soaking all night. You had time to cook and garden and do the things that really mattered when you were there. Not like in London where you were always rushing off to the office or catching a plane in search of the driest or hottest or coldest or most miraculous places on earth.

'I'm definitely coming down in favour of the Scottish castle,' said Lydia, calling out from the bedroom. 'The weather can be dodgy anywhere in the UK, so unless we were thinking of chartering a plane for everyone to go somewhere hot . . .'

There was a hint of a question in her voice, which Rupert was quick to answer.

'No.'

'So in that case, I think the castle. Entirely in keeping with your dour Scottish roots and relatively economical. I know we need to keep a bit of a lid on it, and we don't want to compromise on the honeymoon. Or the London home.'

She appeared in the doorway, wearing a bathrobe, arms folded as she outlined their wedding plans. She was like his business partner, or his accountant, or one of those scary PAs who used to be the power behind the corporate throne in the days before women had proper jobs.

'I'm going for a shower,' said Rupert. 'I can't be thinking about this right now.'

He patted her on the shoulder on his way out – he didn't want to be unkind – and went into the bathroom, stripping out of his travel-stained clothes, turning on the shower and standing under the powerful jet of hot water. It was no good, he was going to have to tell her he couldn't go through with it. The only question was, how? How did you walk out on the wedding you had just spent three weeks hearing about? How could you break off the engagement that you had only announced a month ago to a room full of approving friends?

His friend John had done it from the driving seat of his sports car after Sunday lunch with the future in-laws. Engine throbbing, he had dropped the bombshell, then it was foot down on the gas and he was out of there. Rupert could never be so cruel. Maybe he should just suggest they continue as they were, backing down from the wedding but not going as far as ending the relationship. He couldn't bear to make a scene. But even as he was convincing himself, he knew this was impossible. You could live with someone for years without any talk of getting married, but once the idea had been mooted and the deal agreed, there was no going back to the way things were.

He finished his shower and dressed and combed his hair. It was jet lag and exhaustion that was doing this to him, he needed to rest and come to his senses. It had hardly been a spur-of-the-moment thing, his engagement to Lydia, and if he felt rather underwhelmed by the whole thing, it must simply be that you didn't get that excited about things once you were forty. By leaving it so late to get married, he had leapfrogged straight into discontented middle age, bypassing the young-love stage altogether.

By the time Lydia left to go shopping, Rupert had chased away his dark thoughts. He had found two crumpets in the freezer that he had toasted and spread with butter, and was now lying on the sofa, watching football on the telly. For the first time in three weeks he was alone, and the silence reassured him. Outside, the grey sky was a comforting reminder that here was a temperate land, unlike the violent climatic extremes he had just visited. He was a temperate, reasonable English person about to get married to a vivacious, clever, attractive woman. He wanted for nothing materially, and if he was finding his job vexing, well, he was only like most people, and lucky to have the job in the first place.

When his phone rang he was still in the comatose state induced by watching sport on an English winter's afternoon when it gets dark at four o'clock, his body still bridging the gap between two continents.

'Hallo,' he said sleepily, eyes still fixed on the TV.

'So you're back?'

It was Jane. In a shot, he snapped back to life; all thoughts of football and illusions of contentment went straight out the window. He couldn't marry Lydia when the mere sound of another woman's voice was enough to turn him to jelly. He sat up and swung his feet back onto the ground, turning down the sound on the remote. 'You got my message,' he said, idiotically, getting to his feet and pacing towards the window, as if in hope of seeing her in the street outside.

'Yes. I was unreasonably pleased to hear from you.'

'Me too. I am pleased. Ecstatic, in fact. Above and beyond the call of reason. To hear from you, that is.'

'How was your trip?' she asked, after a moment.

How was his trip? Did she mean apart from the fact that he wasn't travelling with her? Apart from the fact that every morning when he woke up he wished it was her lying beside him instead of Lydia?

'As you'd expect,' he said. 'Very cold, and then very hot. What about you?'

'Neither hot nor cold, but something in between. Quite rainy.'

'I see.'

'Do you think it's a bit weird, us talking about the weather?' she asked.

'Not at all. I think it's a fine topic. In the States they have an entire TV station devoted to it.'

'I know, the Weather Channel, I love it.'

'So there's something else we have in common.'

'Yes.'

'We'll be able to talk hurricanes and sleet showers when we next meet.' He bunched his left hand up tight as he said it, pressing his nails into his palm, bracing himself for a refusal, waiting for her to make her excuses, to say that she couldn't meet him again, that she'd been thinking things over and there was no future for them.

Except she didn't say that. Instead, she said, 'How about next Friday?'

He unclenched his hand, felt a rush of blood to his head.

'Next Friday it is then.'

Sunday morning invariably found Will and Jane in bed with the papers. Piled up on their laps, spilling out onto the floor from all sides, awash with magazines and Internet supplements and sections about homes and business and the arts. It frightened Jane to think of it, all those people like Will being paid to produce the endless, spewing words, words, words, that you never had time to absorb. It was always with a sense of personal failure that she gathered them up for recycling, confronted by reams of unread pages.

Going out to buy the papers was Jane's job. Will was not a morning person so it was Jane who carried them back like a weightlifter in two extra-strong stripey nylon laundry baskets, remembering to ask for a receipt so Will could set the cost off against his tax. She didn't mind, it made her feel less guilty about agreeing to meet Rupert again, going back on everything she had decided. When she got his message, all her determination to cut him out of her life had evaporated. She had to see him.

She'd tell him they must just be friends, there was no harm in that.

The mood in their bedroom could be volatile on these mornings, but today it was relatively serene. Will's spirits were dictated by what he read in the papers; it all came down to how the competition was faring. This morning he was in luck, there was a scathingly bad review for a friend's book that set his heart singing.

'Dear oh dear,' he chuckled to himself, shaking the paper out in front of him so he could make the most of the experience. 'I think this deserves another cup of ayurvedic tea, Jane, if you wouldn't mind.' He held his cup out to her, his eyes alight with pleasure. 'Poor old Jeremy, he's going to be mortified. Mind you, I'm not entirely surprised, he is a bit second-rate.'

Jane filled his cup and handed it back to him, then picked up a health and well-being supplement that explained how to achieve shiny eyes from inner peace and eating more vegetables. It insisted you could be even more fabulous if you really, really tried. Then they offered a quiz to assess your stress levels to see if you needed to go on a swanky spiritual retreat in Tibet. The whole tone of the thing was that you were one very special person who deserved endless, narcissistic grooming.

'I'm sick of the papers,' she said, pushing them onto the floor. She thought about Rupert saying how he no longer bothered with them. What did he do, then, on Sunday mornings? What was he up to now? She felt like ringing him to find out.

'Careful,' said Will, pulling on his Chinese embroidered dressing gown. 'Don't go biting the hand that feeds you. Speaking of which, I'd better get upstairs to the thought laboratory.'

He had renamed his workspace since reading that Barratt homes had launched a new development in Peckham under the name of The Galleria.

'Just something light for lunch, please,' he added. 'Don't you go trying to fatten me up with a stodgy Sunday roast!'

'I'm going out, remember?' she called out, but he didn't hear.

She sank back in bed, picking up a travel section although it was her least favourite part of any paper. Journalists gushing about their all-paid-for stay in a luxury hotel. Who cared if the end of the bog paper was folded into a peak or if they scattered scented mimosas on your pillow at night? Will was with her on this, he couldn't stand travel journalism, and would never stoop so low as to be sent on what he termed a tart's freebie. He was fond of pointing out that travel journalism was to travel literature what penny dreadfuls were to Dostoevsky. Like Tolstoy, he considered journalism a brothel from which there was no return, except for his own column, which was a mere sideline to his true vocation.

She turned the page to read the question-and-answer column. A school-leaver wanted to know where in the world he should go and spend his gap year that would be free from terrorism. He had a budget of six thousand pounds, and would like to do something a little different from the usual hippy trail. His sense of entitlement was that of an eighteenth-century aristocrat setting out to do the Grand Tour before coming home to run the family estate. Why don't you get a job in a canning factory to pay for your tuition fees, you spoilt little toad, she thought, moving into the bathroom to run the taps.

Climbing into the bath, Jane planned her day ahead. Her cousin was in town, over from New York, and she had arranged to meet him in the V&A. It was the first place that had come to mind when he rang and he sounded pleased with the idea. 'Tell Liberty I can't wait to see her,' he said, 'but you don't need to bring Will.' Simon had never liked him and after their first, disastrous meeting he had tried to put Jane straight. 'I just don't get it,' he said, 'you can't possibly want to spend the rest of your life with him.' Jane had been very offended and they had barely spoken for a year, but it was all forgiven now. She missed Simon and wished he lived closer.

Liberty came wading through the sea of papers into the bathroom. 'Cartoons have finished,' she announced. 'What can I do now?' She slipped on a pair of high-heeled shoes that Jane had kicked off last night and neglected to put away in the wardrobe. 'Look, Mum, I'm a top model.' She stuck her nose in the air and walked towards Jane, striking a pose and delivering a fearsome scowl, then turning on her heel and sashaying back to the door, swinging her narrow little bottom.

Jane smiled. 'Very good. Is that what you want to do then, when you grow up?'

'Got to get my bosoms first,' said Liberty. 'Then I might marry someone nice and do my exercises and have lunch with people.'

'Lucky we're giving you that expensive education, then,' said Jane. 'There goes a century of feminism down the toilet.'

'What can I do? I'm boredy-boredy.'

'How about tidying up my bedroom? Pick up all those newspapers and put them in that bag in the corner.'

Liberty set about it, gathering the papers, folding them neatly, like a small and slightly manic housemaid. Jane was reminded of the Montessori nursery school that Liberty had first attended, where a lot of expensively crafted wooden objects were imported from Scandinavia in order to teach the children how to put them away. The headmistress had promised the Montessori system provided a tidy mind for life, so maybe they were reaping the benefits of that precious establishment where, the head had once told her in a frighteningly controlled whisper, the voice of the teacher was never raised above that of the children.

'We're going out soon,' she said, 'don't you remember, we're going to meet cousin Simon.'

Liberty looked up from her folding. 'Hooray, I like Simon! Where are we going?'

'To look at some tiny shoes. They're only as big as dolls' shoes, but they were worn by Chinese ladies who tied their feet up in bandages to stop them growing.'

Liberty nodded her approval. She would enjoy it, and Jane need not feel guilty about engineering an outing to the place where she last saw Rupert. Only five more days, and she would see him again.

ELEVEN

On the morning of her date with Rupert, Jane was planning her tactics. She would play it cool, tell him they could just be friends. There was no need to be dramatic about it, friendship was a fine thing. Except that friends didn't usually wake up at 6 a.m. in excitement at the thought of seeing each other.

'I know how the world began,' said Liberty from her soapbox in the back seat of the car.

'Do you?' Jane was always grateful when Liberty claimed to have the answer. It meant she didn't have to cast around for one that was accurate but also comprehensible to a seven-year-old.

'Yes. Monkeys were thrown out of a volcano, then they turned into people.'

'Mmm, nice idea. Kind of Darwin meets Big Bang.'

They were just coming up to Hyde Park, and Jane thought maybe she should unload Liberty at Speaker's Corner, so she could share her theory of evolution with a wider audience.

'Mum?'

She was off again, on her philosophical half-hour. Thank goodness they didn't live any further from the school, otherwise it could turn into a full hour of high-level debate.

'Yes?'

'What is the point of living if you are going to die?'

She was going for the big ones this morning.

'That's a very good question. I think I would say, the point is you should try to lead a useful life.'

'Is that what you do?' Children were ruthless, they hadn't yet learned that it was bad manners to question the meaningless lives of their parents.

'In a way. I earn money to pay for things, and I look after you. That's useful.'

The streets round Leinster Square were clogged, as usual, with the cars of useful parents pouring their hopes for the future into their children. When Jane was growing up, children were accommodated into their parents' lives. Now it seemed it was the other way round. The child was the tyrant king, and woe betide the parent who didn't put them first.

Most of the children were looking tanned this week, after the Christmas break. The skiers had white goggle-marks round their eyes, while the winter-sun brigade were all-over honey brown. Jane had joined the mothers for coffee on the first day back, so knew all about the benefits of Club Med mini-club versus going it alone in a villa with only the nanny to entertain the children. 'No, we stayed at home this year,' she had replied to their questions, as if this were an act of astonishing originality.

Liberty slammed the car door shut and Jane turned

the car homewards, back to her useful life spent translating books to pay the fees for Liberty's horrid school
for spoilt brats. No, stop it, she chased the madness from
her head. The school had been chosen for good reasons,
and she worked not just for the money, but because she
enjoyed the mental stimulation, and working from home
gave her so much freedom.

Freedom to do what, exactly? This is what she wondered
as she parked the car and let herself into the house that
smelt of laundry and last night's dinner. Freedom to sit
alone in front of her computer? Freedom to let in the
gasman? Freedom to get ahead with preparing an interesting supper of sustainably farmed Norwegian cod?

Her brother Simon had been amused to hear about
her life.

'You've become a real home-bird,' he had said over
lunch at the V&A, 'and when I think how intimidated I
was by you. You were always the high-flyer.'

'Oh, rubbish,' she'd said, 'you've always been cleverer
than me.'

'But you were the A student. Mum was so proud of
you. She was proud of me, too, in the end, but you were
the steady performer.'

They had talked then about their mother, how glad
she had been to see Jane taking opportunities her generation had never had. The chance to walk out the front
door in a sharp suit and be clever all day. Earning the
money to pay someone less clever to come in and clear
things up at home.

Well, that was all over now and the sharp suits were
gathering dust in the wardrobe. In the best music-hall

tradition, she had turned into her mother, holding things together at home and doing the best she could for her daughter. Patterns repeated themselves.

Rupert rang at ten thirty. She pushed her chair back from the table and held the phone tightly to her ear in anticipation of the pleasure of seeing him again.

'Are you working?' he asked.

'Of course. You too?'

'Sort of. Richard's just gone out, so I can speak freely and tell you how much I HATE MY JOB!' He shouted the words and she giggled.

'Why don't we have lunch this time?' he said. 'I've never seen you eat, I think it could be sexy.'

'Wouldn't count on it, I'm a messy eater.'

'I remember a friend of mine left his wife because he couldn't stand watching her eat. It's something you need to clear up early on in a relationship.'

'We're not in a relationship, remember.'

'No, of course not. I've told Richard I'm having lunch with a prospect, so that's what you are.'

'Makes me sound like something out of *The Crucible*. Goody Prospect.'

'Do you know Racine? It's in the Brompton Road, opposite the V&A. French food in a rather stern setting, solemn rows of dark tables. The mussels in saffron broth are quite something.'

Three hours and a great deal of preparation later, Jane was able to agree with him that the saffron broth was indeed quite something. And so are you, she thought, seeing him again for the first time in three weeks. He said he was glad she agreed with him, and she noticed that when he smiled the skin around his eyes broke into laughter lines of unconditional enjoyment.

He was telling a story against himself now, about being the only unfashionable person in the hotel in the desert. 'I took the same shorts I always take on holiday, but everyone else was in a djallaba, leaving me to be the token fat Englishman.'

He couldn't care less about appearing gauche, very different from Will who would never invite ridicule by casting himself in an unflattering light.

'It was one of those minimalist hotels where you can never find the door handle or the light switch. Switches aren't aesthetic so they have to be hidden under a flat panel, apparently. So was the minibar: I had to press every bit of wall space before I found it.'

She should stop drawing comparisons, it wasn't fair. Of course it was more fun to listen to the stories of someone you barely knew rather than tread the familiar paths of conversation with the person you lived with. It was too easy to exaggerate or romanticise. She shouldn't read too much into it.

'I'm so happy to see you again,' she said. 'It's such a treat to meet for lunch . . .' She wanted to let him know that happiness was something that could be measured out in small doses, that it didn't require any life-changing decisions. 'It's all you can ask, isn't it?' she went on. 'Live each day as if it were your last, because one day it will be. And know that at least you had the saffron broth.'

Rupert was not prepared to play the game, he couldn't trivialise his feelings.

'It's no good,' he said. 'I don't think I can go through with it. This wedding business.'

Jane said nothing.

'Lydia's got it all worked out, even the menu. It seems we're going understated like Kate Winslet with champagne and bangers and mash, as I'm sure you were dying to know. It all seems so final, and I just don't see how I can. Not with the way I feel about you.'

She tore off a piece of bread and tried to be sensible. 'Don't say that,' she said. 'We hardly know each other, please don't bring me into this . . . we mustn't get serious.'

'I want to be serious . . .'

'No, you don't.'

'Yes, I do.'

He caught her hand across the table and the touch of him made her catch her breath. She shook her hand free, and sat back, reasonable, trying to calm things down.

'But it's not real, is it, you and me?' she said. 'It's just something we've dreamed up. I'm sure a shrink would say we are projecting our fantasies on each other, or transferring our longings, or whatever.'

'I don't care what a shrink would say. Anyway, that's what love is, isn't it? What else is it if it's not about projecting fantasies?'

'Love doesn't come into it. Love is what I have for my daughter. Unconditional love, of the throw-myself-under-a bus-for-her type.'

'And for Will?'

'Will is the father of my child.'

Though even as she spoke the words, she thought how unappealing they sounded. The sombre progenitor, the paterfamilias, the name filled in on a birth certificate. Why was she still with him?

'If I didn't know I was doing the right thing,' she said, 'I might feel sad.' She took a sip of water. 'Because I think that you and I could have been very happy together, in other circumstances. In fact, I'm sure we would. Much happier than I am with Will.'

She had said it. For the first time, she had admitted that her life with Will was not the fairytale she pretended it was. For ten years she had counted herself lucky to have him. Until recently, when she had come to see him in a different light.

'But you can't undo things,' she continued, 'and I can't wish I'd never met Will. I've loved him very much. He is Liberty's father, he's half of her, and I could never wish not to have loved him, that would be like wishing I hadn't had her. You must know, don't you, that I'll always put Liberty first. And especially, I would never break up my home. I couldn't inflict that on her.'

She was back in her own childhood now, remembering the moment when her mother had told her that Daddy was leaving them because he had met someone he preferred to her. Then Jane saying it wasn't true, that he couldn't possibly like anyone more than her. To Jane's childish mind it was out of the question that anyone could be preferable to her perfect mother.

Rupert was leaning forward now. 'People do split up, you know,' he said, 'even people with children. It happens all the time . . .'

No. She had to make it clear that this was out of the question.

'I know it's fashionable for couples to break up and tell the kids that whatever happens, they love them most of all. But that's not true, is it? If they loved their kids most of all, they'd stick together, even if they hated each other. They wouldn't just swan off with anyone they fancied.'

'I'm not talking of swanning off. You know that; please don't cheapen this.'

'But we need to be realistic. Whatever you decide to do about Lydia is up to you, but please don't bring me into the equation. I'm not available.'

He sat back in his seat.

'Except sometimes on weekday afternoons,' she added. 'Let's just enjoy it, shall we? It's not like anyone's died. Can't we just rewind to five minutes ago? Back to the fat man in the desert, I liked that bit.'

He smiled reluctantly. 'I still haven't told you about the fat man on the glacier,' he said. 'Reclining before an open fire in a hotel constructed entirely of ice.'

'Oh look, here comes our cassoulet.'

They stopped talking while the waiter placed two steaming bowls in front of them.

'I was imagining cooking a cassoulet for you, in my French house,' he said. 'It was when we'd just got back from holiday, I was thinking of having to go back to work, and I kept thinking of you, sitting in my kitchen . . . and I realised that was all I wanted.'

'It sounds so simple, doesn't it?' she said. 'But it's not. There's all the other stuff. We should just be glad to make the most of our time together.'

'So that's where we are, is it?' said Rupert when the waiter had gone. 'Two people in complicated mid-life situations who occasionally meet up to exchange laughter and comfort.'

'Sounds OK to me,' said Jane. '*Attached female, mid-thirties, loves gardening, food, French cinema – seeks male for occasional midweek sorties. No need to rock the boat.*'

'Have you ever placed a lonely-heart ad?'

'No. You?'

'No. That reminds me, I heard a great story about a bloke on a plane who was sifting through a pile of replies he'd had when he had advertised for a girlfriend. The guy sitting in the next seat bought the reject pile off him for fifty quid.'

She laughed. 'It might have worked out well, who knows? At least he would know they were all single girls looking for lurve.'

'I wish you were one of those.'

'Don't start that again.'

'I do, though. I wish I'd met you through a dating agency; that way you'd be available.'

'You wouldn't have joined a dating agency, you already had someone.'

'So did you.'

'Look, we're here, aren't we, so why not just enjoy it, leave all the other stuff at home. There's something to be said for the occasional treat – we don't have to put up with each other's nastier habits.'

'You sound like a bloke.'

'What do you mean?'

'It's usually men who compartmentalise their lives. Women are supposed to be all or nothing.'

'One compartment's better than nothing.'

'That's true,' he said, picking up his knife and fork, 'and anyway, it sounds like I don't have much choice.'

Part-time love is like social smoking: each occasion just makes you crave the next. When Rupert accepted there was no hope of them walking off into the sunset, it did nothing to diminish his feelings for Jane. He lived from one meeting to the next, feeding off the memory until they could see each other again. As he joked with her in Kew Gardens one rainy afternoon, this was courtly love, and he was the knight laying down the cloak of his devotion over the puddle of their daily lives. The impossibility of fruition lent an edgy sweetness to all their meetings.

Rupert felt bad about Lydia. Adultery would have been less of a betrayal than going to sleep every night with the image of Jane in his mind, less treacherous than confining his happiness to a small compartment of his life that had nothing to do with the woman he was going to marry.

He should call the wedding off, he knew that. But he felt paralysed, unable to act. Lydia had it all organised, and it made no difference to him. He couldn't have any more of Jane than he had now, so why not go along with it? At least Lydia was happy with the arrangement. He hoped his feelings might change, kept waiting to go off Jane; surely it must only be a matter of time before they tired of each other. He had considered putting an end to it, but the thought of not seeing her again made him feel entirely bleak, as though there really was nothing to live for. You had to take what you could from life, not kick aside opportunities for happiness.

These were Rupert's thoughts as he watched Lydia holding forth to their dinner guests about her design plans for the apartment. She was hosting a business dinner party for him, getting into practice as the perfect networking wife. The wife of a banker, that was, not the wife of a gardener. He was well aware of the motivation behind tonight's little dinner. Clive the butler had been hired to answer the door and take people's coats, though Rupert thought this unnecessary for eight people who were all in full possession of their faculties.

So far, they were just six in the drawing room, which had been decorated with lilies and a Chilean throw that did a reasonable job of disguising the beige sofa. Lydia had invited Marie-Helene de Montfort, the banker turned housewife who had invested in Rupert's fund after re-arranging the cancelled lunch which had thrown him together with Jane. Rupert's partner Richard was there with his wife Caroline, and then there was Mark, a morose but wealthy dotcom entrepreneur.

'I've commissioned an artist to come up with a humorous interpretation of Rupert's coat of arms,' Lydia was saying. 'We're looking for a mixed-media mural to run the length of the sitting room. He was quite taken with the demi lion rampant holding a fusil with a cock motif, he might introduce some sexual ambiguity there.' She fiddled with her engagement ring. Not quite a rock, but pretty damn near. Just this side of tastelessness. 'The important thing these days is to wear your ancestry lightly, send it up while at the same time celebrating its rich history.'

Watching her perform, Rupert remembered what a

good show she had put on that weekend they had driven down to East Hampton for dinner at his boss's beach house. Lydia had made them all laugh with her stories about shopping for shoes in Barneys, and Rupert's boss had told him afterwards how lucky he was to have a girl like that. Everyone enjoyed it so much they had stayed until 11.30, wildly late by American standards.

'How far back does your family actually go, Rupert?' asked Richard. He couldn't get enough of nobility, loved the idea of toffs dating back to a handful of dynasties, as opposed to tikes like himself who were spawned out of nothingness. His wife's distinguished family tree hung proudly in their own baronial entrance hall, but he had never bothered to trace his own. No point in finding out you were sprung from a parlourmaid and an illiterate coalman.

Rupert was reluctant to encourage this conversation. He didn't know what all the fuss was about.

'I daresay my family goes right back to the monkeys, same as everyone else's,' he said.

'There's a monkey on his coat of arms, actually,' said Lydia, 'standing between two chevron gules – that's red goats to you and me – and a bare-breasted woman with an ostrich plume. She's wearing a kirtle azure, which means blue skirt in Heraldic.'

'I, too, am from a noble family,' boasted Marie-Helene.

'*Noblesse de robe* or *noblesse d'épée*?' asked Richard. 'That's what you have, isn't it, for new and old nobility. Unlike me, I'm just new-money nobility. *Noblesse de filthy lucre!*' He grinned winningly, but the Frenchwoman didn't seem to think he deserved an answer.

Richard changed tack, he didn't want to offend her. 'How long have you been living here, Marie-Helene?' he asked.

'Six months,' she replied, 'in a tiny dolls' house in Chelsea. My husband can no longer bear to set foot in the salon, it is so small.'

'You should move out to the country,' said Caroline, 'plenty of space out our way.'

Marie-Helene looked at her as though she were from another planet. Parisians understood that the country was for weekends and holidays, certainly no place for a smart woman to bury herself away. 'No, I am not a provincial person,' she said, 'although I must say London is like a third-world city. How can you live in a place where they only collect the garbage twice a week? I walk down my street and all I smell is old meat rotting in the dustbins. What are we supposed to do with our chicken carcasses between Friday and Tuesday? Tell me that.'

'Boil them up and make glue?' suggested Richard.

Marie-Helene scowled at him. 'I am surprised you do not have the plague here,' she said, 'and finding fresh vegetables, it is impossible, I have to drive all the way to Borough Market just to get some decent salad . . .'

'She's right there,' whispered Mark, 'it's a bloody disgrace, this country.'

Clive the butler moved in to top up the glasses. It got on Rupert's nerves, having him hovering in the background, dressed up to the nines in his dicky bow and tails when all the guests were wearing what his years in the States had taught him to refer to as smart-casual. All except Caroline, who never came out without a stiff bit of taffeta to hold her together.

'And then the maid was away so I went to the supermarket myself,' Marie-Helene went on. 'I filled my chariot and when I got to the checkout I said it was for delivery and they said they didn't do deliveries and offered to call me a taxi! Of course, I walked out.'

'Why don't you go back to Paris, then?' said Mark. 'It's got to be better than here.'

Marie-Helene puffed in disapproval. 'Even in Paris, things have become terrible. It's the same everywhere now, nobody understands good service.'

It was a miracle how she managed to get out of bed of a morning, Rupert thought.

'I know what you mean,' said Mark, 'you can't even get a decent hotel these days. Whenever I come back from the Cipriani or Parrot Cay and ask myself, yeah, but was it really, *really* special, I have to be honest and say, no, it wasn't.' He nibbled at an olive then removed it from his mouth to stare at it critically.

'I don't know what you're on about,' boomed Caroline. 'We've had some marvellous hotel holidays, and there's nothing I like better than loading up at Sainsbury's and bringing it all home to the kitchen.'

The final guest was Dr Firth, the handsome psychologist, who was shown in with more than servantly interest by Clive. Lydia had invited him along as light relief; she couldn't tolerate a whole room of money people, and the good thing about a posh shrink was that he could move up and down the social spectrum. More importantly, he could be relied on to keep her entertained. His *pièce de résistance* was demonstrating a panic attack, taking a series of deep, short breaths and slowly rising from his seat as they crescendoed faster and faster to a gasping finale.

'Good God, Andrew, you sound like you're having sex,' said Lydia. Clive looked up from serving the individual lemon tarts, which were garnished with raspberries. He must have been distracted by Dr Firth's performance, because when Rupert came to eat his dessert he noticed that a couple of stray baby new potatoes had found their way in among the fruit.

In bed that night, Rupert was consumed by self-loathing. I am a coward, he thought, as he lay beside Lydia in a post-coital cocoon of separateness and stared at the ceiling. I am a coward, and a bastard, and a liar. A more sensitive person than Lydia might have realised that his heart was no longer in it, that he no longer cared about the sex and the wedding plans and all the rest. Yet Lydia seemed entirely impervious, blissfully locked into her own sweet existence that was going entirely to plan.

'I'm so glad you talked me out of moving,' she said in the dark. 'You were quite right about my flirtation with the hot tub, it was ridiculous. Much more sensible to stay here, especially now the maximalist décor is really coming together.' She shifted in the bed, unable to sleep with everything that was churning in her brain. 'The castle is booked and I've got a fantastic calligrapher lined up to write the invitations, she did Madonna's wedding. So the only thing left to settle now is the honeymoon.'

Rupert stared upwards in a misery of indifference.

'I had wondered about the new hotel in Antigua by the people who did One Aldwych, but then it was all over the Sunday supplements, and I realised that that is the whole problem. You can't find anywhere these days that's not overrun by people you frankly wouldn't choose to have lying on the next sun-lounger. But then I came across a solution.'

She propped herself up on one elbow and leaned over her honeymoon companion, the one who would be paying for it all. There was no shame in it; she considered he was getting excellent value for money. Like those infuriating women in the L'Oréal ads, she was worth it.

'There's this travel club that operates out of New York,' she went on. 'Normally there's a waiting list but I know someone who can get me in. You pay a fifteen thousand dollar joining fee, then five thousand dollars a year membership, and they find you places to stay that aren't listed in any brochures.'

'So you still have to pay for the holiday on top of that?'

'Of course. But at least you know there won't be any dorks at the next table who read about it in a magazine.'

Maybe now was the moment, thought Rupert. He should tell her that actually he had been thinking that it wasn't an awfully good idea for them to get married after all. He'd been having doubts for a while, and now that he'd fallen in love with her old school friend, it really was out of the question.

Instead, he said: 'It's late, let's talk about it in the morning.'

In the morning he would think of something, or a *deus ex machina* would intervene and sort it out without him needing to take action. A freak earthquake would swallow Lydia up or she would be coated with fairy dust and fall for someone else. Then a flying carpet would carry him and Jane to a turreted eastern city, leaving their old lives behind them.

Oh well, thought Lydia, at least he's not saying no.

'I thought we could go to France for Easter,' she said as a palliative, 'keep the costs down'. That should please him, there wasn't much to spend your money on over there. 'We could invite some friends,' she went on, 'maybe Jane and Will. She's such a good friend to me, in a wholesome sort of way. And Will can be good fun as long as you don't take him too seriously.'

Jane come to France with them? Could fate really be serving him up such a delicious proposition? Rupert lay still in the dark, quietly scheming, getting to grips with this new possibility. Jane would have lunch in his kitchen just as he had dreamed, wearing her jacket that matched his tablecloth. He could show her his garden, just as he had planned it. The only difference was, she would be there with Will, and he would be with Lydia. The redundant partners, the spoilers, the flies in the soup. Even so, there was no way he was going to knock it on the head.

'Yes,' he said, in a voice that was over-casual, 'Jane and Will seemed very nice. Why don't you ask them?'

TWELVE

Sunday afternoon found Jane and Will and Liberty in one of those so-called communal gardens that are hidden away in the snobbier parts of London. You might think from the name that these were democratic pleasure grounds for all-comers, but nothing could be further from the truth. In fact they were strictly private, for keyholders only, while everyone else remained outside, noses pressed against the railings. The keeper of the keys was invariably someone who spoke like Prince Charles and got very snooty about what you could and couldn't do in the gardens.

One thing you were allowed to do in Ladbroke Gardens was hold a children's birthday party. Liberty had been invited by her school friend Lolly to take part in a teddy bear's picnic. Five hundred chocolate teddy bears had been hidden among the bushes, and the children were supposed to find as many as they could before returning to Lolly's house to watch a troupe of acrobats and a three-man magic show, followed by tea, when someone from a well-known boy band would be singing 'Happy

Birthday'. As these things went, it was really rather modest.

Will didn't normally stoop to attending children's parties, but he was making an exception since he vaguely knew the birthday girl's father from university. Mark Thomas was one of those old-fashioned northern meritocrats who had climbed out of grimness, encouraged by a self-taught father who read improving books when he got back from the pit. He won his grammar-school place and Cambridge scholarship in the days when education was still the poor child's passport to success. After a stint at the BBC, Mark had become a hugely successful thriller writer. Like Will, he was on to his second family, and like Will, he remained a socialist. It was galling that Mark had earned enough from his middlebrow books to buy himself a cavernous house in Notting Hill even after the cost of a divorce, but Will forgave him. At least being less rich left him the intellectual high-ground.

They stood talking together now, the travel writer and the thriller tart, grey-haired old dads, watching the children running around, stuffing the teddy bears into party bags, their eyes alight with greed.

'Little beggars,' said Mark. 'How many have you got now, Will?'

'Three,' he said, 'two boys and a girl. Jane was keen to have more, but I told her, "It's all right for you to say that, but don't forget I've already been there."'

'Tell me about it,' said Mark, nodding in sympathy over women and their outrageous demands. 'I was a softer touch than you, though, I've got seven. Wouldn't be without them, mind.'

Will watched Jane coming towards them, holding some evergreen leaves and bark samples that she had stripped off the trees. She always did that when she visited gardens, she liked to take home samples and identify them from a large guide to trees that she kept by the bed, like a nerdy girl-guide with her stamp collection. Will found it rather sweet. She was wearing a long cream sweater-coat that she had found in a charity shop and a cloche hat that made her look young and vulnerable. He introduced her to his friend, and was pleased to see the gleam in Mark's eyes.

'Thank you for inviting Liberty,' she said. 'I do envy you this garden, but I am rather mystified. For all the cultural diversity everyone claims for Notting Hill, I can see nothing but white people in here.'

'Good God, Jane,' said Will, embarrassed, 'I do wish you wouldn't talk like my grandmother. People aren't identified by their colour any more. Anyway, that's nonsense.' He gazed around, trying to prove her wrong. 'Look, there you go, over there!'

A black man had just arrived through the gate and was being greeted by everyone he passed.

'Ah, yes, that's our piano teacher,' said Mark, 'he's a great guy, knows everyone.'

Poor bloke, thought Jane, he couldn't get a moment's peace with all that lot fighting over him.

Her phone rang, and she stepped back to answer it.

'Only *moi*,' said Lydia. 'Where are you? I'm lying butt-naked on a slab with my acupuncturist.'

So beat that if you can. Even on a Sunday afternoon Lydia liked to be competitive.

'Good job I haven't got a video phone then. I'm in Ladbroke Gardens as it happens.'

'Listen, we were talking about Easter and we wondered if you and Will would like to come and join us in France. We'll be staying at Rupert's house in the South.'

Jane was lost for words as her secret world came ebbing dangerously close to her real life. She had seen Rupert just two days ago and he hadn't said anything. They had walked over the bridge to the Tate Modern to see a weather installation, hanging like a luminous orange cloud. She couldn't imagine spending several days together with him and Will and Lydia, she wasn't sure she was up to that.

'Hallo? Jane, can you hear me?'

It must be the house with the check tablecloth, thought Jane. The one he had told her about, with the iron gates and the green shutters and the garden where he grew his Beale's roses. He must have put Lydia up to this, he must have told her to invite them. What was he playing at?

'That would be nice,' she said guardedly, fiddling with a piece of silver-birch bark that she had picked earlier, and dropping pieces of it onto the ground. 'We'd obviously have to bring Liberty,' she added.

Dammit, thought Lydia, she'd forgotten about the child. She turned to restrain the acupuncturist who was being a little too intrusive with his needles.

'Sorry Jane,' she said, returning to her phone, 'Sami was getting a bit carried away. Of course you can bring Liberty if you want, but doesn't she have to go to school?'

'Not at Easter.'

'No, I suppose not.'

Lydia thought quickly. It would be churlish to withdraw the invitation, and one child wasn't going to ruin things, was it? It could just play in the garden, or watch telly. It might even work in her favour to prove to Rupert what a bore it was having children. He seemed to be hoping for them to start a family right away. Or he used to be, he hadn't mentioned it recently.

'Right, that's settled then,' she said.

'I'll need to check with Will,' said Jane, 'I don't know how he's placed . . .' Although she could guess that Easter with Rupert would not figure high on Will's list of things to do before he died.

'Oh, don't you worry, he'll be up for it,' said Lydia. She was sure that Will would want to come; she could tell he still fancied her from the way he had flirted with her at the party, kissing her goodbye on the neck just below her ear to prove he still remembered her favourite places. It would be good to have a frisson running as an undercurrent. Anything to break the monotony of a week *a deux* in the French countryside. 'Let me know then,' she continued, 'quite soon if you would, so I can wheel in some replacements if you can't make it. I don't want to be stuck out there with only my fiancé for company, darling though he is. After all, I've got a lifetime of that heading my way.'

Jane felt a stab of jealousy. She wished she had a lifetime of Rupert to look forward to, she couldn't think of anything nicer. It was clear she would be accepting the invitation, she couldn't throw up the chance of spending a whole week with him, even in such strange circumstances. 'I'll call you back,' she said.

Jane put her phone away and walked back to join the men. 'Time to go back for tea, I reckon,' said Mark. 'I'll get Vanessa to herd them up.' He wandered off to help his wife, a tiny blonde thing chosen to complement his own rugged physique. Will turned to wait for Jane.

'That was Lydia on the phone,' said Jane, thinking she might as well broach the subject right away, 'inviting us to Provence for Easter. Rupert's got a house there, apparently.'

'Is he going too?'

'Of course, they're engaged.'

'Engaged! At their age, I ask you. It's quite grotesque, like they're a blushing couple of teenagers.'

'So, what do you think?' she asked.

'What do you think I think?'

'I don't know, that's why I'm asking.'

He pretended to ponder the question. 'Let me see, Easter, springtime, when a travel writer's thoughts turn to journeys, to undiscovered lands . . . or else to a banker's anodyne second home that is bound to epitomise the worst style tendencies of Provençale life. I'd say it was a bit of a no-brainer, wouldn't you?'

Jane decided to appeal to his well-developed sense of meanness. 'It's a cheap option to take Liberty on a week's holiday.'

He thought about it again. He'd be off soon on his proper travels. And at least Lydia could be entertaining. They might even find an opportunity to relive old times: why not, it might be fun, and he would enjoy getting one over on the banker. Maybe he'd give her a call next week, meet her for lunch and see how the land lay.

'Fair enough,' he said, 'you can tell her we'll come.'

*   *   *

'So,' said Jane to Rupert on the phone a few days later, 'I finally get to see your house in France.'

They were supposed to be meeting up later at the sir John Soane Museum, but she couldn't wait to speak to him.

'I told you I'd take you there one day,' he said, swivelling round in his office chair so he didn't have to look at Richard, 'but it wasn't my idea to invite you both. Lydia thought you'd be good company. I couldn't argue with that, though I'm not sure old Sinbad would be my first choice of holiday companion.'

He took a sip of water from the bottle on his desk; just thinking about Will made Rupert go hot under the collar. He always referred to him as Sinbad now, demonising him as an old sea-bandit.

'So it wasn't your idea, then?' said Jane. 'I wondered what you were up to . . .'

'I know what I'd like to be up to,' he muttered quietly, checking to make sure Richard wasn't listening in, 'I'd like us to be going there, just the two of us.'

'Never mind . . .'

'What do you mean, never mind? We can't go on like this, you know that.'

Jane doodled on an envelope. She knew he was right, but she didn't want to hear it. 'We'll talk about it later,' she said. 'Are you still all right for this afternoon?'

Rupert saw Richard was off the phone and waiting to talk to him. 'Of course,' he said, more calmly. 'What are you doing now?'

'Working. And thinking about my garden. I'm going to

plant a hot summer-bed, with only yellow and orange flowers.'

'Are you? I hope you're going to include geum borisii, gorgeous deep orange flower, hummocky green foliage . . .'

'It's on the list.'

'Coreopsis verticillata is very striking. And Gertrude Jekyll was very keen on using dwarf evening primroses with geum borisii, you could back it with some purple leaves, like stinking hellebore.'

'Too tasteful, I'm only going for the really bright stuff. I want it to be truly garish!'

'African marigolds then. Yellow Climax, with double, globular flowers, you can't get more garish than that!'

Richard was standing beside his desk now.

'Got to go,' said Rupert in a businesslike voice, 'I'll see you later.'

Jane hung up and pushed aside her gardening books. She was translating a book on Lacan now, a French psycho-analyst feted by the the *soixante-huit* generation, a kind of Freud for hippies. She was just getting to grips with the Hysterical Discourse when the doorbell rang. Probably someone selling dusters. Will told her to ignore them, but she felt sorry for them, cold-calling like that, trying to sell stuff at twice what you'd pay at the supermarket.

She opened the door and looked up to see Rupert, standing big in the doorway, arms crossed.

'What are you doing here?' she whispered in delight, looking round to see if anyone was watching. She didn't even know her neighbours' names, though, so they were hardly going to snitch on her. 'We're supposed to meet later, at the museum.'

'I just had to see you.'

'You're mad. How did you know Will wasn't here?'

'A hunch. Anyway, I knew it would be you who answered the door. Can I come in?'

'I don't know . . . I suppose so.'

He grinned. 'Very gracious of you. So this is your home. You've seen mine, but I've not seen yours, it's only fair.'

He stepped into the hall and she closed the door behind him. It was odd seeing him there by the Perspex balustrade, out of his setting. For a moment she thought he was going to sweep her up in his arms and ravish her there and then, but he just said, 'Which way to the garden?'

She pointed down the stairs and followed him into the kitchen.

'Your office,' he said with a smile, looking at her computer and the messy pile of books, then opening the French windows.

'Behind the shed, right?' he said, walking outside and down the path until he came to the hot bed, newly dug over and marked with wooden sticks. 'I just wanted to check the site, you have to be careful about drainage for coreopsis, and they prefer some shelter. But that's OK, you've done your homework.' He looked up. 'You can invite me in for a drink now, before we go out to lunch.'

'Are we still going to the museum?'

'Of course. I never break a date.'

In the kitchen, Jane took a bottle of wine from the fridge and uncorked it. She felt clumsy and self-conscious, it was mean of him to sneak up on her like that when she wasn't expecting him. She hadn't even got changed yet, but maybe her pyjamas could be passed off as a tracksuit.

She poured out two glasses and threw him a packet of Wotsits. 'I'll just go and get ready,' she said, 'don't answer the phone or anything, will you?'

Rupert sipped his wine and started flicking through the book on Lacan. 'Don't worry about me,' he replied. 'If anyone comes I'll just hide in the garden shed.'

She left him to it and went up to the bathroom, stepping out of her pyjamas and into her underwear, then a brown wool suit, nothing flashy. As she applied her make-up in the mirror, she kept expecting him to appear behind her. If he came up now, she would have no choice, he would have forced her hand. It would be out of her control, unplanned, just one of those things she never meant to happen. She applied a peachy blusher; still no sign. Then an apricot lipstick. She wished he would.

He's not coming, she thought as she applied her mascara, listening out for his step on the stairs. If he hasn't come by the time I've brushed my hair, I'll know he's not coming.

Down the stairs she went, demure, correct, hair in a good-girl neat bun.

'Hi,' he said, looking up from his book, at ease as though he were in his own kitchen. 'Is it me, or is this Lacan fellow seriously weird?'

'He's weird,' Jane agreed, 'very hung up on language, it's like because "je veux" sounds like "cheveux", he reckons that hair is an expression of desire.'

'But only if you're French.'

'Exactly. Shall we go then?'

Rupert stood up. 'That's a nice coat,' he said, nodding towards her fitted jacket.

She smiled. 'Normally we call this a jacket,' she said, 'coats tend to be bigger.'

He shrugged. 'As you know, clothes aren't my bag. I just meant you looked lovely, that's all.'

She blushed.

'Shall we leave by separate entrances?' he suggested. 'I could escape through the back gardens.'

'Don't be stupid.'

She wished he had been stupid, that he had carried her away so she didn't have to think about the consequences.

He followed her out to the car.

'I'm going to park near the school,' she said, 'then we can get a bus.'

'Fine by me.' He got into the passenger side and put an expansive arm round the back of her seat. 'I'm putty in your hands,' he teased, 'just do with me what you will. And meanwhile I shall enjoy taking in your profile, which I don't often have the opportunity to admire.' He saw a straight temple, a gentle retrousse nose and lips that curved into a firmer line than you noticed from the front.

She glanced sideways at him as she pulled out. 'Stop it, you're embarrassing me.'

'All right.' He looked ahead instead. 'So, a week together in Provence. Who'd have predicted that? What does Will think about it?'

'He's keen for us to go now there might be some money

in it. I've set up a meeting with a French comedian who's looking for a translator. He's at La Garde Freinet, not far from you. I'm going to see him on the Tuesday. Leaving you free to bond with Will. You never know, you might become best buddies.'

Rupert pulled a face.

'At least we'll get to see each other every day,' she said.

He stared stonily ahead. 'And how do you think that will make me feel? Knowing you're there, but not for me.'

'It's what we agreed, remember,' she said gently. 'The point is that we can do this, we can go on holiday all together, because we haven't let things . . . develop. It is perfectly within the bounds of our friendship.'

'Friendship!' He laughed. 'I feel like that Victorian painting, *The Long Engagement*, with the po-faced vicar standing next to the girl he's supposed to marry in about fifty years once he's saved up . . . I tell you what, why don't you just stick me in a frame and hang me up in that museum we're going to? It's where I belong.'

Three hours later they were saying goodbye at Holborn tube.

'That museum's fabulous, isn't it?' said Jane. 'Makes you want to turn back the years and become a Victorian collector. Though obviously with access to antibiotics.'

'I suppose I could have been, if I'd been born earlier,' said Rupert, 'like my grandfather: he filled our house in the country with a whole load of paintings and stuff he bought on his travels.'

'Yet here you are in the twenty-first century with your

hedge fund. It still makes me think of cockerels cut out of privet. Or a row of beech edging a green field, or box plants edging a herb garden.'

'I wish.'

'Don't you miss being able to go to your country house, though?' she asked. 'It must feel odd, having it rented out to strangers.'

'Yes and no,' he said. 'It's quite a bind, a big house like that, it comes with a terrible sense of duty. And memories of being by myself in the school holidays – I'd look forward to coming home at the end of term, and then be enormously bored when I got there. And I don't see the point of having forty-seven rooms when you can only be in one at a time. You end up sitting in one room and worrying about what needs doing in all the others. I prefer a simpler life.'

'I'm not sure Lydia would agree,' said Jane. 'I don't think "simple" features among her life goals.'

'That's true, but then she hates the country, except for the snob value of me having a country seat. It suits her the way it is, rented out. But you're right, a simple life is not what she's about, very far from it. Lydia likes her life to be as crammed and as complicated and filled with stuff as it can be. Which is her charm, of course, all that energy. Saving me from my simple tendencies to wear drab clothes and stay at home. But let's not talk about my fiancée.'

'No.'

'Better get back to work.'

'Me too.'

He couldn't bring himself to leave. 'Have you ever thought of stopping work?' he asked.

'Do I get the impression you're looking for an excuse to avoid going back to the office?'

'Of course.'

'Not really. I like it and I need the money. I couldn't spend my life hanging round tile shops or looking for the ultimate sofa. And if I didn't work, my daughter would become the entire focus of my life, which isn't fair on her.'

'No.' He kicked a stone against the gutter. 'Listen, Jane, I haven't told Lydia this, but I'm thinking of starting up a business. Exporting plants to France and offering a gardening service. You know how envious the French are of English gardens, and they really don't have a clue about garden design, apart from formal rigid box-beds in front of classical chateaux. All their best gardens have been done by Englishmen. The typical self-made French affair is a wall of evergreen enclosing a dull expanse of grass they call a *parc* with a solitary clump of pampas grass stuck in the middle.'

'I think that sounds wonderful. But you'll have to be a little more tactful if you want to get their business.'

'Oh, I will, but it's a growing market over there, they're gagging to be shown how to do it.'

'And this new business, would you run it from France?'

'Yes.'

'So you wouldn't be living in London?'

'No.'

There would be no more Friday-afternoon trysts. She wouldn't see him any more.

'I see,' she said.

* * *

While Rupert and Jane were talking over his plans for a new business, Lydia was putting in a rare appearance at the office. It wasn't necessary to be there, she could just as easily research her articles at home, but it was important to show her face once in a while. She especially enjoyed leaving early, reminding those obliged to stay behind that she got to choose her own hours.

So Will was lucky to catch her there when he rang the magazine. He no longer had her mobile number, it was years since they had been on intimate phone terms.

'Will, what a surprise!' she bellowed at him, for the benefit of the girls sitting at desks around her. It was important here to speak loudly on the phone, to sound confident and as if you knew everyone.

He had forgotten about that grating voice, and was momentarily put off. The last time he'd seen her had been at the engagement party when the general noise level would have flattened the sound of a foghorn. But what the hell, it would be fun.

'I'm just round the corner,' he said, 'and thought you might fancy joining me for a drink.'

She looked at her watch: it was 12.45.

'Still as mean as ever I see,' she said. 'I won't meet you for a drink but I might take you up on lunch. Although I don't want to push you into wanton extravagance when you should be saving up for our Easter holiday.'

'All right then, lunch,' said Will, smiling down the phone. 'I'm in the Soho wine bar.'

Will looked up as Lydia came in five minutes later, turning a few heads with her striking red hair. She certainly knew how to make an entrance, and her dress sense was terrific. Unlike Jane, who seemed to be getting less and less interested in clothes.

'Ha-llo,' he said, raising an ironic Cary Grant eyebrow.

'Hallo to you, Will,' she replied, sitting down opposite him as he poured her a glass of wine. 'This is all a bit of a surprise. May I ask to what I owe the pleasure?'

He sniffed the gooseberry high notes of his wine before replying, 'Do I need a reason? As Pascal so eloquently put it, "Man is born for pleasure: he feels it, no further proof is needed". Or in French, "*L'homme est ne pour le plaisir: il le . . .*".'

'All right, all right, no need to show off. I see you're still doing a good job of playing Mr Boasty. Cheers!'

They clinked glasses.

'You obviously believe I still have something to boast about,' he said. 'Why else would you have invited me to your fiancé's clichéd holiday home in the sun? What I'm really curious to know is whether it is my fine conversation you are after, or something more . . . primal.'

Lydia threw her head back and laughed. 'Oh, I see,' she said. 'You've invited me today to see if you can prearrange a little bit of "how's your father" for the Easter holidays. The answer's no.'

He shrugged. 'Pity. But it was worth a try.'

'I'm engaged now, you know.'

'Oh don't worry,' he said, 'I've no intention of snatching the ageing bride from the altar, far from it. I was merely proposing some light relief from the rather stolid charms of your betrothed. Or are you going to tell me he's dynamite in the sack?'

'I'm not going to tell you any of my bedroom secrets, if it's all the same to you.'

'Fine,' he said, picking up the menu. 'Shall we order?'

'And I might remind you that Jane is my oldest friend.'

'Didn't stop you before.'

'That was when I was going through a turbulent time.'

'Beautifully turbulent, as I recall . . .'

The waiter came to take their order and Lydia made a point of choosing from the upper end of the menu. She folded her arms as if in defence of her position, as though further justification were necessary. 'Rupert's a lovely guy,' she said, 'and he is a proper gentleman, in the best sense of the word.'

'Don't give me that *Burke's Landed Gentry* bollocks,' said Will. 'Ghastly jumped-up types, most of those phoney crests were only invented in the 1960s, you shouldn't be taken in by the latin mottos and rampant demi-lions.'

'His goes back to the seventeenth century, actually. But I'm not talking about that. I mean he's a nice, considerate person.'

The words flopped damply onto the table. 'Nice' and 'considerate' were not big on sex appeal, bringing to mind bearded men who worked in the social services. She moved swiftly on. 'And, yes, he does give me a . . . certain lifestyle. And financial security.'

That marvellous euphemism. She loved it the same way she loved all those other words: cash, liquid assets, bonds, global macro returns. 'Incubator funds' was one of her favourites: tiny, fragile bits of premature money, hot-housed to grow into full maturity. Thinking of Rupert's vast sums of money never failed to perk her up and quell the doubts that occasionally reared their ugly heads, whispering *was she sure about this marriage*? She sometimes wondered if he wasn't a bit staid for her, a bit slower off the mark than she was, a little bit *boring*, even. Though the word only had to creep into her mind before it was immediately discarded. It was too easy to dismiss someone as boring, and anyway, what did that say about her? Would Lydia Littlewood become engaged to someone who was a bit boring? Of course not.

'So, to answer your question,' she continued, 'the reason I invited you and Jane to come on holiday with us was as friends, for intelligent company. It takes a suspicious mind like yours to look for an ulterior motive.'

'Not so much suspicious as hopeful.'

He wondered what it would be like to make love to her again. There was a particular pleasure in rediscovering an ex, a comforting mix of nostalgia for the good times and the fresh excitement of a new conquest. It was like revisiting a city you hadn't seen for a few years, familiar yet stamped by the passage of time. Lydia didn't look as though she would disappoint; she hadn't yet reached the age when the damage kicked in for women.

'I must come clean,' she said, 'and admit I completely forgot about your daughter when I invited you. I hope she won't be bored, there's nothing for her to do there. Mind you, there's nothing for adults to do either, apart from gaze at the hills and buy olives, it's not exactly St Tropez. I would say bring the nanny to keep her entertained except you haven't got one.'

'Don't worry about Liberty,' said Will, 'she'll be happy enough, and Jane's a very hands-on mother. A bit too much, I sometimes think. Always a temptation for women, to immerse themselves in their children and lose sight of themselves. I saw it happen with my ex-wife, and now I'm afraid Jane's going rather the same way.'

He thought about Jane frowning behind her computer at the kitchen table, surrounded by piles of ironing and dictionaries, wearing her old cardigan as she toiled her way through the psychology textbook she was currently translating. Quite different from the woman who was sitting opposite him now, chic and brightly dressed, with the sharp sexiness that comes with a healthy ego.

'Liberty's rather like me in many ways,' he went on, 'she has a very strong personality.'

Lydia pulled a face. 'That's one thing that really gets on my nerves about parents,' she said. 'They always claim their kids have got strong personalities. I'm never really sure what it means, anyway, a strong personality.'

'It means she knows her own mind and has an enquiring intelligence. As I said, she's a chip off the old block!' He smiled in acknowledgement of his own fabulousness.

'You really think you're something, don't you?' said Lydia. Seeing him sitting there so pleased with himself, she thought how unlike Rupert he was. Rupert hated to be the centre of attention, and was almost dysfunctionally modest. It had seemed exotic when she'd first met him in New York. Compared to the American men who wasted no time in giving you their full CV and list of selling points, he appeared to be an advertisement for bumbling English understatement. 'Oh, I'm just a gorilla with a calculator,' he had said when she asked him what he did. The moment she'd got home she had run a Dun

& Bradstreet check on his credit-rating and found out that he was doing extremely well for a gorilla. Even without taking into account his family money.

Now they were back in the UK, his modesty seemed mundane, verging on defeatism. She missed that American confidence, that energising feeling that you could become whatever you wanted. Looking across at Will, she got a sense of that energy.

'We're two of a kind, Lydia,' he said, 'which is why we could never live together. We're both hungry for experience. I'm not cut out for a quiet life of conjugal bliss any more than you are.'

Lydia pretended to be shocked. 'That's no way to talk to a girl on the verge of getting married.'

'Don't worry,' he said, 'I know what that wedding's about. You have a fine business head on those pretty shoulders. Which I seem to remember were always shown to advantage above a décolletage.'

She obligingly slipped off her jacket to reveal a burgundy plunge neckline that made the most of her sculpted shoulder-blades. This holiday might prove to be more fun than she had expected.

THIRTEEN

In the Easyjet departure lounge of Gatwick airport, Will was acting snooty. So what if the tickets cost a fraction of what you'd pay for a decent flight? There were some things in life that you didn't stoop to, and that included no-frills airlines. He sipped his filthy coffee, piss-thin in a polystyrene cup, and glanced around him at the horrid evidence of democratisation gone mad. Who on earth had decided that Joe Public should be able to travel to Marseille for £15.99? Where did that leave the mystery and romance of travel? The world was a better place when only a tiny elite could think of boarding a plane, before mass tourism had opened up abroad to the great unwashed.

'I don't know why you didn't book Air France,' he complained to Jane. He liked the Air France hostesses, they were the only ones who understood service, all icy politeness and expensive perfume. They knew how to keep their distance, unlike the girls on British Airways with their infuriating perky familiarity and sing-song voices. Though BA would be far preferable to what he was enduring today. Easyjet: the very name was enough to make you heave, never mind the bilious orange logo.

'I told you, if you want to pay the difference, that's fine with me,' said Jane.

He didn't reply. Family holidays came out of her budget, and he wasn't going to start forking out for that as well as everything else. He wasn't made of money, not like bloody Rupert with his rampant demi-lions and multiple homes.

'You could have got a later flight at least,' he said at last, 'you know I'm not a morning person.'

'The six forty was cheaper,' said Jane crisply, hating him for making her sound like a prim penny-pincher, 'and it makes the most of our holiday.'

'I want to go to the toilet,' said Liberty, looking up from her comic.

Jane stood up to go with her, leaving Will to sulk over his newspaper. She looked back at him, cross and out of sorts, his battered briefcase lying on his lap like a badge of intellectual superiority.

During take-off, Liberty stared out of the window in fascination at the receding landscape while Jane squeezed her daughter's hand tightly and tried not to think about air disasters. She had never heard of an Easyjet plane crashing, and there was no reason why that should change today. Once they were up above the clouds, Liberty plugged herself into her Discman like a miniature teenager, and sat back with her eyes closed, quite at ease in this modern world that was constantly on the move.

The sight of her daughter made Jane happy. She stroked

the back of Liberty's hand, running her fingers over the thin white line above the wrist where she had been stitched after falling from her bike. She had a parent's intimate knowledge of her child, could identify the precise location of the chicken-pox scars behind her knees and the mole on her back, the way her second toe grew longer than the first. But, in a few years, her daughter would grow tall and leave home. She would no longer require her mother's cosseting, except perhaps when things went wrong, when someone let her down, when she had her own child.

And then what? Would Jane settle down to a comfortable old age with Will, who at this moment was sitting beside her, writing in the leather-bound notebook that he never travelled without. She found it impossible to imagine how it would be when they no longer had Liberty at home. Perhaps they might move house, to something smaller back in Notting Hill, or maybe to the country. If things went well, they might be able to afford both. To be honest, she really didn't care.

She closed her eyes to sleep and thought about Rupert. He would be waiting for them, having arrived last night with Lydia to open up the house. She couldn't wait for him to show her the garden, the kitchen, the view from the terrace as he had described it to her. She had a picture of it in her head that was already tinged with nostalgia, filled with regret for the life with him she might have had if things had been different.

The plane touched down on time and in bright sunshine. Jane unfastened Liberty's seat belt and gently shook her awake.

'Mercifully short, at least,' said Will, standing up and stretching his arms behind his head. 'Do you realise you couldn't get from Shepherds Bush to Soho in a taxi for the price of that flight? It does make you wonder what's wrong with the world.' Half an hour later he stood apart, looking pained in his crumpled linen suit, while Jane and Liberty queued at the car-hire desk.

Outside, it was warm, the kind of spring day that makes British people wonder why they don't move to the South of France. The kind of spring day that makes so many decide to do that very thing.

'Not exactly Scott and Zelda, is it?' Will said as they got into the Fiat Multipla, which was shaped like a frog, with three seats spread across the front row. 'Bloody ridiculous thing, what on earth made you choose this?'

'It was on special offer.'

There was a brief tussle when Liberty was denied the extra front seat on safety grounds and strapped into the back, then Will was issued with a road map while Jane got behind the wheel.

'We need to head for Aix on the A51, then the A8 going east,' she said.

Will sighed. A Fiat Multipla on special offer from Avis rent-a-car, it wasn't exactly poetry. He wished he was back in the 1920s, winding his way down through the mountains in a curvy open-top sports car, catching glimpses of the Mediterranean, sparkling blue through the grey-green Cézanne landscape. That was before the Côte d'Azur was ruined. At least they were heading inland and would be spared the excesses of coastal development.

He checked the map then shook his head in disapproval.

'We should have flown to Nice instead of Marseille, it makes far more sense. We could have stayed for longer on the motorway, it would have saved us at least an hour.'

'It's about the same, I checked on the map.' She was sick of the way Will left all the planning to her and then criticised the end result. She would like to be the one relaxing in the passenger seat, offering her opinion on his choice of route.

'You need to take that turn-off,' he said half an hour later, as they whizzed past the motorway exit.

'You could give me a bit more notice!' said Jane. 'I'll have to go on to the next one now.'

'I thought you knew we wanted the D560 for Barjols. There's no need to shoot the messenger, I'm merely pointing out that you appear to have missed the turning.'

Once they were off the motorway, the road began to twist and turn, heading up into the hills through a series of villages, backed by forests and rolling hills. It was surprisingly green, and danced in the sunlight, which was coming through strongly now the morning mists had lifted. It was quite enchanting, and even Will didn't find anything to complain about, in spite of his best attempts to pick out evidence of tourist pollution.

The best he could manage was foreign numberplates. 'Look at that,' he said, as they drove through a particularly charming village. 'Dutch cars, Belgian cars, and of course the ubiquitous British. I don't suppose there's any such thing now as a real French village. Did you know the French call us *Les GBs* after our car stickers?'

'Yes, I did actually,' said Jane, irritated. 'You may recall that I have a degree in modern languages and also work as a French translator.'

'We don't reciprocate, though, do we?' he continued. 'It's not as if we call them "the Fs". Though I suppose that's because they never come to England. When was the last time you saw a French car in Britain?'

For the rest of the journey, he entertained Jane with an analysis of the rise of the British motoring holiday, with a special mention for his particular pet hate, the touring caravan, which clogged up the roads and defaced the countryside, the late-modern equivalent of Betjeman's bungalow eczema. The Dutch were even worse offenders, he told her, and widely loathed by the French for stocking up on their wretchedly bland cheese and ham before leaving home and spending the minimum in their host country. In some campsites, you even got a Dutch van selling the stuff *in situ*.

His tirade went uninterrupted until they drove past the entrance to a castellated restaurant high on a hill, at which point Will leaned across Jane to take a better look. 'Now that is Michelin two-star, and well worth a visit. I might see if I can get a free dinner, say I'll review it for the paper.'

It was shortly after this and only a few kilometres away from their destination when Jane heard a bang and realised she must have driven over something. 'Did you hear that?' she asked. 'I hope I haven't got a puncture.'

Her fears proved well-founded as she felt the car lurching to one side, but they managed to limp on to a lay-by, where she parked and got out to inspect the tyre which was deflating softly before her eyes.

'It's a damn nuisance,' she shouted back to Will, 'though I suppose it could be worse. I could be by myself with darkness falling and the wolves creeping out of the trees.'

'The wolves I could cope with,' said Will, 'but I do hope you're not expecting me to change a wheel.'

'Oh come on, Will, everyone knows how to change a wheel. Even me, luckily.'

He held up his hand in self-defence. 'Give me my due, Jane, you know perfectly well I don't do cars.'

'Well you're a load of bloody use then.'

She found the toolbox behind the seat, then slid deftly under the car with a spanner to release the spare wheel. Luckily she hadn't dressed up for the flight; she couldn't imagine her equivalent of Will's grey linen would respond too well to such treatment.

In spite of her confidence, it proved more difficult than she'd imagined, and after several attempts with the jack, she realised she would need to call for help. Will was reading in the passenger seat, having done his duty by finding her the relevant page in the car manual. Liberty was sleeping, still catching up on her early start to the day.

She took her phone from her bag and called Rupert's number, walking away from the car.

Will stuck his head out of the window and asked her what she was doing.

'Getting some help,' she said.

'Who from?'

'Rupert.'

'Why don't you call the French AA?'

'I don't need the AA, I just need someone with a bit of muscle and common sense.'

'I wouldn't count on him being any more use than me.'

'I would.'

'How come you've got his number?'

'I'm well-organised, remember. All-round handyman and travel rep, and I never travel without the right numbers. Rupert, thank goodness,' she said when he answered, 'I need you.'

'I need you too,' he said, and she could hear the pleasure in his voice. 'Are you nearly here? I've just put some coffee on.'

'No, I mean I really need you.' She explained about the flat tyre and her failure to engage with the jack.

'No problem, where did you say you were?'

'Just a bit after a posh restaurant called the Tour de something, with a load of flags flying.'

'Give me fifteen minutes.'

Jane got back in the car to wait. Fourteen minutes later he arrived in a battered old Jeep, tooting his horn as he came down the hill, pulling across the road to park in front of them.

He jumped out of the car and came towards them, a picture of masculine capability. He was wearing old jeans of the functional variety and a faded denim shirt that Jane felt inclined to rip from his broad body.

'Good to see you Will,' he said, extending his hand through the passenger window. 'What an extraordinary car,' he added. 'Was this your choice?'

Will's jaw tightened as he shook Rupert's hand. 'Jane assures me it was on promotion,' he said, as though the words were a personal affront. 'I leave these things to her, though needless to say I wouldn't have chosen such a ludicrous vehicle. But cars are not my thing, especially not when they go wrong.'

'Of course, I remember now, you don't do cars.'

Will glared at him. Was he taking the piss? And how did he know that Will didn't drive?

'Lydia told me,' Rupert added quickly, 'she said that Jane was the driver.' He looked across at her, sitting nervously behind the wheel. 'Come on then, Jane,' he said, 'let's get on with it.'

Will picked up his book, anxious to distance himself from this humiliating episode. 'I'll leave you to it,' he said. 'I don't think it takes three British tourists to change the wheel of a rental Fiat Multipla.'

'No indeed.'

Jane followed Rupert to the back of the car and watched him work. 'I've never seen you out of a suit before,' she whispered. 'It suits you.'

He looked up at her, his red-blonde hair falling over his eyes as he turned the wheel. 'Clothes have never been my thing,' he said, straightening up and wiping his oily hands on his jeans, 'I've never seen what all the fuss is about.'

'Nor had I until I saw you just now in your rugged outdoor wear,' said Jane. It reminded her of all those Harrison Ford movies, real men battling with real tasks.

He touched her lightly on the cheek and her heart missed a beat.

The wheel was soon in place, and the punctured tyre replaced beneath the chassis.

'All done then,' he said, sliding out from under the car, 'you can follow me for the rest of the way.'

He got back into his Jeep and set off up the hill, pausing for a minute to wait for Jane to catch him up. She started the engine and drove up behind him, admiring the set of his shoulders silhouetted against the windscreen. How did she get herself in this situation? Driving in convoy behind the man she desired, while locked in grim silence with her life partner, who was still rigid with irritation at having to be rescued.

She should have called out a proper mechanic in over-alls instead of making him look like a pansy in front of that bloody banker, Will thought. He was the explorer, after all, the one who was supposed to take charge in unforeseen circumstances. He should never have agreed to this holiday.

They reached the brow of the hill, then followed Rupert down the gently winding road, shaded by grey-green trees. Jane had never expected it to be so lush, you could grow anything here. Liberty was awake now and back on chatty form.

'That man is good at fixing cars,' she said.

'He only changed a wheel,' said Will, 'it doesn't take a rocket scientist to unscrew a few bolts.'

'And then he fixed Mum's other car too. Didn't he, Mum?' She tapped her mother on the shoulder.

'Did he? I don't remember,' Jane said brightly, her voice brittle in anticipation of what might follow.

'Yes, he did, when you came to get me from school and you couldn't find your keys and he came by in a taxi to give them back to you.'

'Oh yes, that's right,' said Jane in a giveaway nonchalant voice, 'so he did.'

She glanced quickly across at Will, but she needn't have worried. He had pulled the vanity mirror down and was performing his anti-ageing exercises, which involved sticking his forefingers inside his upper lip and moving them about in order to maintain the elasticity.

'It's true, isn't it, Daddy,' Liberty went on, like a dog with a bone. 'That man is good at fixing cars.'

'If you say so, sweetheart,' Will said indulgently. 'And I must admit cars are not my own strong point. But then I never had pretensions to being an oily rag. Each to his own, I say, or, as we are in France, *A chacun son truc.*'

Jane's relief at not being blown out did not extend to hearing Will slag off Rupert as a rude mechanical. 'I wouldn't say that being able to change a wheel qualifies you as an oily rag,' she said. 'I would say it was all part of being a fully functioning human being.'

'Whatever,' said Will.

They reached Rupert's village and followed him through the main street, past the old market place and the fountain spring and the stone troughs where the women used to come to do their washing. Then up a side street which led into open country, with views down to the valley. A few minutes later he turned up a steep stony track which led them through high metal gates into a forecourt shaded by cypress trees, beyond which stood a sumptuous stone *mas*. A row of generous windows with soft green shutters gave out onto a terrace lined with massive terracotta pots bleached pale by the sun, filled with lavender, rosemary, cistus, sage, and other herbs that Jane couldn't wait to identify. From the terrace, steps led down to a discreet pool like a giant fish pond, hedged in by flower borders, and beyond that the lawn stretched seamlessly into the distant landscape.

Jane stepped out of the car and looked around her. It was so entirely perfect, she couldn't see how she could ever leave. Rupert was watching her anxiously, reading her response.

'What do you think?' he asked.

'I think . . . it's like all my escapist fantasies rolled into one. I don't know why you would want to live anywhere else.'

'I'm working on it, as you know,' he said quietly. He led her up to the house, stopping on the terrace to look at the early rock roses coming through, and the herb garden, aromatic with basil and thyme, lemongrass and tarragon. 'I'd have a proper vegetable garden, if I lived here all the time,' he said. 'Ten sorts of tomatoes and ratte potatoes, and garrigue strawberries do very well round here, you know, those orangey-red ones, small oval shape.'

It was cruel of him to draw so clear a picture of a perfect life that she had decided she could not share with him. It was like wheeling a trolley of delicious food past a fasting man, tormenting him with delectable smells of what he must refuse.

Lydia came out of the house to greet them, wearing a pale pink suit and holding a jug of steaming coffee. She set it down on a table and came towards them, the sun reflecting off what appeared to be a pair of metal sandals.

'Darling, how lovely to see you,' she said, giving Jane a quick head-to-toe appraisal from behind her sunglasses. Clearly a trip abroad had done nothing to improve her dress sense.

'Nice flip-flops,' Jane replied, following the modern convention that women should always comment on each other's shoes.

'Thanks,' she said, 'they're Louis Vuitton. What have you done with Will and the child?' Jane looked around guiltily; in her excitement she had forgotten all about them.

'Liberty's found a playmate,' said Rupert, pointing down to the lawn where she was throwing a stick for a large dog. 'Don't worry,' he added, seeing Jane's anxious face, 'he belongs to the caretaker, he's perfectly safe with children. And Will's around somewhere.'

'There he is,' said Lydia, 'over there, poking round the *maison d'amis*. I'll go and tell him to come for coffee.'

She went off to get him in her narrow pink skirt, leaving Rupert and Jane alone on the terrace, suddenly shy.

'Can I see the kitchen?' she said. 'Now, while no-one's here.'

'Of course.'

He led her indoors and there it was, just like he'd said, a blue and white gingham cloth spread over a large farmhouse table that sat comfortably in the middle of a kitchen rich in old charm and short on mod cons. A vase of wildflowers stood on it, and Jane guessed, correctly, that Rupert had gathered them for her.

'I deliberately didn't bring that jacket,' she said. 'I didn't want anyone else making the same comparison.'

'Me neither. That's our memory. The first time we met, seeing you on those stairs, I could tell you were looking for something.'

'My lens.'

'More than that.'

'No, not more than that. I was looking for my lens.'

'You don't believe, then, that people give off vibes of availability?'

'Of course not. I wasn't available then, and I'm not available now.'

He walked round the table to where she was standing and put his arms around her, pushing her gently against the old range cooker.

'I think you are, though,' he said hotly, kissing her neck, 'I think you are, in your heart. But you just won't admit it.'

She sank into his kiss, closing her eyes and thinking how easy it was, to love and be loved. How tantalising, how seductive to come and live here with him. She could set up an office in a room leading out onto the terrace and in summer would work outside beneath an umbrella, a bottle of chilled rosé by her elbow. In the evening, they would cook together, or walk into the village to share a *bouillabaisse*.

Except they wouldn't, because she had a daughter, and that daughter had a father and if there was one thing Jane believed in, it was her child's right to be brought up in an solid, two-parent home. She didn't want Liberty to go through what she had. Hearing her father speak tensely to her mother, before taking her off for a day in town, all guilt and compensation, smothering her with treats before he brought her back and went home to his new wife. She wasn't going to put Liberty through that.

'Show me the rest of the house,' she said, releasing his hands from behind her back, 'tell me all about it, I want to know everything.'

As he walked her through the rooms, she thought how different it was from her visit to Rodmell, when she had been obliged to feign interest in Alison's paint-finishes and endless stories about tracking down knick-knacks. Here she was pushing Rupert for details, wanting to know exactly where everything came from. The furniture was from his family's country estate, which explained why it all fell together so casually, worn pieces of indifferent furniture mixed with the odd antique, none of it screaming to be admired the way that Alison's house was. He told her he had bought the house on a whim ten years ago, when he had been driving through the area on the way to a friend's wedding. It reassured Jane that this had been before he met Lydia. It brought alive a whole part of him that had nothing to do with the guilty, reluctant fiancé that she knew. It showed him in the light of someone free-spirited and open to possibility; the same way that the house now showed her a new way of living, if only she chose to follow it.

By the time they got outside, Lydia and Will had finished the coffee so Rupert took the jug off to make some more. Liberty was still playing with the dog, over-joyed to have found a surrogate pet.

'I'm glad you made it,' said Lydia, shrugging off her light jacket to reveal a low-cut tee shirt, 'it can get a bit tedious stuck out here by ourselves. Rupert's not bothered, he fiddles around in the garden, but I get restless. Though at least the weather's been fantastic, you do sometimes get that down here in April, a fore-taste of summer.' She lifted her feet onto a chair, pulling up her skirt to tan her legs, watching Will's reaction from behind her sunglasses.

'Do you know any of the locals?' asked Jane, sitting down at the table.

Lydia pulled a face. 'There's no way I'm getting on that merry-go-round. Half of them are expats, boring old farts who have retired out here. They spend all their time having dinner at each other's houses and repeating the same conversations.'

'I can just imagine,' said Will with distaste, eying up Lydia's thighs, 'Jane has this deluded fantasy that she'd like to move out somewhere like this, but I always say to her, that's all very well but who would you see?'

'I wouldn't mind mixing with the expats,' Jane said. 'I'm not sure how fascinating our London friends are, to tell you the truth. And there must be some French people round here.'

'Not what you'd call A-list,' said Lydia. 'Nothing you'd cross the road to invite to your barbeque.'

'Uugh, barbeques!' said Will. 'Unspeakable things. Meat burned on the outside, raw inside, or else dry as boot-leather, only made palatable by the slapping on of chilli sauce. And such an eyesore, those hideous constructions that people build in their gardens.'

He scanned the terrace as if in hope of finding one.

'Don't worry, Will,' said Lydia, 'you won't find anything so modern here.'

Liberty came running up the steps to the terrace, her eyes alight. 'Mummy, there's a swimming pool, please can I go in, *please*?'

'Have you said hallo to Lydia?'

Liberty shyly turned to face her. 'Hallo.'

'Hallo there, Liberty,' said Lydia in the patronising tone of those unused to children. She spoke slowly and loudly as though to someone deaf or foreign. 'How you've grown! And don't you look just like your dad?'

'Dominant genes,' said Will smugly, wondering why Lydia had suddenly started speaking like Joyce Grenfell.

'Can I go in your pool, please?'

'Of course.'

'I'll get your costume,' said Jane, 'come with me, the bags are still in the car.'

Liberty went skipping along beside her. 'I love it here, Mum,' she said, 'do you love it?'

'Yes, I do,' Jane replied, 'I really do.'

'Aren't you going to join her for a swim?' Lydia asked Will in her normal voice.

'Nope. Not pools. I swim in rivers and oceans and lakes, but never in pools. For me they represent the artificial taming of the landscape, symbols of petty domestication . . .'

'Ours isn't a pool, it's a *bassin*,' she interrupted. 'It's made of stone and it's grey, not that artificial blue, so I think you'd be all right.'

He gave her a superior smile. 'I'll pass all the same, thank you.'

*   *   *

That evening, they went into the village for dinner at a restaurant. Will was relaxed and expansive, his good mood enhanced by Rupert's refusal of his half-hearted attempt to split the bill.

'Well, this could be a lot worse,' he said, restoring his credit card to the safety of his wallet. 'You can say what you like about the French, but they certainly know about food. One remembers their gastronome Curnovsky who said that to do justice to his job he would need to have twelve mouths and twenty-four anuses.'

'Thank you for that, Will,' said Lydia, 'though you do see his point. I think if I lived here all the time I would be the size of a house. Let's face it, there's precious little else to do other than stuff your face. Apart from write to the mayor to complain about the neighbour's extension or the frequency of the rubbish collection.'

'I disagree,' said Rupert. 'It's far more satisfying to lead a simple life, not always be chasing around after things you'll never have.'

'I think it was Bertrand Russell who said that being without some of the things you want is an indispensable part of happiness,' said Jane. Will looked at her as if to ask who had rattled her cage. He was the one who came up with the clever quotations.

'What nonsense,' said Lydia. 'It's getting the things you want that makes you happy, and I for one would rather cry in a Rolls Royce than laugh on a bicycle. Once you've given up the chase, you might as well just lay down and die. Like that couple over there,' she added in a loud whisper, nodding towards an elderly couple who were tucking into their dinner without exchanging a word. You can't tell me they're happy.'

Four pairs of eyes were suddenly focused on the unfortunate couple. Only Liberty took no notice, intent on colouring in the picture book that Jane had brought along to keep her quiet.

'They're stuck, that's what they are,' Lydia added. 'They come out here to retire, and then one of them will drop dead and leave the other one even more miserable.'

As she spoke, the woman leaned over and said something to her partner. He leaned towards her and murmured something in reply, at which she laughed. Jane saw the love in her eyes.

'They're happy enough,' she said softly, 'they've got each other.'

Rupert was sitting opposite her and he turned back and caught her eye.

'Happiness, schmappiness,' said Will scornfully, 'it's been downhill all the way since the right to happiness was written into the American constitution. As though it's a pot of gold that can be found as long as you get the right rainbow. I don't buy it, myself. Life is a cruel and purposeless charade that ends in death. The point is, how best to entertain yourself until that moment.'

'That's a rather bleak view,' said Rupert. 'Perhaps you should be seeking psychiatric help.'

'Not at all! People should realise it's normal to feel bored and depressed. The ones who need psychiatric help are the self-delusionists who believe they should be feeling happy. They're the ones who are deranged.'

'So how do you intend to struggle through the rest of the pointless charade that is your life?' asked Rupert, amused.

'The way I always have. By travelling and immersing myself in my art. Bringing enlightenment to people's lives, entertaining them with stories from other cultures. I offer a broad view of the world, not the limited glimpses afforded by the deckchair of a retirement home in the sun. You won't catch me measuring out my life in the coffee spoons of small domestic comforts.'

He drained the last of his cognac and put his arm round the back of Jane's chair in a gesture of self-satisfaction. Jean-Paul Sartre pushing back the barriers of intellectual understanding on a balmy southern night. This holiday was proving more enjoyable than he had imagined. Jane moved away from him fractionally and stroked her daughter's silky hair.

'We should go,' she said. 'Liberty's getting tired.'

'Oh, there you go again,' he said impatiently. 'Just as things are getting interesting, you have to put a dampener on it.'

'You stay,' she said, standing up, 'I'll take her back.'

'Fancy another one, Rupert? You can't claim the old excuse that you need to be up early for the office. I know what you banker types are like in London, always rushing off early to prepare for another day of money-grubbing.'

Rupert ignored the jibe. 'No, I'll go back too. I don't want them walking home alone in the dark.'

'Old-fashioned gallantry, eh? The true English gentleman, alive and well in the South of France. Maybe you'll be able to change a few wheels on your way.'

'I'll join you in another glass,' said Lydia. 'We are on holiday, after all.'

There was a scraping of chairs and good-night kisses

as Rupert and Jane left the table with Liberty and headed off into the darkness.

'Just like old times,' said Will, once they were out of earshot. 'Do you think Rupert minds playing the noble escort?'

'Dear Rupert,' said Lydia with satisfaction, 'he does love to do the decent thing.'

'Where decent rhymes with faintly boring?'

'Now, now.'

'They just don't get it, do they?' said Will, summoning the waiter to bring them two glasses of cognac. 'The first hint of animation and they go creeping off like a couple of party-poopers.'

'At least you've got me to drink the night away with.'

'At least I have. And I don't mind telling you that I am beginning to feel stifled by domesticity. Don't get me wrong, I love my daughter, but it's just the endless routine of it all. It's becoming clearer to me every day, I'm just not cut out for regular family life.'

'Family life.' Lydia shuddered. 'It just sounds so depressing.'

'Don't get me started on the vocabulary: after-school club, kids' menu, parenting classes, family room, mini yoga, Baby Gap . . .'

'What I really can't stand are those baby-on-board stickers,' said Lydia. 'It's like, feel free to smash into everyone else's car.'

'And the curse of the five o'clock shadow falling over kitchens around the land as kids sit down to chicken nuggets and raw carrots, tended by their martyred mothers.'

'Making big casseroles and freezing the leftovers,' sneered Lydia, 'looking forward to the high point of the week that is the family walk in the park.'

Will sighed in recognition. 'Jane's a great girl, and at least she doesn't make a fuss about me doing my own thing. But you don't create literature by respecting regular meal-times and early nights. There's no getting away from the fact that dull people make the best parents. I see myself more in the mould of the glamorous, visiting father returning from his exotic travels with a silken dress for his little princess.'

He stared into the distance, thinking himself into the role. It was making more and more sense to him. You didn't catch Byron cutting short his travels through Greece in order to be home for Sunday lunch. That was a clerk's life, the life of the salaried family man. Pooter he was not.

'Rupert has always said he wants kids, but I'm not that keen,' said Lydia. 'I can just see him getting into the ante-natal classes and hunching over a pushchair. But it's not my bag, I'm afraid, much too limiting. Everyone I know who's had children has become so boring. It's like they go overnight from being a really good laugh to someone who's half dead. Then they claim it's improved them, that they've calmed down, or they've mellowed, as though that's a good thing.' She took a sip of her cognac. 'I don't like mellow, I like spiky. And I don't like same-ness and routine, which seems to me pretty much what having kids boils down to. I like variety. There's a big world out there, so much to do, so many things to have and places to go.'

Will leaned forward, intimately. 'My own philosophy entirely,' he said. 'Drink up and let's get another, the night is yet young.'

Away from the restaurant, Rupert and Jane were walking slowly down the village street, breathing in the soft night air and the scent of the blossom. Liberty had found her second wind and was running ahead of them, making a game out of not stepping on the lines between the paving stones.

'That was a lovely dinner, thank you,' said Jane. 'I hope you weren't offended by Will, he does like to provoke an argument. I don't know why he's got such a thing about bankers.'

'No, he's quite right about that,' said Rupert, 'I can't wait to get out of it.' He swiped a branch of a tree as they went past. 'And I couldn't give a damn what he says about me. But what I don't understand is how he can go on about life being so meaningless. When he's got you. I don't know what's the matter with him.'

'He's only being an existentialist,' said Jane. 'It's nothing personal.'

'Mummy, look!' Liberty had stopped in front of a stone gargoyle by the old pump. She pulled a face to match it, and skipped up on top of the water trough, walking along the edge, balancing with her arms.

Rupert came up behind Jane and slipped his arms round her waist, hidden in the darkness. 'Come away with me, Jane,' he murmured into her hair, 'come and live with me here and be happy.'

She felt his breath warm through her hair and allowed

herself to imagine it. Falling into bed with him every night, watched over by the shepherdesses on the wallpaper. Taking breakfast on the balcony, seeing the seasons change in the garden they created together. Having dinner together every night, growing old and tender with him like the couple in the restaurant.

'I can't,' she said.

'Yes you can, give me one good reason why you can't.'

'She's standing in front of you.'

Liberty had turned round now and was facing them with her arms outstretched, a small figure in her flared trousers adorned with sparkly flowers that they had chosen together, her face perfectly trusting.

'She's the centre of my life,' said Jane. 'I have to put her first.'

Rupert stood back, gracefully accepting defeat. There was no way he could compete with a seven-year-old girl.

The three of them turned up the road that led to the house, hearing the night crickets sing in a darkness you never saw in London, stars shining brightly in the biggest sky Jane had ever seen. As they turned into the drive, past the caretaker's cottage, the dog barked on cue as if to justify the *chien mechant* sign that hung on the gate and Jane realised that everything she wanted was right here. She didn't care about the bigger outside world, she didn't need to explore the frontiers of far-off lands like Will, or climb the glittery ladder to A-list glamour like Lydia. She'd be perfectly happy to spend the rest of her days in a faded floral frock, helping Rupert to import English roses for the sunkissed gardens of Provençal expats.

*   *   *

Jane took Liberty up to bed, then checked her phone messages. One from Alison to say she was up in town for the day and how about lunch; that was a lucky escape. Then Marion, hoping she was having a good Easter. Then someone with tortured vowels whose name she didn't catch wanting to know if Liberty was '*a bite*' this week. She replayed it, and listened more carefully. 'There's a message for you from Cosima's mum,' she called to Liberty who was brushing her teeth in the bathroom next door, 'inviting you to stay. That's nice, isn't it, maybe you can go next holiday.'

Liberty appeared in the doorway, her eyes wide. 'Oh no!' she said. 'I could have ridden her pony.'

'Never mind, there's always next time,' said Jane, cross with herself for bringing it up. 'Anyway, you're having a nice time here, aren't you?'

'Yes, and there's a swimming pool here; I don't suppose Cosima's got a swimming pool,' said Liberty, turning back to her tooth-brushing.

I wouldn't count on it, thought Jane. I'd put money on a pool and a tennis court and probably a full-size gym.

She tucked Liberty in and went downstairs. Rupert had set out a pot of tea on the terrace, and lit tall citronella candles to ward off mosquitoes. When she came out and saw him sitting there, the valley spread out below him in star-studded darkness, it was like a déjà vu of how she had imagined it would be.

'Is she all right?' Rupert asked, watching Jane's silhouette against the light of the house. She looked so delicate in her sleeveless blouse, he could encircle her upper arm in his hand.

'Fine. Just a bit annoyed to be missing out on a riding opportunity. There was a message from a friend back home, inviting her.'

'There are some stables in the next village,' he said. 'We could take her tomorrow.' And maybe leave her there for an afternoon, he thought, while he took Jane off and showed her in no uncertain terms why she had to change her mind.

'She'd love that,' said Jane. 'Horses are something you can't do in London.'

Another reason to leave the city. Another reason to change her life.

'Good, that's settled then. Tea?' He poured it out and settled back in his chair to watch her. She looked at him suspiciously.

'You're enjoying this, aren't you?' she said. 'You're enjoying showing me how perfect my life would be here.'

He shrugged. 'You can see how it would be, I'm not an illusionist. You feel at home here, don't you?'

'Like I've lived here all my life.'

'Well, there you are.'

'Tell me about the flower business,' she said. 'How would you work it?'

He drew up his chair and began to explain his plan, the growers he would use, the margins, the market he would be aiming for, the combination of direct mail and outlets. There was a big market, he had already established that, people who had traded in the rat race for the pleasures of everyday living, and what finer example of that could there be than a garden? He would also offer a garden design service, and employ a team of local people to do the hard digging, though he wanted to do it himself as well, he liked to get his hands dirty.

She listened, chipping in and making comments and suggestions, which plants would work and which might not be so good. It seemed very real and well thought through.

'You seem to have it all worked out,' she said.

'Oh, I do. Once I've got my partner lined up, I'm all ready to go.'

'Your partner?'

'You of course. You know all about gardening. Plus, I'm in love with you.'

'You don't give up, do you?'

'Remember what Churchill said. Never, ever, ever give up.'

It was two o'clock when Will and Lydia returned. The barking dog warned of their arrival, followed by loud laughter as they approached the house, slightly the worse for wear.

'Well, well, you're still up, are you?' said Will, stumbling round the corner onto the terrace. 'What about that, Lydia, there we were worrying about them fretting about us, all alone in their beds, and here they are hobnobbing over the candlelight. Not up to anything, are you?'

Lydia slumped down next to Jane and kicked off her metal sandals. 'I tell you, those shoes are killing me, I don't know what it is with them.'

Will walked unsteadily to the edge of the terrace and stared down into the valley. 'Look at that, eh, paradise lost and paradise regained. Got any brandy, Rupert?'

'I think you've had enough,' Rupert replied, 'though I realise by saying that I risk falling neatly into the boring-old-banker box you've carved out for me.'

'Merchant Ws, as we used to call you!' Will was chortling at the memory. 'Do you remember that, in the Eighties, how we used to laugh about merchant wankers?'

'Not everyone can have an interesting job like yours,' said Rupert. 'Not everyone's got your talent.'

Will melted at the compliment. 'Thank you for that, Rupert,' he said, 'but there's no need to do yourself down. Some of us have got to work in the finance sector, each to his own, I say. And we artists all need our men in grey suits to do the money thing.' He turned unsteadily. 'Well, if you're not going to offer me a nightcap, I might as well go to bed. Good night, Rupert, good night, sweet ladies, good night, good night . . .'

He staggered into the house, leaving an uneasy three-some sitting round the table.

'Is the child OK?' asked Lydia, rubbing her sore foot. 'I have to say it was quite well-behaved in the restaurant.'

'She,' said Jane.

'What?'

'She, not it. I wouldn't refer to you as "it".'

'No, obviously not since I'm a fully fledged person. I'm inclined to take the Victorian view of kiddies, treat them as unisex until they reach the age of reason. You've seen those old photos of little boys with long golden hair and flowing white dresses.'

'I'm going up,' said Rupert, 'and I suggest we all do the same.'

'You're right, I need to rest this foot,' said Lydia. 'See

you tomorrow, Jane.' She hobbled away, crossing the old terracotta tiles of the living room, then up the stairs to bed.

Rupert blew out the candles and locked up while Jane carried the tea things through to the kitchen and rinsed them in the butler sink, setting them out on the heavy wood draining board.

'Right then,' said Rupert, turning off the light and following her up the stairs. 'Sweet dreams,' he said when they reached the landing, kissing her softly before they turned away, into their separate bedrooms.

Will was snoring loudly, his grey hair spread wildly over the pillow like a dying monarch. Just a few years ago his hair had been jet-black, contrasting with the billowing white shirts he wore in those days, like a glamorous pirate. He used to wear them unbuttoned to his chest in a look he based on the French intellectual Bernard-Henri Levy, a potent mix of brains and raw sex. He'd been dressed like that when he took Jane to see Theatre de Complicite at the ICA. She'd been in love with him then, her very own European, pushing back the frontiers of cultural diversity.

She switched her attention to her daughter, sweetly rosy in the little bed that had been set up for her, so she could sleep like a medieval dog at the feet of her masters. Liberty sighed in her sleep, a gentle, pure, milky sound, compared to her father's guttural breathing.

Jane put on the nightie she had bought specially for this holiday, a spinsterish thing, all white lace and ribbon, the sort you found in shops selling Provençal potpourri and chunky soap made from olive oil. It was the type you were meant to store in a drawer with lavender bags. Climbing into bed, she was like a chaste young girl in the virtuous ecstasy of taking holy orders. For the sake of her child, she would lie like this, in the quasi-matrimonial bed, for the rest of her life.

FOURTEEN

The next morning brought more dazzling sunshine, breaking over the hilltop and falling like a blessing on the terrace where Rupert and Jane were having breakfast. It was that exquisite spring sun that was never too strong, not yet obliging you to move your chair into the shade or seek shelter in coolly tiled indoor rooms.

Rupert had been out to buy croissants and banettes, loose twists of bread still warm enough from the oven to melt the butter as Jane spread it, pale and creamy, for Liberty's breakfast.

'She'll be back in a minute,' said Jane, 'after she's played with the dog. He makes a fantastic nanny, you can see where Barrie got the idea from, for *Peter Pan.*'

'Did you sleep all right?'

He meant, had she had sex with Will.

'Fine, thank you.' She was able to meet his gaze. 'How about you?'

'A bit disturbed. Lydia's suffering with her foot, she's calling a doctor out to see what's wrong.'

'A home visit, isn't that rather dramatic?'

'Not in France. It's only in England that you have to be nearly dead before they'll come and take a look. More coffee?'

He filled her cup, then his own. She turned her face up to the sun and closed her eyes, happy to know as the warmth flooded into her that she had a full day ahead to do as she liked.

'There's nothing like it, is there, the first sun of summer?' she said. 'I know you're not supposed to do this any more, what with wrinkles and killer rays, but it just feels so good.'

He wished she would come nearer and lie down with her head in his lap so he could stroke the hair back from her face and examine the faint freckles that had appeared since her arrival. Better still, he would take her upstairs and lay her out on his bed, and run a full check all over her body, committing to memory the exact location of every mole and blemish and distinguishing feature. He'd done it so often in his dreams, he was curious to match it against the reality.

'No sign of your partner,' he said, 'though I can't bear that expression except in business. Howdy partner, it always makes me think of cowboys.'

'I don't think we'll be seeing him for a while,' said Jane, her eyes still closed. 'He's not a morning person at the best of times, and he was certainly putting it away last night.'

'We've all been there,' said Rupert magnanimously. At least the drink had put Will out of action; he couldn't bear the thought of him making love to Jane, seducing her with his clever remarks.

'Where did you meet him anyway?' he asked, turning a croissant between his fingers. He wanted to leave it alone, but he couldn't.

'Publishing party. I couldn't believe my luck. Those things are so awful, people always looking over your shoulder for someone more interesting to talk to. And he just stayed talking to me all night. I was so thrilled . . . him a famous travel writer and me a nobody.'

'I wish you wouldn't talk like that,' he said crossly, 'like you're a bit of dirt at the bottom of the food chain. You're worth a hundred of him.'

'You're just biased,' she said, pleased. It was nice to have someone bolster her up for a change. She hadn't had much of that since her mother died, apart from Liberty's passionate, unconditional love, which delighted her but at the same time sometimes threatened to overwhelm her.

Liberty came running up to them now, her eyes wide, the important messenger bearing news.

'There's a man here,' she panted, out of breath, 'in a white car.'

Moments later, the man in question appeared behind her. It was the doctor, carrying the traditional black bag that always invoked Jane's irrational fear of all things medical. The bag of death, filled with needles and tubes and sharp implements for removing bits of human tissue that could then be displayed in small Petri dishes.

Rupert led him away to see the patient, and Liberty sat down to tuck into her breakfast.

'What's the matter with Lydia?'

'She's hurt her foot.'

'Did a horse stand on it? Cosima hurt her foot when her pony stood on it.'

'No. That reminds me, how would you like to come with me to see some stables and see if you can go pony riding some time?'

Jane was practically knocked off her chair by Liberty's enthusiastic response.

'I left a message on their answer phone,' said Jane. 'When they call back we'll see when they can fit you in.'

The doctor was swift in his verdict. One look at the swollen black foot and a feel of the pain at the top of Lydia's leg was enough to make him ask to take a look at her footwear. She sent Rupert downstairs to retrieve the sandals from where she had kicked them off last night. There was no doubt about it, said the doctor, inspecting the metal straps of the very upmarket flip-flops, she was suffering from a poisoned foot. It was the folly of fashion designers, he explained disapprovingly, to use metal for shoes, so patently unsuitable for the purpose, so damaging to the fragile epidermis. He wrote her out a prescription for antibiotics along with the usual six ancillary panaceas that the French had come to expect, and advised her to rest the foot and calm her fever.

'You must admit it has a certain poetry,' she said later, after limping outside to install herself on a sun-lounger. 'Done for by Louis Vuitton. I wonder if I could sue?'

Will appeared shortly after, showered and restored, in a pair of cream trousers. He gave everyone a brave smile then dragged a deckchair to the far end of the terrace where he sat down in a do-not-disturb kind of way with the new French translation of Plutarch's letters, which was his idea of holiday reading.

Rupert picked up his car keys. 'I'm going to run into the village and get this prescription made up,' he said. 'Anyone care to join me?'

He knew he was safely addressing an audience of one. Will waved his hand dismissively and Lydia was clearly going nowhere, while Liberty was at the bottom of the garden, throwing sticks for the dog.

'I'll come,' said Jane with a nonchalant shrug. 'Might as well.'

'You don't think they're getting a bit too pally, do you?' said Will from his deckchair, watching them disappear round the corner of the house.

'Those two?' Lydia snorted. 'There are many words you could use to describe Rupert, but home-wrecker is not one of them. And Jane is hardly the type to go sniffing round other people's fiancés, they are both loyal to a fault.' Loyalty was not high on Lydia's list of must-have qualities. It was way down alongside dull virtues like sticking with it, counting your blessings and being kind to animals.

She lowered her Chloe sunglasses and gave him a provocative look. 'You, on the other hand, are an altogether more dangerous proposition.'

It was good to know he still had what it took, but Will was too hungover to bother with Lydia. 'You just rest that foot,' he said, returning to his book, 'I don't take advantage of the disabled.'

Jane jumped happily into the Jeep beside Rupert. A trip to the local pharmacy was hardly a dream date, but she was alone with him, and the thrill was as acute as when her first boyfriend had walked her to the ice-cream shop.

Rupert got out to open the gates and stopped to exchange a few words with the caretaker who was engaged with a hedge-trimmer. From their gestures Jane guessed they were discussing the happy relationship between his dog and Liberty, who were running races up and down the garden.

Rupert got back behind the wheel and the caretaker nodded to her as they drove past. She lowered the window and spoke to him in French about the dog and the garden. His wife appeared, a stocky woman with the aubergine-coloured hair that seemed a favourite with the locals. They eventually made their escape, amid much smiling and waving.

'You see, you even speak French,' said Rupert. 'It was meant to be.'

In the village, he backed skilfully into an unfeasibly small space between an old Renault and a bashed-up white van. It was pathetic to admire a man's ability to park a car, but Jane couldn't help it. Obviously what women wanted was intelligent conversation and men who understood them and shared a commitment to gender equality. But for pure sexiness you couldn't beat old-fashioned male competence.

'I'll wait here,' she said.

'Fine, I won't be long.'

She wanted to stay in the car so she could watch him cross the road and walk down the street. When he came out of the shop she would compare him with the other customers and give them all marks out of ten.

The village was bustling with Easter weekenders, and the pharmacy was busy. First man out hardly counted, too old and gnarled. Second man, not bad in a French strutting-cock sort of way, low centre of gravity, pointy shoes, five out of ten. The third man was young and gawky, thin in a way that lacked energy, as opposed to wiry thin, four out of ten. Next up was obviously an incomer, probably Dutch, with too much facial hair and a dodgy money-belt, four again.

She remembered a game she used to play with the girls at work. It was during the sales conferences, those depraved events when a hundred employees would hole up in a hotel and brag about how much they had drunk. You had to pretend someone was holding a gun to your head and forcing you to go to bed with one of the reps. Which one would you choose? How they had laughed. Some years later, the game became more sophisticated. Names would be produced from a hat and you had to decide whether to shoot, shag or marry the individual in question. Her thoughts briefly flickered back to Will, lounging on Rupert's terrace. She frowned for a second, but brightened again when she saw Rupert come out of the pharmacy, filling the doorway, broad and English, looking unkempt with his hair falling over his face, his shirt unironed. Objectively, thought Jane, he would be a six or a seven, maybe an eight a few years back. But she was no longer being objective. He opened the car door and threw the bag of medicine onto the back seat.

'Shall we get some bread for lunch?' he said. 'Maybe a couple of *fougasses*? Why are you laughing?'

'I'm not laughing.'

'Smiling, then.'

'I love you.'

He climbed in beside her and she smelt the now-familiar scent of his embrace. 'Good,' he said, 'so can we stop messing around now?'

When they got back to the house, Lydia was still on the sun-lounger, a pile of magazines beside her.

'God, I'm bored,' she said. 'It's all very well loafing around when it's your choice, but as soon as you're told to put your feet up, the whole thing becomes tedious beyond words.'

Rupert went in to fetch a glass of water then came out and opened the boxes of medicine, counting out the correct doses on the garden table.

'You are a sweetie,' she said as he handed her two tablets, 'I can see how wonderful it will be in our old age. You can push me around in a wheelchair and get one of those pill-boxes with compartments for each day of the week.'

Rupert smiled guiltily. He knew it wouldn't happen, but had no idea how he was going to break the news. Until he did, it had to be business as usual.

'It's a shocking thought,' Lydia went on, 'being old. You don't need to think about it in the city, far too much going on. But when you come somewhere like this, all there is to do is sit around and wait for death. Have you noticed how many old people there are in this village?'

'I like old people,' said Jane, who had settled down into the chair beside Lydia and was trying to act normally, to calm her thoughts into some sort of pattern. 'I like the way they can say what they want,' she added. 'They've got less to lose, I suppose, it makes them more reckless.'

'Come to think of it,' said Lydia, 'I don't think I've spoken to anyone over fifty since my grandmother died. How old's Will, by the way?'

They all looked at him across the terrace where he was engrossed in his book.

'Fifty next year,' said Jane. He'll be sixty soon, she thought, he'll be drawing a pension and I'll be responsible for him. She had never thought of it in those terms before.

'I'll make some coffee,' she said, getting to her feet, suddenly anxious to be doing something.

'Oh by the way, the stables rang,' said Lydia. 'I got Will to bring the phone out here, so I didn't have to move. They can't take Liberty this week, all the horses are booked on a *stage de perfectionnement* for experienced riders. I love that about the French, don't you? You're either on a course for beginners or else a course of perfection, there's nothing in between.'

'That's a shame,' said Jane. 'I shouldn't have said anything to her, I ought to know by now not to mention anything until it's for certain.'

'Don't beat yourself up about it,' Lydia shrugged. 'She might as well get used to disappointment, plenty more of that to come.'

'Spoken from the heart,' said Will, who had moved in to join the conversation now they had moved safely away from the subject of age. 'Never mind coffee, Jane, it's nearly lunchtime, better make it a bottle of rosé instead.'

*   *   *

They had salade nicoise for lunch, the olives plump and black, the eggs fresh, but Jane had no appetite. She tore off a piece of the *fougasse* they had bought that morning and chewed on it mechanically, but her mouth was dry and she couldn't swallow. She busied herself instead with Liberty, ensuring she ate properly, watching her concentrating as she loaded her fork with small mouthfuls. Jane was unwilling to make small talk with the adults, it seemed so artificial.

Will was more than compensating for her silence. He talked about Plutarch's letters and the loss of subtlety they suffered in translation; the difference between the two old French languages, *langue d'oc* and *langue d'ol*; the way that second-home owners were killing the spirit of Provence.

You windbag, Jane thought, you insufferable, boring old windbag.

Across the table, Rupert was stacking the plates, his fingers strong and deft. 'Did you know they're prosecuting the *Sapeurs Pompiers*?' he said, changing the subject. 'They were talking about it in the pharmacy this morning. It seems they're on commission for putting out forest fires and someone caught two of them down in the valley with a jerry can of petrol.'

'How very enterprising of them,' said Lydia. 'It must be the most interesting thing that's happened here since the war. Would you mind bringing my manicure set, Rupert, while you're up? I might as well paint my nails, there's bugger all else to do round here, even for those who aren't handicapped.'

'There's riding,' said Liberty. 'I wish I could go riding.'

'Never mind,' said Jane, 'there's always next time.'

'Next time?' Lydia teased. 'That's a little presumptuous of you, Jane, to assume we'll invite you again.'

'Only joking,' she added, mistaking the cause of Jane's embarrassment for something more straightforward, 'you can come again. Even the child is less bother than I expected. Would you like me to do your nails, Liberty?'

Liberty nodded, honoured to be included in the grown-up-girls' club, and when Rupert returned with the bag she sat solemnly still, hand outstretched, while Lydia buffed and polished her small fingernails.

'I'll do the dishes,' said Jane, glad for a chance to escape.

'I'll help you,' said Rupert and he followed her into the kitchen.

'I can't stand this,' she said, once they were out of sight of the others. 'I feel so treacherous, creeping around behind their backs.'

'It'll be OK, just wait and see,' said Rupert, putting his arms round her, 'it'll all come right in the end, it's just the detail needs sorting. We know what we want, and that makes everything easy. It's the not knowing that's so difficult.'

Jane thought of all the years she had spent convinced that Will was the one. She had been deluding herself with the energy of one who wants to believe. But who was to say she wasn't doing the same again now, with Rupert? What is love anyway, but the desire to believe?

'I hope you're right,' she said, 'because I can't see what's going to happen at all. It's all such a mess . . .'

*   *   *

By the time they got back outside, Liberty's little nails were shiny crimson. She waved them at her mother in delight. Jane pulled her onto her lap, wanting to hold her still in time, to freeze her in this moment. Will had moved away from the table and was talking on his phone, pacing up and down the terrace, jangling the coins in his pocket. Jane watched him dispassionately as she sat holding her daughter. He seemed a stranger to her, this man who had shared her bed for so many years. They had built a life together, she had jumped into line with his aspirations, washed his shirts, espoused his views, and yet she had no idea who he was. When he returned he had a new vigour in his stride, his shoes clicked importantly across the stones.

'I hate to be a party-pooper,' he said, though he didn't look like he was hating it at all, 'but it looks as if I may have to break up this idyll. That was my agent, it seems that Rob Bryson is in London and wants a meeting with me. I need to be at Sketch tomorrow night. No-one else will do, apparently. He wants me to act as a special advisor on a film on Amerindians. According to Ed, I can dictate my terms.'

'Not THE Rob Bryson?' Lydia was impressed. 'How very mainstream of you. And here's me thinking you were a marginal intellectual.'

'Who's Rob Bryson?' asked Rupert.

'Dear Rupert,' said Lydia, 'I sometimes think you live on another planet. He's only the hottest producer in Hollywood, darling.' She turned to Jane. 'Rupert's only interested in old films,' she explained, 'or else European art-house affairs where nothing ever happens. You might as well watch paint dry.'

Jane and Rupert were careful to avoid eye-contact.

Will was bustling around now, making plans. 'I'll leave in the morning,' he said. 'Jane can run me to the airport, and I'll get on the first flight.'

He saw the confusion on Jane's face and mistook it for disappointment. 'If you don't mind, that is, Jane?'

'No,' she said, 'of course not.'

Poor old thing, he thought, she'd been looking forward to this week together, and it was true he didn't get to spend much time with Liberty. A generous thought came to him.

'Hang on,' he said, 'here's a suggestion. Why don't I take Liberty back with me? That way, she can go and stay with Cosima after all and get to ride that damn pony we're sick of hearing about. What do you say, Liberty?'

'Oh, yes please!' Liberty fell into a theatrical beseeching position. 'Please can I go, Mummy?'

'I don't know,' said Jane, 'I don't think I can change your ticket, and anyway, Cosima might have invited someone else now.'

'Why not ring her and see?' said Will, 'and don't worry about the ticket, I'll buy another one. I've a feeling I'm about to get lucky.'

Hardly believing her ears, Jane went inside to fetch her phone. She had her meeting tomorrow at La Garde Freinet, so it would be convenient for Liberty not to be around. She couldn't imagine Lydia would be that delighted at having to play nanny for the day.

'That's settled then,' she said, coming back outside. 'Cosima's mum says you can go whenever you like. She's even said she can pick you up if you go tomorrow, as she's going to be in London.'

'Hooray!' Liberty pretended to be a horse and set off galloping round the garden.

'Lucky you,' said Lydia. 'I'm really rather tempted to come with you.' It wouldn't be much fun once Will had left. Just her and Rupert having to entertain Jane. 'Maybe we should all go back to London?' she said. 'Enough's enough, and we've made the point, we've had our taste of the South.'

'But Jane's only just arrived,' said Rupert. He didn't want her snatched away so soon.

'And I've got to go and see this writer tomorrow,' said Jane. 'I'd rather not cancel.'

'That's settled then,' said Will. 'I'll go and get packed.'

Upstairs, Jane watched Will packing his bag with an alacrity he hadn't shown on the way out.

'This could be very big, you know,' he said. 'I know it's a bore cutting the holiday short like this, but you don't say no to Rob Bryson.'

Jane was struck by the speed of his transformation from highbrow intellectual to rabid groupie, panting at the thought of getting in with the big boys.

'I thought you hated his films,' she said, 'and I thought you despised those writers who wanted to get into movies.'

'You realise what this could mean,' said Will, ignoring her. 'Mark Thomas can keep his miserable six-bedroom house in Notting Hill: if this works out, I'll be able to buy up his entire street.'

Liberty came into the bedroom. She had put on Lydia's poisonous metal sandals and was twirling around, pouting like a model and holding up her painted nails for inspection.

'Take those off at once!' said Jane. 'I don't want *you* going home with a black foot.'

Liberty obediently kicked them off and jumped onto the bed.

'Help me pack your things,' Jane said. 'Pass me the clothes out of that cupboard.'

Liberty got down to open the wardrobe. 'When are we going, Daddy?'

'Tomorrow, my love, first thing. Jane, could you bear to fold these shirts for me, you know how useless I am at that sort of thing?'

She took over from him, carefully folding the shirts like a proper lady's maid.

'You'll need to take some more trousers to Cosima's,' said Jane. 'Those joggers and a pair of jeans; will you be able to find them?'

'Course she will,' said Will. 'She's a lot more independent than you give her credit for. It will do her good to get out of your skirts for a few days. Leave you free to get on with some work.'

FIFTEEN

Jane blinked hard and tried to focus on the road ahead. She didn't like to think how long she had been awake. After a sleepless night it had been a relief to get up at six and gently wake Liberty, coaxing her into her travelling clothes. Leggings, with a spare pair in her backpack just in case. She had been happy enough to go off with Will; it was Jane who'd had to fight back the tears. In seven years it would be the first time they had spent more than one night apart, which she knew was wet beyond belief, but that was how it was.

They were a party of three taking the plane in the end. Lydia had decided there was no point in staying on with her gammy leg: if it got worse she'd rather put her trust in the Chelsea and Westminster A&E than some travelling French quack. And she had her wedding plans to get on with. It meant that when Jane got back to the house, she and Rupert would be alone together for the rest of the week. She told herself that it was fate; she hadn't engineered it, that was the way it had worked out.

The lunch in La Garde Freinet had been a welcome diversion. Instead of worrying about Rupert and whether Will would take proper care of Liberty, Jane had been treated to a passionate defence of the delights of smoking, which had lasted from the main course to the petits fours, washed down by two bottles of rosé.

'I like you,' the writer had said to her halfway through the second bottle. 'I can see we are going to have a long and profitable relationship. But honestly, you should take up smoking, it is so good for the brain.'

And now here she was, halfway home to Rupert, alone in the Fiat Multipla. It seemed so long ago since they had arrived, with Will fussing and complaining. It felt exhilarating to have no passengers, just the road map lying open on the seat beside her. She was her own navigator now.

She decided to pull over and take a break, and call home to make sure they'd got back safely.

Liberty answered the phone, and excitedly told Jane that she had packed her bag herself and put in three pairs of joggers. Then Jane made her put Will on so she could run it through with him and make sure she had the right things.

'Don't fuss,' he said, 'she can always borrow anything she's forgotten. I don't imagine her little friend is short of clothes.'

'That's not the point, I don't want her turning up unprepared, it looks like we don't care. And don't forget her cream and her panda.'

This is what it's like for divorced couples, she thought. Fretting down the phone, worrying whether your child was being properly looked after.

'All right, all right,' he'd said, irritated, 'I'm sure we'll manage.'

She could tell he was already regretting his suggestion that Liberty travel back with him. He wanted to be psyching himself up for his big night out, instead of which he was taking instructions on what to pack for a seven-year-old's country-house party.

'What time's Cosima's mum coming?' Jane asked.

'About seven. She'd better not be late.'

'And how's Lydia?'

'Miraculously better. Didn't mention her foot, practically skipped off the plane. I think she's just happy to be back in London.'

'I'll call you tomorrow, then. Good luck for tonight.'

'Thanks.'

'Bye then.'

'Bye.'

She sat for a moment and pictured the familiar sight of Will and Liberty at home. She ought to be there, fixing dinner and helping Liberty get ready for her trip. And yet here she was, parked in a lay-by in a village somewhere between Marseille and God knows where, completely alone. What did she think she was doing? Rupert. She must call Rupert now, tell him she was on her way. She needed to hear him, to remind herself why she was there.

His voice sounded distant when he answered; it must be the line. Which was funny, because Will had sounded like he was standing right beside her.

'Hi, it's me,' she said. 'Just to say I'll be half an hour or so.'

'Good.' There was a pause, then he said, 'Everything all right?'

'Yes, fine. The lunch went well. I just spoke to Will, they got back OK.'

'Yes, I know, Lydia called.'

Of course she did. They were engaged, after all.

'I'll see you soon, then. Do you want me to get anything? Bread?'

What a dreary little woman she was.

'No, it's all taken care of.'

'Right,' she said brightly, 'I'll try not to get another puncture, don't want to drag you away from the stove.'

'Drive safely.'

'I will.'

That was a weird conversation, she thought as she started the engine. He sounded so formal, as though they were strangers. It was as if now there was no obstacle in their way they didn't know how to behave. She was going home to him for dinner, like couples did. It was banal, not what they had been used to. Careful what you wish for, because it might come true, wasn't that what they said? And she wasn't at all sure now what she wanted.

The journey took longer than she expected, marked by several pauses to consult the map. Jane could have done with Will there, at least it would have given her someone to blame every time she took a wrong turn, and there were plenty of occasions. There seemed to be so many roads leading nowhere that didn't feature on the map.

By the time she arrived it was getting dark and the lights were on in the house, guiding her in as she negotiated the gateposts. Rupert came out to meet her as she unfolded herself from the car, stretching out limbs that were tense from the journey and the fear that she might never arrive.

'There you are,' he said, 'I was starting to get worried.'

There was nothing formal about him now. His shirt was untucked as he came towards her, and before she had time to think he had her pressed up against the car, kissing her, then sinking to his knees, pushing up her tee shirt and burying his head in her belly.

'No more excuses,' he said, gripping her waist, then sliding his hands down inside her linen trousers, 'you've got no-one to hide behind now.'

'No,' she said, pulling him to her, 'I don't suppose I have.'

She woke to birdsong and the smell of coffee and for a moment couldn't remember where she was. Then Rupert put the tray down and climbed under the sheets beside her.

'I knew it,' he said, 'I knew it would be like that.'

She propped herself up on one elbow. 'Like what?' she asked, teasing.

'Like that,' he said, sliding a thigh across her legs so she was trapped by the weight. 'I knew it the moment I saw you. I knew if ever I had the incredible good fortune to get you into bed, it would be the happiest thing I had ever done. Ever.'

She ran a hand down his back and felt smooth skin over warm firm flesh.

'I was worried,' she said, 'but I need not have been . . .'

'Why were you worried?'

'I worried we might be stuck in that unrequited thing, you know, the perfect love blighted by circumstance. Only works when you can't have it. I thought it might be a big let-down when it came down to it.'

'It wasn't, though, was it?'

'Well . . .'

His face fell and she took pity.

'Only joking. Move over, you're giving me a dead leg.'

He pulled his leg back and put his arm round her instead.

'And anyway,' she went on, 'aren't you supposed to ask me how it was for me?'

'Nope,' he said, 'that's only for losers. If you need to ask, then you really have no idea. Now, sit up, and I'll pass you your coffee.'

She did as he asked and he plumped the pillows up behind her, making her comfortable, smoothing her hair, looking at her as if she was the most wonderful piece of work.

'I can't believe it,' he said, 'look at me, grinning like an idiot.'

'You'd better believe it,' she said, 'otherwise I might think I've made the most terrible mistake.'

Two hours later, the coffee was stone-cold and the sun was streaming in through the window. Jane watched the way it played on the shepherdesses that decorated the bedroom walls with their long dresses and poetically arched crooks. *Toile de jouy,*' she said, 'that's the phrase I was looking for. I love that wallpaper, I'd choose it every time for my bedroom.'

'This *is* your bedroom,' he said sleepily into her shoulder.

'It is for now.'

He lifted his head to kiss the side of her neck. 'What shall we do today?'

'How about nothing?'

'Nothing it is.'

And so it was for the next three days. Beneath the gaze of the *toile de jouy* shepherdesses they explored a thousand new ways of doing nothing. They had been given the most luxurious of presents: time together, giftwrapped in sunshine and privacy. Every morning they would wake and then remember they had all day ahead to do exactly as they pleased. They were drunk on it, the freedom, the selfish oblivion to everyone and everything else. Jane could close her eyes and describe every detail of her lover's body, their entire life was in that bedroom.

Except for every evening at six o'clock, when Jane returned to the room she had slept in with Will. She kept her phone there, and would first check her messages before ringing Liberty to hear about what fun she was having with the horses, and what she had eaten for tea. She rang Will just once. He was full of his film project, the meetings that were being set up with those he described without irony as 'people who matter'.

'What about you, then?' he had added as an afterthought. 'What are you up to?'

'Oh, you know, this and that,' she had said, grateful for his lack of curiosity, 'nothing really . . .'

And then she had closed the door on the hotline to

her real life, and returned to the heightened world she had created with Rupert, where each moment was savoured and prolonged. This is happiness, she thought, true happiness is here and now, allowing no intrusions from what has gone before and what may come tomorrow.

'Shall we go out?' Jane asked on the fourth day. 'There's a garden we should look at.'

'If you insist,' he said, his head in her lap. 'You're the boss.'

They drove through the hills in search of a remote bastide garden, established in the seventeenth century. On the way, Jane talked about love.

'I read a thing about couples,' she said. 'Most couples get together for prosaic and practical reasons. Like, they're both available. But that's not enough, each couple has to think it's unique and predestined.'

'Like us.'

'And so, every couple invents its own myth, about how they got together.'

'A contact lens.'

'And the couple will only last as long as both parties go along with it. When one person destroys the myth, the couple is finished.'

'So what's your myth with Will?' He was confident enough now to mention his name.

'Eliza Doolittle. He was my Professor Higgins. What about you and Lydia?'

'Brits in New York. I was the caricature of the bumbling Englishman abroad, and she was my glamorous redeemer.'

He thought about those days and it seemed a lifetime ago. 'And what about us?' he asked. 'What's our myth?'

She laughed. 'That we're unique, of course, and predestined for each other. Or that we're trying to re-create the Garden of Eden. Look, we've arrived.'

They got out of the car and walked up through an ancient stone arch, stopping to admire some self-seeded alpines that clung to its side.

'It's supposed to have been designed by Le Notre,' said Rupert, 'but I'm not so sure. The arrangement of parterres doesn't seem quite in keeping. I wonder if it's moated, I'll just go and check.' He went off to look at the boundaries, leaving Jane to admire the herb garden.

'It's definitely moated,' he called out, catching her up, then realised she was in conversation with a man in shorts and sandals with socks.

'I was just saying to your wife, that is possibly the best display of sempervivums I have ever seen,' he said to Rupert, turning to point them out.

'Tell him I'm not your wife,' Jane whispered with a giggle.

'It's like I said,' Rupert told her as they moved away, 'the only people who know about gardens round here are the English. But there are enough of them to provide my entire client base.'

On the way back to the car, Jane paused to call Liberty and listen to her account of the day's triumphs. As she said goodbye, she remembered stories she had read about women who walk out on their families. Women who pack a suitcase and leave their sleeping children, gambling on love. Sometimes they came back, years later, for tearful reunions. Often, they lived with only the memory of their children. They made their choice and accepted the consequences.

＊　＊　＊

On her final morning, Jane woke with a sick feeling in her stomach. The Monday-morning, end-of-holiday feeling, except a hundred times worse. It was time to get real.

'Let's walk down to the village,' she said, 'break me in gently to the outside world.'

As they walked down the drive. Jane slipped her hand inside the back of Rupert's belt, wanting to feel his flesh, storing up the memory.

Rupert took her to the *Bar des Sports* and ordered coffee. 'I love this place,' he said. 'I was thinking about it the day I met you, wishing I was here instead of in the office. And now here we are, out in public. May I say, you look quite good with your clothes on. Though better without, obviously.'

'And you look better without the suit and braces. I should get those braces framed as a souvenir of our first meeting.'

'You can have them,' he said, 'they're no use to me.'

'Sentimental value only.'

'Very sentimental.' He took a sip of his coffee. 'And now I can chuck them away, along with the Turnbull and Asser shirts. You do realise, Jane, that I'm not going back.'

They had carefully avoided talking about the future, but now there was no getting away from it. Jane shifted on the bar stool, wishing they could continue to live in the present, wishing they were back to where they were two days ago.

'Oh,' she said.

'And neither are you, not permanently.'

'Aren't I?'

'Aren't you?'

She frowned, her mind crowded by complications.

'I think perhaps . . . we shouldn't rush things . . .'

He grew impatient now, crashing his cup onto his saucer. 'What do you mean, shouldn't rush things? Come on, Jane, we're grown-ups now! I've found what I've been looking for, I thought you had too? Or is that just a nice little display you've been putting on for my benefit for the past few days . . . ?'

'Of course not!'

'Well then!'

'It's just . . .'

He paused. 'I'm waiting . . .'

'It's just there are things I need to sort out . . .'

'So sort them out. And quickly.'

'It's all right for you,' she said, 'you don't have a child.'

'I'd like one, though,' he said, 'I'd like us to have a child. What do you want to do, hang around prevaricating for another ten years until it's too late?'

'You know I love you . . .'

'Thank you for that.'

'But it's not very feminist, is it, me turning my life upside down to follow you? We're not supposed to do that any more, seek fulfilment through loving a man . . .'

He threw back his head and roared with laughter. 'So it's sexual politics, now, is it? Why don't we just sit down and plan a symposium. Get Germaine Greer along to show us the way.'

'She'd tell me to get myself a lithe young boy to play with, not a man on the cusp of middle age.'

'You say the kindest things.'

She squeezed his hand. 'I don't want a boy, I want you.'

'Good. So tell me what the alternative is. Ending your days alone, knowing you've done the right thing? What could be more wretched than that?'

'Growing old with the wrong person,' said Jane, thinking of Will, 'that could be very . . . dispiriting.'

'Quite.'

She leaned forward to kiss him. 'I will sort it out, I promise. I bet you wish you'd chosen someone without any baggage, it would be so much simpler.'

'I like your baggage, if by that you mean Liberty. I think she likes me too, so far, doesn't she?'

'Of course she does.'

Though even as she said the words, Jane was thinking, you will never be her father. Will was Liberty's father, and the thought of what she was planning to do made her queasy with guilt.

After lunch they walked back up to the house.

'I'd better get packed,' said Jane.

'Leave your toothbrush, that way I know you'll be back.'

'Are you trying to hold me to ransom?'

'Absolutely.'

She disengaged herself and went back into her bedroom. Her clothes were still neatly folded in the wardrobe, she hadn't had much need for them lately. She put them in her bag and collected her things from the bathroom, leaving the toothbrush as promised. It was a lucky token, a promise to herself that it would be all right, that she would come back and everything would work out. Then she checked her messages. The first one was from Will.

'Jane, I'm at the hospital with Liberty. She's had an accident, but don't worry, she's going to be all right.'

SIXTEEN

Jane plumped the pillows up behind Liberty and looked anxiously at her pale little face. She had only eaten half her toast.

'Now, are you sure I can't get you anything else?' she said. She wanted to feed her up until she got the roses back in her cheeks.

Liberty shook her head. 'Not hungry.'

It was two weeks since Jane had arrived to find her daughter stretched out on a hospital bed, her leg already set in the preliminary plaster. It was a bad break, in two places, but the advantage of young bones, the doctor had explained, was that they mended so much better than old ones. Jane had been overcome by gratitude and wanted to kiss his coat. She rarely had dealings with people who did important jobs, and it made her wonder why she worried about the things she did. Watching the nurses bustling around, doing what needed to be done, she was ashamed of the narrow self-absorption that had recently consumed her. She had sat there, through the night, holding Liberty's hand and thanking the God she didn't believe in that nothing worse had happened to her.

Now, at home in her own bed, Liberty made a miaowing noise and stretched out her arms.

'Do you prefer me as a cat or a human?'

Jane smiled, relieved to see her back on form. 'A human, definitely.'

Liberty grinned, enjoying the undivided attention of her mother. She had grown attached to the purple plaster on her leg, it made her feel special, in spite of its limitations.

'Mum, I will be able to go on a horse again, won't I?' she asked.

'Of course you will.' Though even as Jane said it, she was thinking of other, more terrible possibilities. Broken spine, coma, a lifetime of communicating through a flickering eyelid. She kept remembering the scene from *Gone with the Wind* where Scarlett's daughter lies in a still heap of crinolines and curls after being thrown from her pony.

'I'm so sorry I wasn't there when it happened,' she said. 'I just felt so awful when I got Daddy's message . . . you poor, brave little creature.'

Liberty looked pleased. 'It wasn't too bad,' she said. 'Daddy came quite quickly to the hospital and sat with me for a bit. But then he had to go outside to make a phone call and he fell; it was a shame he was wearing those shiny shoes.'

Will was calling to her now from the galleria, his voice was rising up the stairs. 'Jane! Jane!'

She picked up Liberty's breakfast tray. 'See you in a bit, just call if you need anything.'

Liberty picked up her book and waved goodbye to Jane as she went down into the galleria where Will was sitting at his desk. His bandaged left foot was resting on a cushion.

'I'm sorry to be a bore,' he said, putting down his book, 'but is there any chance of a cup of camomile?'

She flinched at his self-pitying tone. Liberty was her concern, not him. What did he expect anyway, wearing brand-new leather soles on the rainy steps of the hospital; it was obviously asking for trouble. He'd been in such a hurry to phone his agent that he'd missed his grip and gone crashing down, ripping his new Vivienne Westwood trousers while he was about it. And while he was bundled off in a wheelchair to get his foot X-rayed, Liberty had been left alone with only Cosima's mother for company. Poor woman, she'd done her best, but it was more than she had bargained for when she'd invited her daughter's friend to stay, playing next-of-kin in Accident and Emergency.

'Sure,' said Jane, trying to be gracious, 'do you want anything to eat?'

Will frowned, thinking about what might tempt his jaded appetite. 'Perhaps a little grapefruit, properly pared, would go down well.' He sighed and looked down at his foot. 'What a damn nuisance this is, of all the inconvenient times for it to happen . . .'

'It's those killer shoes. You and Lydia are both paying the price for your fancy footwear . . .'

He looked cross. 'Thanks for the sympathy. And may I remind you that if you'd been there for Liberty I wouldn't have had to rush away from my meeting and my metatarsal would still be intact . . .'

'I know, and I feel terrible. Not, it must be said, about your metatarsal, but about poor Liberty. It won't happen again, I assure you. She is my number-one priority from now on.'

Jane went down to the kitchen and picked a grape-fruit from the fruit bowl. She took a sharp knife from the drawer and began the fiddly process of removing not only the skin and pith but also the membranes that separated the segments. Then she had a better idea: there was a tin of grapefruit in the cupboard. She shook the canned fruit into a bowl and placed it on a tray, together with a teapot, into which she measured three teaspoons of camomile, just the way he liked it.

While she waited for the kettle to boil, she thought about what she had to do. She'd realised she had no choice the moment she'd got Will's message. On the way to the airport she had run through it all so many times in her head. While she had been enjoying a self-indulgent lunch with her lover, her daughter had been in desperate need of her. It was all very well to rationalise, to say it was just a simple mistake, that she had forgotten to take her phone. That accidents happened and no-one could be there 24/7 for their child. That wasn't the point. The point was that she had been placing her own happiness above that of her child's, and Liberty's accident had come just in time to remind her that she was not a free agent. She was not the heroine of a romantic drama, able to follow her heart. She had responsibilities.

She carried the tray upstairs, past the front door where two pairs of crutches, little and large, were propped side by side. Her two invalids. For the sake of one, she'd put up with the other. She reminded herself that before she'd met Rupert she had been quite happy with Will. She could get that feeling back if she tried, the feeling that she was lucky to have him, the feeling that they were a happy family, the three of them.

'Here we are,' she said cheerfully, 'tea and segments.'

Will looked up from his screen. 'That sounds ominous,' he said, peering into the bowl.

'We're out of fresh,' Jane lied. 'I'll be downstairs working if you need anything.'

In the kitchen, she switched on her computer and checked her emails. Nothing from Rupert, why should there be, he didn't even know her address. They had always said it was too risky, many people found out about their partners' infidelity through raiding their inbox. Infidelity. The word used not to apply to them, but they could no longer claim they were just friends. Jane opened the file of the comedy she was translating and set to work. It was so familiar, the old routine, sitting at the kitchen table with the washing machine humming. The pile of bills stacked up beside the toaster. The floor littered with crumbs and toys, quietly demanding her attention. She'd see to it once she'd finished this scene, when she had her mid-morning coffee. The framework of her old life, she'd get used to it again. It wouldn't feel like this forever, the raw sense of loss would soften and fade.

She must tell Rupert now, it wasn't fair to keep putting it off, hoping something would happen. She listened up the stairs, making sure that Will or Liberty weren't calling her, then took her phone out into the garden. The wisteria was in bud now, against the back wall. Another month and it would be hung in extravagant mauve swathes all the way up, setting off the small primrose-yellow blooms of the rosa banksia that matched its height. Jane called Rupert's number. She had only spoken to him once since her return, a brief call to say she had arrived at the hospital, that everything was all right. She had told him then not to call her, she would call him. She wandered down to the end of the garden, to the hot yellow summer-bed, where the African marigolds and nasturtiums and geum borisii were gathering force, preparing for their June explosion.

He answered at once. 'There you are . . . how are you my darling?'

The sound of his voice made a nonsense of her cool resolve.

Through her tears, she told him. 'I'm sorry, Rupert, I really am so very sorry . . .'

It was remarkable, thought Lydia, how much she could get done with Rupert out of the way. Even with her sore foot, she'd managed to clear out an entire wardrobe in his bedroom, bundling up the clothes for charity, filling two carrier bags with shoes alone. He was terrible about throwing things away, but she knew he'd be grateful when he returned from France. He never wore the stuff anyway, or at least not in her presence. She knew she wasn't marrying a clothes horse, but there were limits. You couldn't expect her to be seen in public with someone wearing a three-piece suit, and as for those tank tops . . .

She flung herself back on the bed and admired her

handiwork. A whole empty cupboard, with enough hanging space to accommodate her shoulder-season wardrobe. The winter and summer things could go in the spare bedroom, there was plenty of room, far more than she had been used to in her own flat. She stretched out her legs and lifted them slowly, one at a time, tightening her stomach muscles. The wedding dress was closely fitted, with a row of tiny buttons running down the back. She couldn't afford to put on any weight and risk them pinging off as she went up the aisle.

Some people thought it was laughable for a thirty-seven-year-old atheist to be having a church wedding, but not Lydia. There was nowhere near the same drama at a registry office and she wasn't going to turn down the chance to be filmed in the proper setting, organ blaring, early autumn mists rolling in over the Scottish hills. You had to make the most of it, go out with a bang, before settling down to married life.

She picked up the red book from her side of the bed and flicked through the lists. Everything was taken care of, more or less. The invitations were printed and boxed up in the corner of the bedroom, waiting to go out to the calligrapher. Caterers, reception, flowers, photographer, guest list, done, done and done. Surely there must be something she'd overlooked. With so little left to arrange, it seemed quiet, almost anti-climactic. She felt she was in mourning for the early exciting stage of making plans.

She swung her legs round to Rupert's side, down on the shag-pile carpet. That would be gone soon, thank goodness. Flicking through the reading material stacked on his bedside table, she tried to form an impression of the man she was to marry: back copies of *The Economist*, a book on the art treasures of the V&A, flower catalogues, with tight lists of Latin names, and something called the *Checklist of Birds of Northern Europe*. He had marked it in several places, noting the date and place of sighting, the way she imagined train spotters went about their sad business. She thought about Rupert crouching in the undergrowth with fellow twitchers. Bill Oddie perhaps. It wasn't something she wanted to dwell on.

It was unhealthy to spend time like this alone, brooding. Lydia picked up the phone to call Jane. She was going there for dinner tonight, and needed to check what time. Poor Jane, she'd had a terrible shock with Liberty's accident, but that was kids for you, you couldn't wrap them up in cotton wool. Personally, she thought Jane had gone a bit overboard on the guilt trip, it wasn't as if it would have made any difference if she'd been at home in London instead of hanging around in the South of France. Lydia half thought that Rupert would come back too, but he still had something to finish off in the garden, he said. Better for him to get it out of his system and go back to work refreshed. She didn't want him going down that dropout route again.

The answer phone was on, Jane must be working. Lydia left her message, then wondered what she should do now. She couldn't go round the shops with her foot as it was. There was always that article she was researching on modern manners, but the deadline was weeks away and she was still supposed to be on holiday. Surely there was something else that needed sorting out for the wedding.

She turned over on the bed so she was kneeling on all fours and began pushing out her right leg behind her, then bending the knee to push the foot towards the ceiling in little bursts. Of course! There was one thing she hadn't even started to think of yet, the seating plan. Even without knowing the final numbers, it was possible to work out a rough draft. Abandoning her exercises, Lydia rolled off the bed and limped into the sitting room, where she took a piece of paper from the printer. She drew twenty small rectangles on it, then consulted her guest list. This was one big job: what a good thing she'd thought of it now, while she had the time.

When Rupert rang, she was deliberating about how best to mix up the guests. Should everyone be forced to mingle, or was it better to keep people on tables with people they knew?

'What do you think, Rupert?' she asked him down the phone. 'To be honest, I think we should keep separate tables, don't you? Don't you? Hallo?'

He had gone silent on the other end. Eventually he spoke.

'It's no good, Lyd.'

The flat tone of his voice told Lydia all she needed to know.

'I should have done this earlier,' he went on. 'It's my fault, entirely my fault, I just couldn't seem to find the right way . . .'

'Stop it right there.' Lydia's defence mechanism was fully engaged now. Somehow, she knew, she'd been expecting this. Her mind was racing ahead, but Rupert wouldn't be stopped.

'I think we've been too carried away by the plans,' he said. 'We haven't thought through the reality . . .'

'No. You don't know what you're saying, Rupert, you're not thinking properly.'

There was a pause.

'You're tired, that's all,' she said. 'And it's not doing you any good rattling round down there by yourself. Come back to London, you'll feel differently then.'

'No, I won't.'

'You will, I promise. I know you're fed up with your job, but you can leave it. I didn't realise it was getting you down so much.'

'It's not just the job . . . Oh, Lydia, I feel so awful . . . I can't tell you how sorry I am.'

Lydia put down the phone and stared at the piece of paper in front of her. Two hundred and fifty names, written in pencil in her neat handwriting. Slowly she scrunched the paper into a ball, then threw it across the room, towards the bin. She didn't cry. She'd managed to hold it together pretty well on the phone, she thought. Her head throbbed as she tried to get to grips with what had happened. Her future had just been entirely erased, she was looking at a blank canvas again. She'd have to cancel everything, of course, but nothing that a few phone calls couldn't fix. She wasn't angry, and she wasn't sad. What she was feeling, she realised with surprise, was relief.

'So, you blew him out!' said Will admiringly later that day, when Lydia had joined them for drinks in the galleria. 'Very sound move, if you don't mind me saying so. Nice-enough guy, in his way, but not right for you, darling.'

Jane topped up their glasses with caipirinha, a potent cocktail of limes and sugar-cane brandy. It was what they drank in Brazil, to work them up into the carnival spirit, but it wasn't having that effect on her.

She listened to Lydia's account of ending the engagement. Rupert must have rung her this afternoon, just after they had spoken. He'd been putting it off, but her call to him must have spurred him on. She had proved that you could deliver bad news down the phone. If you were going to break someone's heart, you didn't need to be fussy about how you did it. Although Lydia didn't appear to be too heartbroken.

'It just wasn't adding up,' she was saying, waving her glass. 'He seems to be going through some kind of midlife crisis, all this talk about becoming a gardener, clearly a cry for help. And I didn't feel like being the one who picks up the pieces, does that sound awful?' She knocked back her drink, pleased by how convincing she sounded. She almost believed it herself, now, that she had been the one to call it off.

'Better now than just before the service,' said Will. 'You're a bit old to play the flibbertigibbet bride, changing her mind at the eleventh hour.'

'I've got to call everyone tomorrow to cancel,' said Lydia, 'then it's back to the drawing board. Out there alone in the big wide world. You two don't know how lucky you are, with your cosy little set-up.'

Though even as she said it, Lydia was thinking how exhilarating it felt to be back in the field; already she was tuning in to the exciting scent of possibility.

'I do like your hair, Will,' she added, 'it's so . . . virile.'

Will smiled and caressed his shaved head. He'd had it done yesterday after spotting the beginnings of a bald patch. He'd never been able to imagine himself without a ponytail, but he loved his new look. Thrusting male, Hollywood A-list.

Jane glanced across at Will and tried to feel grateful for her cosy little set-up. It was too soon. Next week, next month, certainly by next year, she would be glad she'd made the right decision. But at this moment she felt like walking downstairs and jumping into her car and driving non-stop to Rupert's house in Provence. It would only take her twelve hours and 58 minutes, and £46 in motorway tolls; she had checked on www.viamichelin.com this afternoon while she was pretending to work.

Liberty came upstairs with a bowl of Japanese rice crackers, bumping her way up on her bottom, dragging her leg behind her. Jane smiled at the sight of her.

'Look at you,' said Lydia as she was offered the bowl, 'aren't you a good girl? Here, I've brought you some make-up samples.' She pulled them out of her bag.

'Thank you,' said Liberty. 'We're going to Brussels.'

'School trip,' said Jane, 'me too. I'm an accompanying mother.'

Lydia pulled a face. 'Rather you than me.'

'We're going to get lace. Mummy had to come because of my leg, otherwise they said I couldn't go.'

'There goes my free week,' said Jane. 'Still, it's a good excuse, isn't it? A week away with my lovely daughter.' She was hoping the break would do her good, help her to get herself together.

'Can I be a bridesmaid when you marry Rupert?' Liberty asked Lydia. 'My cast will be off by then.'

Jane intervened. 'Lydia's not getting married after all,' she said, comforted by the thought.

'Why not?'

'Because she's not.'

Liberty nodded thoughtfully, then took herself off to experiment with the make-up samples.

Will was still fretting over the idea of himself and Jane as the prototype steady couple. 'When you talk about our "cosy little set-up", Lydia, I hope you're not seeing us as . . . stuck. Because we've always prided ourselves on standing apart from all that, reinventing ourselves as we go on . . .'

'Have we?' asked Jane.

'You know we have! We've always refused to go by the rule book.'

'I know you've always refused to marry Jane,' said Lydia, 'but there's nothing special about that, just you being mean.'

'It's a state of mind,' said Will, 'being open to possibilities. In all aspects of life. It was in that spirit that I resigned from my column today.'

It was the first Jane had heard of it. 'You did what?' she said, astonished.

Will poured himself a top-up. 'I was going to tell you,' he said evasively, 'but I wanted to do the deed first.'

'You've been writing that column for as long as I've known you,' said Jane.

'Exactly. Time to move on, don't you think?'

The question hung in the air.

'What did they say?' Jane asked. 'Did they offer you filthy amounts of money to stay?'

Will had assumed they would, but in fact they had seemed rather relieved. Kept telling him he could go as soon as he liked, they wouldn't stand in his way. If he hadn't got the other thing up and running, he might have felt rather put out.

'It's not a question of money,' he said grandly, 'I need to prioritise my serious writing, and this film project brought the whole thing into perspective for me. Grubby little business, journalism.'

'Shall we eat?' said Jane. 'It should be ready by now. I've done a Cajun recipe, think New Orleans.'

They went down to the kitchen and Liberty burst in like a midget from Versailles in one of Jane's old nighties, her face dusted white with talcum powder, a bright smear of red lipstick and eyes luridly painted with Lydia's make-up samples.

'You look scary,' said Jane, 'that talcum powder's not supposed to go on your face, I don't think.'

Liberty scowled beneath her mask. 'Where is it supposed to go?'

'Anywhere else, just not your face.'

'That eyeshadow looks gorgeous on you,' said Lydia, 'I'll bring you some more next time I come.'

Flattered, Liberty hoisted up her nightdress and sat down beside her.

Jane had correctly predicted that the stiffness of the cocktails would prevent Will from noticing that her Cajun speciality was in fact takeaway Kentucky Fried Chicken, removed from its cardboard box and arranged decoratively on a bed of salad. She watched him pick over it, enthusing about the exotic blend of spices and invoking the unique combination of French and African influences that informed the cuisine of the deep south.

'Marvellous, Jane, very unusual,' he said. 'You see what I mean, Lydia, about us insisting on an adventurous spirit, in food as in everything else.'

As Will and Lydia started to talk about the paper, and who might take over his column, Jane thought about Rupert. What was he thinking right now? She should be there to help him through all this, it was unbearable to think of him by himself. He might be in his garden now, the roses would just be coming into bloom.

Will and Lydia had moved on from work and he was quizzing her about Rupert, about why she had changed her mind.

'You don't think he was seeing anyone else, do you?' he asked.

'Rupert? Come off it, Will, he's hardly Casanova, is he now?'

'Don't ask me, you can't expect me to have an opinion. Let's ask Jane, come on Jane, what do you think, was Rupert seeing someone else? Is that why he's gone a bit funny?'

'A bit funny?' Jane repeated, avoiding the question.

'You know, all this life-change thing that Lydia was talking about.'

'No idea,' she shrugged, 'it seems to be something you'd know more about, with all your exciting new plans.'

'You're right there,' Will said, 'just you wait, this film deal is going to be huge.'

'Big changes for both of us,' said Lydia. 'Just you, now, Jane. What have you got up your sleeve?'

'Oh, you know, just more of the same,' said Jane, passing round bowls of *mousse au chocolat* which she'd made from a packet, 'I've got plenty of work on, and looking after Liberty, of course.'

Poor thing, thought Lydia. I may have been unexpectedly dumped, but I don't envy Jane her life, not one little bit.

SEVENTEEN

The next morning, Jane was packing for the school trip, reading from the list provided by the teacher.

'Funny place to go, Brussels,' she said to Liberty, counting out six tee shirts, 'famous for mussels, beer and lace, none of which is that interesting for a class of seven-year-olds.'

'And chocolate,' said Liberty. 'Miss Evans said they had delicious chocolate.' She was playing with her dolls on the bed, Barbie in a bridal gown, all gleaming white satin and lace, and prince Ken in a turquoise tunic, silver crown and anachronistic preppy haricut. Liberty kept pressing a button on his back to make him deliver his smooth-talking lines in a clean and deep American accent. *I love you . . . will you join me at the ball?*

'It's a shame Lydia's not marrying Rupert,' said Liberty. She pressed the button on Barbie's back which set off 'The Wedding March', tinkling around the room.

'Yes,' said Jane insincerely.

'I like Rupert.'

'Me too.'

Liberty picked up Barbie and stuffed her under a pillow, trying to drown out the sound of the music.

'Why doesn't she want to marry him any more?' she asked.

'I'm not sure,' said Jane, 'but it's better to find out now rather than later.'

'Otherwise she'd have to get divorced.'

'Or else, not be very happy.'

'It's a good job they haven't got any children.'

'Rupert and Lydia?'

'Because when people have children, they have to stay together, don't they? Even if they don't like each other any more.'

Jane wondered if this was directed at her. 'Do they?' she asked.

'Yes. Even if they're not married.'

'Is that what you think?'

'Of course!' Liberty abandoned Ken and turned her attention to the Sylvanian Families she had assembled neatly on the floor. Mummy and Daddy bear and their bear children, Mummy and Daddy dog and their dog children. All dressed up in skirts or trousers, mimicking their human counterparts.

Jane had forgotten how reactionary children were. More resistant to change than the stuffiest old Tory. Put them in charge of the world and there'd never be any progress.

'But what if, say, the wife was mad and kept attacking her husband?' Jane asked. 'You couldn't expect him to stay with her then, could you?'

Liberty gave her a clear-eyed look, letting her know

she was missing the point. 'If she was mad, she would be put in hospital, or else in prison.'

'I see. But they might just be two ordinary people who didn't get on any more. Or think they made a mistake . . .'

'They shouldn't make a mistake, they're grown-ups.'

Liberty made Atilla the Hun look liberal.

'The mummy must make sure the home is nice and that she looks pretty,' Liberty went on, picking up the toy lady bear and smoothing down her headscarf, 'then the daddy won't want to leave.'

Steady on, thought Jane, this is getting onto very dodgy ground. 'The thing is, Liberty,' she said, 'you're only a child and there are lots of things you don't understand . . .'

Jane stopped herself there. She was sounding like an apologist for divorce, employing the very arguments she so adamantly opposed. Instead, she should be looking to the future, to the time when her present unhappiness would be a dim memory. Her fling with Rupert would be accorded its proper status as a dizzy episode in an otherwise uneventful life. Maybe one day she might tell Liberty about it, when she was old and grey. While the grandchildren were having tea, she might draw Liberty aside and show her a photo, tell her what very nearly happened, how she came within a hair's breadth of being brought up in the South of France. Liberty would thank her, she would be grateful that her mother had taken the view that parents should stick together come what may, that she had prized her daughter's happiness above her own.

'I'll go and pack the sponge bag,' Jane said, 'then we're all done.'

In the bathroom, she applied her anti-ageing, retinol-enhanced magic potion, and dipped into a smaller pot that promised special protection for the fine skin around the eyes. She then took her tweezers and tweaked out a hair that had just started to grow on one side of her chin. The first signs of age; it was as if her body was giving out warning signs, telling her this was it, it was downhill from now on, she had better make the most of it. She peered closely at the mirror for further signs of decay.

'Vanity, thy name is woman.'

She started as Will came in behind her.

'You made me jump,' she said, 'I thought you'd gone out.'

He looked at her reflection appraisingly. 'Not too bad, are you? Holding up quite nicely, I'd say. I think you may have lost some weight.'

'Thanks.' She smiled at him, he was making an effort to be nice, after all.

'I thought I should update you on my plans,' he said, turning his attention to his own reflection, lowering his chin and running a hand over his shaved head. It felt hard and virile beneath his fingers. 'As you know, I've resigned from my column. Sorry to drop that news in front of Lydia, by the way, I meant to speak to you first about it, but everything's been moving at such a pace . . .' He paused and leaned forward, frowning at what looked like a blackhead on his forehead. No, relax, it was just a fleck of dirt. 'It's all to do with this film project,' he went on, 'they want me to go over and spend some time in Hollywood.'

'How long?'

'Hard to say. A few months. But I'll come back for the odd weekend, and you might like to bring Liberty over for a break in the summer. They're putting me up in a suite, there'd be plenty of room.'

Jane imagined them creeping around the hotel, trying not to be in the way. 'You'd be working, though.'

'Obviously,' he said, talking to the mirror again. 'They're not paying me to take an extended holiday with my family.' He was wearing a plain white tee shirt beneath a loosely structured suit, with its sleeves pushed up, like Bruce Willis. 'What do you think?'

She wasn't sure if he meant his appearance or his career plans. 'I think it sounds very exciting, well done.'

'It could just be the start. I may well decide to move over there permanently, and if it works out, you might like to join me. You might finally achieve your dream of leaving London. Though we don't want to get too ahead of ourselves,' he added. Better not to make rash promises. 'The thing about your work is you can do it anywhere,' he went on, meaning anywhere I choose to lead you.

It was true that a few months ago she would have jumped at it. Now, the idea of a new life with Will just left her cold. It was all she could do to carry on as they were.

'But you're so attached to London,' she said, 'all that stuff in your column about it being the only city you could call home.'

He shrugged. 'You've got to take opportunities when they present themselves. Don't want to lie on your deathbed wishing you'd done things when you had the chance.'

She couldn't argue with that. 'What about Liberty? She might turn into a valley girl. Or become a drug addict, someone from a Bret Easton Ellis novel.'

'Don't play the anti-American ticket, Jane, you sound like the *Daily Mail*. Anyway, this is just for a year or so, there's no need to rush into any decisions.'

'A year? You said a few months.'

'To start with, yes. And you can stay here, if you like, in the long-term. There's no need for you to uproot if you don't want to.'

He doesn't want us, she thought. So much for her effort in holding together the family unit. He was buggering off to Hollywood and she and Liberty could do as they liked. They were expendable.

'When are you leaving?'

'Next week. Gives me just enough time to sort everything out here.'

'Including us?'

'I've never had to sort you out, Jane, you're so damned efficient.' He smiled at her. 'How's your packing coming on?' he asked.

'Nearly finished.'

'Good, only I might need a bit of help getting organised.'

He left her to it and went back down to the galleria. That had gone quite well, he thought. Kind of welcoming and noncommittal at the same time. He wanted to keep the family on board, but he needed to be realistic about the future. Alone in Hollywood, he couldn't rule out the possibility of a bit of love interest. He felt a flicker of horniness. A writer in Hollywood, all those Californian girls with blank eyes and easy ways. Himself as a kind of intellectual Beach Boy, winning them over with his huge vocabulary. He conjured up an image of himself sitting on a surfboard on Venice Beach, holding forth like Socrates, drawing in the sand for the benefit of a crowd of admiring beach babes.

He shifted in his seat and went online to take another look at the hotel he would soon be calling home. It floated up before him, speaking of endless possibilities. The size of his suite was about twice that of the galleria. The phone rang.

'Will, it's Chas.'

'Chas, hi.'

'Hang on a minute, just got a call through on the other line.'

Will tucked the phone under his chin and clicked on the screen, running through the hotel facilities: gym, sauna, personal trainers on site, it might not be a bad idea to up his fitness level.

'Sorry about that,' said Chas.

'No problem, what's new?'

'Well . . . not good news, I'm afraid.'

'Oh?'

'Those fuckers at the studio . . .'

'What?'

'Basically, they've changed their minds. Decided they've got someone else they want to use, don't ask me why.'

Will's hand froze on the mouse. 'They can't do that,' he said. 'It's all worked out. I've just given notice at the *Messenger*.'

'Ouch,' said Chas, 'that was a bit premature.'

'But I was supposed to be leaving next week, for Christ's sake.'

'If you'd discussed it with me, I'd have told you. Don't count on anything until you've signed the contract.'

Will jumped to his feet in a panic, feeling his shorn head, vulnerable and exposed. It had been tempting fate, shaving off his ponytail like that.

'You told me,' he said, 'you told me to tie everything up as soon as possible.'

'I said, get prepared, that doesn't include handing in your resignation,' said Chas evenly. 'First bit of advice I give all my clients is don't give up the day job.'

'Listen, mate!' Will was shouting at him now. 'You were the one who got me into all this, it was you who was talking like it was all in the bag. Don't you think that as my agent you might have advised me a bit better?'

'Don't shout, Will, it's really not my fault . . . These things happen.'

'Fuck you!' Will threw the phone down and realised he was shaking. He poured himself a shot of vodka and downed it quickly, then poured another. He walked over to the window and stared out into the grey and rainy street. This time next week he should have been basking in the Californian sunshine. He was to have taken his place in that lurid blue Hockney-swimming-pool land-scape. In his head he had already formed the scenes: working in a huge studio alongside powerful executives, then returning to host a thong-clad soiree round the pool. He was to have been the intellectual English writer in Hollywood, a latter-day Isherwood, except straight and minus the yoga. And now it had all been snatched away.

He remained at the window for some time, motionless, wondering what to do. He watched an old lady pushing along a four-wheeled shopping basket, pausing to lean on it, while a group of boys were mucking around on bikes, performing wheelies. The usual banal sights.

Dear old grimy London, he thought at last, it could be worse. At least you saw people on the streets here, unlike Los Angeles, where everyone was sealed inside their cars. It wasn't really him, that half-baked West Coast idiocy, he should see this as a blessing in disguise. He'd ring the paper now, withdraw his resignation. Then he could negotiate a six-month sabbatical some time soon, to get on with his book. He was a writer, after all, not a film lackey. He felt a theme for next week's column coming on: *Losers go to Hollywood*. The dumbing down of the American film industry, with particular mention for those shits who had just messed him about. How there was more talent in one BBC studio than in the entire American entertainment business.

Feeling much better, he went back to his desk and called his editor, explaining that he had changed his plans, waiting for the warm sighs of relief as she welcomed him back into the fold.

'I'm sorry, Will,' she said when he'd finished, 'but we've already made other arrangements.'

'So, un-make them!' he said. 'You can't tell me you've done anything irrevocable since yesterday. As I know only too well, nothing is definite until it's signed and sealed.'

There was an awkward pause.

'The thing is, Will,' she said, 'there's been the feeling here for a while that maybe . . . it's time for a change.

We need to be hooking in our younger readers, and some-times your angle is a little bit . . . of its time, shall we say. We've already given your column to a very exciting new writer . . .'

'Another twelve-year-old, like you, is it?' Will said, before hanging up for the second time in ten minutes.

He shouldn't really be drinking vodka at this time in the morning, but then again these were exceptional circumstances. Will topped his glass and sat down to think again. The book, of course. He'd have to get a new agent, naturally, and not before time. Bloody Chas. Until he'd got the deal, they could manage on Jane's money. Jane, bless her. What a good job he'd left the door open when he told her about moving to America. That could have been a very costly own goal.

He called out to her, but there was no reply. She must still be upstairs, finishing the packing. Setting the glass down on the desk, Will went up to the bedroom to find her, but the case had gone and the bed was neatly made.

'Jane!' he bellowed down the stairs. Running down, he could make out the suitcase standing by the door. He continued down into the basement where Liberty was eating a sandwich and Jane was wiping down the surfaces in the businesslike way of someone preparing to leave.

'There you are!' he said in relief. 'I thought for a moment you'd gone off without saying goodbye.'

'Five minutes,' said Jane, looking at her watch.

She was looking good, he thought, in her long sheep-skin coat. And Liberty in her civvies instead of that damn uniform. He felt a surge of affection for them both, the way he did whenever he felt a bit out of sorts.

'There's been a change of plan,' he said, 'you might actually be seeing a bit more of me than we thought.'

'I don't think so,' said Jane. 'Go upstairs, Liberty, and get your things together for the journey.'

Liberty obediently went off, leaving her parents alone together.

'I've been thinking, Will,' said Jane, 'and I realise that I've waited far too long. If it wasn't for Liberty, we wouldn't still be together, we both know that.'

Will started to protest. Was she out of her mind? After everything he'd done for her, everything he'd taught her, the quality he brought to her daily life.

'I used to think that Liberty was reason enough,' Jane went on, ignoring him, 'you know my view that a child should be brought up by both parents. But seeing how easy you find it to walk out makes me realise that my illusion of us as a happy, functional family is a lie. I don't want Liberty growing up with us as an example of a normal couple. I don't want her to think that what we have is a good, loving relationship, when it's nothing of the sort. So I'm leaving you.'

'You're what?'

'I'm leaving you. Of course you can see as much of Liberty as you like, and I don't want any money, we'll manage.'

'What do you mean, you're leaving me? You're nothing without me, you've said so yourself many times!'

'And you let me believe it! Look, Will, when we met I was so impressionable, and I thought you were just so glamorous. You still are, of course,' she added, feeling a sudden rush of pity, 'but you've got to admit I was a pushover. Making me fall in love with you was like taking candy from a baby, as you have pointed out to me on more than one occasion.'

Will stared at her, casting around wildly for something to say that would stop everything from crashing down around him.

'But I honestly feel it's over now,' Jane was saying. 'Let's be grown up about it. I'm no longer your little protégé, and you . . . well, you're you . . . hugely clever, and in with all the right people, and now with a fabulous future in the film world. You know it makes much more sense for you to go there by yourself, free of any ties . . . you more or less said so, earlier on.'

'But that's just it, Jane,' Will interrupted, 'I'm not going, it's fallen through. They've pulled the plug on me.'

He explained what had happened.

'I see,' said Jane slowly, 'what a shame, I'm so sorry.' She thought it through. 'But that doesn't really change anything between us, does it? I'd still have reached the same conclusion, even if you weren't going.'

'You can't leave me now! I've supported you for all these years and the minute I want something back, you tell me you're swanning off!'

'Will, the house is yours, your money's yours, all you've ever given us has been a roof over our heads, and that's all I ever asked for.'

She was heading up the stairs now.

'But I need you to support me, while I write my book,' he said desperately, laying all his cards on the table.

'Sorry. You'll just have to dig into your savings, and don't pretend you haven't got any . . .' She knew about all those secret funds and Mini Cash ISAs that he kept quiet about, filing them away where he thought she wouldn't see them.

'Hang on,' he said, 'you could at least show me how the washing machine works.'

'Treat yourself to a new one,' said Jane, 'and a dishwasher, while you're about it.'

Liberty appeared at the front door. 'Say goodbye to Daddy, we'll see him soon,' said Jane.

Liberty kissed Will goodbye then Jane helped her into the taxi.

'Waterloo, please,' said Jane. She closed her eyes, and when she opened them they were halfway down the street and Will was out of sight.

At the Eurostar check-in an excited party of little girls and their mothers were congregated at the bottom of the escalator that separated international departures from run-of-the-mill commuters. Miss Evans was standing in the middle with a clipboard, ticking off the arrivals.

'That seems to be everyone,' she said, raising her voice, 'could we please have the children lined up behind me, and the three mothers who are joining us: Mrs Khan, Mrs Phillips, and Mrs Rhys-Baker.'

Liberty tugged at Jane's sleeve. 'What about you?' she hissed.

'Don't worry,' said Jane, and turned to Miss Evans. 'Excuse me,' she said, 'I think I'm down as one of the mothers. Don't you remember, you said I should come because of Liberty's leg being in plaster.'

Miss Evans looked dismayed. 'Oh, so I did, I'm so

sorry, I completely forgot! I must have got confused because Mrs Phillips wasn't down to come, but then she was particularly keen to, because of Xanthe's separation anxiety, and I was thinking we needed a third mother . . . I'm terribly sorry, Mrs Thacker, but I don't think we need you after all . . . and I haven't got a ticket for you.'

Liberty squeezed Jane's hand. 'You have to come, Mum,' she whispered. 'What about my bath? You have to put that plastic cover thing on my leg.'

'Can't I come along anyway, as an extra?' Jane asked. 'I could go and get a ticket now.'

Miss Evans looked flustered. 'It's the accommodation,' she said. 'I don't know how it would work. I'm sharing a room with Mrs Khan, then Mrs Phillips is sharing with Mrs Rhys-Baker, I know the hotel is fully booked . . . oh dear, this is all so very last minute, maybe we could get you a room somewhere else . . .'

Liberty was pulling at Jane's hand again. 'MUM,' she said, 'let's just not go.'

'What?' Jane crouched down to talk to her daughter. 'But you've been looking forward to it,' she said.

'I don't care, I don't want to go any more.' Liberty looked down at her shoes, then up again to meet her mother's eyes. 'I don't want you staying in a different place . . .'

'They might be able to swap it around, or you could come and stay with me at a different hotel . . .'

'No. Please, let's just not go.'

'We really should be going through now,' said Miss Evans.

'All right,' said Jane, relieved. 'If you're absolutely sure, Liberty?'

Liberty nodded, and Jane turned back to Miss Evans. 'I think it's probably better, in the circumstances, if we don't come,' she said. 'I do hope you don't mind, only I think, with Liberty's leg, it was probably a bit ambitious, and in view of the mix-up . . .'

Miss Evans looked relieved. 'Well, if you're sure . . .'

'Yes, we're sure.'

'I am sorry about the confusion.'

'Don't be, it really doesn't matter.'

And she and Liberty retreated to the café, where they ordered two croissants and two *pains au chocolat*, and sat eating them as they watched Liberty's classmates filing through the ticket machines.

'Do you mind?' Jane asked, dunking her croissant in her coffee.

Liberty shook her head. 'I'd rather be with you.'

'And I'd rather be with you than with all those other children. And I certainly wouldn't fancy sharing a room with Mrs Khan or Mrs Phillips.'

'Or Mrs Rhys-Baker.'

'Or Mrs Rhys-Baker. Though I daresay they wouldn't fancy sharing with me either.'

They ate on in companionable silence.

After a bit Liberty asked, 'Mum, is Daddy going to America?'

'I don't think so.'

'So what will we do?'

Jane looked at her carefully. 'I don't know,' she said.

'Are you and Daddy really going to live in separate houses?'

Jane didn't ask her how she'd worked that out. She

had to tell her the truth. 'Yes, we are. But don't worry, it'll be all right.'

'I know.'

Jane felt as if a great weight had been lifted from her chest. She thought about what Rupert had said, about the hardest thing being to know what you really want. Once you knew that, the rest was easy. She looked at Liberty's trusting face staring up at her and realised that everything was going to work out. There was no longer any need for her to settle for the next best thing, no need to throw away her chance of happiness and claim it was all for Liberty's sake.

She looked up at the departure board. There was a train to Paris leaving in thirty minutes. From Paris, it was three hours to Marseille by TGV, and then about an hour in a taxi. They could be there by nightfall.

'I did wonder, Liberty,' she said, 'whether we might go and see Rupert. What do you think?'

She waited, hoping for a favourable reply. Although she realised that she had already made her decision.

'I'd like that,' said Liberty.

Rupert had just finished watering the pots on the terrace and was sitting down for some reheated *pot au feu*, though he had little appetite. After two weeks of waiting, he now had to face the truth. Jane wasn't coming.

He tried to picture her at home. What was she doing now. Was she at her desk, or watching television, or sitting in her garden? The wallflowers would be out now, the first blaze of colour in her hot summer-bed. He steered away from imagining her with Will. Lydia had told him earlier they had been quite inseparable at the hospital, united by their concern for Liberty. He hadn't wanted to hear about that. Jane had asked him not to call her until she had sorted things out, and he had respected that though it had been hard. And now she'd told him she was staying with Will. For all he knew they were enjoying a second honeymoon, you did hear that, couples becoming even stronger after an affair had ended.

An affair. The words were so cheap, so throwaway. He hadn't told Lydia there was someone else, there was no point. He couldn't have married her anyway, it would never have worked. His only regret was not ending it sooner, instead of dragging it out like the miserable coward he was. He still felt bad about doing it by phone, he had planned to go back to speak to her, but hadn't trusted himself. Once in London, he knew he couldn't have resisted finding Jane and begging her to change her mind, but that would have been unfair on her, and at least he could say he'd behaved honourably towards her, which was all that counted.

Soon he would be able to engage in his life here. People had been very kind, he'd had no end of dinner invitations, but he didn't have the heart for it without Jane. A nice Icelandic couple in the village were particularly keen to rope him in for a Wagnerian blonde they had staying, but he had managed to keep them at bay so far.

It was getting dark and he could only make out the white roses against the dark mass of the borders. He picked up his plate and glass and was heading back to the house when he saw the headlights at the gate. His first thought was that it was the Icelanders, come to fetch him for dinner. If he won't come to us, we'll have to go to him, they must have said. He stood and watched; he could hardly pretend he wasn't at home, you couldn't get away with that down here. Someone was getting out and opening the gates, then the car door was slammed shut and it was coming up the drive towards him. It was a taxi, he saw that now.

He watched in disbelief as Jane opened the door and stepped out onto the drive, followed by a sleepy-looking Liberty. He'd imagined the scene so often, he couldn't believe it was really happening. The driver was opening the boot, taking out Jane's suitcase. She was walking towards him uncertainly, her arm round her daughter.

'Is it still OK?' she said, though she knew she didn't need to ask. She had come home now.

He opened his arms and gripped them both in a clumsy embrace.

'It's more than OK,' he said. 'I was beginning to think you'd never make it. Come into the garden.'